fm Leg Br

"When Kathleen Kane writes a book,
it's a big warm hug . . ."*

**Praise for Kathleen Kane's bestselling Home-
spun romances . . .**

MOUNTAIN DAWN
Winner of The Paperback Forum
1993 Romance Reader's Choice Award
Voted *Best Americana Historical* by
the readers of *The Paperback Forum*

"Four and a half stars. *Mountain Dawn* is filled with rich, tender
moments that tug at the heart. Ms. Kane has woven a brilliant tale
of loyalty and courage. This reader was totally captivated by the
lively, all too human characters." —*Affaire de Coeur*

"A delicious, suspenseful tale . . . Ms. Kane has penned a
charming one-night read." —*Romantic Times*

SMALL TREASURES
"Five gold stars. Absolutely delightful . . . A standing ovation for
Ms. Kane. Author, author . . . take a bow!" —*Heartland Critiques*

"Its charming love story and engaging characters will delight and
disarm readers." —*Romantic Times*

"An entertaining story, well worth your time." —*Rendezvous*

"A book to treasure!" —*Ann's World*, cablevision TV*

**And don't miss Kathleen Kane's wonderful novels in
the heartwarming romance series, A TOWN CALLED
HARMONY . . .**

KEEPING FAITH
"Another indisputable winner for Ms. Kane . . . a gently evolving
tale of love and passion." —*The Paperback Forum*

COM
"An author to watch for in

Titles by Kathleen Kane

Charms

KATHLEEN KANE

DIAMOND BOOKS, NEW YORK

This book is a Diamond original edition,
and has never been previously published.

CHARMS

A Diamond Book / published by arrangement with
the author

PRINTING HISTORY
Diamond edition / January 1995

ISBN: 0-7865-0068-9

Diamond Books are published by The Berkley Publishing Group,
200 Madison Avenue, New York, NY 10016.
DIAMOND and the "D" design
are trademarks belonging to Charter Communications, Inc.

PRINTED IN THE UNITED STATES OF AMERICA

10 9 8 7 6 5 4 3 2 1

PROLOGUE

Red Deer, Montana
"Durn near got ya *that* time!"

Leda James flipped her wild red hair back over her shoulder, glanced up at the old man, then continued to tug at the hem of her blue and green striped skirt until it ripped free of the nail it had caught on. She frowned at the long tear in the wide, ruffled hem and muttered, "What?"

"Good God, girl! Din't ya hear that gunshot?"

Leda blinked, caught her breath, and stood up. Gunshot? She laid one hand on the jumble of necklaces lying against her chest and blew a stray lock of hair out of her green eyes. Looking into the wizened, leathery face of the old man standing at her elbow, she said, "A gunshot?"

He pointed at a dark hole in the porch post beside her. "Looka that! It's a bullet, girl, and it come close to callin' your name."

She stared at the hole and whispered, "Fate."

"What's that?" he asked.

"I said it's Fate, Jubal." There was no sense in denying it any longer. Her time was at hand. Now all she could do was get her life in order before it ended.

1

One near fatal "accident" she could ignore. Maybe even two. But in the last two weeks, she'd managed to escape death three times.

First, there'd been the runaway wagon that had so narrowly missed her. Then, just a few days ago, she'd gone to the cemetery to visit her mother's resting place and nearly fallen into an open grave. Why, when that stranger suddenly bumped into her, she would have tumbled into that gaping black hole in the ground if she hadn't quickly grabbed at him to steady herself.

Of course, Leda'd felt just terrible that she'd saved herself at the cost of sending the stranger crashing into the grave. She shook her head slowly, remembering the poor man's cries for help. Why on earth would anyone have piled jagged rocks in the bottom of a grave, for heaven's sake?

The poor man had left town with a broken arm and it should have been *her*.

But this last incident had finally convinced her that more than a spate of bad luck was at work. Leda leaned in closer to the newel post, lifted her hand, and ran one fingertip over the bottom of the deeply imbedded stray bullet. Why, if she hadn't bent over suddenly to unsnag her skirt from that rusted nail, she would be on her way to lying beside her mother in the graveyard right now.

There had to be a reason for her near misses and the only reason she could find was that it was Fate telling her to get ready.

"You all right, girl?"

Leda looked at the old man and forced a smile. No point in worrying him. "Thank you, Jubal," she said. "I'm fine."

"All right, then." He shook his graying head. "But I got to say, Leda James, you are about the *luckiest* durn female I ever come across!"

Luck.

Her fingers curled around the twenty-dollar gold piece hanging from a chain around her neck. Nestled among the colored beads, the coin stood out like a talisman. Perhaps, she told herself, Jubal was right. If not for her lucky coin, she probably wouldn't have survived *this* long.

In an instant, her mind rushed back to the morning she'd found that coin, three weeks before. The day her luck had changed. It was right after she'd bumped into the woman boarding the dawn stage.

"I'm *so* sorry," Leda said and reached for the elegant woman's bag, now lying in the dirt.

"It's quite all right," the other woman snapped and grabbed the bag from Leda's hands before she could even finish brushing off the layer of street dust.

The stagecoach horses, standing in their traces, stomped their hooves against the dirt and the hollow sound seemed to echo down the deserted Main Street.

Leda'd often taken a dawn walk through the silent town and usually ended her stroll in the cemetery, where she could have a nice chat with her mother. She'd never seen anyone on one of her walks, save the driver of the dawn stage. Until that day.

"Are you taking the stage?"

The elegant woman shot her a furious look before she answered, "Of course! Why *else* would I be up at this ungodly hour?"

Leda paid no attention to the woman's obvious ill temper. After all, not *everyone* enjoyed being up and about before the world came to life.

Instead, Leda reached out for the woman's bag again. "At least let me give your bag to the driver. I feel awful that I've gotten it all dirty and now it's ruining your beautiful dress!" Leda's gaze swept over the woman's sky-blue gown without envy. Instinctively, she began to brush at the delicate fabric with the palms of her hands.

The object of her attentions jumped back, startled. "That won't be necessary," she answered and curled her fingers tightly around the wooden handle of her bag. "Now if you will *kindly* excuse me, I would like to board the stage."

The woman turned, put one dainty foot on the wooden step, then pulled herself into the stagecoach with her free hand. Once she was seated, she laid her bag on her lap and stared thoughtfully out the window at Leda.

"You live here? In town?"

"Yes." Leda pointed to the opposite end of the narrow street. "In the small green house at the edge of town."

The passenger's eyes narrowed thoughtfully.

"Movin' out!" the driver called as he climbed to his perch. As soon as he'd lifted the reins, he cracked them above the horses' backs and the stage lurched into a roll.

Something shiny caught Leda's eye and she glanced down. A gleaming new gold coin lay in the dirt at her feet. No one else was around, so she told herself it *had* to have fallen from the woman's satchel. Leda picked it up and looked after the rapidly moving stage. The woman was still watching her from the window. But already, she was too far away to call back.

As the last bit of dust settled back to earth, Leda decided to have the blacksmith in town punch a hole in the coin so she could wear it around her neck for luck. And before she'd finished that thought, Mr. Sloane, the banker, staggered out of his office, bleeding from a nasty cut on his forehead and shouting that he'd been robbed.

In the rush to care for the injured man and then to find the sheriff, Leda'd had time only to wonder why the Fates would so bless one person and curse another on the very same day.

She blinked suddenly and let the coin fall back into the nest of necklaces draped around her neck. Pushing the memory of that day to the back of her brain, Leda shook her head.

Fate. Everything came back to Fate.

No. As much as it pained her to leave her mother, Leda knew what she had to do. If her time was drawing near, she wanted to spend what little time the Fates granted her with the only family she had left.

Straightening her shoulders, she began to walk quickly toward the boardinghouse. If she hurried, she could be packed in time to catch the afternoon stage. And in one short week, she could be in Tanglewood, Idaho, with her uncle Garrett and his children.

A sad smile curving her lips, Leda told herself that she would do her best to make good use of however much time the Fates allowed her.

She only wished that she might have been allowed to find *him* before she died.

CHAPTER 1

Tanglewood, Idaho—two months later
"You're *here*!"

Leda James jumped up from behind the small table and stared openmouthed at the man entering her uncle Garrett's store. In the space of a quickly drawn breath, she'd forgotten all about Flora Lloyd and her reading.

"Leda?" the outraged woman sputtered. "Leda! You set back down and finish this! You can't leave me hangin' that way!"

But the young woman wasn't listening.

Hungrily, Leda looked at him. Tall, lean, with sandy blond hair and pale blue eyes, the stranger stared back at her. No, she corrected herself mentally, he wasn't a stranger. Not to her. Not really.

Her heart pounded erratically and she forced herself to take long, even breaths. Hadn't she been waiting for him more than half her life? Hadn't his face haunted her dreams almost nightly for years?

Not daring to look away for fear he might disappear as suddenly as he'd arrived, Leda took a half step toward him then stopped. The air in the tiny store was charged with the same power that filled the sky just before a storm.

Even Flora had stopped screeching.

Goosebumps raced along Leda's flesh, standing straight up on the surface of her skin. For a moment, she let her gaze trace the so familiar line of his strong jaw. Then her eyes shifted to linger on the full lips she'd waited what seemed forever to kiss.

Without wasting another moment, Leda grinned and raced across the room to him and threw herself against him. He staggered back, slamming into the door behind him. Ignoring her uncle's shout of surprise, Leda felt her man's arms close around her, steadying her. Tilting her head back, she smiled up at him.

"You're here. Just like she promised," she murmured. His eyes narrowed, his brow furrowed, he simply stared back at her, seemingly lost for words. It didn't matter, she told herself. What did they need with words now?

Her hand on his freshly shaven cheek, Leda pulled his head down to hers and kissed him. Her lips moved over his familiarly and she moaned deep in her throat. His touch was just as she'd known it would be. Soft, warm. Her stomach flopped, her blood rushed through her veins, and she heard a definite ringing in her ears.

For what seemed an eternity, she clung to him, her mouth moving over his, despite his lack of response. But when her lungs were straining for breath, she finally pulled away. Still pressed tight against him, she stared up into his eyes again and felt herself drawn into the pale blue depths. Briefly, she imagined how wonderful it would be if only they'd been given *years* to be together instead of weeks . . . maybe days.

She swallowed heavily. All these years, she told herself. The long days and even longer nights of wanting, dreaming, planning. She remembered how often she'd amused herself by wondering how he would appear. And where. Would he be mortally wounded and only *she* would know how to save him? Would he stumble onto her doorstep in the middle of a thunderstorm begging refuge?

Leda sighed. Now, when it was too late for any of her dreams to be realized . . . he walked into her life with the simple act of opening a door.

As she looked at him, a stab of confusion sliced through her. He looked angry. In fact, now that she paid closer attention, every inch of him screamed out with tightly leashed fury. Could it be that he'd been searching for her, too, all this time and was angry that it had taken him so long to find her?

She brushed the thought aside. Whatever the cause of his temper, it didn't matter. Surely he would see that. Nothing mattered now that he had finally found his way to her.

And even if the Fates had chosen to bring them together when all hope was lost, Leda James was not one to question *Destiny*. Whatever the reason for the timing of their meeting, she would simply accept her chosen one's arrival as the gift that it was.

"Leda girl," Flora asked worriedly, "are you all right?"

"Oh yes," Leda answered, her gaze never moving from the man in front of her. "I'm wonderful, *now*."

His head drew back and he stared at her, openmouthed. Slowly, he reached up, pulled her hands from behind his neck, and said, "My good woman, what in heaven are you thinking?"

"You even *sound* as I imagined you would."

"I beg your pardon?" She saw his questioning glance dart from her uncle to Flora, then back to her.

Shaking her head slowly, she licked suddenly dry lips and said quietly, "But you're too late, my love."

"Late?"

His voice, deep and rough, filled her and it took every ounce of her courage not to look away. But, she told herself, if she had to break his heart, she must at least look him in the eye.

"Yes," she said, despair choking her. "I can't marry you now. You see . . . I'm going to die."

*   *   *

Die?

Maxwell Evans stared down at the tiny woman still leaning up against him. What on earth was going on? First, a
total stranger throws herself at him, kissing him as if he
were her long-lost husband, in front of *everyone,* for God's
sake . . . then she calmly announces she can't marry him
because she's dying? Well, who *asked* her to marry him,
anyway?

"Garrett," he said, appealing to the other man, "would
you mind telling me just what is happening?"

The storekeeper was no help. He looked as lost as Maxwell felt.

"I don't know," the big man finally managed to say. "I
never seen her act like this before."

Her smile still in place, the woman stared at him with
all the hunger of a starving man for a shank of beef. She'd
pressed herself so tightly against him that the innumerable
necklaces of multicolored beads she wore around her neck
gouged into his flesh despite the heavy fabric of his shirt
and vest.

"She didn't tell me you'd be so tall," she whispered.

"Forgive me," he said, still trying to draw back.

"Oh no," she corrected quickly, "I *like* it."

"Well." Maxwell nodded and tried again to take a step
away. "I'm happy you approve."

Her waist-length red hair fell in loose waves around her
shoulders and her incredibly green eyes shimmered with a
haze of unshed tears. Burnished copper freckles dotted her
creamy complexion and her full lips trembled slightly with
her every breath.

She shifted in his arms, rubbing her generous breasts
against him. Immediately, his body responded and Maxwell
knew that she had to be aware of it. As close to him as she
was, she could probably tell exactly how many coins he
was carrying in his pockets! She seemed to melt into him
then and the contented sigh that left her told him she had
no intention of moving anytime soon.

Good God.

Had the entire world turned upside down, he couldn't have been more confused. Never in his life had he experienced anything remotely like the last few minutes.

He'd gone to Malone's store for the sole purpose of confronting the woman who'd appropriated his patients during his two-month absence from Tanglewood. Not knowing what to expect, he'd nevertheless been surprised to find a freckled . . . *pixie* dressed up as some sort of gypsy!

And there wasn't a doubt in his mind that *this* woman was the one that old Mrs. Fairfax had described to him only an hour ago as a "miracle worker." Even discounting her odd attire, she was the only stranger in the store.

Maxwell raised his gaze once more to Garrett Malone, standing behind his counter, arms folded across his barrel chest. Curiosity was etched on his features and Maxwell could hardly blame the man. Though he *would* have appreciated a little assistance.

At the table in the far corner, behind sacks of flour and sugar, sat Flora Lloyd, the gunsmith's wife. Her already thin lips were pursed in a straight line of aggravation as she studied Maxwell and the woman still pressed against him.

Maxwell lowered his gaze, took the pixie's elbows in his hands, and tried to set her back from him. But she was a limp weight. Suddenly it dawned on him.

Hadn't she said that she was dying?

Then surely she must be ill.

For heaven's sake, he told himself, as a *doctor* shouldn't he at least find out what was the matter with the woman? His anger disappeared and he willed his body to stop reacting to an obviously distressed woman.

"Are you ill?" he finally asked.

"Ill?"

She leaned her head back again and smiled up at him. He tried desperately to ignore the fact that her green eyes were tilted slightly at the corners.

"Yes," he answered, speaking slowly and distinctly. After

all, he had no idea what *type* of affliction she suffered from. "Are you feeling unwell?"

"Oh no." She shook her head fiercely, sending deep red curls into an abandoned dance about her features. "Not at all."

"Then . . ." Confused as ever, Maxwell again tried to set her from him. This time, she complied and stood on her own two feet. The top of her head barely reached his uppermost vest button.

For the first time, he got a good look at the rest of her unusual clothing. A plain white shirt, open at the throat and at least two sizes too big, was tucked into the waistband of a wide, full skirt. His eyes widened in horror at her choice of fabric—a garish blend of multicolored stripes and flowers that fell to the floor and rested across the tops of her feet . . . clad only in a pair of men's red wool socks.

Maxwell closed his eyes momentarily for strength, then let his gaze wander back up the woman. The countless ropes of beads and charms she wore around her neck intrigued him. He found himself wondering how such a small person could possibly support the weight of so many necklaces.

Still, he thought with determination, that really wasn't the point right now. The woman's health was in question. Her physical health of course. As far as Maxwell was concerned, there was *no* question about her mental health.

She didn't have any.

The insipid smile on her face as she continued to stare at him was proof enough of that!

He glanced at Garrett and noted disgustedly that the man hadn't stirred an inch. Instantly, he decided to stop looking to *that* quarter for help.

"What took you so long?"

Maxwell's gaze snapped back to the pixie. *Him?* What took *him* so long? At what? "I beg your pardon?"

"I asked you where you've been? Why didn't you come to me before?"

Those green eyes of hers fastened on him in silent appeal. He had the distinct impression that she was looking into his soul. Shuddering slightly, he shrugged off the nonsensical feeling.

"I am sorry, my good woman," he began with only a cursory glance at the storekeeper across the room, "but I really don't see how I could have arrived any earlier than I did. I only returned home last evening and—"

"No." She shook her head vehemently.

"But you *did* ask where I'd been and I—"

"No, my love," she said quite clearly.

"My love?" Maxwell frowned and shot a quick look at Flora Lloyd. Grimly, he realized that she'd heard the pixie's endearment. He squelched a groan.

"I *meant*," the redhead continued, "these last few years. Why did you wait until *now* to find me?"

The stares of the others in the room drilled into him and Maxwell felt their fascination. What was the matter with them? Didn't they realize the woman was mad? For heaven's sake! Was he the *only* one here with an ounce of common sense left?

He fought desperately to hold on to the rising tide of his own frustration and managed to say evenly, "I was unaware that I was supposed to be searching for you."

"You mean you didn't know?" Her breath caught and she laid one small hand on his chest. He felt the featherweight touch all the way to his bones. "Until this very minute, you didn't know?"

Her eyes filled again, and with the sheen of unshed tears, Maxwell's patience snapped.

"Didn't know *what*?"

She smiled gently, tilted her head to one side, and said quietly, "That we were destined to be together."

"What?" Good Lord. This couldn't be happening to him.

"It's true. I've known about you for years. I've waited for you *so* long." One tear slipped from the corner of her eye and rolled down the curve of her cheek. "And now, when we've finally found each other, the Fates have snatched us apart again."

"Fates?" She looked as though her heart were breaking.

Jerking a nod, she said in a strangled voice, "Yes. But why they're being so cruel, I don't know."

"Cruel?" In the back of his mind, Maxwell realized that he sounded like a parrot, repeating single words of her impossible speech, but somehow he couldn't help himself.

She nodded again and he watched the red curls bob up and down.

"It *is* cruel, don't you think? To bring us together just before I'm to die?"

Die. There she went again. A madwoman. Here, in Tanglewood. And, he told himself wryly . . . *no one* seems to care.

Finally, against his own better judgment, he asked, "What makes you think you're going to die?"

"I've seen the signs."

"Signs?" *Stop that!* he told himself silently.

"Yes, it's been made clear to me. That's why I've come home, you see."

"Home?" He surrendered to the inevitable. This had to be some kind of joke, he told himself. But a quick glance at Flora Lloyd's thin-lipped disapproval assured him that the woman wasn't laughing.

"To Uncle Garrett."

Max shot the man a look. *Uncle?* Garrett Malone shrugged his massive shoulders but didn't say a word.

"I wanted to be with my family when the end came." A heavy sigh escaped her and Maxwell had the distinct feeling that he was trapped in the middle of a very bad stage play.

This couldn't be real. *No one* actually *believed* in this nonsense. Did they?

He looked around the room frantically, hoping that someone would come to his aid. But there was no help coming.

"My dear woman," Maxwell started, deciding the only way to handle the situation was to take a firm hand. He took a step sideways and continued. "We are *all* going to die." Off to his left, he heard Flora sputter anxiously and he quickly added, *"Someday."*

"True," the gypsy said and closed the space between them, "but the Fates decide who will die and when. They've made their choice and now I'll have to leave you all alone."

Maxwell rubbed one hand over his jaw. Somehow, he'd lost control of the conversation. None of this was going at all well. He'd expected to come in, tell the meddler who'd gone poking into his practice that he was back, and leave again. As it looked now, the most he could hope for was simply to *leave*.

"Leda."

At last! Maxwell thought and looked hopefully at Garrett.

"Yes, Uncle?"

"Why don't you let the doc here get on home now? Don't you think you've given him enough to think about for one morning?"

"But—"

"Leda," Garrett went on, "we still got a lot of work to do." He shot a quick look at the doctor. "You got plenty of time to talk this thing over, the two of you. No need to do it all at once, y'know."

"I suppose," she agreed, then turned her liquid green gaze back on Maxwell. "Would that be all right with you, my love?"

"Uh, yes. Of course." *Anything* to get out of that store.

"*And,* missy," Flora added, rising from her chair like an avenging angel, "I'd like to remind you that I've already paid for my reading! It's high time we got back to it."

Reading? Maxwell wondered. What kind of reading? His gaze slipped past Flora to the table beside her.

Good Lord! What had happened in the time he'd been gone? Had everyone in town lost his mind?

There, in the middle of the table, resting on a small wooden pedestal square in the center of a black cloth, sat a *crystal ball*!

And he didn't have the slightest doubt as to whom it belonged.

CHAPTER 2

"Is that what I think it is?"

Curses and swears, Leda thought. The man's shout was enough to shatter windows! And she'd thought his anger gone. As he continued to sputter and wave one hand at her crystal ball, Leda watched him, fascinated.

Imagine that, she told herself silently, a *doctor*. That was one thing her mother hadn't mentioned. Of course, she admitted, as her intended stalked across the room to shout at her uncle, her mother'd also neglected to warn her about the good doctor's *temper*. Ah well, those were minor points, surely. Besides, even the most talented of seers, like her dear mama, couldn't be expected to get every little detail right.

Though Leda'd always known, deep in her heart, that he would one day show up, it was nevertheless astonishing when it finally happened. He was just as her mother'd drawn him, that long-ago night when she'd told her daughter about the man destined to be her husband. Remembering that faded pencil sketch, Leda could hardly wait to retrieve it from her trunk and examine it again.

This time, she could compare it to the living, breathing man in front of her.

She smothered a chuckle. "Breathing *fire*" would certainly be a more appropriate description of the doctor at this moment. His face mere inches from the storekeeper's, Leda watched as her Uncle Garrett's calm, unflappable nature slowly worked its soothing effect on the younger man.

"Doc," Garrett was saying, "you're gettin' all het up over something that surely ain't worth the effort."

Well, Leda thought. She wasn't sure she liked *that*.

"Garrett, I came over here to find out who it was that'd managed to pilfer my patients away from me in less than two months!"

Leda's beloved turned briefly to glare at her. She smiled back.

"And what do I find? I find a crazy woman, who kisses strangers, refuses marriage proposals that haven't been made, and talks of dying!"

Garrett's lips quirked slightly and the doctor snapped at him.

"*Nothing* about this is funny, Garrett!"

"I guess that's all in how you look at it, Doc," the other man countered.

Maxwell glared at the other man, but it didn't do the slightest bit of good. That amused smile of his never left Garrett's face.

"*Now,*" he said quickly, sucking in a gulp of air, "I see a crystal ball of all things, set up in your store!"

"That's right."

"Huh?"

"I said, you're right. It *is* my store." Garrett's massive shoulders rose and fell in an impressive shrug.

"Well, of course," Maxwell conceded.

"And Leda is my niece . . ."

The niece in question watched for the doctor's reaction and saw with relief that he seemed to be calming down. Good, she told herself. Under the temper, he was a reasonable man. That would make things much easier between them for whatever time they had together.

"All right," the doctor finally agreed, "your store. Your niece." He spun around suddenly to stare at the woman in question. "But the people in this town are *my* patients!"

"I don't think I care to be talked about as if I were a side of meat," Flora tossed in from the corner, "and I'm sure the rest of Tanglewood would agree with me, Doctor."

"I didn't mean it *that* way, Mrs. Lloyd."

"I should hope not!"

My goodness, he was a handsome man, Leda thought admiringly. And in a temper, his cheeks blossomed with the nicest color. Taking a few steps closer, she held out one hand toward him. "Of course the people here are your patients, my love. And I didn't *steal* anyone from you either. I never had any intention of *hurting* anyone." She gave him a smile. "I only wanted to help . . ."

"Don't call me that," he shot back, "and you didn't *hurt* me."

"I'm so glad," she answered. "Don't call you what?"

"Your . . . love."

"Oh, does that bother you? Well then, perhaps you wouldn't mind telling me your name?"

His head tilted to one side, he looked at her for a long moment before challenging, "Don't you *know* my name?"

"No. If I did, I wouldn't have asked."

"You mean you can't *see* it in your"— he jerked his head at the offending article—"crystal ball?"

"Of course not." She stepped even closer and laid one hand on his arm. "It's not a ledger, you know. Merely a guide to help me help others."

"Uh-huh."

"You *do* understand!" she said, delighted.

"Oh, I understand more than you'd like to think, I imag-ine."

"Doc . . ." Garrett growled out a warning.

Leda didn't even glance at her uncle. Instead, her gaze was locked on her intended.

"Tell me this, then, Miss . . ."

"James. Leda James." She smiled and added quickly, "And yours?"

Frowning, he said grudgingly, "Maxwell Evans."

Her brow furrowed, she tilted her head back and stared at the ceiling for a moment as she whispered his name, liking the sound of it on her lips. "Max," she finally said aloud and looked back at him. "I like it." She nodded firmly. "Max."

The doctor frowned more ferociously this time. "It's Maxwell. Or *Doctor* Evans."

"Oh, that's much too stuffy for a man like you."

She hadn't known it was possible for a man to look both offended and flattered at the same time.

"But Max suits you very well."

Her uncle gave a strangled cough and Leda made a mental note to talk to him about it at the first opportunity.

"On the contrary, Max doesn't suit me in the slightest."

"Oh! You mean no one else calls you Max?"

His pale blue eyes narrowed and his lips curved into a slight frown. "Of course not."

"That's even better, then!"

"What?"

"Well," she said cheerfully, "if no one else calls you Max, it can be my special name for you."

Strange, she told herself, but his cheeks were beginning to fill with color again. Whatever was wrong?

"Miss James, leaving my name aside for a moment, perhaps you could answer one question for me?"

"Of course, Max. What would you like to know?"

"How is it you have *seen* that we're to be married, but you don't know my name?"

"Oh!" She flashed a quick smile at her uncle, then turned it full force on the doctor. "*I* didn't see our marriage."

"Ah-hah!"

"My mother did."

"What?"

"Yes. She told me all about you when I was ten years

old." Leda closed the last small bit of space separating them. "Of course, she left out a few things . . ." Laying her hand on his chest, she was pleased to feel his heart pounding erratically. No matter his manner, it was clear that he felt far more than he was willing to admit. "So, you see? I *have* been waiting a very long time."

He stared down at her as if she had two heads.

"Uncle?" she asked, never moving her gaze from Max. "Tell him about Mama."

Maxwell's gaze slipped to the man behind the counter, but Leda continued to stare up at him.

"Well now, Doc." Garrett spoke slowly, haltingly. "My sister Eileen . . . well . . ."

"What about her?"

"Leda's right about that," he finally admitted on a long sigh. "Eileen *did* have the sight. Just like our grandmother before her."

"For heaven's sake, man!" Max's voice sliced through the stillness with the deadly accuracy of a bullwhip. "Surely you don't *believe* in such nonsense yourself!"

Garrett shrugged. "Not a question of believing or not. It just *is*."

"Good Lord."

His eyes came back to meet hers and Leda saw the battle being waged within him. She stifled a sigh. So, she told herself grimly. He *didn't* believe. It would have been so much easier if he had.

"Look," the doctor said, sidestepping away from both Leda and her uncle. "I don't know what kind of game you two are playing . . ."

"Game?" Leda took a step toward him.

He took two back and started edging his way to the door. "And if this is some kind of a joke, I must tell you I don't find it the least bit funny."

"This isn't a joke, Max."

"Maxwell." When he'd backed his way to the door, he stopped briefly. "But whatever your reasons, Miss James,

I'll thank you to stay away from my patients. *And* from me!"

Then he was gone.

Several seconds crawled by before Garrett Malone spoke quietly. "I'm sorry, Leda. The doc ain't such a bad fella, really, y'know. But—"

"It's all right, Uncle." Leda stood still, her gaze locked on the open doorway and the town beyond. "Remember, I've known about *him* most of my life. He just found out about *me*." She turned her head suddenly to smile at her uncle. "It will take Max a little time to get used to the idea, that's all." Silently, she prayed that the Fates would allow her enough time to wait him out.

"Leda . . ." The big man started shaking his head.

"Uncle Garrett," she challenged with a grin, "*you* should know better than anyone that you can't change Fate. Don't you have the three sons Great-grandmother promised you? And aren't you living in a land far from Ireland?"

The burly man's lips curved in a reluctant smile. "That I do, Leda darlin'. And as I remember it, when my granny told me what was to be, I laughed until I thought my chest would burst." Shaking his head, he turned for the storeroom door to his right. "Wherever she is now, I know Granny Doyle is havin' the last laugh!"

Her smile stayed with her until Garrett disappeared from sight. Then thoughtfully, Leda looked back at the doorway where Max had escaped. The last laugh, she thought idly. This time, it would be *her* turn.

"Leda!"

She spun around, sending the necklaces around her neck into a wild swing. "Flora," she said guiltily, as she watched the angular woman shift from foot to foot impatiently.

"Well," the woman snapped, "you *do* remember me! Do you think, now that you've got *your* future taken care of, we could finish talkin' about *mine*?"

Leda grinned. *Everyone*, it seemed, wanted to know their future. Everyone, that is, except Max Evans.

*   *   *

The very *tidiness* of the room was a reproach.

Maxwell sat at his desk and stared at his impeccably clean office. By this time of day, he'd usually seen any number of patients and the floor was marked with their dusty footprints.

There were typically two or three people sitting in his waiting room talking softly among themselves while waiting their turn to be treated.

Maxwell sighed heavily and cast one quick look through the open door to the waiting room. Empty. Just as it had been since he returned home three days ago.

Leaning back in his chair, he idly twirled a pencil between his fingers as he studied his problem. He well knew what the problem was. Or rather, *who*. What he didn't know was how to deal with her.

And what was he supposed to think of his patients? For five years, he'd lived and practiced medicine in Tanglewood. He'd seen the townspeople through diseases, broken bones, births, and deaths. He'd listened to their complaints, accepted payment in chickens and apple pies when they couldn't afford anything more . . . in general, he thought, he'd been an excellent doctor to these people!

He frowned and glared at the still room. The silence was deafening. "Here, then, is your reward, *Doctor*," he muttered thickly, "for your superb care of these good people. They've left you for a woman who reads *tea leaves,* for God's sake!"

Oh, fine, he told himself. *Now* he was becoming one of those pathetic creatures who not only talked to himself, but answered his own questions, as well!

He dropped the pencil to the desktop and rubbed his jaw tiredly. His return home hadn't gone the least bit as he'd expected it to.

All the way back from Boston, Maxwell'd planned the next five years of his life. After seeing to his late father's affairs, Maxwell had been more determined than ever to be a different sort of doctor than his father'd been.

Not that the elder Dr. Evans hadn't been a wonderful physician, of course. He was.

Maxwell's features softened in memory of the countless times his father had gone without sleep or food or both so that he could better spare time for the people in his care. He'd become such an integral part of his patient's lives that neither he nor they could have survived without the other.

But, Maxwell reminded himself, at least his father's patients believed in *loyalty*. He'd known several of the old man's patients to travel ten or twenty extra miles to see "Doc Evans" rather than seek out a closer, more convenient physician.

He snorted and the sound seemed to echo in the quiet of the old house. Loyalty certainly had nothing to do with the folks in Tanglewood.

After five years, he'd been gone less than two months to settle his late father's estate and see the man decently buried . . . and his practice had all but dried up completely.

So much for loyalty.

If he'd lost them to another doctor, he might at least be able to understand it. But to lose his patients to a would-be gypsy more comfortable with a crystal ball than a stethoscope . . . well, there *were* limits!

Hmmph. Gypsy. His lips quirked as he remembered her fall of red hair and the freckles dancing across her face. Hardly the type one would expect to find draped in shawls and beaded necklaces. She looked as though she'd be more at home in a schoolroom than anything else!

Not quite, his brain taunted as he recalled all too clearly the feel of her lushly curved body pressed against his and the warmth of her lips moving on his mouth. No, hardly a schoolgirl either.

Maxwell shifted uncomfortably in his chair. Just thinking about the woman's kiss and the way her green eyes lit up

when she spoke was enough to make his body tight all
over again.

"Oh no," he said firmly and shook his head violently to
underscore his determination. She wouldn't get to *him* as
easily as she had the others in town!

As for his attraction to her . . . Maxwell was willing to
acknowledge that it *was* formidable . . . but he would simply
ignore it. After all, attraction was easily enough explained.
He was a normal, healthy man and Leda James, he told
himself, was most *certainly* a healthy woman.

For an instant longer, he let himself remember that kiss
she'd greeted him with. But running close on the heels of
that memory came another. He snorted again.

She couldn't *marry* him? For God's sake! Who asked her
to? A completely *outrageous* woman!

Not the kind of woman he wanted.

Or needed.

Maxwell had long known the kind of woman he would
eventually settle down with. He'd made plans. Thought
it all out. Things *that* important in life could hardly be
left to chance. Nodding, he told himself that he needed a
calm, refined, *dignified* woman who would be an asset to
his career.

Hardly an accurate portrait of Leda James, he thought
with a smirk.

In his mind's eye, he saw his dream family again. A tall
woman—as yet faceless—but elegantly dressed, surrounded
by three tidy children. Two boys, one girl. And in the middle of that disciplined group . . . himself, smiling smugly.

Suddenly, though, his treacherous brain replaced the
faceless dream wife with Leda James's image. Maxwell
shuddered as his wife's fashionable costume was replaced
by Leda's *eccentric* finery. Then, as his imaginary children
shifted and changed, he groaned aloud.

His fine, strapping sons were suddenly . . . slovenly. Hair
too long, shirts untucked, holes in their britches . . . and
his *daughter*! His delicate, dainty daughter *now* wore an

ensemble similar to her mother's. On the little girl's lap was a crystal ball and perched on her shoulder . . . a black cat!

Horrified by his own mind's conjured images, Maxwell leaped up from behind his desk and hurried from his office. He had to see Garrett Malone. The man *must* send his niece away. *Far* away.

Leda bent over Gladys Fairfax's twisted fingers. Gingerly, she rubbed the cut side of half an onion over the swollen knuckles. She heard the old lady suck in a breath between clenched teeth and immediately gentled her touch.

"Have you been feeling any better at all, Gladys?"

"Hard to tell, Leda."

The woman's gray hair had straggled free of her outdated black bonnet. Beneath her knitted black shawl, Gladys's shoulders were slumped as if with the cares of the world, but her faded blue eyes were sharp.

"I understand," Leda murmured sympathetically.

"Don't see how you can," Gladys snapped back. "A body as young as yours could likely do most anything without a care! Me"—she sighed and winced as Leda transferred her attentions from one hand to the other—"it's gettin' so's I don't hardly step foot outside my house no more."

"You come here," Leda looked up and grinned.

"Don't you get smart with *me*, young woman!" Gladys sniffed and her beaked nose quivered with the effort. "I only come 'cause I promised to give them onions of yours a fair try."

"And I appreciate it."

"Ain't you about done yet?"

"Almost," Leda said, then asked, "Why don't you go on telling me about your son? We were interrupted on your last visit."

"Hmmph! Don't I know it? That Flora Lloyd . . . you'd think she'd have enough to worry about with that husband of hers and all them kids! What in heaven does she want to know her future for?"

"People like to plan ahead, Gladys. It gives them comfort."

"I always say, the Good Lord likes surprises . . . and who are *we* to try to outguess Him?"

Leda smiled inwardly. The old woman was just lonely. Oh, her arthritic hands pained her enough, true. But if she could only step outside herself a bit . . . get involved with more than her own aches and pains . . .

"You were going to tell me about your son?" she prodded.

"I ain't that old, missy! My mem'ry still works just fine, thank you."

"I'm sure," Leda said and carefully rubbed the onion juices on a particularly large knuckle on the woman's second finger.

"There really ain't much to tell about Lester, y'know," the woman conceded slowly. "Since he married up with that *woman*, he don't have time for his ma at all."

"But didn't I hear something about him wanting you to move to San Francisco to live with them?"

"Oh"—Gladys waved her free hand in dismissal—"that was just his way of easin' his conscience. That female he married don't want no truck with me, I can tell you!"

"But *I* heard your daughter-in-law was a fine woman."

"Who told you that?"

"August Haley."

"Hmmph!" she snorted. "I thought as much! That man's a worse gossip than any woman I ever met! Don't know why he don't spend more time in his telegraph office instead of wanderin' around flappin' those lips of his! 'Sides, how's he know Geraldine anyway?"

"Oh," Leda answered, hiding her smile behind the fall of her hair, "when your son and his wife were here last year, August says that Geraldine made it a point to meet the folks in town. Said she wanted to make sure that there were plenty of neighbors to help you out if you needed it." Risking a glance at the woman opposite her, Leda was pleased to see a surprised expression cross the weathered, lined features.

"Hmmm . . ." Gladys was silent for a moment before saying brusquely, "*Told* ya she don't want me livin' with her and Lester. She's just makin' sure that some *stranger* will be handy to do what Lester *should* be doin'."

"Now, Gladys—"

"What in the name of heaven are you doing to my patient?"

Leda looked up, grinned in welcome, then turned back to her task. "Hello, Max. I'm rubbing onion juices on Gladys's hands."

"I can *see* that!" he shouted back. He sniffed and wrinkled his nose in distaste. "What I want to know is *why!*"

She glanced at him, her lips quirking slightly. "You didn't *ask* that," she pointed out.

"You can read minds, supposedly. I'm sure you knew what I meant."

"Oh." She set the onion down for a moment and stretched the kinked muscles in her neck. "I can't read minds, Max. Only the future."

He opened his mouth but before he could speak, Gladys cut him off.

"Dr. Evans, if you want to see Leda here"—she jerked a nod in the younger woman's direction—"you'll have to wait your turn like ever'body else."

"You mean I need an *appointment*?"

"Oh," Leda tossed in quickly, "not really. As soon as I'm finished with Gladys, we can talk."

"But she ain't about to hurry on *your* account, neither, young man!" Gladys Fairfax glared at him and Leda watched the changing expressions on Max's face with interest. Briefly, she saw anger, confusion, frustration, and disbelief chase each other across his handsome face.

Finally, though, he seemed to calm down a bit. Leda took that moment to look her fill of him. She'd just passed

through the longest three days of her life. It had taken every
ounce of her self-control not to go running off to see him.
But she'd realized at last that he *did* need time to adjust to
his Fate. She couldn't expect to just show up unannounced
on his doorstep so to speak and have him feel the same
spark of Destiny that had filled her.

One lock of his honey-blond hair fell over his forehead
and she wondered idly if he even knew it. Standing there
in his perfectly fitted black suit with a gold watch chain
stretched across his vest, he looked the very image of a
solid, respected professional man. Only the high color in
his cheeks gave proof to his indignation of only a moment
before.

Such a handsome man, she told herself thoughtfully. Oh
Mama, you were so right. He is everything you promised
he would be. And well worth the wait.

So many times over the past few years, Leda'd turned
down offers of marriage from otherwise nice, well set-up
men. And as the years passed and she became more used to
the idea of being "on the shelf," there'd even been moments
when *she'd* doubted, when she'd asked herself if she had
passed up her chance for happiness in exchange for her
mother's prediction of true love.

Now, though, looking up at Maxwell Evans, Leda was
glad she'd waited. Even knowing that she was destined to
die soon, she wouldn't have missed the chance of finally
meeting him, touching him, for anything.

"Leda girl!"

Shaken out of her thoughts, she turned to face Gladys.
Imperiously, the old woman was holding her right hand out
as if she expected it to be kissed. Instead, Leda picked up
the onion half, took the woman's hand in hers, and began
the slow treatment again.

"An *onion*," Maxwell muttered thickly.

"The juices are good for all manner of things," Leda
explained, ignoring his skeptical tone.

"Certainly can't do no worse than you done with all your pills and such, Doc," Gladys said firmly.

"Mrs. Fairfax—" Maxwell started.

"Hush now," the old woman snapped. "I ain't in *your* office. I'm in Leda's."

"Her *office*?"

CHAPTER 3

Her *office*? Maxwell repeated it silently and *still* couldn't believe he'd heard correctly!

Quickly, his pale blue eyes flicked over the general store. Floor-to-ceiling shelves, packed full with every conceivable piece of merchandise, from books to harnesses, lined the walls. Jars, filled with everything from flour to hard candy stretched out along the scarred but polished counter. The distinctive scents of tobacco, leather, even pickles from the nearby barrel, mingled together like old friends, welcoming everyone who entered.

A good, well-stocked, friendly little store. But an office? Hardly.

Saddle blankets and drawings clipped from old magazines dotted the plank walls. Hanging from the overhead beams were saddles, spurs, drying herbs, and ropes of all sizes.

His gaze snapped back up. Herbs? Since when did Garrett Malone dry herbs in his store? His lips twisted in a parody of a smile. He already knew the answer.

Since Leda James arrived in town, no doubt.

Naturally, he thought with a quick glance at the two women seated at opposite sides of the small table. A woman with her very own crystal ball would of course insist on fresh herbs!

Maxwell bit down on the inside of his cheek. Mentally, he began a slow count to ten, hoping that it would bring him some sense of calm. Then a breeze drifted in through a hole in the front windowpane, and drove the sharp, over-powering scent of sliced onion at him.

He wrinkled his nose and gave up counting altogether. It was no use, he admitted. It was simply *impossible* to stay calm!

His gaze drifted back to the good-sized hole in Garrett's front window. Thoughtfully, he studied it. He was almost sure it hadn't been there a couple of days ago.

"It was an accident."

He looked at Leda and found her staring up at him. "What did you say?"

"The window. Weren't you wondering how it got broken?"

Exasperated, he shot back, "Are you trying to tell me you *knew* what I was thinking?"

She laughed and he hated himself for enjoying the sound.

"Of *course* I knew!"

"But—"

"Max, you *were* staring at the hole with a scrunched-up look on your face!" Leda smiled at him and he noticed how the sparkle in her eyes shone brighter with her delight. "I didn't need a crystal ball to guess what you were think-ing."

"Oh."

Leda shook her head and Maxwell found himself watch-ing the light play on her hair as the waves of curls danced with her movements. He kept watching her even after she lowered her head to concentrate on Gladys Fairfax's hands. As she worked, she talked.

"It was the strangest thing . . . that window, I mean," she began.

"You *could* say so," Gladys agreed.

"What?" Maxwell demanded, forcing himself to stop staring at the woman's hair. After all, he'd seen red hair before. Hadn't he?

"Well," Leda said and smoothed onion juices across Gladys's wrist bone, "yesterday afternoon, one of the local farmers came in for supplies—"

"Tom Shipley," Gladys tossed in.

"Ah." Maxwell nodded. Tom Shipley. The crankiest man in Idaho Territory. It had taken Maxwell almost two years to win the man's trust.

He shook himself mentally when he realized that Leda was speaking again.

"And as he was leaving, I had the strongest feeling that he was in danger." Leda set the onion down and looked up at Maxwell.

"Danger?" He frowned. "What kind of danger?"

"Well"—she chewed at her lip for a moment before continuing—"I just *knew* that if he left through the back door, where his wagon was parked, that something *terrible* would happen."

Amazed by the woman's certainty in her own notions, Maxwell was nonetheless interested in the finish of the story. "And . . ."

"And I convinced him that it would be much safer if he left by the front door and let Uncle Garrett's son Sean bring the Shipley wagon around." Her brow furrowed, she stared into space. "So Tom walked out the front door and hadn't taken more than a step or two when a *huge* dog, at a dead run, came out of nowhere and crashed into him."

"Wonder where that dog come from," Gladys murmured thoughtfully.

Shaking her head, Leda said, more to herself than the others, "Most unusual." Inhaling sharply, she went on. "Well, naturally, Tom lost his balance and fell backward into the window."

"Oh, naturally," he commented and wasn't surprised to see his sarcasm drift right past her.

"Wonder where that dog *went*," Gladys said to no one in particular.

Leda nodded at Maxwell. "His head hit the window, I'm afraid."

"The dog's?" he asked. "Or Tom's?"

The pixie laughed again. "*Tom's,* silly."

"His *head*?"

"Uh-huh." She nodded, then brightened. "But the cut wasn't *too* deep."

"Cut?" He was doing it again. Parrotting everything she said.

"Back here." Leda half turned in her chair and drew an imaginary line across the back of her head. "Of course, I had to cut off quite a bit of his hair to be able to sew him back up—"

"*You* stitched his wound?"

He couldn't believe it! Two years. It had taken nearly two years to get to the point where he was now allowed to listen to the man's chest with a stethoscope! Through a shirt, of course. It'd probably take another *ten* years before the old bastard would be willing to unbutton for a doctor!

Maxwell had consoled himself with the certainty that it wasn't *him* personally Shipley didn't trust. He'd always told himself that if the old man severed an *artery,* he'd probably demand qualifications from a doctor before allowing the wound to be closed.

Apparently, he was wrong.

"Of course I did." She turned back around and smiled up at him. "He was bleeding all over the boardwalk. It seemed the only proper thing to do."

"It never occurred to you to go for a *doctor*?"

"Oh!" She covered her mouth with her fingertips. "Isn't that silly? You know, it never *did*." Then she shrugged and graced him with a dazzling smile. "But you know, the town's been without a doctor since I got here. I guess I didn't think."

"I guess not." Maxwell's hands curled into helpless fists.

He could hardly blame her, he supposed. After all, she did what was necessary. But what about the *rest* of Tanglewood? They knew he was home. They knew he was a doctor. Why hadn't *they* come for him?

"How did you know how to do it?" he asked, when he had control of his emotions again.

"Well, it's not that much different than stitching a hem, is it?"

A hem.

"Although Tom Shipley certainly isn't the most *grateful* of men, I must say."

"Grateful?" His voice grated on his own ears.

Gladys snorted.

Maxwell snapped a glance at her.

Looking back at Leda again, he asked, "Would you mind telling me what he had to be *grateful* for?"

"Max, my love," Leda said with a slight shake of her head, "weren't you listening? I already told you. If I hadn't been here, he would have gone out the back door to certain doom!"

"So he should be grateful that he was merely *maimed*?" He threw his arms wide. "If not for you, he wouldn't have gone out the front door, wouldn't have been attacked by a dog, and certainly wouldn't have cracked his head open!"

She laughed again and Maxwell ground his teeth together. She paid no more attention to his anger than she would to a child's temper tantrum.

"Hardly *maimed*. It was just a little cut. Why, when I take the stitches out in a couple of weeks, he'll be good as new." She chewed at her lip again. "Of course, he'll probably want to wear his hat all the time until his hair grows out. I'm afraid I'm not much of a barber . . ."

Gladys snorted louder this time and didn't bother to hide her amusement. "Barber? Hon, I've seen *scalpin's* done neater than what you did to that ol' cuss!"

"Gladys!" Leda tried to look offended.

"Oh botheration, girl." The old woman chuckled. "Folks

in town got a real kick out of seein' that pile of buzzard bait done in by a dog. And that bandage of yours was just the topper!" She looked up at Maxwell and grinned. "This child had so much paddin' on them stitches, ol' Tom couldn't get his hat on a'tall! That's how we got such a good look at that blamed haircut she give him. I tell you, Doc . . . he looked like an old hound with the mange."

Leda's laughter spilled out into the room again. "I *am* sorry about his hair, Gladys. But who knows *what* might have happened to him if he'd gone out the back way like he wanted to."

"Uh-huh," Maxwell offered, his voice tightly controlled, "and I don't suppose you happened to notice if anything unusual occurred at the back entrance, did you?"

"Whatever for?"

"Well, for one thing, you might have held your evidence up to Tom Shipley to convince him that you were right."

"Max, dear"—she sighed patiently—"don't you understand? *Nothing* happened at the back entrance."

"Exactly!"

"Because," she continued quickly, "Tom wasn't there."

He opened his mouth to speak then snapped it shut again. Staring down at her wide-eyed, innocent expression. Maxwell wondered how he could argue with that kind of logic. She actually *believed* everything she was saying. She *believed* that if Tom Shipley had walked out the back door, something more serious than a crack on the head would have happened to him.

Maxwell inhaled slowly, deeply. Two months. She'd only been in town two months. His brain taunted him with the fact over and over. Two months and she was on a first-name basis with Gladys Fairfax. He frowned sullenly. The old woman had never given *him* leave to call her Gladys.

Hell, the infuriating woman even called Mr. Shipley by his Christian name! For the first six months Maxwell'd been in Tanglewood, he wasn't sure the crotchety man *had* a first name.

Somehow, she'd wormed her way into the heart of a town that Maxwell'd labored to be a part of for five years. And she'd done it in record time. His jaw clenched for fear he'd start shouting again, he glared at her.

There she sat, he thought, as pleased with herself as a cat with kittens, *bragging* about how she'd stitched up one of *his* patients! Not only that, his mind screamed, she'd already made plans to take the stitches out, as well!

He'd just see about *that!*

"So, *Doctor* James," he said, sarcasm dripping from every word, "just when did you plan on going to Mr. Shipley's farm?"

Leda reached for a small wooden chest sitting on her right. As he watched, she lifted the lid. Inside were several dozen small cotton bags, each closed tightly with a drawstring. And around each drawstring was a small slip of paper.

She pushed the bags around with her finger until she found just the one she was looking for, then closed the chest again and set it back down. Turning to Gladys, she held out the tiny cloth bag.

Before the old woman could take it, though, Maxwell snatched it from Leda's hand. With both women staring at him as if he'd lost his mind, he asked again, "When were you going out to the Shipley farm?"

"Oh, I couldn't *possibly* find the time to go all the way to Tom's farm." She cocked her head and smiled up at him. "But he promised to come here to the store himself in a couple of weeks."

"*He's* coming to *you*?"

"Of course! Ordinarily, I wouldn't have minded going out into the countryside at all . . ."—She sighed tiredly—"But there seem to be so many people needing my help lately."

"I see." Naturally she was busy! She'd stolen all of his patients! But in two weeks, when Tom Shipley came to town, Maxwell himself would be waiting to take the stitches out. Though he was willing to understand how she might have felt obliged to sew Tom up . . . there was no reason at all that *he*, a *doctor*, shouldn't be the one to finish the case.

"I knew you'd understand, my love." Her expression sobered instantly. "Besides, in my final days, I'd like to save my strength as much as I can."

"Of course." His fingers tugged at the bag's drawstring. Idly, he noted the name "Gladys" written on the tiny slip of paper. What now? he asked himself.

"Now, Leda girl," Gladys piped up, "don't you start that dyin' nonsense again, y'hear?"

"Thank you, Gladys," Leda answered quickly and gave the old woman's hand a pat. "You're a dear friend, but there is no arguing with Fate."

Maxwell snorted, lifted the bag and sniffed the contents. He sniffed again. What in the name of heaven was in the bag? He couldn't quite place the smell. Truth to tell, he couldn't really smell *anything* but onions!

Snapping the drawstring shut again, he held tight to the bag and said shortly, "What is this? Have you taken to prescribing medication now?"

"Doc," Gladys shot back, "you got a real nasty tone to your voice sometimes, you know that?" With a speed belying her age and arthritic joints, the old woman snatched the bag from his hand and held it close to her bosom. "A body would think you'd be pleased that I finally found me something to give me a little comfort from the pain!" She pushed herself up from the table, straightened her shawl slowly, and glared at Maxwell until he stepped out of her way.

"*You* never give me nothin' that helped as much as what Leda here gives me."

"Mrs. Fairfax," he started lamely but stopped at the warring gleam in her eye.

"Not one more word, young man." Her gaze slipped to

Leda momentarily. "Thank you, child," she said quietly.

"You're welcome, Gladys. Now you remember what I told you to do with the onion tonight . . ."

The gray head nodded firmly. "I'll remember!" She turned to leave, but managed to give Maxwell one last frosty stare.

He waited until the old woman had stepped out onto the boardwalk before whispering harshly, "What was in that bag?"

"Tea."

"Tea?"

"Tea."

"And *that* cures her pain?" He shoved one hand through his hair then rubbed his chin viciously. "You expect me to believe that?"

Leda smiled softly and stood up. "The tea is raspberry with a touch of basil. It's a soothing tea, good for aches and pains of all kinds. But I believe the preparation does her more good than anything else."

"What?"

"It gives her something to do. Something to think about. Makes her feel less helpless."

"Gladys Fairfax? Helpless?"

Leda smiled again and stepped closer. "She's lonely, Max. As we all are when we're separated from those we love."

He cleared his throat and looked down at her. She was entirely too close. A faint scent of roses seemed to surround her. Funny that he could hardly smell the onions when she was near.

Onions. Hadn't she said something to Gladys about onions?

"What, uh . . ." he said and tried to move back a pace. "What did you mean when you told Gladys to remember the onions tonight?"

"Oh," she answered, closing the gap between them and laying one hand on his chest, "she's to cut an onion in half

and leave the open halves in her room. Then throw them
away in the morning."

"Uh-huh," he said, trying to ignore the warmth of her
that seemed to seep down into his bones. "And what good
will *that* do?"

"The cut onion will soak up the illness and pain in the air.
Then when she throws them away tomorrow, she'll throw
away the pain, as well."

Nonsense. Utter, complete nonsense. He'd never heard
such a pack of claptrap in his life. If he had the slightest
amount of sense, he would see her locked up for her own
safety.

For God's sake! Onions, teas, *dying*!

She certainly didn't seem in any danger of dying to *him*!
On the contrary, from where he stood, she appeared to
be just about the *healthiest* woman he'd come across in
some time!

He stifled a groan as she leaned into him.

"I'm so glad you came to see me, my love," she whispered.

"Maxwell."

"Max."

He bit his tongue.

"It's been *such* a long three days." Her fingers slid up
his chest to his throat.

Like tiny match flames, he felt the warmth of each of her
fingers as they moved over his flesh.

"And we've lost so much time already . . ."

"Time?" he repeated and silently cursed himself.

"Time forever lost, Max." Her other hand snaked up
his chest to his shoulders and cupped the back of his
head. "And who knows how much time we have left to
us . . ."

"Yes, well . . ." How in the *devil* had they gotten off on
such a tangent? He'd come to the store filled with righteous
indignation and now . . . He groaned inwardly. Now, all he
could think of was how good she felt. He'd never known

the kind of wild desire that coursed through him at the mere sight of her.

Oh, he'd wanted—and *had*—his share of women over the years. But no woman had ever had the effect on him that this one crack-brained lunatic did.

"Miss James," he started, congratulating himself on the strength of his voice.

"Leda," she breathed and stroked his cheek gently.

"Very well. Leda." Reluctantly, he reached up and grabbed her wrists. Holding them tightly, he swallowed and said, "You don't even know me, Leda. Didn't anyone ever tell you that it was foolhardy behavior to tempt even the *best* of men?"

She smiled, wider this time, and he couldn't help but notice the tiny dimple in her cheek.

"And you *are* the best of men, my love."

"You must stop that."

"What?"

"Calling me that. Your love."

"But you are." She pulled at his hand, still holding one of her wrists prisoner, and forced him to touch her chest. "Can't you feel my heart pounding?"

He swallowed heavily. He could feel it . . . and more. That was the problem.

"Can you really say that you don't, Max?" She stood on her toes, lifting her face toward his. "This tie between us. This magic . . . I know you feel it, too, my love." Her lips pressed against his gently, reverently.

He steeled himself for her touch and even then his head swam at the first contact of his mouth on hers. Even stronger than the first time she'd kissed him, he felt the jolt of their joining shake him to the bone.

For what seemed forever, her lips dusted across his with the lightest of touches. As if she were waiting for him. Waiting for him to acknowledge what she thought existed between them.

Maxwell fought harder than he'd ever fought before and

still his control deserted him. With a groan deep in his throat, he dropped her hands and pulled her to him. Slanting his mouth over hers, Maxwell eagerly fed the flames consuming him. Her breath puffed against his cheek, and when she parted her lips for him and his tongue first invaded her, he felt as though he'd come home.

A home that he'd never expected. A home unlike the one he'd always planned for himself. A home that could, eventually, destroy him.

And with that thought burning into his brain, he jerked free of her. He tried not to notice the smile on her face or the happiness shining in her eyes.

His chest heaving with the effort to breathe, he looked down at her and saw her for the danger she was.

Not to his practice, his livelihood. But to his soul.

Leda knew it the moment he pulled away. It wasn't a "vision." It was simply that on some level, deep within herself, she *felt* what he felt.

Like nothing she'd ever known before, she wanted to savor this connection with him. She wanted to explore every bit of it. To glory in the knowledge that she'd finally found the man she was meant to be with. But she couldn't.

At least not yet.

Not until she was sure his misgivings were gone. There was something in him that fought against her. It was in his arms when he held her. Almost as if he were fighting himself, instead of her.

Now watching him, she saw worry and regret in his eyes. If she only had *time,* she thought sadly. If they'd only met years ago, when the world would have stretched out before them with open arms.

She smothered a sigh and told herself that it was pointless to torture herself with what-might-have-beens. It was better to accept what Fate handed you and take pleasure in it than to be miserable with wanting more.

Max took a step back from her, and she could see that

in moments, he'd be running for the door. A soft smile curved her lips as she reminded herself that he wasn't the *first* nonbeliever she'd had to deal with.

Only the most important.

"Miss James," he finally said.

"Leda."

"Miss James."

She sighed and waited as he pulled in a deep breath before speaking again.

"This . . . *prescribing* for my patients has got to stop. Do you understand?"

Her eyes widened at the unexpected shift of the conversation. How he must have struggled inwardly to find something to talk about besides their soul-shattering kiss. Poor Max, she thought helplessly. He has so much to learn.

"All right, Max," she agreed pleasantly. "But you know, I don't really 'prescribe' medicines at all. I just like to help."

"I've *seen* what you consider 'help,' Miss James. And I think the people of Tanglewood can get along quite nicely without it."

Her shoulders lifted in a slight shrug. She didn't see anything wrong with offering help to people in need . . . and she wasn't about to stop, no matter *what* he thought.

Beloved or not, he was in no position to deny *her* Destiny. On the other hand, though, she also didn't think now was the best possible time to tell him that. Instead, she said, "If you think so, Max. But—"

"No buts. All this nonsense with teas, *onions* of all things!" He waved a hand at her little table.

She saw how his mouth tightened just *looking* at the crystal ball. Well, that was one more thing he'd have to get used to. For the life of her, Leda couldn't understand what it was that had him so *irritated*. Was it help in general that he objected to . . . or just *her* help?

Idly, her fingers toyed with her good-luck coin. She moved it back and forth over its chain and tried to think

what to do. She certainly didn't want to get on Max's
bad side, but then again, she couldn't very well turn down
people in need, could she?

"Are you listening to me?"

"Yes," she said and looked up at him. The truth was,
she enjoyed listening to him. Even the timbre of his voice
did strange things to her. It was as though the very sound
slipped inside her and tugged at her heart.

Deliberately, her gaze fastened on his mouth and, for a
moment, she let herself remember the taste of him. The feel
of him pressed close against her. Oh, there was so much her
mother hadn't told her.

Leda'd never dreamed that meeting the man promised to
her would be so much like finding a missing part of her
own soul.

She saw him shift position uneasily then and forced herself to empty her mind. Like it or not, she would have to
go slowly with him.

At least at first.

"Good," he said with a firm nod, as if pleased with
her attention. "I'm happy to see that you've decided to
be sensible about this." He took another half step back
as though he were still leery enough of her to keep his
distance. "After all, no one in their right mind could *really*
believe that an *onion* can absorb disease!" He crossed his
arms over his chest before continuing. "I don't know what
kind of game you're playing, but . . ."

Leda wasn't listening anymore. She let her gaze slip
away from him. Staring blindly at the towering shelves
behind him, she gave her mind free rein. There was *something* she was supposed to remember. But what? Onion,
Max'd said. Her brows drew together and she rubbed her
thumb over her bottom lip. What was it? What had she
forgotten?

Onion . . .

"Curses and swears!" Pushing past Max, Leda ran for
the door.

"Where are you going?" he shouted. "We haven't finished yet!"

She tried to stop, but her red wool socks slid across the polished floor. Waving her arms frantically for balance, Leda reached out with one hand for a nearby shelf to steady herself. When she finally came to a wobbly halt, her necklaces swung out in a wide arc and she had to push her hair out of her eyes.

"I'm sorry, Max. But I just remembered something I forgot to tell Gladys!"

"What?"

"About the onions!" Leda shook her head. "Honestly, when I'm around you, I forget everything else."

He cleared his throat uncomfortably. "Well, what is so important that you have to run off while we're having a discussion?"

"I told you. The onions. I forgot to tell Gladys not to touch them with her hands when she throws them away tomorrow morning."

"What *possible* difference can that make?"

"Oh, Max." She sighed helplessly. "If her hands touch them, all the bad air they've soaked in overnight will just rub off on *her*."

"Of all the . . ."

She grinned, waved, and said, "I'm sure I'll see you later, though? You can finish lecturing me then, all right?"

Lecturing? Max frowned but she wasn't there to see it. She'd already run out the door, across the boardwalk, and into the street.

He leaned closer to the front window and looked out through the spider-cracked glass. Her gaudy skirt hiked up above her knees, her legs bare but for the red socks, Leda ran down the middle of the road headed for Gladys's house.

Breath held, Max watched her hair stream out behind her like a shining red curtain. His jaw clenched, he noticed that several *other* men were paying much too close attention to Leda's very shapely legs.

CHAPTER 4

Montana-Idaho border
"What do you *mean,* you lost her?"

Cecelia Standish looked at the two men opposite her and, not for the first time, fought down the urge to slap them senseless. Of course, knowing how little sense her henchmen possessed, it wouldn't have to be much of a slap.

She would be able to accomplish her goal of retiring to Europe much more quickly if she hired men who were able to think for themselves. But she couldn't afford to take that chance. An intelligent man would be difficult to handle. And much more likely to try to take control of her little operation.

No, she told herself, it was better in the long run, no matter *how* maddening, to deal with these two cretins. At least *this* way, she didn't have to watch her back.

Her gaze snapped quickly over the older of the two, noting the gaudy checked suit jacket he wore over well-patched jeans. His whiskey-clouded eyes shone in appreciation as he stared back at her, but she ignored it.

The younger man, tall and skinny with an habitual twitch in his right eye, began to speak and she braced herself for the inevitable excuses.

45

"Well now, boss," Cooter said with a pleading glance at his partner, Deke. "We done like you said an' all . . . but she just up and took off." He shrugged and his ill-fitting coat slapped around his too thin frame. "Nobody seems to know where she went."

"Marvelous." Her dry voice cracked over them like a bullwhip.

Cooter winced and cast yet another look at Deke. But the older man looked unconcerned. Sometimes Cooter envied his partner's bad ear. Hell, he was practically deaf. Unless the boss was to screech and yell at them, Deke wouldn't hear a blessed thing.

And the boss *never* yelled.

She didn't have to.

He ran one finger under his collar and wished for the tenth time in so many minutes that he was *anywhere* but where he was.

Oh, the money was good. There was no denyin' that! Hell, ever since him and Deke had hooked up with the Queen, they never lacked for eatin' money. There'd even been a few times, when she wasn't around, that him and Deke had really cut loose.

He almost smiled as he recalled that week in Cheyenne. Between the drinkin' and the gamblin' and all them fine girls that worked at the Silver Dollar . . . well, they'd about wore themselves out! Lordy, what he'd give to be back in sweet Cindy's talented arms right now.

But he wasn't.

And unless he started talkin' fast and thinkin' even faster, he didn't have a hope in hell of *ever* seein' the likes of Cheyenne again.

"I've *tried* to explain to you two how important it is to find that woman." Her tone told him she was about out of what little patience she had.

Ol' Queenie was at it again. Talkin' to him like he didn't have a brain in his head. He shot another quick glance at Deke and swallowed his frown. For all that the man made a good travelin' partner . . . he was no help at all dealin' with the boss.

"I know all that," Cooter said in what he hoped was a soothing tone. One thing he couldn't afford to do was make her mad. " 'Cause that female picked up a coin you dropped and—"

"So!" the elegant woman opposite him interrupted. "You think to blame this debacle on *me*!"

Cooter wasn't sure what "debakel" meant, but he was fairly sure it didn't bode no good at all for him.

"No, ma'am," he said quickly, trying to head off her temper before she really got rollin'.

"That's better," Cecelia said, then added, "Don't call me ma'am either. I am not your elderly grandmother."

"No, ma'am, uh . . . boss."

The elegant woman glared at him for a moment before speaking again. "If you and your half-witted partner here"— she waved a long-fingered hand dismissively at Deke—"had taken care of that bank manager as you should have, *none* of this would have happened." She strolled around the tiny cabin she'd bought for the express purpose of having a hidden meeting place. And as she walked, her voice rose with every step. "*Then* the woman would never have put me and that robbery together. But no! You two can't even hit a man over the head properly! He was up and out the bank door screaming for help while my stagecoach was still rolling down Main Street!"

"Now, Cecelia," Deke finally managed to say.

Cooter couldn't believe it! He turned and stared at his partner. The man at last works up the nerve to talk and says the one thing he shouldn't.

"That's *Miss Standish*," she snapped, twirling around to face the older man. "You demented, inept bungler!"

Deke winced and even his salt-and-pepper whisker stubble seemed to shrink a bit. Cooter almost felt sorry for him, but then he remembered how the fool had muffed his shot at the gypsy woman.

Silently, though, he acknowledged that his own idea of a rock-filled grave hadn't done much better. In fact, his arm still throbbed somethin' fierce.

He watched Cecelia as she strode purposefully around the cabin. Once she got past her mad, he knew she'd have a plan. And whatever she came up with, it would be a beaut. He'd at least discovered *that* much in the time he'd been workin' for her. And a little touchy she might be, but as long as the money was good, he'd stick around.

"All right," she finally announced through gritted teeth. "We'll have to forget about our little gypsy for the time being.

"There's another job I want to talk to you two about. *If,*" she said, glaring at them pointedly, "you think you'll be able to handle it without blundering *too* badly?"

Cooter grinned and just stopped himself from clappin' Deke on the back. Now they were gettin' down to it. All her plans swung around big money. Besides, he'd be just as happy to forget about that redheaded gypsy altogether. He was beginnin' to think she was bad luck for them.

The dog was back.

He erupted suddenly from the surrounding woods and flew at Leda as though he'd been shot from a cannon. She hardly had time to gasp in surprise before she was flat on her back.

No one had seen him since he'd knocked Tom Shipley into the store window. And he would have been hard to miss.

Her face only inches from the animal's, she squinted against his hot, panting breath and excited slobber. He held her down firmly, with his forefeet planted solidly on her shoulders. As if from a distance, she heard her cousin's worried voice asking, "Leda? Leda, you all right?"

Since she didn't have the breath to answer right away, Leda instead looked up into big brown eyes, nearly hidden by a fall of dirty white hair. The massive dog's tongue hung

from one side of its open mouth and its wide chest moved
in and out rapidly with its short, raspy breaths. Covered in
dirt and grass, the beast looked as though he'd been on his
own for quite a while.

He also looked delighted to be where he was.

She grinned when the beast dipped his head and washed
her face with one long stroke of his tongue.

"I'm fine, Dennis," Leda finally said on a half laugh as
she turned her face to avoid another washing.

"Whose do you suppose he is?"

She glanced at her cousin and smiled. Dennis, the youngest of her uncle Garrett's boys, was also the most cautious
of the three. His lake-blue eyes were fixed on the dog. And
as she watched him, he began chewing nervously on his
thumbnail.

"I don't know, Denny. Maybe he doesn't belong to anybody." Struggling to sit up, she pushed at the mountain of
hair trapping her.

"Leda!" Dennis urged quickly. "Watch out. He might be
mean, y'know."

"How can you look in this face and think it mean?"

"Looks don't mean nothin'," he countered with another
step back. "My last teacher, she was real pretty. But that
woman had a switch in her desk and she didn't mind usin'
it neither."

"Well, Denny," she said on a groan as the dog sat down
on her belly, "if he was planning on having me for his
dinner, he's certainly had time enough already." The dog
stretched out atop her and laid his big head on her shoulder.
Leda groaned again, louder this time. "Besides, by the feel
of him, I'd guess he doesn't need much more to eat!"

Tentatively, Dennis stepped closer and reached out one
hand toward the dog. Immediately, the beast lifted his head,
turned toward the boy and sniffed. With a wriggle that set
every hair on his body waving and brought a fresh moan
from Leda, the animal left his perch, lay down in front of
Denny, and rolled onto his back.

"See, Denny? He wants to be friends." Leda struggled to a sitting position, looked down at the dirt covering her best blue shirt, and grimaced. Then with a shrug, she began to tug her necklaces back into place.

Glancing at her cousin, she saw him fall to one knee and carefully stroke the big dog's chest and belly. His paws sticking straight up, the animal twisted and writhed on the ground, clearly enjoying the attention.

Denny's delighted laughter spilled into the afternoon air and Leda paused for a moment to enjoy the sound. In the two months she'd been in Tanglewood, it was the first time she'd heard Dennis laugh.

According to her uncle Garrett, the boy had been badly shaken by his mother's death two years before. In fact, of all his sons, Dennis was the one who most concerned Garrett. It wasn't natural, he said, for a boy to be so quiet. So sad all the time.

Leda smiled thoughtfully as she looked at her young cousin.

Maybe, she told herself, this was Fate's way of helping Dennis. What other explanation could there be? In a town the size of Tanglewood, a dog *that* big would surely be noticed if it belonged to anyone nearby. And after Tom Shipley'd been hurt, no one had recognized the animal.

Her brain racing, Leda had already mentally bathed and combed the dog and made it a bed in Dennis's room when the boy spoke and shattered her thoughts.

"Leda?"

"Hmmm?"

"He's wearin' a collar."

Disappointment colored Denny's voice and Leda knew he'd been making swift plans for the dog too. She moved closer and looked where the boy pointed. Under the dog's tangled, matted hair there was some sort of rawhide collar around his neck. A glimmer of regret shot through her. Would Fate really dangle a prize like this in front of a child and then snatch it back?

"He *does* belong to somebody, don't he?" Dennis said wistfully.

"I don't know, Denny," she answered, smoothing her hand through his shaggy black hair.

There was nothing to be done about it. Like it or not, she had to check to see if there was a name etched on that collar. Sighing, Leda reached for the rawhide strip. Dennis began to chew at his thumb again.

When she touched the leather, though, the dog jerked slightly and she had to speak quickly, softly, to calm him down again.

Frowning, Leda slipped one finger beneath the crude rawhide collar and winced. The leather strap was much too small for such a huge animal. It was digging into his skin and choking him, slowly.

Horrified, Leda sat back on her heels and stared down into deep brown eyes that now seemed to be asking for her help.

"You poor thing," she whispered and stroked one hand down his side. He snuffled, and now that she'd seen the strangling collar he wore, Leda realized that he hadn't barked once either time she'd seen him. "And no wonder," she said softly, "no doubt you can hardly breathe with that thing on you. It's a miracle you've been able to swallow enough food to keep you alive this long."

"What is it?" Dennis tore his gaze away from the dog but continued to pet him when the animal rolled over and laid his immense head on the boy's knee.

"The poor dear's choking." Leda shook her head, gave the dog one last pat, and stood up. "That collar was meant for a much smaller dog than this one."

Dennis looked back down at his new friend. "But why would somebody do that to him?"

"Oh," she said quickly, "I don't think his owner meant to hurt him, Denny. Whoever it was probably put that collar 'round his neck when he was a puppy. Then, the dog must have gotten separated from his people." She shook her head sadly. "And as he grew, the collar began to strangle him."

"Well, take it off, Leda," Dennis demanded.

"It's too tight, Denny. It'll have to be cut off him, I think."

Jumping to his feet, the boy looked up at her anxiously. "Then let's go home. We can get a knife there."

Leda nodded thoughtfully as she stared down at the dog, watching first one then the other of them.

"We could. But I think we'd best take him to Max."

"The *doctor*? Why?"

"He'll have sharper knives than us, for one thing." She looked at her cousin. "And for another, that collar's so tight now, I'm afraid I might hurt him if I try to cut it off myself."

"But the doc's a *people* doctor!"

"Nonsense! Max will be happy to help this poor creature. You wait and see."

Dennis shook his head slowly, his too long black hair falling into the deep blue eyes so like his father's. "I don't know, Leda. The doc don't much like animals, I don't think."

Leda laughed. "*Everyone* likes animals, Denny."

"Not the doc." Staring at the dog, still lying at his feet, he added, "Once Mrs. Tracy brought her cat to see him and he told her to keep it outside 'cause animals had 'germs' on 'em."

"Germs?"

"That's what he said." Dennis shrugged. "I didn't see no germs and I looked for 'em too. 'Cause I figured I could put some in Sally Myer's lunchbox. But there wasn't any."

"Well," Leda said firmly, "I'm sure there was some sort of mistake. I *know* Max will help our friend here."

"Did you 'see' it?" Dennis turned hopeful eyes on his cousin.

"No . . ." She had to admit, Leda thought, she hadn't had any kind of vision about this poor beast or Max's willingness to treat it. But, she told herself as she remembered her beloved's eyes, she *knew* he would be more than happy to help.

"What is that . . . *dog* doing in my office?"

Dennis stepped back a pace and kept one hand on the animal's neck.

Leda threw her arms around Maxwell, gave him a quick hug, then stepped back herself, smiling up at him.

"Will you stop doing that?"

"What?"

"That habit you have of throwing yourself at me without the slightest provocation."

She smiled. "I just can't help myself, my love. I've waited so long for you that every time I see you"—she shrugged helplessly—"I just *have* to touch you."

"And stop calling me that."

"My love?"

He sighed. For heaven's sake. The woman was unstoppable. No matter what he said or did, she went blithely on her way, doing as she damn well pleased. Maxwell clenched his jaw. She hadn't even bothered to come by and finish their "discussion" of a few days ago. He refused to admit, even to himself, that what he'd been doing was "lecturing."

No, he'd thought she'd forgotten all about him and his well-deserved complaints. Oh, he'd seen her, off and on over the last few days, flitting from one place to the next, all over town. He'd watched the townspeople greet her with smiles and laughter.

From behind his office windows, Maxwell had watched the town and her and realized that *he* was the outsider. Not Leda James. Five years he'd been in Tanglewood and he couldn't remember the last time someone had greeted *him* as effusively as they did her.

And he couldn't even blame them. In spite of his best intentions, he'd found himself looking for her more times than he cared to think about. There was simply something about her that called to him. She somehow touched a part of him that he hadn't thought about in years.

Staring at her now, though, he fought down the suspicious curl of pleasure winding through his chest. She'd avoided him for days and then, when she finally *did* show up at his office, she brought along with her a dog of momentous proportions and dubious health.

He frowned slightly as he looked down at the drooling mass of filth plopped on its generous rump in the middle of his office. Maxwell could almost *see* fleas leaping off that disgustingly dirty body to take up residence in his curtains.

He just managed to keep from scratching.

"And that's why we brought him to you," Leda finished.

"I beg your pardon?" He'd missed the entire explanation and somehow Maxwell was sure it would have been interesting.

"His collar," Dennis supplied.

"Collar?" Did they mean to say that the beast actually had an *owner*? Good Lord. His brows shot upward. The mind boggled at what the *owner* must look like.

"Max dear," Leda said patiently, "I just told you about the collar. The rawhide strap? And how it's choking this poor creature?"

"Choking?" He didn't even *attempt* to stop parroting her this time. Instead, his gaze shot to the dog.

Without another word, Maxwell dropped to one knee in front of the hairy beast and to his credit didn't pull back when the animal pushed its dirty nose under Maxwell's chin.

Carefully, gingerly, his fingers slipped under the dog's dirt-streaked hair, searching for the collar. When he finally found it, he inhaled sharply and let his hands drop to his sides.

She was right. The poor animal *was* strangling.

His lips pressed in a tight line, he studied the dog silently for another moment or two. Then he pushed himself to his feet, walked to the nearest glass-fronted cabinet, and yanked one door open.

Five shelves, each draped with fresh white linen, faced him. On the shelves were a number of medical instruments. Maxwell's gaze swept over them and finally settled on a razor-sharp scalpel. Holding the cold silver knife delicately, he glanced over his shoulder at Leda.

"Is this the dog that attacked Tom Shipley?"

" 'Attack' is a strong word, Max dear."

"Appropriate, though."

"Not really." Leda took a step closer to the animal and stood beside him defensively. "He didn't mean any harm."

"I suppose not," he admitted grudgingly. If the animal was vicious at all, he would have shown it by now. And he certainly wouldn't have allowed a stranger to touch a neck that *must* be painful.

Maxwell shook his head. Even though he himself hadn't much use for animals—much too messy to his way of thinking—he also wouldn't stand by and let one suffer.

"Look at him, Max." She glanced down at the animal and smiled when the beast returned the look. "See how well mannered he is?"

"Hmmm." True. He hadn't budged an inch since plopping down onto Maxwell's once clean floor. But then again, perhaps all the dirt on his coat was weighing him down.

Kneeling beside the first patient he'd had since his return to Tanglewood, Maxwell spoke in a slow, soothing tone. "Easy now, boy. We'll have that thing off you in no time at all."

"Don't hurt him!" Dennis said quickly.

Hurt him? Maxwell almost smiled. He'd have to be crazy to hurt an animal that size. Even as that thought entered his brain, he tried to figure out just what kind of animals had come together to produce such a monstrous dog.

A pony? And what?

He shook his head as if to clear away the ridiculous notions and instead concentrated on the task before him.

Carefully, his practiced fingers slipped under the tight rawhide strap, lifting it away from the dog's throat. The animal whimpered and tried to tug itself free, but Maxwell's voice and sure fingers settled him again.

His scalpel sliced through the old leather with a whisper of sound and the dog jerked back, shaking its head. Maxwell stared at the offending collar, hanging from his fingers. "It must have been strangling him for years," he murmured thoughtfully.

"Oh, Max!" Leda said. "Just look at him!"

Glancing up, Maxwell watched the dog lift its hind leg and scratch at his neck. The big brown eyes rolled back ecstatically and Maxwell would have sworn the animal sighed in pleasure.

A reluctant smile curved his lips and he tossed the offending collar to the examining table behind him. One moment later, he told himself he should have been paying closer attention.

A *woof* deep and rough enough to scrape a man's bones sounded out just before the dog hurled himself at his savior. Flat on his back, Maxwell stared up into a grinning dog face and grimaced at the drool raining down on him.

"He's thanking you, my love!"

"Assure him, as you drag him off me," Max grunted, with the pressure of at least one hundred pounds wriggling on his chest and stomach, "that he's more than welcome."

"Can I keep him, Leda?" Dennis knelt down beside the dog and the fallen doctor and looked up at his cousin. "Do ya think Pa will let me keep him for mine?"

"I'm sure he will, Denny."

"Oof!" The beast planted one foot on Maxwell's groin as he got up and leaped at the little boy. A wave of pain rolled over Maxwell and even the sound of Dennis's long silent giggles wasn't enough to cheer him.

"Are you all right, my love?"

He looked up into her garden-green eyes and jerked her a nod. He didn't dare risk trying to speak.

"Shall I help you up?"

He shook his head violently. Lord, don't let her move me, he thought desperately.

"Well, if you're sure you're all right, then," she said, "Denny and I will go give this beast a bath before introducing him to Uncle Garrett and the boys."

With his jaw clenched against the pain that still hadn't crested, Maxwell told himself that the dog would need at least a *river* of water to come clean.

"Are you ready, Denny?"

"Yeah," the boy answered and laughed again as the beast swiped its new master's mouth with a long, wet tongue.

For a moment, Maxwell thought of cautioning the boy about germs, diseases, and just how dirty animals were. Then he changed his mind and willed his muscles to relax against the dirty pine floor. Even his eyes hurt.

"Thanks, Doc," Dennis offered.

Maxwell nodded.

"Leda said you'd help Arthur."

"Arthur?" Leda asked.

"Uh-huh," the boy answered. "That's his name now. Arthur. Anyhow, Doc," he went on, "I didn't think you'd help. I surely didn't. But Leda here said she knew you wouldn't turn your back on no creature. Not even a dog."

Briefly, Maxwell let himself look up at her, and for a moment, he enjoyed the proud gleam in her eyes. Then he reminded himself who and what she was and looked away pointedly.

He couldn't take the chance of becoming too accustomed to her.

Pain continued to blossom and spread throughout his body and he fought to keep from moaning aloud.

"Would you like me to help you tidy up?" Leda asked.

If he'd had the strength, Maxwell would have laughed. Tidy up? This from a woman who stood before him, covered in dog drool, dust, and red wool socks.

Somehow, he managed to croak, "No, thank you."

"If you're sure . . ."

"I am." Please, he added silently. Just *leave,* so he could groan in peace.

"Then we'll be off!" Leda began herding Dennis and Arthur toward the front door, then paused a moment, turned back, and dropped to one knee beside him. "Thank you, my love. It meant so much to me *and* to Denny."

Then she kissed him.

A brief, warm, gentle kiss that was over and done almost before it had started. And yet, he felt her touch shoot through his body with the wild abandon of a Fourth of July skyrocket gone berserk.

When she left, Maxwell lay on the floor with neither the strength nor the inclination to get up.

CHAPTER 5

Sheriff Dan Nichols sat slumped at his desk, staring down at the telegram he'd already read five times. A stray lock of dark brown hair fell over his forehead and he brushed it back impatiently.

"Trouble?"

Dan glanced up through narrowed eyes at the older man across from him. Silhouetted against the morning sunlight slicing through the jailhouse windows, the nosy old coot shifted from foot to foot eagerly. Even with his face in shadow, August's still sharp, faded green eyes seemed to shine with anticipation.

The sheriff had forgotten that August Haley was still in the office. Of course, he wasn't surprised. The man always found some excuse to linger after delivering a wire. Hell, the only reason August became a telegrapher in the first place was so that he could know folks's business before *they* did.

And since August already knew damn well what that telegram said, Dan figured he had nothin' to lose by saying, "Yeah. Could be."

"Yessir, Sheriff," August piped up in a wheedling tone nearly as thin as his scrawny body. "As soon as that come in for ya, I says to myself, August, I says. There's trouble comin'.'"

Dan cocked one eyebrow, lowered his gaze, and read the wire one more time.

BIG HOLDUP HERE STOP SLICK JOB STOP NO IDEAS
STOP SEVERAL JUST LIKE IT OTHER TOWNS LAST
COUPLE MONTHS STOP HEARD ABOUT THE GOLD
SHIPMENT HEADED YOUR WAY STOP KEEP YOUR EYES
PEELED STOP WILL WIRE MORE INFORMATION IF I
GET IT STOP SIGNED MIKE CONNOR SHORT HILL
MONTANA STOP

Mike wouldn't have bothered sending a wire unless he thought there was a good chance that *his* bank robbers would be ending up in Tanglewood. Dan sighed and glanced back at August. The hell of it was, without more information, there wasn't a damn thing he could do about it.

His gaze flicked to a tattered calendar on the far wall. In just over three weeks, Wells Fargo would be arriving with a long overdue payroll shipment of gold for the miners at Lost Creek.

Granted, as gold shipments went, it wasn't nearly the size some big town might get. But it was big enough for Tanglewood. And plenty big enough that somebody might want to make off with it.

And the hell of it was, there was no way to keep it a secret.

Everybody already knew about it anyways. Half the town was lookin' forward to its arrival. Unpaid bills would be settled at last and no doubt a lot of that gold would find its way to the Red Dog Saloon, Garrett's store, the barbershop, and bathhouse . . . shit.

"Ya figure ya ought to be out hirin' on some deputies, Sheriff?"

"What?"

"Deputies," August repeated. "Don't ya think you're gonna need some help around here?"

"For what?" Dan snatched the wire off the pile of papers strewn across his desk, opened his cluttered top drawer, shoved the paper inside, and slammed the drawer shut again. "A bank robbery that *might* take place? By nobody knows who? Only God knows when? What am I s'posed to do, August? Shut down the town?"

"Well," the telegrapher whined, "ya *could* ask Leda."

"Ask her what?"

"Ask her if we're gonna get robbed, that's what!"

"Hmmph!" Dan liked Leda well enough. Seemed like a nice woman and he enjoyed her predictions as much as anybody else. But he'd be damned if he'd treat the town's safety and livelihood to a woman's *dreams*.

The old man rubbed his whisker-stubbled jaw and let his eyes roll up to study the ceiling. "Well, ya *could*—"

"What I *could* do, August, is get back to work," Dan said, cutting him off. He'd never get any thinking done while the old gossip was there. "And I suggest you do the same."

Straightening abruptly, August sniffed, lifted his chin, and reached for the doorknob.

Before he could do more, though, the heavy oak door flew open and August, eyes wide in surprise, staggered clumsily into the wall behind him.

Dan grinned, smothered a chuckle, and turned to look at the man in the open doorway. "Mornin', Maxwell."

"Dan," he said and stepped into the room, closing the door after him, "I've got to talk to you."

"Jeez, Doc!" August pushed himself away from the wall, clutching one elbow tightly. "You needin' customers so bad you got to go out and break a bone so's you can fix it?"

"August. I didn't see you."

"Ain't surprised, the way you come pushin' in here!"

"Are you hurt?" Maxwell asked and took a half step toward the older man. "Let me see."

"Just you hold on, Doc!" August stepped wide around him. "My old bones been through enough already, thanks to you."

Dan chuckled again and this time the old man heard him.

"Think it's funny, do ya? Why, I might be ruin't for life!"

"The way you go stickin' that long nose of yours into folks's business," the sheriff countered, "that 'life' of yours might not last much longer."

August stiffened and stretched his spindly neck. "Reckon I can tell when I ain't wanted."

"It'd be the *first* time."

The older man lifted his chin, snorted, and stomped out.

Dan winced when the door slammed. Tilting his chair back on two legs, he lifted one booted foot and propped it against his desk. Forgetting all about the worrisome telegram for the moment, he asked, "So, Maxwell. What'd you need to talk about?"

"Leda James."

Laughing, the sheriff shook his head. "Now why doesn't that surprise me any?"

"Dan," Maxwell started and ran one hand over his neatly combed hair. "Something's got to be done about the woman."

"Like what?"

"*Something. You're* the sheriff, you tell me!"

Dan looked hard at the man on the opposite side of the desk. His plain, black suit was, as always, neatly pressed without a trace of the dust that seemed to cling to everyone else in the country. Every hair in place, even the man's gold watch chain draped at a precise curve across his vest, and yet . . . there was something different.

Then he noticed that Maxwell's hands were clenching and unclenching at his sides. Interesting, he told himself. For the first time in five years, Maxwell Evans was *not* his usual calm, controlled self.

Easing his chair back to the floor, Dan propped his elbows on the littered desktop, rested his chin in his hands, and said, "Why don't you tell me what she's done, Max-well?"

"What she's done?"

"Yeah. She seems a good sort to me. Likable. Friend-ly."

"Oh," the doctor countered as he began to pace the floor, "she's *very* friendly. So friendly, in fact, that she's managed to take all my patients."

"Surely not *all*," Dan countered with a small grin. "Why, I heard you had a patient just the other day. Saved a poor fella from chokin', didn't you?"

Maxwell inhaled sharply, tugged at his jacket, and stared at the sheriff until the man stopped smiling.

"That . . . *dog* wasn't a patient. He was a—"

"Poor creature in need of help?" Dan offered. "At least, that's what Leda's tellin' folks in town."

"She's *telling* people about that beast?"

"Sure is." Dan chuckled softly again. "And paintin' you out as a regular hero too."

"Lord!" Maxwell sighed. "I knew I shouldn't have let that animal into my surgery."

"Take it easy, Doc." Amazing, the sheriff thought. He'd never imagined Doc Evans to be capable of so many emo-tions. The man went from anger to helplessness back to rage again in a matter of seconds.

In fact, this was one of the longest conversations the two of them had had in the five years Maxwell'd been in Tanglewood. He blinked and shook off his wandering thoughts when he realized the doc was speaking again.

"All I did was slice off a collar that was close to strangling the dog. That's *all*," he added as if explaining a horrible crime.

"Well, Leda tells a much more excitin' tale, I *must* say."

"I can well imagine," he sighed. Shaking his head in frustration, he went on. "That must be *one* of the reasons she's found it so easy to steal my patients from me."

"Steal?"

"Yes, steal!" One lock of sandy-blond hair fell from its appointed place but Maxwell didn't appear to notice. "What would you call it? I sit in my office all day with nothing to do but clean my unused instruments while *she* hands out homemade remedies from behind a crystal ball in a general store!"

Dan smiled but let it slip away quickly under Maxwell's glare. "I don't see how you can say she stole your patients, Doc. Looks to me like she's just offerin' to help folks who come to her. She's not exactly settin' outside your door with a pistol, forcin' folks to go to Garrett's place instead."

"She might as well be!" Maxwell grumbled under his breath for a minute, then said aloud, "In the week or so I've been back, I've had exactly *one* patient. That dog.

"I can't tell you how many people I've met on the street who sing Leda James's praises to me. How much better they feel now that *she's* in town. How I really should think about learning a few things from Leda." He sighed and seemed to deflate a little. After a moment, he shrugged and added, "I don't know what to do anymore, Dan. My practice is about dead and I can't even blame the woman who's killed it."

"Huh?"

"You were right," he said unbelievingly. "She *isn't* sitting outside my office with a gun. People go to *her*. And why shouldn't they? I mean, of course, not for the crystal-ball nonsense . . . but the rest of it. She smiles, tells them what they want to hear—"

"And she's sure prettier than you," Dan said thoughtfully.

Maxwell glared at him.

"Calm down, Doc."

"I *am*," he shouted, then took a long, deep breath before finishing more quietly, "calm. What I want to know is, what are you going to do about it?"

"Nothin'."

"*Nothing?*"

"That's right, Maxwell. Nothin'."

"But—"

"She ain't hurt anybody, has she?"

"Not that I know of, but—"

"Nobody but *you* has complained."

"So far, but—"

"And it ain't against the law to help folks."

"It certainly is if you're claiming to be a doctor!"

Dan's eyebrows lifted slightly. "Far as I know, she never has said that. Has she?"

Deep red color flushed Maxwell's cheeks and Dan watched as the other man's hands began tightening into useless fists again.

"No," the doctor finally admitted, "she hasn't. She only passes out foul-smelling teas and onions and pretends to know the future!"

"Yeah, I know. She already told me mine."

"*You* too, Dan?"

This time, when he laughed, he made no attempt to hide it. "Hell yes, me. Why not?"

"Because it's nonsense. That's why."

"Now, I don't know about that," the sheriff countered quickly. "The future she read for me sounded just about right."

Maxwell sighed and after a long pause seemed to force himself to ask, "All right, Dan. Tell me. What is your future? Fifteen children? Are you going to strike gold? Or perhaps become a judge?"

"Nope. Even better." Dan laughed. "When Idaho becomes a state . . . *I* am gonna be the first governor!"

"Good Lord."

Another burst of laughter shot from the sheriff's throat before he added, "I should think my 'office' deserves just a tad more respect, Maxwell."

The doctor cocked his head and frowned. "It's nonsense, Dan! Just as I said before. Nonsense!"

Another lock of Maxwell's hair slipped out of position

and joined the first. Still, Dan realized, the doc hadn't
noticed. Unusual.

"Maybe it's nonsense," he said. "Who knows?"

"*I* know. It's impossible to tell the future."

"C'mon, Max."

"Maxwell."

"You can't say you never wondered about the future."

"My future will be whatever I make of it," he snapped
back. "And if Miss Leda James keeps interfering with my
livelihood, that won't be much."

"That's not what *she* says."

Maxwell froze. "What do you mean?"

"Accordin' to *her,* you're gonna be a real big man in this
territory."

"What?"

"Oh, yeah." Dan was beginning to enjoy this. He'd never
seen the good doctor so at a loss. Strange how much havoc
one woman could cause a man. "She says you're gonna start
a fine hospital and folks'll come from all over just for you
to take care of 'em."

"She said that?" Some of the angry color drained from his
cheeks and Dan saw confusion in the other man's eyes.

"Sure did." He hid his smile as he finished. " 'Course, she
also says that it's a pure shame you didn't find her sooner.
'Cause now you're gonna have to do it all on your own."

"Huh?"

"Yeah, what with her dyin' soon and all . . ." He looked
at Maxwell slyly. "Says you won't be able to be married
like you was supposed to be."

"Good God."

Dan laughed louder as Maxwell dropped helplessly into
the closest chair.

Leda sat on a small hill at the edge of town and looked
down at Tanglewood, shining in the afternoon sun. She
drew her knees up to her chest and wrapped her arms
around them. A soft smile curved her lips as she let her

gaze wander over the tiny town that had come to mean so much to her.

The cluster of buildings that huddled around the one and only street looked as neat and still as a daguerreotype. Except that in a picture, the glorious color would be missing.

Now, in early May, the surrounding slopes of land were a rainbow of wildflowers. Stands of deep red Indian paintbrush jutted up from fields of delicate lavender lupin. And an occasional splash of bright pink fireweed danced with tall, fragile-looking blue larkspur. Leda sighed then inhaled deeply, trying to capture everything around her, make it a part of her.

She glanced quickly at the towering trees encircling the small clearing that was Tanglewood. For just a moment, as she admired the pine, fir, and spruce trees in their varied shades of green, Leda felt a stab of regret that she wouldn't be there to enjoy the splendor of the autumn.

Even as she imagined the brilliant golds and reds of the larch, birch, and aspen trees, though, Leda admitted silently that she would regret missing *every* season.

Oh, she told herself that autumn, with its sharp cold wind, the rattle of dead leaves, and the promise of snow was her favorite time of year. But when winter blew in, covering the world in a soft white blanket, Leda was sure that the stark, bare bones of the trees against a slate-gray sky was the most beautiful thing she'd ever seen. By spring, with wildflowers scenting the air and a soft wind dusting off the mountainsides, she loved the season of new beginnings. And the summer. Leda smiled and found herself hoping the Fates would let her live long enough to enjoy the heat of the sun and the pleasure of diving into a cool lake one more time.

Sudden tears filled her eyes and Leda bit down hard on her bottom lip. She would miss so much.

Then a gentle breeze lifted a tendril of her hair, twisted it about her cheek, and teased her into remembering to take pleasure in the present. She blinked back her tears, drew in a long, shuddering breath, and determined again to enjoy every day that she was given.

Smiling, she looked down on the town she called home now. The town she'd chosen to spend her last days in.

Tanglewood.

Slowly, she looked from the livery with its freshly white-washed fence to the rooming house across the street. As she watched, Selma Tyler stepped outside and swung her broom over the steps with the same determination as ancient warriors had wielded their swords. Behind Selma's big, two-story structure, back among the trees, sat Gladys's house. Silently, Leda reminded herself to visit the older woman later.

Beyond Selma's was Max's office, then the bank and Garrett's store. Farther down the street, hidden from view by a stand of birch trees, was the mill. In the still afternoon air, the steady creak of the water wheel seemed like the heartbeat of Tanglewood.

Beyond, in the schoolhouse yard, the children were playing, and on the other side of the street, Walter Bunch washed down the windows of his bathhouse/barbershop. About fifty yards behind the barbershop, set back from the street, was the Red Dog Saloon. Squeezed in between Walter's place and Lloyd's gunsmith shop, the tiny, little-used jailhouse waited.

A sudden movement caught her eye and Leda looked down toward her uncle's store. Garrett, fourteen-year-old Sean, and twelve-year-old Michael stepped into the street, fishing poles laid across their shoulders.

Leda grinned when Dennis ran to join them, followed closely by Arthur. The clumsy dog insisted on walking between Garrett's feet, as if testing its new owner's patience. Even from a distance, she could see her uncle's temper building as he faced down the animal crouching at his feet.

Arthur looked completely humbled until Garrett started

walking again. Then with complete disregard for its own safety, he slipped right back under the big man's feet. Leda thought she heard Dennis's laughter and she knew that as long as that dog could make the boy smile, Garrett would put up with anything.

She should be up and heading for town, she knew. Leda'd promised Garrett that she would mind the store while he took his sons fishing. But somehow, she just couldn't bring herself to move. It seemed almost sinful to sit inside a store on such a glorious day.

Without thinking, she let her eyes slip back to the doctor's office. Max. Her heartbeat quickened merely at the thought of him. Even the sunlight beating down on her back was no match for the warmth that flooded her as his image rose up in her mind.

He didn't fool her. Oh, he pretended to be stiff and uncaring. But she knew he was hiding a wealth of love deep inside him. It was there in the gentle strength of his hands. In the patience he showed, even to a frightened dog. Even his bluster and temper were proof of his warm heart. If he *truly* didn't care about anyone or anything, he'd have no reason to carry on.

She rested her chin on her knees and buried her bare toes in the long grass.

"Oh, Mama," she whispered, stealing a glance at the cloud-dotted sky, "does it really have to end now? When I've finally found *him*?"

She waited, breath held for a long moment, hoping for an answer. A vision. A sign. But there was nothing.

Abruptly, she threw herself back on the grass, stretching out her arms and legs and closing her eyes against the sunlight. As another, warmer breeze drifted over her, Leda smiled, imagining Max's hands gliding across her flesh with the same gentle touch.

But when the sun slipped behind a bank of clouds and the very air around her darkened, Leda's smile faded away. Despite the warm grass beneath her, a slight chill crept up her spine. She opened her eyes to a mass of gray clouds being whipped across the sky by a wind no longer gentle. In the far distance, thunder rumbled angrily.

"Is that my answer, then?" she whispered brokenly. Pushing herself to her feet, Leda stood and tucked her hair back from her face. In the silence that followed, she searched her heart for a reason to hope. But she couldn't find one.

The Fates had decided. No matter how much she wanted to stay with Max, she couldn't change her Destiny. And she knew it. Hoping for anything else was foolishness. Pure and simple.

Perhaps in another life, she and Max would get the chance Fate had denied them this time.

"Curses and swears," Leda whispered under her breath just fifteen minutes later. She slowed her steps to a halting pace as she passed the livery. The blacksmith, Cyrus Finster, shoved at a huge wooden crate until it stood flat against the plank wall of the livery.

Wearing only his leather apron over a well-worn pair of jeans, Cyrus's tanned, muscled back belied his more than fifty years. Leda watched for another minute or two as the man carried another crate and stacked it atop the first. He was building a makeshift ladder.

She tilted her head slightly and let her gaze shift out of focus. In seconds, a clear, detailed "vision" came to her. In her mind's eye, she saw Cyrus scale the crates, and stretch out one arm for the open loft door above him. Then the image wavered, like a mirage taunting a dying man in the desert. Leda concentrated, willing the "sight" to clear itself.

When the concealing mists lifted, Leda saw Cyrus fall. His broad body landed in the dirt and was crushed by the uppermost crate of his shaky tower as it toppled from its perch.

She gasped, shook her head and started walking toward him before the "vision" had completely died away.

"Cyrus!"

He turned around and smiled. "Afternoon, Leda. What can I do for you?"

"You can use your ladder instead of these crates."

"What?" he asked as he wiped the sweat off his brow with his forearm.

"Cyrus, I've had a terrible vision."

His bushy gray eyebrows drew together. Turning his head to the side, he looked at her from the corner of his eye. "That so?"

"Oh, yes. You mustn't climb on these crates. You'll be hurt." She paused, reached out, and laid one hand on his arm. "Maybe killed. The vision wasn't clear."

The big man's weathered, lined face creased in a kind smile. "Now don't get yourself all worked up. I done this lots of times."

"Maybe so," she countered, determined to convince him, "but *this* time, something dreadful will happen. I just know it, Cyrus."

"I 'preciate it, Leda. I surely do. And it's real nice of ya to come tell me about it. I'll be extra careful today. I promise."

"Please, Cyrus," she interrupted, "you have a ladder here, don't you?"

"Well, yeah . . ." His gaze flicked to the far corner of the livery. "But it's way back there, got lots of stuff piled up against it." He offered her another smile. "Lots easier to just stack these ol' boxes than to go in to diggin' out my ladder."

Even as they stood there talking, Leda felt the vision returning. Once again, she saw Cyrus's body fall. She saw the heavy crate land on his back and neck. Then everything around her went black.

"Leda?" he asked hurriedly. "You all right?"

She inhaled, forced the terrible images from her mind, and somehow managed to nod at the worried man opposite her. "I will be, Cyrus. If you'll just use your ladder."

He frowned.

"Please?" she added, thinking that she would say or do *anything* to make him agree. Didn't he know that she was trying to help him? Oh, why was it that people didn't believe when she most needed them to?

"It's that important to ya?"

"Yes, Cyrus." She nodded fiercely and brushed her hair out of her eyes. "It is."

He exhaled in a rush, glanced back at the crates behind him then shrugged. His deeply tanned features twisted in a tired frown, but he said, "All right, then. I'll do it your way."

"Oh, good." She patted his arm and added, "You'll see, Cyrus. If you'll just use the ladder, all will be well."

"If you say so."

Grinning now, Leda asked, "Would you like me to help you drag that ladder out from behind everything?"

His lips quirked. "No. I can manage." Glancing at her naked toes sticking out from beneath her skirt, he added, " 'Sides, with those bare feet of yours, there's no tellin' what you might step on back there."

She curled her toes in the dirt. "I'd be careful."

He shook his head. "Nope. You get on. And you don't even have to stick around to keep an eye on me. I promise I'll use the ladder."

"Why, Cyrus!" Eyes wide, she grinned up at him. "I never doubted that you would. I trust you completely."

The big man rubbed one hand over his short gray beard, sighed, and said, "You best get along now, Leda. I got plenty to do." Then he turned, stepped into the shadowed livery, and disappeared.

Breathing a relieved sigh, Leda left the stableyard and slowly continued on her walk toward the store. She felt as she always did after successfully helping someone with her "gift." A small, warm glow filled her and she told herself that even though she was fated to lead a short life, at least she'd been able to be of service.

There was only a tiny stab of regret when she realized that her mother's mother's mother's gift would end with her. There would be no more girl children to carry on. There would be no one to share her secrets with. To teach about the Fates and Life and Death and the Life Beyond.

With one sad glance at Max's office as she passed, Leda moved on.

"Foolishness," Cyrus muttered thickly. "That's all this is. Foolishness, plain and simple."

If he hadn't promised Leda that he'd use the ancient ladder now propped against the side of the livery, this task would have been finished an hour ago.

"What the hell was wrong with the crates?" he wondered aloud for no one to hear. "Seems to me they was a lot sturdier than this ol' thing."

He winced as the wood beneath his feet creaked out in protest. Cyrus glanced uneasily at the ground some ten feet below. Clenching his jaw, he told himself not to look down again and tightened his grip on the sides of the ladder.

Old slivers of wood poked and prodded at the palms of his leathery hands. He took another step up, gently resting his foot on a rung that looked none too stable. As his weight settled on the narrow piece of wood, he sighed.

It held.

He snorted a half laugh, shook his head, and stepped up again. Hell, what did it matter if he climbed a ladder or a stack of boxes? It didn't. Not to him. And if it eased Leda James's mind a bit, he'd climb the damn ladder for her.

Cyrus whistled a disjointed tune and kept his gaze locked on the weathered plank wall in front of him. Place needs a good coat of paint, he thought and promised himself to get right to it as soon as he could.

Must be close to the loft door now, he told himself and shuddered to think just how high he was. Had to be at least twenty feet. Beads of sweat that had nothing to do with the heat broke out on his forehead.

It was his own fault. If he just hadn't left that damned rope in the corner of the loft last time he was up there, none of this would be happening. It was pure hell gettin' old . . . losin' your memory that way.

He lifted his left foot, moved it to the next rung up, and stepped.

He heard the splintered snap.

He felt the rung give way and his foot slide free into empty air.

He staggered and lurched and clutched at the ladder. His left foot swung in a wide arc, as he searched hopelessly for a foothold.

The ladder shifted, pulling away from the wall and with his left foot dangling, his right seemed determined to join it.

"Ooooh . . ."

Like a flag in a weak breeze, the ancient ladder moved back and forth lazily. Eyes wide, Cyrus tried futilely to balance himself. His thick fingers clasped tight around the rotting wood, he held the ladder close to his chest as he fell to the dirt and straw below.

CHAPTER 6

"Don't tell 'er, Doc."

Maxwell's eyebrows shot up almost into his hairline. "Don't *tell* her?"

Cyrus winced, cupped his left arm with his right hand, and nodded. "She'd feel bad, Doc. And it wasn't her fault, I don't guess."

Muttering under his breath, Maxwell turned from the man seated on his examining table. He moved quickly to the front window, threw back the curtains, grabbed the lower sash and lifted. As a welcome breeze flew in, Maxwell propped a small wooden rod under the window frame to hold it open.

Wrinkling his nose against the peculiar odor that still hung in the office air, he turned back to his patient.

At last. A patient. Yet even as he thought it, he reminded himself that this patient had slipped in the back door like a thief and was now trying to swear his doctor to secrecy.

All to protect the sensibilities of a certain well-known would-be gypsy.

"Then why would she 'feel bad'?"

"Like I told ya, it was her who got me to use that ladder in the first place."

Maxwell shook his head. As he ran practiced fingers over the blacksmith's shoulders and back, he sniffed again. Frowning, he realized the stench remained, despite the open window. He only hoped Cyrus Finster didn't notice.

He'd never win his patients back if they were convinced that his home and office were little better than a pigsty.

" 'Sides, you know how notional females get, Doc."

Maxwell frowned and determinedly ran his fingers gently down the length of the blacksmith's injured arm. Thankfully, no. He had no idea how *notional* females got. He'd made it a point *not* to find out.

Except for the occasional "duty" of having to squire one woman or another to social functions, Maxwell had managed to steer clear of any woman who might be harboring delusions of marriage.

He carefully straightened the injured arm and ignored Cyrus's low-pitched moan.

Between medical school, helping with his father's practice, and then traveling west to start up his own, Maxwell hadn't had time to pay court to anyone. And when there *was* time, he'd had no desire to be ensnared by an eager female. He'd learned long ago how to elude husband-hunting women and their even *more* predatory mothers!

When he decided to take a wife, he'd do it on his own terms. Leda James's predictions notwithstanding.

No, the only women he'd bothered with over the last few years weren't notional at all. They knew exactly what they wanted and how much to charge for it.

Maxwell's fingers moved over the blacksmith's muscular arm thoroughly, testing and probing gently. For the moment, he pushed thoughts of women in general and Leda James in particular to the back of his mind.

Straightening up, he said, "I don't know how you managed it, Mr. Finster. But the arm isn't broken."

The blacksmith blew out a rush of air and shook his head with relief. "That there is good news, Doc. I got so much work to finish this week—"

One hand up for silence, Maxwell interrupted. "I didn't say your arm was perfectly all right, Mr. Finster. As a matter of fact, it's not."

"Huh? If it ain't broke, then—"

"It hasn't been snapped in two like a twig," Maxwell countered and saw the big man wince in imagined agony. He went on, though, being a firm believer in honesty, no matter how harsh, with his patients. "But there may very well be a small break that I can't see or feel."

"But there might be nothin' too. Right?"

"Right." Before the pleased man could scoot down from the examining table, Maxwell added, "Of course, if *I'm* correct and you go ahead and use that arm as you would normally, it might very well snap in two."

"Jeez, Doc," the blacksmith said, wincing again. "Do ya have to keep sayin' it like that?"

"What?"

"What you said. 'Bout my arm snappin' like a twig." Cyrus shook his head slowly. "Kinda like you enjoyed the idea."

"Of course I don't want to see that happen, Mr. Finster," Maxwell answered. "But on the other hand, I also don't want to see you injuring yourself any further. The only way to do that is to make sure you understand the severity of the problem."

"Oh, I understand, all right. I just don't know how come you got to say things so flat out." He frowned and even his gray beard looked to be bristling. "Ya could kinda warm a man up to it, like. No need to go worryin' a body so."

Maxwell inhaled slowly. He hadn't meant to distress the man. "I'm sorry, Mr. Finster. Next time, I'll 'warm up to it.' "

"*Next* time? There won't be no next time."

There will if you don't stop arranging your actions to suit "visions," Maxwell warned silently.

"Lordy," Cyrus whispered, his ruddy face still pale with the imagined image of his strong arm hanging limp at his side. "What d'ya want me to do?"

"I want you to wear this sling." Maxwell reached for a square of linen, folded it into a triangle then knotted it and slipped it over the man's head. As he carefully eased Cyrus's injured arm into the linen, he went on. "And do as little with the arm as possible for at least a couple of weeks."

"Weeks?"

"Yes, weeks." Maxwell nodded and crossed his arms over his chest. "After that, I'll take another look and we'll see how you're feeling."

"But Doc, I got work to do."

"Not for two weeks you don't."

"Damn it all to hell and back."

The blacksmith looked as though he could bite through his anvil and Maxwell couldn't really blame him. Still, the man should have known better than to listen to Leda James.

"If you don't mind my asking, how did you manage to break your fall? By rights, a drop like that should have killed you."

Cyrus looked up at him and smiled sheepishly. "Prob'ly would have, 'cept when that ol' ladder swung out wide, she dropped me smack down into the manure pile."

Maxwell sniffed. *That* explained the offensive odor that had followed Cyrus Finster into the office. For the first time, Maxwell noticed bits of filthy straw clinging to the big man's pants. Even Cyrus's thick iron-gray hair was dotted with Lord knew what.

Good God.

"Yeah, guess you could say I was lucky," the blacksmith said and slid off the table.

"Oh," Maxwell agreed wryly, "*most* fortunate."

As Cyrus headed for the door, he turned back one last time. "Now remember, Doc, don't go tellin' Leda about my fall, all right?"

"Don't you think she'll notice the sling, Mr. Finster?"

For heaven's sake. The man was nearly killed and all he was worried about was protecting Leda James's feelings.

Cyrus glanced down at his injured arm, then back up to the younger man. "Oh, I'll think of somethin' to explain it."

"I'm sure."

"Well then, thanks, Doc. I'll see ya in a couple of weeks."

Maxwell nodded grimly and watched his patient leave by the back door. With every step the burly man took, pieces of straw and manure dropped to the once pristine office floor. Sighing, Maxwell grabbed up the nearby broom and began swiping at the wood planks.

First, he had no patients because Leda James had bewitched everyone in town. Then she brought him a choking dog as some sort of consolation patient. Now, he got a patient who was only injured *because* of Leda James's interference. *And* the man's main concern was only that the fortune-telling madwoman's feelings not be hurt.

Fortune-teller.

Onions.

Visions, indeed! The woman was clearly dangerous. But apparently, he was the only one in town who noticed. He'd tried to be understanding when she was merely killing his practice. Now, though, she seemed bent on killing his patients.

And what was wrong with everyone? Didn't they think it strange that a woman threw herself at a perfect stranger? Didn't they find it a bit odd that this same woman talked constantly of her own impending death?

Unbidden, an all-too-real picture of the dangerous pixie rose up in his mind. Her wild, untamable hair half hidden by one of her ridiculous shawls, her green eyes looking up at him with adoration, even the pale gold freckles across her nose were clear and distinct. Her full lips were curved in a secretive smile that Maxwell found himself unconsciously returning.

He shook his head suddenly as though the action could

rid him of her memory. What on earth was happening to him? If he wasn't careful, he just might find himself drinking her teas, setting out onions all over his house, and walking barefoot down the middle of Main Street!

A strangled laugh slipped from his throat.

No, that wouldn't happen, he assured himself. But he also realized that Leda James wasn't about to stop passing out her remedies and advice. He'd hoped to wait her out. To let the people of Tanglewood realize for themselves that what they needed was a *real* doctor. But there was no sign of that happening anytime soon. Maxwell glanced around his empty office and told himself that if something didn't change quickly, he would have to close his doors.

He'd studied long and hard to become a doctor. He'd sacrificed a personal life for the good of his practice. He'd come to a tiny town in the middle of nowhere because he knew he'd be needed.

And he wasn't about to give up in favor of a redheaded gypsy with more necklaces than common sense! No matter *how* attractive she was.

But, he thought resignedly, his practice *was* dying, if not dead already. Though he'd never been paid much for his services, now he was getting *nothing*. Somehow, he had to find a way to save his livelihood *and* his sanity. And there was only one thing left for him to try.

Compromise.

Gently, carefully, Leda rubbed the surface of the crystal ball with the edge of a black cloth. When she was finished, she leaned her elbows on the tabletop, cleared her mind, and stared into the colorless ball.

With Garrett and the boys fishing and no customers in the store, she'd decided to indulge herself.

In seconds, images began to form. Images of Max. Max in his office, gently tending to an injured Arthur. Max in the store, astonishment written plainly on his face after she kissed him for the first time.

She blinked and the images changed. Now she saw the Max of her dreams, bending low to claim her mouth with his own. Max's arms closing around her. His breath on her cheek, his hands against her back, pressing her close to him. She watched helplessly as the two figures in the crystal swirled together, becoming part of each other as the lines of the image grew fainter and fainter until it finally disappeared altogether.

Leda sat back suddenly and shook her head. What she'd seen had nothing to do with the crystal and she knew it. These pictures of her beloved appeared every time she closed her eyes. Awake. Asleep. His features seemed burned into her brain.

It was as though at first sight of him, a connection had been formed between them. Something so deep and strong that had it been given a chance to grow, it would have blossomed into a love more rare than she'd ever dreamed possible.

But there was no chance for them. The signs were too clear to miss. All the accidents she'd had. The near-misses. Although, Leda thought, she hadn't had a brush with death in the two months she'd been in Tanglewood. If anything, her time in the small town had been filled with a reassuring warmth. Maybe, she thought. Maybe.

No, she warned herself quickly. It wouldn't be wise to pin false hopes on *that*. Soon enough, the Fates would come calling on her. There was no way to avoid it. Deep in her heart, Leda knew they'd only waited this long to give her a chance to prepare.

Better she accept what couldn't be changed. As she had before she'd found Maxwell Evans. Thinking and hoping otherwise could only make their final parting even more painful.

Maxwell stopped just inside the open doorway, his gaze fastened on her. A single shaft of afternoon sunlight shot through the store's front window, bathing her in a golden glow. Her long red hair hung loose around her shoulders, falling in waves of lazy curls that lay across her full breasts. The ropes of colored glass that she wore around her neck sparkled in the sunlight, making hundreds of tiny rainbows against her white shirt every time she drew a breath.

He raised his gaze to hers and found her deep green eyes, shining and wondrous, locked on him. He couldn't look away, couldn't force himself to turn from the gleam of anticipation he saw there. When she pushed herself slowly to her feet, Maxwell found himself holding his breath.

As she crossed the room to him, his gaze still joined to hers, he nevertheless noticed the sprinkling of freckles across her small, straight nose. He saw the color in her cheeks and felt his breath stagger when she licked her lips. She moved with an easy grace, soundlessly in her bare feet. The full red and black skirt she wore clung tight around her hips then fell to sway lovingly around her legs with every step. Even the air in the room seemed still, expectant.

Just before she reached him, he told himself that maybe coming to see her wasn't such a good idea after all.

"Max," she breathed and laid a hand on his arm.

"Maxwell," he countered, his throat suddenly too tight to speak clearly.

"I'm so glad you came to see me. I've missed you."

He swallowed and looked down at her. Surprisingly, Maxwell realized that *he* had actually missed *her* as well. He was becoming much too accustomed to looking up and seeing her. He'd even spent too much time lately looking out his office window hoping for a glimpse of her as she hurried up and down the street. Always busy. Always smiling.

A faint scent of roses drifted to him and he inhaled it greedily. At his sides, his fingertips brushed together and he just managed to keep from reaching out to touch the silky length of her hair.

"You must have felt me thinking about you," she said with a smile.

He stifled a sigh. He was actually getting *used* to hearing her say such outrageous things.

"Miss James," he started.

"Leda."

"Very well, Leda." He forced a smile and took a quick step to the side. "I've come because I want to talk to you about something."

"Yes, Max?"

He opened his mouth to protest, then thought better of it. Besides, he was getting used to his shortened name too.

"Leda, I'd like to propose—"

"Oh Max, please don't." She cut him off.

"What?" He looked at her, confused. He hadn't even had the chance to offer his compromise and she was refusing it already? "Why ever not?"

She gave him a sad smile before saying, "I thought I explained to you before that I can't marry you. And really, to hear a proposal I couldn't accept would simply be too difficult to bear."

Marry me? he thought. Good God.

Hurriedly, he tried to explain. "You misunderstand, Leda."

"Hmmm?"

"By 'proposal,' I meant . . . an offer. A proposition, as it were."

"Yes?"

Clearly, she still didn't understand what he was trying to say. "I'm not talking about a proposal of marriage. I'm talking about a *business* proposal."

"Business?"

"Yes." He walked the few steps to the store counter and gave silent thanks that he and Leda were, apparently, alone in Malone's Mercantile. Idly, he pulled a piece of rock candy from one of the shining glass jars facing him, then turned to look at her.

She hadn't moved.

"I'd like to suggest a sort of 'compromise' between us."

"What do you mean?"

"It's very simple, really." Maxwell's fingers toyed with the piece of candy. "When someone comes to see you"—he hesitated—"*professionally*, I would like you to send them to me afterward."

"Whatever for?"

Because *I* am the doctor, he wanted to shout. Instead, he offered, "So that I may look at their complaints too."

"In case I miss something, you mean?"

"Yes. Exactly." Anxiously, he waited for her answer. Though not a perfect solution by any means, if she agreed, this compromise would at least keep his practice going. Until the citizens of Tanglewood finally realized that Leda's home remedies were no substitute for real medicine.

As the seconds passed, Maxwell lifted the piece of candy to his mouth and ran his tongue over the irregular, hard surface. The sweet flavor ran down his throat and he smiled. It was really very good, he told himself. He couldn't even remember the last time he'd eaten candy.

"Max?"

"Hmmm?" He looked up and found her standing right in front of him. Taking the hard sugar from his mouth, he realized he hadn't been paying any attention. "I'm sorry. Did you say something?"

Leda grinned. "Yes. I said I think it's a wonderful idea."

"You do?"

"Oh yes. Why, with the two of us working together, there's no telling *how* much we can accomplish."

"Together?"

"Uh-huh." She reached past him for the candy jar and pulled out a piece for herself. Tucking the crystallized sugar into a corner of her mouth, she went right on talking.

"And when I bring our patients to you, you can teach me so much."

"*Our* patients?"

"Uh-huh." Her full lips smacked over the candy and she tilted her head back thoughtfully. "And you know, Max? I think it would be best if I simply bring my supplies to your office. That way, I won't have to carry everything back and forth every day."

"Your supplies?" He heard himself parrotting her again and didn't bother trying to stop.

"Yes, my teas and things." She waved one hand airily. With her other hand, she pulled the candy from her mouth, ran her tongue over it one more time, and confided, "You know, he would never say anything of course, but I *do* take up quite a bit of room in Uncle Garrett's store."

"Uh-huh."

"And the people coming and going *do* tend to get in the way of his customers."

"Naturally," he murmured, desperately trying to think of something to say. This wasn't right. This was supposed to be a compromise. Not a conquest.

"And best of all," Leda said, laying one hand on his forearm, "we'll be together every day."

"Yes," he whispered, "yes, we will. Won't we?"

His mind racing, Maxwell stared blankly at the wall above and behind her. What had he done? Hadn't he just made a bad situation worse? For heaven's sake. He hadn't meant to invite her to set up shop in his office!

"Oh Max, it will be wonderful, the two of us. Working together."

Helplessly, he nodded.

"Spending our days together."

He forced a stiff smile.

"I've waited so long, Max."

He looked down into her eyes and noticed for the first time that they weren't just green. They were an unusual blend of green. As she spoke, they seemed to change from a dark forest-green to the soft, muted color of a spring garden.

Maxwell drew in a long, deep breath and fought against the unwelcome rise of desire building inside him. Through his own fault, he would now be spending even more time with her. And for his own sake, he would have to learn to control his baser instincts. No matter *what* the provocation.

"I knew it would be like this, my love."

My love.

"The night my mother told me about you, she promised that you would be the love of my life." Leda smiled gently and laid her hand on his chest. "She said that your heart would know me. That once together, nothing would pull us apart."

She believed it. All of it. And Maxwell couldn't think of a solitary thing to say in response.

CHAPTER 7

Long after Max left, Leda stared at the open doorway, but she didn't even notice the bright shaft of sunshine pouring into the store. She was much too busy thinking.

Now that her beloved was finally beginning to realize that he couldn't fight Destiny, Leda felt like celebrating. A slow smile crossed her lips. Of course, she knew that he wasn't totally convinced . . . not yet. His expression as she talked about their new venture had told her that much.

But that didn't matter. The only thing that mattered was that Max had come to her. It was *his* idea that they work together. It was curious, though—how he'd changed his mind about her and the help she gave people so quickly.

Leda popped the piece of candy back into her mouth and rolled it around on her tongue. Elbows on the counter behind her, she tilted her head and stared blankly at the empty doorway. In her mind's eye, she saw Max's face as he suggested their compromise. He'd looked . . . hesitant, as if he'd thought she wouldn't accept.

Then, she remembered, when she *had* accepted, it was as though a shutter had dropped over his eyes. In fact, now that she took the time to really *think* about it, Max hadn't appeared the least bit pleased.

"Well, curses and swears," she said softly. "Why would the man *make* an offer he didn't want me to take?"

Leda pushed away from the counter, walked to the front door, and leaned against the jamb. As she watched, Flora Lloyd left her husband's shop and hurried down the boardwalk toward the schoolhouse. Hiram Adams, the banker, left his establishment right next door, scuttled across the walk then practically ran across the street to the sheriff's office. Walter Bunch's cat stretched in the sun in front of the barber shop and the heartbeat of Tanglewood, the mill wheel, squeaked in a familiar rhythm.

Everything was as it should be. Everything was the same as it always was. Everything and everyone. Except Max Evans. Leda didn't have the slightest notion what had prompted Max's offer and suddenly she didn't care.

Whatever his reasons *or,* she told herself with a grin, his regrets . . . the deal was made.

And once she'd had the time to talk to him, she knew she'd be able to convince him that everything she'd told him about Fate and Destiny was true. When a plan began to shape itself in her mind, Leda allowed it to blossom and flower. In moments, she realized that she'd had the power all along to prove to him that their Destinies were entwined.

All she needed now, she told herself, was five minutes alone with him.

Quickly, she stepped back, shut the front door, and hung a Closed sign in the window.

Maxwell spent the rest of the afternoon in the rooms above his office. With the curtains drawn tightly closed, even the waning sunlight was locked outside. But he didn't mind. The growing darkness was the perfect companion for his mood.

After pacing the length of his living quarters more times than he could count, Maxwell was no closer to a solution than he'd been hours ago. He frowned, glanced around at his spartan home, and told himself he was overreacting.

Ten quick steps took him past the wardrobe that held his five identical black suits. He stepped around the solitary overstuffed chair set directly in front of an empty hearth and ignored the congealed plate of food he'd left untouched on his bedside table.

He stretched out on his narrow bed, staring sightlessly at the whitewashed ceiling. Flinging his arms behind his head and bracing himself on the flattened pillow, Maxwell relived that awful moment in Garrett Malone's store.

The moment when Leda said the one little word that had shown him what a fool he'd been to go to her in the first place.

"Together."

Frowning, he tried to figure out exactly what had gone wrong with his plan. It had seemed so simple. So straightforward.

Until Leda took it over.

One eyebrow lifted slightly as he told himself that he had no right being upset. If he'd learned anything in the last two weeks or so, it was that the woman was a constant source of surprises. He should have been prepared for this. He should have expected it.

He should have thought the whole compromise offer through—then discarded it. No, he quickly amended, compromise was the only answer to his dying practice. Besides, he asked himself, how better to fight a fire—than *with* a fire? Still, though, if he'd been more prepared, he could've nipped Leda's counterproposal in the bud.

Now he was caught in a trap of his own making!

"Damn it," he muttered to the empty room, "she was supposed to *send* patients to me . . . not become my partner."

How could they be partners? An impossible image leaped into his already tired brain. He could see it all clearly. As he bent over a patient, listening to his heartbeat, Leda would be slumped over a crystal ball, or reading palms, or rubbing onion juice all over the poor patient.

Good God.

But that wasn't the main thing worrying him and he knew it. Oh, certainly, she'd be a bother in an examining room. But he could deal with that. Somehow.

No. It was the effect she had on his person that had him so concerned.

He couldn't even pinpoint exactly what it was about her that he found so disquieting.

Her eyes? Her lips? Those ridiculous red socks she wore?

His body tensed even with the memory of her, and Maxwell suddenly realized just how difficult his and Leda's "partnership" was going to be.

Outside, footsteps sounded on the stairs. Cautiously, he got out of bed and quietly crossed the room.

"He ain't here, Leda," Dennis complained as he climbed the flight of stairs leading to the doctor's house.

"We don't know that," she countered quickly, her feet practically running up the weather-worn steps.

"His curtains're drawn shut," the boy pointed out. "He's prob'ly out tendin' somebody."

"Well, it will only take a minute to find out." A gust of wind lifted her hair and slapped it around her face. Impatiently, Leda plucked it free and tossed it back over her shoulder.

"But I'm hungry," the boy whined.

"I know, Dennis. And I'm willing to bet that Max is too." She turned and looked back at her nephew, still dawdling three steps behind her. "He must be tired of eating at Selma Tyler's rooming house."

"So?"

"*So,*" she shot back, "it's the neighborly thing to do, inviting him for supper."

"We never done it before," he said mutinously, brushing his wind-ruffled hair out of his eyes.

"Well . . ." Leda's lips pursed. She knew very well why she wanted Max to come to her uncle's house for supper.

Besides wanting to celebrate their new arrangement, she was hoping to get a few minutes alone with him. Now that she had a plan of action, she didn't want to waste any more time.

But she couldn't tell *Dennis* that. "Don't you think," she said with sudden inspiration, "that the *least* we owe Max is a good meal for how he helped Arthur?"

A long moment passed and Leda watched the boy, waiting. His brow furrowed, lips pursed, he considered her question for what seemed forever.

"Oh, I guess so," he finally conceded.

"Good." She turned forward again and ran up the last few steps to the landing just outside Max's door.

Shuffling his feet, Dennis joined her there a moment later. When she gave the door three sharp raps with her knuckles, Dennis offered, "He don't eat anywhere but Mrs. Tyler's, y'know."

"I know." She didn't add that she'd asked around town to get her information. Nor did she add that she'd been told by more than one person that Max ate alone, every night. That even in a sometimes crowded dining room, he kept to himself despite any friendly invitations he might get. "That's exactly why I think he might like a change."

"Leda, the doc don't like people much, y'know."

"That's silly, Denny." Her hand dropped to her side and she stared down at the boy. His big blue eyes shifted away uneasily. "How can you say that?"

He rubbed the toe of his scuffed-up black shoe over the clean, freshly painted white landing. Shrugging, he said quietly, "The doc, he just don't mix much with folks, is all."

"Denny Malone." Leda shook her head.

"It's true, Leda. Honest. All the time he's been in town, I don't believe I ever seen him go to anybody's house 'cept when they was sick."

"Were."

"Were."

"Well," she said, turning back to the door and knocking again, harder this time. "Maybe he's shy."

"The doc?" he said, disbelief evident in his voice.

Leda knocked a third time and her knuckles began to ache.

"Mrs. Lloyd says that the doc is 'standoffish.' What's that mean, 'zackly?"

"Standoffish?" She looked at her young cousin. "Flora said that?"

"Uh-huh. Said she thinks he thinks he's too good for the likes of Tanglewood."

"She *said* this? To *you*?"

"Not 'zackly."

"What exactly, then?"

"Well, she was sayin' it to Mr. Haley." He looked down at the toe of his shoe and added, "And I sorta listened."

"Hmmm." Leda's brain raced for a moment or two then she smiled at the boy. "You were wrong to listen, Denny— but Flora was wrong about Max too."

"Ya think?"

"Yes, I do. Max is good and kind and smart." She smiled softly, lost in thoughts of her intended.

She believed everything she'd just told Denny. She *felt* it to be so. But even if she didn't, surely all anyone had to do was look into Max's eyes to see what a fine man he was. Of course, she could understand how Max's temper might put some folks off. And true, he *did* sound fairly . . . "stiff" when he talked. In fact, Leda couldn't remember hearing him call anyone in town, except her uncle, by their given names.

Still, that didn't mean he didn't like people. Only that he was . . . uncomfortable with them. Leda smiled to herself. She could help him with that. He only needed to learn to step outside himself a bit. To meet folks halfway. And together, she and Max would be able to do *anything*.

She just knew it.

"Aw c'mon, Leda." Dennis's impatient voice shook her from her wanderings. "Let's us go eat, huh? Pa and the others're waitin' on us."

"In a minute, Denny."

"Ya want me to go check at the livery? If his horse ain't there, we'll know for sure he ain't home."

Was he gone? Curses and swears! she thought in disgust. She'd been shut up in Garrett's kitchen all afternoon fixing a supper that any cook in a fancy restaurant would be proud of. All for nothing.

She frowned at the unyielding door.

"Leda?" the boy repeated. "You want me to go look at the livery?"

"No," she said finally just as the boy was turning to leave. "You don't have to. I'll check."

Deliberately, Leda laid the palms of her hands flat against the closed door. Closing her eyes, she concentrated, straining to feel Max's presence in the room beyond. The sun-warmed wood burned into her hands but she didn't move. She opened her heart and her mind, reaching for Max. Minutes passed slowly and Denny's foot was tapping when she let her hands drop.

"Well?" the boy asked impatiently.

"No," she said, staring dejectedly at the door in front of her. Now her plan would have to wait. But only until tomorrow, she told herself firmly. "He's gone. I can feel the emptiness of the room. If Max was home, I would know it."

"How?"

"We're in love, Denny." She smiled despite her disappointment. "It was Fate that brought us together and nothing can separate us."

"You and the doc?"

"Yes." She threw one more glance at the closed door. "If Max was at home, I would *feel* his love for me through any barrier."

The door flew open. Maxwell leaped out onto the landing and shouted, "Ah-hah!"

Leda gasped, clutched at her throat, and staggered back, her eyes wide with shock.

Denny yelled, "Shit!" and stumbled backward toward the stairs behind him.

Maxwell's arm shot out and his fingers curled in Denny's shirt before the boy could fall. Once he had the youngster steadied, though, he turned triumphantly to Leda.

"What do you say about your 'visions' now?" he crowed.

"Curses and swears!" she shouted, still struggling to catch her breath. "You like to scared me out of ten years!"

Maxwell crossed his arms across his chest, leaned back against the wood siding, and looked at her, victory shining in his eyes.

"Scared you?" he repeated, his head cocked and his eyebrows lifted almost into his hairline. "Now how could I scare you? Didn't you *feel* my presence?"

Lips pursed mutinously, Leda watched him. It was the first time she'd seen him without his black coat on. Her gaze moved over him quickly, thoroughly. Strange, she thought, how a plain white shirt could make his shoulders seem so much broader. The long sleeves were rolled back to his elbows, exposing surprisingly strong, tanned forearms. His top collar button was undone and his shirttail hung outside his pants. His usually neatly combed hair looked as though a bird had tried to build a nest in it and the cocky look on his face made Leda want to kick him in the shins.

Handsome he might be, she told herself, her mouth suddenly dry. But that didn't give him the right to go leaping out at folks from behind closed doors!

"Well?" he asked, one corner of his mouth sliding up into a self-satisfied smirk. "I heard you tell Dennis that if I was inside, you would *feel* it. What happened?"

Leda glanced down at her young cousin and found the boy's bright blue eyes fastened on her questioningly. He wanted to know too. She silently acknowledged that *she* wouldn't mind an explanation either. She couldn't understand it.

But she wasn't about to admit that to Max! Instead, she planted her hands on her hips, leaned toward him, and accused, "You were *hiding* your presence from me."

"What?"

"You heard me, Max. You did it on purpose."

"*I* didn't do anything." He straightened up and looked down at her. "*I* was sitting in my room, minding my own business. *You* were the one playing magic tricks."

"I was not doing magic tricks."

He grinned. "Apparently not well, at least."

"Leda," Denny piped up, "how come you didn't know he was there? He scared you too, didn't he?"

"Well, yes, Denny. He *did* scare me a little."

Max snorted.

"*But*," Leda went on quickly, ignoring him, "I didn't know he was there because he didn't *want* me to know he was there."

"Huh?" The boy's face scrunched up in confusion.

"I agree," Max tossed in. "Huh?"

She frowned at him then demanded, "Don't try to deny it, Max. You were hiding your essence from me."

"Essence?"

"Yes. You blocked your inner self from answering my call."

"Call?"

"Can he do that?" Denny said, with an admiring glance at the doctor.

"It would seem so," Max answered before she could.

"Yes, Denny. He can." She raised her gaze to meet her beloved's. "What I'd like to know is *why* he did it."

Maxwell faltered for a moment under her direct stare. For some reason, he felt exactly the way he had when his father had caught him at some mischief or other. The last lingering shreds of the rush of triumph that had filled him only minutes ago dwindled away. Now, he was left looking as foolish as he felt.

But, for heaven's sake, he hadn't been able to help himself. As soon as he'd heard her telling the boy that she would be able to *feel* Max's love for her through any barrier—well, he'd *had* to fling open that door just to watch her face.

And for one brief moment, it had been worth it. He'd finally caught her out. At least he'd *thought* so. But how could he argue with the kind of logic she used? He *had* been hiding his "essence" from her. Whatever *that* was.

Now, he told himself with a glance at the triumphant shine in her eyes, he was forced to explain ignoring her repeated knockings. Just how had she managed to put him on the defensive?

"I," he started, mentally groping for an excuse, "was asleep." Max almost winced. That sounded lame even to *him*.

"Asleep?" Her tone carried the lack of conviction evident on her features.

"Boy, Doc!" Denny grinned. "You sleep harder'n me!"

"Hmmm," Leda added.

"Yes, well. I, uh, haven't been able to sleep much lately." Another lie. He'd had more sleep in the last week or so than ever before in his life. That's *all* he'd had to do, thanks to Leda James pilfering all his patients.

"Leda, you gonna ask him now?"

She didn't take her eyes off Max, and he had the unreasonable desire to shuffle his feet and look away. But he didn't. He forced himself to stand upright and meet her direct gaze.

Since he'd heard their whole conversation, he knew that she was about to invite him for dinner. All he had to do was refuse politely, then they'd be on their way and he could retreat into his room.

"Leda and me, we come to ask you to supper," Denny finally said when he'd given up waiting for Leda to speak.

"Thank you, Dennis," he started, "but—"

"Have you eaten already?" she cut him off.

"Yes, yes, as a matter of fact, I have."

She looked past him into his room. "I didn't see you go to Selma's," Leda said.

"No, I was, uh, tired. She sent me something on a tray." That, at least, was true. Selma'd sent her oldest boy, Billy, with his supper an hour ago.

"Oh." Leda let her gaze move over the dark room behind him. When her eyebrows lifted suddenly, Maxwell knew that she'd spied the uneaten plate of food.

"I wasn't very hungry either," he said quickly.

"So I see."

"Bet ya are now, though. Huh?" Denny moved in closer. His round, freshly scrubbed face split in a wide smile as he said, "Leda's got ham and beans and potatoes with corn bread and a apple pie for dessert." He paused and licked his lips for emphasis. "And her corn bread's about the best thing you ever tasted, Doc."

It sounded wonderful. Certainly far better than the now cold supper Selma'd sent him. And Maxwell knew he should accept their invitation. At the very least, it would help to dispel a few of the things he'd heard Denny say about him.

Standoffish?

Didn't like people?

A *fine* thing for folks to think of their *doctor*!

Leda coughed slightly. She was waiting.

Maxwell's stomach rumbled and he knew she'd heard it when she smiled.

"Well, Max?" she asked softly. "Will you join us?"

"I don't—"

"Are you scared now?" Those copper arches above her eyes lifted.

Her challenge hung in the charged air between them. From the corner of his eye, Maxwell saw the boy looking from one to the other of them, waiting anxiously for a decision.

Was he scared? he asked himself. A voice in the back of his mind screamed out, "Hell yes!" Too much time with her could only be asking for trouble. On the other hand, maybe it would be better all the way around if he just tried to get used to her presence as quickly as possible.

Besides, he thought, he'd be damned if he'd admit to *her* that she scared him.

"All right, Denny," he heard himself say, his gaze locked with Leda's. "I'd be happy to join you for supper."

Leda's lips quirked slightly.

"Let me get my coat," he said.

"No need, Doc," the boy answered and tugged at Max's shirttail sharply before releasing him again. "It's just us. Let's get goin' now before Sean eats all that corn bread!" The boy made enough noise for four children as he clattered down the steps. At the bottom, he looked back up at the two adults and smiled. "Boy, wait'll I tell Sean and Mike about how you scared us, Doc! That was really something!"

Maxwell gave the boy an absent smile.

"Are you ready?" Leda asked quietly after Dennis ran off toward home.

"Yes. I'm ready," Max said, and for some reason, he felt as though he were agreeing to far more than supper.

CHAPTER 8

"I don't agree," Maxwell said and tried, unsuccessfully, to push Arthur's shaggy head off his leg. Instead, the huge dog rubbed its hairy chin against Maxwell's thigh and stared up at the man through adoring brown eyes. Sighing, Maxwell resigned himself to the growing patch of drool on his trousers and turned back to the discussion at hand.

"But it was your idea," Leda insisted before taking a sip of hot raspberry tea.

"I'll have to say she's right, Doc." Garrett tamped tobacco into his pipe and looked at the man sitting opposite him. "From what Leda told me, you *asked* her to work with you."

Inhaling sharply, Maxwell took a moment to try to gather his thoughts. Although, he told himself, it was difficult at best trying to think after eating such a big meal. True to Dennis's promises, Leda James did indeed make the best corn bread he'd ever tasted. And the way Garrett's boys put food away, Maxwell'd practically had to fight to get his share.

Strange, he'd never really noticed how uninspired Selma Tyler's cooking was before tonight. Now, he doubted that he'd ever be able to look at the woman's stew and rock-hard biscuits without comparing it, unfavorably, to the meal he'd just eaten.

And he even had to admit that he'd been enjoying himself with the Malone family. That is, until he, Garrett, and Leda had retired to the parlor with their after-supper tea. It wasn't until then that Leda'd brought up the subject of their working together.

He knew that all he had to do was tell her, outright, that he had *no* desire to work with her. That all he wanted from her was that she leave his patients alone. Oh, he'd said it all before, true. But something told him that if he pulled no punches, if he was brutally honest without giving her a chance to interpret things for herself . . . she would finally believe him.

Somehow, though, he found he couldn't quite bring himself to crush her that way. She seemed so—*pleased.* So happy that he had, in her mind at least, come around to her way of thinking. And strangely enough, Maxwell'd also discovered that he was reluctant to see the smile on her face fade away. He would have to settle, he told himself, for trying to find a way to at least slow down her plans.

Especially now that she'd decided what his office *really* needed was an extra room, set aside specifically for *her* needs.

"Now, Garrett," Maxwell said and set his teacup down on the doily-covered table beside his armchair. "What I *actually* said was, I wanted a compromise between us."

The older man lit his pipe, puffed at it for a moment or two, then asked, "What kind of compromise?"

"I'd had in mind more of a, well . . . a referral of sorts."

"What?" Garrett looked confused and the doctor could hardly blame him.

Trying to keep his gaze from straying to Leda, Maxwell focused on her uncle. "I thought that Leda could send people to see me, after she'd seen them and done what she could."

"Isn't that what we're talkin' about here?"

"Yeeesss," Maxwell agreed, "but it seems to me that keeping our 'offices' separate would be better for the patients."

"Don't see how," Garrett admitted.

"But Max," the gypsy cut in, "I thought we decided that it would be much easier for us both to be in the same place."

"*You* decided," he reminded her quietly and frowned when her smile faltered.

"Sorry, Doc," Garrett said and leaned back in his chair, "but I just don't see what the big hoo-hah is. What difference does it make if she's in the store or at your place?"

"Precisely my meaning!" Maxwell shot back and felt a small thrill at having made an important point.

"Then"—Leda shook her head—"if even *you* agree that there's no difference, I think our first decision should stand."

"What decision is that?" he asked, though he was sure he knew the answer already.

She laughed delightedly. "For me to move my things into your office, of course."

"But there's no room."

"I don't need much."

"We'll be crowded."

"We'll be together."

He was losing. He felt it as surely as the dog drool soaking into his pants.

Arthur sighed, shook all over, and settled in deeper. Maxwell spared a worried glance at just how close the big dog's mouth—and teeth—were to his crotch. When he spoke again, he kept his voice low. This was no time to upset the animal.

"Leda," he said and tried not to notice how lovely she looked in the soft glow of lamplight. "If you would just listen—"

"Oh, Max!" She cut him off again. "You don't have to thank me."

"Thank you?"

"Yes."

She leaned forward and curled her bare feet up under the hem of her skirt. In her bright pink skirt and soft cream-colored blouse, Leda looked like a spring flower against the backdrop of the faded green fabric of the chair she was seated in. Her red hair tumbled over her shoulders and Maxwell wondered idly if it felt as soft as it looked.

"I know how much this means to you," she said.

"Means to me?" he finally croaked.

"It's just as important to me too. Oh, it will be wonderful, Max. You'll see."

Defeated for the moment, Maxwell dropped his head against the chairback. While Leda chattered on, he let his mind go blank and allowed his gaze to drift away from her disturbing presence. It was probably best if he didn't listen right now anyway. Anything she said was bound to upset him.

Instead, his gaze wandered over the warm, welcoming parlor of the Malone house.

Garrett was one of the two men in town he considered a friend. Yet *this* was the first time in the five years Maxwell'd been in town that he'd been inside his friend's house.

He frowned thoughtfully and wondered why that fact had never bothered him before. But now that he stopped to think about it, everything he'd overheard Dennis saying to Leda was right.

Oh—not the part about his not liking people. He liked them fine. But what the boy had said about Maxwell never going to a person's house unless he'd been called there as a doctor. Now, remembering all the refused invitations over the years, he wondered if he hadn't done himself a disservice.

Silently, he compared the stark emptiness of his own rooms above the office with Garrett's noisy, cluttered home.

It didn't take long to decide which he preferred.

The sounds of a battle between brothers drifted down the stairs and mingled with Garrett's and Leda's low-pitched voices. Framed daguerreotypes lined the mantel over the empty fireplace, and rag rugs, their colors dim and muted from repeated washings, lay scattered on the shining wood floor.

Schoolbooks, slingshots, and other assorted children's possessions littered the tabletops, and coats and sweaters of varying sizes hung from an overloaded halltree. Idly, Maxwell stroked Arthur's head, bringing a deep rumble of appreciation from the animal.

Garrett's pipe tobacco scented the still air, and as Maxwell took another sip of raspberry tea, he decided that he really didn't miss his usual cup of coffee.

"Don't you think so, Max?"

"Hmmm? What?" He shook himself from his wanderings and looked up into the amused faces of his hosts.

"I said, the sooner we start, the better," Leda repeated. "Don't you think so?"

"Well," he hedged, "I, uh—"

"Pa," Sean yelled as he raced down the staircase and jumped over the bottom three steps to land heavily on the floor of the hall.

Maxwell sighed at the reprieve and looked up when the boy stuck his head around the corner.

"I'm gonna go for a walk. That all right?"

Garrett glanced up at the ornate mantel clock before looking back at his oldest son. "It's near eight o'clock, Sean."

"I won't be long," the boy said quickly.

"Where you headed?"

"Oh," Sean said and Maxwell noted that the boy didn't meet his father's gaze as he finished, "nowhere special."

Another set of footsteps sounded out on the stairs and Michael scrambled around his older brother to slide into the parlor.

"*I* know, Pa. *I* know where he's goin'."

"Shut up, you," Sean hissed and made a grab for the twelve year old.

Maxwell hid a smile behind his hand. All three of Garrett's sons were smaller versions of their father. But Sean, at fourteen, was all sharp angles and bones. An embarrassed flush colored his cheeks and his voice cracked when he said, "I just want to go outside for a bit, Pa. That's all."

"That ain't all," Michael crowed and ran to his father's side.

Arthur jumped up from his post at Maxwell's side. In a lumbering trot, he moved to the boy and planted his wide behind down on Garrett's feet. Mouth open, tongue lolling, the animal watched Michael as the boy's father tugged his feet free.

"All right, you two," Garrett said, loud enough to carry over both boys' shouting voices and the dog's excited whining. "Sean, what's goin' on here?"

"Nothin', Pa. Honest."

"He's goin' callin' on Jenny Lloyd, that's what."

"Michael." Sean's voice cracked again, but the threat was no less meaningful for that.

Garrett smothered a smile, glanced at his oldest boy, and said quietly, "Go ahead then, Sean. But you be home before nine."

Sean grinned, shot Michael one last dirty look, then grabbed his coat and raced out the front door.

"Hold on here," Garrett said when he snatched Michael's suspenders before the boy could take off after his brother. "Where d'ya think *you're* goin'?"

"C'mon, Pa," he pleaded, wiggling his black eyebrows. "Lemme go watch."

"Get upstairs, mister. Watch yourself do your sums for school, instead."

"Aw, Pa." Michael shuffled his feet. "Sean's gonna kiss her, I'll bet, and I won't get to see it."

"That's too bad."

"Aw . . ."

"Kissin's not somethin' you go to watch, like a horse race or a fight . . . It's somethin' private. Personal."

Maxwell looked at Leda and found himself staring into her deep green eyes.

"Why's he wanna kiss dumb ol' Jenny Lloyd, anyhow, Pa?"

Garrett chuckled softly. "I'm thinkin' you'll find that out for yourself in no time a'tall."

"Not me," the boy swore. "Sean acts like a dang fool every time Jenny's around!"

"Yes, well."

"What's kissin' like, Pa? Is it fun?"

Maxwell inhaled sharply but couldn't drag his gaze from Leda's. The soft smile on her face told him that she, too, was remembering that shattering kiss they'd shared. Yes, he thought. Kissing could be fun. It could also be dangerous.

"Well, with the right person, *sure* it's fun." Garrett laughed. "Why else would folks want to be doin' it?"

Why, indeed? Maxwell asked himself and smothered a groan when Leda's tongue darted out to move across her lips.

"Beats heck outa me, Pa!" Michael said.

"I'll remind you of *that* in a couple of years, boy-o," Garrett said and pushed himself up from his chair. "As for now, let's you and me go upstairs with Denny. I'll look over that homework of yours."

"Aw . . ."

"G'night, Maxwell," the man said as he and his son started across the room. "I'm sure I'll be seein' you tomorrow."

Maxwell answered him, but he simply wasn't certain of what he said. All he could think about was that he and Leda were alone in the suddenly much too small parlor. He practically leaped to his feet, took a step, and stumbled over Arthur.

"Are you all right?" she asked and gracefully rose to stand beside him.

"Fine, fine," he said, stepped around the dog and walked toward the front door. Why was it so much farther away now than it had been a few minutes ago?

"Are you leaving, Max? So soon?"

"Yes, yes, I think I'd better, really." Closer, closer.

"But I wanted to talk to you about something."

"I'm, uh"— he forced a yawn—"really very tired, Leda. Tomorrow, perhaps?" Only a few steps more.

"But, Max—"

"Thank you so much for supper, Leda." His fingers curled around the doorknob and turned. "It was wonderful, really." One step, over the threshhold. "Best I've eaten in a very long time." Another step, push the door closed.

She grabbed the door, successfully stopping him from shutting it. Laying one hand on his forearm, she looked up at him. "All right. We can talk tomorrow, then."

Tomorrow, he told himself. And she'd be with him all day.

"I'm glad you came tonight, Max."

The warmth of her touch and the shine in her eyes was almost more than he could bear.

Before he could step back, she rose up on her bare toes and brushed his mouth with hers. He felt the lightninglike charge of the brief contact all the way to his bones.

"Good night, Max."

He swallowed heavily and prayed his voice would work. "Good night, Leda." Quickly, before he could do anything foolish, Maxwell turned away. When she went inside and closed the door, the bright splash of lamplight across the open ground disappeared as if it had never been. Then he walked across the lonely patch of darkness toward his even darker, lonelier rooms.

Cooter slid down from his horse and threw the reins over the hitching rail. Piano music drifted out the open door of the saloon and the familiar scent of tobacco smoke, sweat, and cheap perfume seemed to call to him.

Stretching his aching muscles, he smiled, glanced up at his partner, and said, "You gettin' down tonight, Deke? Or you plannin' on sleepin' in that saddle?"

"Huh?" The older man's brow wrinkled and he turned his left ear toward the man speaking.

Like that's gonna help any, Cooter thought. Deaf as a post. "Get down!" he called out and instinctively looked around to see if anyone was paying attention. But set back among the trees as the saloon was, the two men went unnoticed.

Slowly, Deke climbed down, gave his horse a pat, and tied him next to Cooter's mount.

"Ain't we gonna look around the town first?" he asked, in a voice loud enough to shatter glass.

Cooter winced. For some reason, Deke talked like everybody was as deaf as him.

"Will you shut up?" Cooter hissed at him but at the same time put a finger to his lips in a sign for quiet. "For Chrissakes," he mumbled, "might's well fire a gun at the sheriff. Let *everybody* know we're here."

"What's that?" Deke shouted.

"Nothin'."

"Well, talk up, man!"

"Jesus, Deke!" Cooter looked over his shoulder. "Will ya shut up and think?"

"Hell yes, I want a drink!" The older man snatched his hat off and beat at his dusty clothes with it. "What're we waitin' for?"

Cooter groaned and his right eye twitched nervously as he watched his saddle partner stomp up the three steps to the Red Dog. Once Deke disappeared inside, the younger man turned for another look at the town.

Guess it didn't make much difference if they checked it all out tomorrow. And hell, he could use a drink too. It was a long, dusty ride from the Montana border. And havin' to shout every time he had something to say could dry up a man's throat somethin' awful.

Then the memory of Cecelia Standish's face as she ordered them to get the lay of the land in Tanglewood leaped to mind. Torn for a minute between the thought of *her* anger and the tempting thought of a cold beer, Cooter hesitated.

But only for a minute.

What harm was there in a couple of drinks, anyway? Besides, how would *she* ever find out? Chuckling under his breath, he started up the steps. From inside, he heard Deke yell out, "Hey, bartender! You sellin' that whiskey or is it just for show?"

The night air carried the scent of the mountains.

Seated on the cushioned window seat in her bedroom, Leda curled her bare feet beneath the hem of her plain white cotton nightdress and leaned partway out the window. From her vantage point, she could see the lights burning in Selma Tyler's kitchen, the single candle in banker Hiram Adams's window, and the darkness of Max's rooms.

Her own bedroom was gently lit by the turned-down wick of an oil lamp. Shadows danced on the pale blue walls and across the white crocheted lace bedcover. The old house was quiet, the only sound the wind outside sneaking under the shutters and setting them to tapping against the side of the house.

She sighed and glanced down at the paper in her hand. The lines were faded and the yellowed paper was creased deeply from being folded and unfolded so often over the years. But the image was unmistakable.

Maxwell Evans.

Her love.

The one man Fate had destined for her alone.

Leda smiled and ran one finger lightly over the sketch her mother'd made so many years ago. How many nights had she looked at that picture? How many dreams had she built on the strength of her mother's promise?

"Leda, honey?" A knock at the door followed her uncle's soft voice.

"Come in," she answered just as quietly, mindful of her cousins sleeping in the next room.

Garrett Malone, dressed in a worn gray bathrobe, filled the doorway. He stopped hesitantly before entering her bedroom. "Good, I didn't wake you."

"I can't sleep." She smiled and patted the cushion beside her.

He crossed the room to take the seat she offered, and after a moment, he glanced at the sketch in her hand.

"That's the doc, all right," he said, a smile creasing his features. "My sister was a wonder," he added thoughtfully.

"I wanted to show it to him tonight," Leda confessed. "I thought if he saw it, maybe . . ."

"Well," the big man said with a slow grin, "you got him to come to the house. That's more than I've ever been able to do."

She ducked her head and shrugged. "But he left right after you and Mike went upstairs."

"But he *came*. That's the important part, here. And Lordy, did he *eat*."

Leda laughed gently. "I didn't think *anyone* could match Sean's appetite."

"The way the doc was chowin' down, poor old Sean darn near went hungry!"

She nodded, but her mind wasn't really on supper. Thoughtfully, her gaze slipped down to Max's portrait again. "I was so sure that if I showed him this drawing, he'd believe everything I've told him."

Garrett inhaled slowly as if dreading the need to speak. "Y'know, Leda, some folks don't believe in the things your mother could do, no matter what."

"I know, but—"

"Don't you think you ought to let up on the doc some? I mean, there's time. You got your whole life, yet."

Her lips quirked in a sad smile and she shook her head. "That's just it, Uncle Garrett. There *is* no time."

"Now, don't start that dyin' business again."

Leda patted his big hand with her smaller one. "It's not easy to accept, I know. But believe me, once you do, it makes all the difference."

"You never did tell me, what makes you so sure you're goin' to die?"

"The signs are there," she insisted and, for the first time, told him all about the accidents that had plagued her in Montana.

"Uh-huh." He nodded thoughtfully when she'd finished. "But nothing like that's happened here, has it?"

"No, not yet. But—"

"Then maybe things ain't as set as you might think."

Her brow furrowed, she listened carefully as he went on.

"Leda." Garrett spoke slowly, gathering his thoughts as he went along. "Don't you think maybe that all them signs was just a way the 'Fates' had of gettin' you here? To your family? To Maxwell?"

"Oh—"

"Hear me out now," he went on quickly, warming to his idea. "Maybe it ain't about dyin' at all. Maybe it was the only way Fate could get you here to Tanglewood so's you could meet Maxwell."

Was it possible? Leda searched her heart, hoping that her uncle was right. After all, he'd been raised by Granny Doyle. He'd lived with Eileen until he was married and moved away. He was used to dealing with the "sight." Garrett had been seeing and interpreting signs since before she herself was born.

"See, Leda," he said softly, "there's lots of ways to look at signs, omens. Sometimes, they mean more than one thing too."

"But—"

"No buts." Garrett shook his head and stood up. Looking down at her, he said, "All I'm askin' is that you try to look at the signs from a different spot. See if maybe you were too quick to find a meaning in them."

"Maybe," she whispered.

"That's it," he urged. "Accept the 'maybe.' Don't be in such an all-fired hurry to give in."

Her gaze dropped back to the sketch in her hand. If Garrett was right, maybe she wouldn't have to die. Maybe she could stay with Max and have the family she'd always dreamed of.

Max's paper image stared back at her and it seemed to Leda that even the drawing looked . . . hopeful.

CHAPTER 9

First thing in the morning, Maxwell heard the front door open. Though he couldn't see the entry way from his examining room, he knew exactly who the early-morning caller was.

Leda. She was obviously eager to begin working together.

All through a long, sleepless night, he'd fought against the realization that he wasn't nearly as bothered by her "partnership" plan as he'd pretended to be. Oh, he didn't relish having her teas and onions around. And he would do everything in his power to keep that crystal ball out of his office. He wasn't willing to go *that* far. On the other hand, he'd had to admit, if only to himself, just how much he'd come to enjoy her presence. How much he was beginning to *need* it.

Somehow, Leda James had found a path into a heart that Maxwell had thought was impervious to assault.

And as much as that knowledge terrified him, he was helpless against her relentless protestations of love.

"Max?"

Even her voice sent a shiver of awareness snaking through him.

He pushed himself to his feet, walked around his desk, and crossed the room. When he stepped into the hall, though, Maxwell stopped dead.

Sunlight fell through the open front door, surrounding her in a dazzling, golden halo. When she pulled a heavy black scarf from her head, her bright red hair became like burnished copper. A half smile tugged at her lips and the tip of her nose was sunburned.

Why was it, he asked himself, that her careless appearance seemed so . . . appealing, now? What had happened to the man who'd considered her glorious, untamed hair untidy? Briefly, he wondered what it would feel like to bury his hands in that mass of disorderly curls.

Distractedly, he noticed that she wore more necklaces than usual today. Strange, but he was even becoming accustomed to her bizarre attire. Then, his gaze unerringly dropped to her feet.

The red socks were back.

"Hello, my love," she said, and he fought down his body's immediate response.

"Good morning."

She ran across the small space separating them, threw her arms around his middle, and squeezed. Maxwell staggered only slightly. He was also becoming much too accustomed to her displays of affection. After only a moment, she rose up on her toes, brushed his lips with hers, then settled back down and smiled at him.

"Isn't it a glorious morning?"

His mouth still tingling from her kiss, he returned her smile and told himself that he could think of several *worse* ways to start a day. Then her simple comment struck him. Maxwell realized he hadn't even noticed the morning until she'd arrived. But now, tearing his gaze from her, he looked out at the sun-washed street and agreed heartily with her.

"Yes, Leda. It *is* a beautiful day."

Her hands locked behind his back and slowly, hesitantly, his own arms encircled her small form, holding her close.

His jaw tight, he told himself that a simple hug wasn't a declaration of undying devotion. And yet, with her head snuggled up against his chest, her heart beating in time with his, Maxwell knew it was dangerous.

If they were going to be able to live and function in the same town, let *alone* the same office—he would *have* to learn to be near her without giving in to a desire that seemed to be a permanent part of him these days. And it was becoming more and more clear to him that Leda had no intention of curbing her own impulses.

That fact rather pleased him.

"Y'know, Max," she said softly, "even the smallest kiss from you does all sorts of strange things to me."

Good God.

"Is it like that for you too?"

He inhaled sharply and the familiar, tantalizing scent of roses filled him.

"I beg your pardon?" He finally managed to squeeze the words past the sudden catch in his throat.

"I mean," Leda went on, blissfully unaware of what her conversation was doing to him, "did kissing me make you feel all hot and sort of . . . twitchy inside?"

That was certainly one way to put it, he told himself on a silent groan. As she rubbed her cheek against his shirtfront, his breath caught in his throat. In fact, it was an excellent description of what was happening to him that very minute.

"I, uh," he said, groping for something to say.

Suddenly, she drew her head back and looked up at him. Her eyes shining, a soft smile tugging at her lips, she said, "This is all so exciting, Max."

"Exciting?" The abrupt change of subject hardly registered with him. A silent laugh sounded in the back of his brain. He was even becoming used to the way her mind worked. What a terrifying prospect.

"Yes," she said. "Our first day together as partners. I only stopped by here to say good morning before I go to the store and get some of my things." She sighed. "Oh, it's going to be wonderful, Max. I just know it."

He wanted to ask her if she'd "seen" it, but he kept quiet. The day was going to be difficult enough as it was. There was no point bringing in talk of visions and Fate before they absolutely had to.

"I think I'd better get the . . ."

He wasn't listening anymore. Instead, he allowed his mind to wander. He seriously doubted that she would notice when he didn't answer her. Leda had a way of talking so fast, she answered her own questions.

Besides, looking down into her features, Maxwell found that he didn't want to talk at all. He just wanted to look at her. Hold her. Slowly, he began to notice that her direct gaze had changed. Now, her eyes seemed clouded with desire and he felt her tremble.

Had she said something important? Something he shouldn't have missed?

Deliberately, he cleared his throat and asked in a strained voice, "What? What did you say?"

"Nothing," she replied in a dreamy tone.

"But—" He was sure she'd been talking only a moment ago.

"How can I think, much less say anything," she whispered, "when your hands are touching me like that?"

When her eyes drifted shut, Maxwell paid attention to exactly what he was doing. Without even being aware of it himself, the simple hug he'd given her had become far more. His right hand cradled her behind and his left, he noted with a start, was even now cupping her breast as his thumb stroked a hardened nipple.

Abruptly, he lowered his hands and took a half step back. He couldn't believe it. He hadn't even *noticed* what he was doing. Good God. And after all his high talk about controlling himself. Even now, his body tightened until it was all he could do not to groan in discomfort.

"I don't know what to say," he finally muttered. "I'm sorry."

"I'm not," she replied quickly and moved closer. Reaching up, she cupped the back of his head and drew him down to her.

When their lips met, he closed his eyes, but not before he'd seen the soft smile on her face. Then, Maxwell knew nothing but the completeness of her. Leda's lips parted for him, and as his tongue swept inside her warmth, his arms snaked around her, pulling her tight against him.

This time he was aware of everything. His hands, her mouth, her arms, the soft puff of her breath on his cheek. Her tongue moved against his in a silent dance of welcome. Leda's fingertips drifted across his nape and each touch felt like a tiny flame.

Everything he'd ever been, ever known, called out for restraint, yet he knew he'd rather quit breathing then draw away from her.

Leda's warmth, Leda's lips, her touch were all important to him now and nothing else mattered.

Outside the open door, a wagon rolled heavily down the main street. Its wooden wheels creaked and sounded a call that shattered their illusion of solitude.

Reluctantly, Maxwell raised his head, sucked in air like a drowning man, and released her. Even as shudders of frustrated desire wracked him, he sent a silent prayer of thanks for the wagon's intrusion. If not for its timely arrival, he had no idea *what* might have happened.

Every ounce of the control he'd always prided himself on seemed to have deserted him. It shocked him to the bone to discover just how close he'd come to laying her down on the cold, hard floor and stretching out alongside her.

Leda's head dropped to his chest, and even though his arms now hung at his sides, more empty than they'd ever been before, Maxwell felt her tremors and shared them. Something rare . . . something almost startling in its strength . . . gripped him. He refused to put a name to it. To do that would be to allow everything he'd always avoided to gain a stranglehold on his soul.

He swallowed heavily and felt his throat close.

"Oh, Max," she said, her breath still unsteady, "that was wonderful. Even better than before."

Maxwell concentrated on breathing.

"I *do* love you!" Leda whispered and hugged him tightly one more time before letting him go.

Lord. There it was. The word he'd been trying to ignore.

"Max? Max, my love. Are you all right?"

Her palm touched his cheek briefly and the sensation of her touch was only slightly less strong than the emptiness when she took her hand away.

"Yes," he managed to say, knowing she wouldn't leave him alone until he answered her. "I'm fine."

"Well," Leda countered quickly, "I'm more than fine. I'm wonderful!"

Yes, he thought silently, you are.

"Oh!" Her tone changed and he looked down, grateful that she hadn't said that . . . *word* again. "Before I go to the store for my things, I want to give you something."

Her things. In hours she would be moved into his office. Then they would be together all the time. Lord. How would he survive this?

She began to dig in the voluminous pocket of her skirt. Maxwell tried to disregard the hideous black and red garment and waited patiently. At least while she was so preoccupied, there was a safe distance separating them. And, he had to admit, he was curious. There was simply no telling what she might bring out of that pocket. Mentally, he guessed at the contents. Onions? Tea? Wing of bat? Toe of frog?

"Hold out your hands, please, Max."

Instinctively, he did as she asked and before he could think better of it, she was piling bits and pieces into his cupped palms.

His eyes widened at the first object. Curiosity piqued, he asked, "A horseshoe nail bent into a ring?"

"Horseshoes are good luck, Max"—she shrugged and added—"but much too heavy to carry in your pocket."

"True." That seemed reasonable.

"And a horseshoe nail is almost as good, don't you think?"

"I never really gave it much thought," he admitted wryly, "but I would assume so."

"Me too." She grinned at him and he felt the full force of it like a physical blow. "Well," she went on, "a ring is the sign for eternity, y'know. So, good luck for eternity."

Of course, he silently acknowledged. Still, he had to ask. "Why don't you wear it instead of carrying it in your pocket?"

"It's too big."

Naturally. And, glancing at her dainty hands and slender fingers, he had to admit she was right. She dropped something else into his cupped hands and Maxwell rolled the three glass balls on the palm of one hand. "Marbles?"

"They're Denny's," she said and went back to digging in her pocket.

Well, he told himself, that was completely logical. Why would the boy carry his *own* marbles when Leda was willing to do it for him? As she dropped the next object into his hands, he asked, "A *rock*?"

"A *crystal* rock," she corrected and touched the tip of her index finger to the pale pink stone. "I found it when Mother and I lived in Wyoming."

He couldn't help himself. "And you use it for . . . ?"

"Use it?" She smiled up at him. "Nothing really. It's just pretty. Don't you think?"

Maxwell looked at the stone again and had to admit that the varied shades of pink were *very* pretty. "Yes," he said quietly, "it is." Silently, though, he wondered if he would have seen the beauty of the stone if *he'd* been the one to find it.

Probably not.

When she dropped a small dark blue gemstone on his palm, he stared at it. "A sapphire?"

"Uh-huh." She pushed her hair back from her face with the back of one hand. "My father gave it to my mother and she gave it to me." Tilting her head to one side, she asked, "Did you know that different stones have different meanings?"

He shook his head, captivated by the play of light on her features.

"Well, they do." Leda pointed at the tiny jewel. "Sapphires mean Truth and Faithfulness."

He didn't say anything. What could he say? Then she dropped a small ball of string on his palms.

"And why do you carry string with you?"

"Might need some one day and I'd better have it."

Strange how all of this was beginning to make sense to him.

Once more, she dug into her seemingly bottomless pocket. As he watched her, Maxwell felt a reluctant smile hovering on his lips.

Leda James was, no doubt, the only woman he would ever know who thought nothing of stuffing her pockets like any ten-year-old child. It was just one more facet of her nature that made the woman almost irresistable.

And dangerous.

Head bent, she dug into her pocket again and this time pulled out both a wilted lupine blossom and a small, folded piece of paper.

A grin on her face, Leda announced, "Finally. I knew it was in there!" Carefully, she tucked the paper into the valley between her breasts then quickly took back all of the items she'd asked Maxwell to hold.

When she was finished repacking her possessions, Maxwell silently marveled that she didn't walk at a slant, considering how weighted down one side of her skirt was. Of course, he reminded himself, for all *he* knew, the matching pocket might very well be just as crammed full.

He shook his head slightly and watched her as she drew the scrap of paper free of its nesting place. Deliberately, he kept his mind away from the open vee of her faded rose-colored shirt and the soft, pale flesh it hid. Unfortunately, his body was not so easily distracted.

Shifting his legs uncomfortably, he waited.

Leda held the paper between her fingertips and gently began to unfold it. Sneaking a peek at Maxwell from beneath lowered lashes, she could hardly contain her excitement. She just knew that as soon as he saw the sketch her mother'd made so long ago, he would believe.

She paused only long enough to admire the portrait once more before looking up and meeting Max's curious gaze.

"I wanted to show you this last night, my love."

"What is it?"

"It's the drawing I told you about. The one my moth-er did."

Confusion was etched plainly on his features.

Leda sighed but rushed on. "The night she told me about you. About us."

"Leda . . ." He shook his head slightly.

"Max, my love," she hurried on, "if you'll just look." Stretching out her hand, she held the paper out to him.

"Now, Sheriff," Cooter wheedled, "Deke's right sorry about that little set-to at the saloon last night."

" 'Set-to'?" Dan snorted, propped one boot heel up on the corner of his desk, and looked at the scrawny man across from him. His coat hung across narrow shoulders like a shapeless rag and the man's right eye twitched at an alarming speed. Dan just managed to keep from rubbing his own right eye in response.

Ever since he'd been called to the ruckus at the Red Dog the night before, he'd had a feeling this wouldn't be any ordinary arrest. Oh, he'd had drunks sleeping it off in a cell before. Even drunks who'd done a considerable amount of damage before passing out.

But he'd *never* had a drunk with a nursemaid saddle part-ner hovering around whining and pleading the drunk's case.

"That was a helluva lot more than a 'set-to,' " he finally said. "Your partner damn near tore the place apart."

Cooter rubbed the whisker stubble on his chin and tossed a glance at the door leading to the two cells at the back end of the jailhouse.

"And," Dan added meaningfully, "if you're thinkin' about tryin' to break him out . . . don't."

"Why, Sheriff! No such thing." Cooter straightened up and adopted his most pious expression. "That would be against the law."

"Hmmm."

"How long did ya say you was gonna keep him in jail, Sheriff?"

"Two weeks."

"*Two* weeks!"

"That's right."

"For bein' drunk?"

"No, for destroyin' a place of business and not bein' able to pay for the damage."

"Hell."

"Course, if you can come up with the money . . . you can get him out sooner."

Fat chance of that, Cooter told himself. He'd lost all his money in a poker game with the gambler just before the fight broke out. And Deke didn't have a penny to his name.

"What's goin' on out there?" An angry shout from the back of the building interrupted them.

Cooter scowled at the sound. Seemed as though Deke finally come to and realized he was locked up. Damn fool. What he *should* do, Cooter told himself, was just ride away and let the logger-headed jackass serve his time.

But he couldn't risk that. Shit, if Deke got to talkin', and most likely he *would,* he might let the whole plan slip. And then what? The sheriff and every other man in town who could hold a gun would be waitin' on him and Cecelia when they hit the bank.

Besides, he felt a helluva lot safer with another fella in on Cecelia Standish's plans. He sure didn't want that woman only havin' *him* to take things out on!

No. He had to get his partner out. Somehow.

"Can I go see him for a minute, Sheriff?"

"I reckon."

He took a half step, but the sheriff's voice stopped him again quickly. "Leave your gun here. With me."

An uneasy chuckle slipped past the knot in his throat, but Cooter dutifully lifted his revolver from its holster and laid it down on the cluttered desktop.

"All right. Go on ahead."

He nodded and walked back to the cells. It was all he could do to keep from shudderin'. Just bein' inside a jailhouse was enough to give a man the cold shakes. Why, he could almost hear a iron door slammin' shut on him. Cooter felt the sheriff's hard stare on his back and forced himself to walk slow, easy. One thing he didn't need was the law checkin' up on him too close.

Damn his fool partner, anyway! This was all his fault. And if that durn sheriff started siftin' through old Wanted posters, Cooter told himself, and happened on *his* face . . . hell, he'd shoot Deke himself! If the truth be known, he'd just as soon shoot his partner now as break him out of jail.

Shit. The rattle-brained fool'd ruined Cecelia's plan and there would be hell to pay soon.

Deke's hands gripped the iron bars tightly, and when Cooter walked in, he glared at him, shouting, "What the hell am I doin' in jail?"

"Shut up, Deke." Cooter glanced back over his shoulder. They wouldn't even be able to talk. Not with the sheriff settin' right outside and Deke shoutin' every word.

"My head hurts somethin' fierce," the older man complained loudly.

"I shouldn't wonder. Ya damn near drank the town dry last night!"

The other man snorted a laugh then winced.

"But why'm I in here?"

" 'Cause after you finished drinkin', you commenced takin' the place apart piece by piece."

A long moment passed, then Deke's expression tightened again. "I 'member now. That fella in there last night? The one in the fancy hat? He insulted me!"

Cooter jammed his hands in his pockets to keep himself from reaching out and throttling his partner. "He did not, ya damn fool!"

Deke straightened up, lifted his chin, and shouted, "He asked me to *dance*!"

Sonofabitch. From the office, Cooter heard the sheriff's chuckle and frowned. Deke's ears was gettin' worse all the time! And the worse he heard, the louder he talked.

"He didn't ask you to *dance*!" Cooter yelled at the other man. "He asked ya did ya want to take a *chance*! Fella was a gambler!"

"Chance?" Deke bellowed and ruffled his sparse hair. "Why the hell didn't he say so?"

Cooter didn't trust himself to speak. In his mind's eye he saw the start of that brawl all over again. That gambler'd hardly talked before he was flyin' into another fella, who jumped up and hit a different fella, until the whole place was nothin' more than fists, feet, and teeth.

All because Deke couldn't hear a gunshot if the barrel was stuck in his ear. But this wasn't doin' any good, he told himself. Instead, his tired brain started scootin' around, lookin' for a way out. But the only answer was the one he didn't want to think about.

Cecelia. He'd have to head back to the cabin and wait for her. They needed Deke to pull the next job and they couldn't get him out of jail without cash.

"When ya gettin' me outa here?" Deke shouted, grimacing at the tiny, spartan cell.

"It'll be a while."

"Huh?"

"I *say*, it'll be a while. Few days, at least! I got to go get some money from our 'friend,' 'cause I'm broke!"

"This ain't no *joke*, son!" Deke stuck his face between the bars and shouted at his partner. "You got to get me out!"

"I will."

"What? Why not just bust me out?"

Cooter winced, glanced at the open doorway, and waited for the sheriff to poke his head in. Nothing happened.

"Will you shut up?" Cooter hissed at him. "Or I'll shoot you myself."

"Don't you tell *me* to go to hell! This ain't *my* fault, y'know. It ain't *my* fault I didn't want to dance with no fella!"

His jaw clenched, Cooter inhaled sharply, then exhaled in a rush, hoping to calm down. This wasn't doin' any good, he thought disgustedly. He was just wastin' time standin' around here. Besides, he purely hated the feelin' of bein' in jail. Even as a visitor. There was just one thing for it.

He had to go get Cecelia.

She'd be right put out by all this, he knew. And he sure wasn't lookin' forward to tellin' her either. But it beat the hell out of tryin' to talk to Deke.

"I'll be back," he shouted one last time and turned for the door.

"Cooter! *Cooter!*"

He didn't stop. He just snatched his gun from the corner of the sheriff's desk and kept on walking. The man's interested blue eyes followed him across the room. Cooter tried to ignore the cold chill that swept over him. With a calm he didn't feel, he hurried on through the office, out the door, and onto the street. As he mounted and rode away, though, he heard Deke's voice still callin' his name.

"Max?" Leda stepped closer. He didn't look well at all. Face pale, fingers tight on the edges of the paper, he stared unblinkingly at the sketch she'd handed him. "Max, my love? Are you all right?"

He swallowed heavily but didn't say anything. Leda could almost tell what was going on inside him. The confusion. The denial. But at the same time, she thought with a flare of hopefulness, there was a hint of acceptance on his features. It seemed to her as though he *wanted* to believe, but that everything he'd ever been or known was fighting against it.

Slowly, silently, Max turned from her and began to walk back to his office. He crossed the familiar room with confidence, even though his gaze never left the paper in his hand.

Leda followed him. When he dropped down into the chair behind his desk, she moved to stand just in back of him. She laid her hands on his shoulders and felt the rigid tension in his muscles. He shook his head and she knew that he was trying to deny the evidence before his eyes.

"Do you see, my love?"

"Hmmm?"

"Do you understand how I recognized you the moment you walked into Uncle Garrett's store?"

He inhaled deeply and the tension in his neck increased. Instinctively, Leda began to knead the muscles in his shoulders.

"How?" he mumbled. "When?"

"I was ten years old when my mother drew that picture. That would have made you what? Twenty?"

"Uh-huh." He nodded jerkily, still captivated by the image of himself staring back at him.

It would be all right now, she told herself. Surely now that he had the proof right in front of him, he would be able to believe in their joined Destinies. "Max?"

She leaned over him, ran her finger across the portrait's jawline, then did the same to him.

He turned his face slightly toward her touch.

"Oh, my love," she whispered and kissed his cheek.

                          *   *   *

He heard her. He felt her. Even the scent of roses assured
him that he was wide awake and sitting in his office with
Leda right beside him. But he couldn't be awake.

This *had* to be a dream.

How else to explain this completely unexplainable drawing?

He couldn't seem to tear his gaze away. There was an
incredible fascination about it. How in the world could
a woman he'd never met draw such an accurate likeness
of him?

The paper was old, he thought. The sketch itself was
fading badly. But there was no doubt at all in his mind.
It was *his* face.

"Max darling?"

Lord. He couldn't talk to her now. He had to have time
to think. Too much was happening. Too quickly.

"Max, Tom Shipley just rode past."

"Huh?"

"Tom Shipley." She smiled down at him. "He just rode
past heading for the store. He's probably come about those
stitches."

"Oh. That's nice."

She laughed, a light, delicate sound that filled so many
empty places inside him, it terrified him.

"I have to go to the store now, Max."

"Uh-huh."

"I'll come back as soon as I can."

No, don't, he wanted to say. Leave me alone for a while.
Let me think about this drawing. And your mother. And
you. Let me try to decide what all of this means.

But he didn't. He didn't say anything. Try as he might,
he couldn't get his voice to work.

"Do you want to keep the portrait with you for a bit?"

He nodded. Oh yes, he wanted to do just that. He wanted
to stare at it until he could convince himself that it wasn't
a sketch of him.

"All right, then," she said cautiously.

He watched her as she walked across the room then paused before stepping through the doorway. Looking back at him, she asked again, "You're sure you're feeling well? I could make you some tea."

A strangled laugh choked from his throat. Tea.

Onions, tea, sketches, and visions. Perfect.

He forced a smile. After a long moment, Maxwell managed to say, "I'm fine, dear. I'm . . . fine."

She grinned back at him. "Then I'll just go help Tom. I'll see you later."

He nodded, but thought, She'll see me later?

In a vision? he wondered. Or in the office?

But he didn't say it aloud. He was much too afraid to hear the answer.

CHAPTER 10

Her step bouncy, spirits buoyant, Leda paused for a moment on the boardwalk outside Max's office. He'd called her "dear." Remembering the distracted tone of his voice, she told herself that he probably didn't even know that he'd done it. But that didn't matter. In a way, that fact even made the endearment mean more.

Something deep inside him, a part of him he hadn't even recognized yet, loved her.

She grinned, took two steps then looked up as a horse and rider raced past her. The rail-thin man sat hunched over in the saddle and looked neither left nor right. In seconds, he and his horse were past her and nearly out of town.

Thoughtfully, Leda stared after him. The sudden silence and a few puffs of dirt in the street were all that was left to mark the stranger's passage . . . and yet. She frowned, narrowed her eyes, and recalled the man's profile. There was *something* about him that struck a familiar chord.

But what was it?

Where had she seen him before?

Leda lifted her good-luck coin and rubbed it between her thumb and forefinger. Memory hovered at the edge of her mind, teasing her with vague impressions and distortions.

"Curses and swears," she muttered and dropped the twenty-dollar gold piece back to its place among the dozens of necklaces draped around her neck. Leda'd always prided herself on her memory.

Being able to place the stranger wasn't very important, of course, but it would niggle at her until she'd solved the puzzle, she knew. After all, hadn't she remembered countless herbal recipes, good-luck chants, and the intricate patterns of palm and card readings? She nodded and assured herself that given time, she would remember where she'd seen that skinny young man before.

"But right now," she muttered, "Tom Shipley's waiting for you at the store." She gave one more quick glance to the closed door of Max's office behind her. "And the sooner you get him taken care of, the sooner you can get back to Max."

Her lips curved in anticipation, she began to walk when a sudden movement at the corner of her eye caught her attention.

Directly across the street from her, in front of his gunsmith shop, Julius Lloyd was about to step off the boardwalk into disaster.

"Julius, *no*!" A blanket of dread dropped over her, wiping the smile from her face and sending a dark foreboding shooting up her spine.

The short, dark man looked up and waved.

Leda saw it all so clearly. Julius crossing the street, a runaway team and wagon careening down the hill. The horrified expressions of the gathering crowd and Julius's crumpled body lying in the dirt. She shook her head violently, to clear away the last remnants of her vision.

The gunsmith already had one foot in the street. She had to stop him.

"Don't, Julius," she cried, her hands outstretched, palms facing him. "Go back!"

Perhaps, she thought wildly, the racing horseman who'd appeared so familiar a moment before was simply a phantom rider sent by a generous Fate as a warning.

"Huh?" The older man paused, half on and half off the uneven wooden walk.

She didn't dare cross the street to talk to him. That runaway team could appear at any moment. Anxiously, Leda shot a quick glance first one way then the other. Still no sign of the approaching calamity. But it was coming. She knew it.

"Don't cross the street now," she called. "It's too dangerous."

"Dangerous?" A surprisingly deep laugh shook his small form.

"Yes, Julius." Leda put every bit of her persuasive powers in her voice. But it was much harder to be convincing when you had to shout. "Please, it's not safe. You'll be killed."

That stopped him. Cautiously, he picked up his right foot and stepped back on the boardwalk. His face a shade paler, he said, "Did you say *killed*?"

"Yes, but there's no time to explain." Leda pointed to the left of him. The open space of ground between his shop and the livery corral beckoned. "Please. Go that way."

"Huh? But I'm headed for the mill," he complained and pointed at the opposite end of the street.

"Then go around behind the buildings," she pleaded. "You'll be safe that way."

Warily, the man looked down the street, first one way then the other. At different points along the wide road, five or six horses were tied to hitching rails. There was a buckboard standing outside the Mercantile and two or three people wandering back and forth across the road. A raw-boned dog wandered aimlessly in the dirt, turned in a small circle three times, and plopped down for a nap.

Julius frowned, scratched his balding head, and shouted, "What about them? It's all right for them to cross but not me?"

Leda paused a moment, looked at the others, and concentrated with all her might. But she saw no danger lurking near them. It was only Julius Lloyd in trouble. She felt it.

Turning back to the blacksmith, she yelled again, "I know it seems strange, Julius. But please?"

She watched him and knew that he was weighing what she'd said about being safe against the much shorter route to the mill. Leda held her breath. If he didn't agree, it would be out of her hands. She would have done everything possible to save him. And yet, that would be cold comfort, indeed, if she had to stand by and watch a friend die.

The thought of Julius's wife, Flora, and their five children shot through Leda's brain. Mentally, she sent a frantic plea to heaven that Julius would listen to her.

It seemed forever before he finally sighed, shrugged, and yelled back, "All right, then. If it means that much to you, Leda. I'll go around."

"Thank you!" As she watched him, it seemed that the dark blanket of danger around him began to fade. A burden lifted from her shoulders as she realized that thanks to her "gift," she'd been able to help another person.

Because he was willing to listen to her, Julius would be safe. He'd be with Flora and their children for many more years.

She glanced back over her shoulder and wished for a moment that Max had been there to see it. If he could see for himself what a blessing her "gift" was, maybe he wouldn't fight so desperately against it.

As Julius turned toward the other end of the walk, Leda hurried her steps for the store. Tom Shipley would be waiting.

Julius shook his head and chuckled to himself. That girl's a pistol, he thought. Wait'll he told Flora about this. His wife had been goin' on and on for weeks about Leda this and Leda that.

She had her fortune told so many times, she could do it herself in her sleep. Flora swore by everything Leda said and had even started giving *him* the teas she picked up from the woman.

Julius chuckled to himself. As far as he knew, though, Flora'd never had the slightest speck of "danger" in her readings, even though the woman longed for adventure. It'd surely fry her chicken to know that Leda herself had saved *him* from certain doom.

He stopped at the edge of the boardwalk and glanced back at Leda James. Her red-sock-clad feet flying down the walk toward the store, red hair streaming out behind her as she ran, she made quite a sight. He smothered another laugh.

Tanglewood sure was an "interesting" town since she moved in.

Still watching the running woman, he stepped off the walk.

"Watch out!" someone shouted and Julius spun around. Eyes as big as saucers, he watched in horror as the fully loaded manure wagon backed into him.

He screamed once as he fell.

Was that a scream? Leda stopped and looked back over her shoulder. No. Must be hearing things, she told herself. Her gaze swept over Main Street. She didn't see a thing out of the ordinary. Julius was safely out of sight and on his way to the mill. Must have been one of the horses at the livery, she told herself absently. She smiled and took the last few steps to the Mercantile. Shaking her head at her too vivid imagination, Leda pushed the door open and walked into the store.

"I'm tellin' you," the man said as he walked across the tiny kitchen floor, "I saw it as plain as the nose on your face!"

"Hmmph!" Gladys Fairfax tucked a stray lock of silver hair behind her ear and looked up at August Haley through narrowed, faded blue eyes. His wispy gray hair stood up practically on end, and his long, curved beak of a nose fairly twitched with his excitement. "If it was as plain as the nose on *your* face, August, *then* you might have somethin'."

"No need to be snippy, Gladys." He frowned and sniffed the air pointedly.

"Oh, climb down off that high hump of yours and tell me again, man." She took a seat on one side of her scrubbed white kitchen table and watched him.

Behind him, morning sunlight streamed through the shining windowpanes. A slight breeze ruffled the red calico curtains and the flowers in the pots on the sill dipped and danced. The telegrapher paused beside the gleaming cookstove. Idly, he touched a blackened coffeepot with the tip of his finger. With a quick intake of breath, he yanked it back and shoved the singed finger into his mouth.

Gladys sighed. He could hardly stand still. It was clear to her that the man was *itchin'* to be talking. She hadn't seen him that excited since the day he'd discovered the job that allowed him to be *paid* and snoop at the same time.

Finally, he dropped into a chair opposite her and took a moment to catch his breath. After shaking, then inspecting, his wounded finger, August helped himself to a cookie from the plate in front of him, took a bite, and started talking.

"Gladys, it was broad daylight," he said around the mouthful of cookie. "Not fifteen minutes ago! They was standin' in the doorway of the doc's office, right out where anybody could see 'em!"

"*If* 'anybody' had their busybody nose stickin' in where it don't belong?"

"No such thing! Weren't like that at all," August retorted, clearly insulted. He stretched his scrawny neck, straightened up in his chair, and snatched another cookie.

Gladys frowned.

"I was just passin' by," he insisted, "takin' a telegram to Hiram at the bank." He leaned forward and confided, "Speakin' of that, did you know that big gold shipment's gonna be here in a couple of weeks? I told Hiram he ought to hire some of them miners to stand guard for him. But you know what he said?" August threw his narrow shoulders back and mimicked the banker's high, quavering voice.

"You're s'posed to *deliver* the telegrams, Mr. Haley. Not read 'em."

He snorted. In his own voice, he asked plaintively, "Now all I want to know is, how'm I s'posed to take down telegrams and *not* read 'em?"

Gladys rolled her eyes. Even if there *was* a way to avoid reading the wires that went through his hands, everyone in town knew that August would ignore it. "I don't give a good hang for that gold, August. The only folks in this town who care about it are the miners and them that'll have their back bills paid up."

"Now," he said slowly, "that ain't quite true. The sheriff's mighty concerned about maybe havin' a holdup."

"Hmmph! And I suppose he come to *you* for advice?"

"We had us a talk . . ."

For heaven's sake. Hadn't she just said she didn't care any about that gold?

"Is this what you come over here to tell me?"

"Oh. No, it ain't." He brightened right up. "Like I said, I was passin' by and there they was! I tell you flat out, Gladys"— he jerked a sharp nod and clutched his narrow chest—"liked to stop my heart."

When he reached for a third cookie, Gladys slid the plate out of reach. "August Haley, you're worse than any old woman I ever met."

His gray eyebrows shot up.

But why should *that* surprise her? she asked herself. Thirty years she'd known August, and in that time, she'd never met a body who more enjoyed the sound of his own voice talkin' about things that don't concern him.

This time, though, Gladys decided she'd stop him in his tracks before he could go shootin' that mouth of his all over town. She freely admitted she had a real soft spot for Leda James. And she wasn't about to set in her own kitchen and listen to the old gossip worry the girl's reputation.

"Don't you never get tired," she snapped, "stickin' that nose where it don't belong?"

The nose in question twitched.

"I swear, you carry more tales than that telegraph of yours!"

"I ain't carryin' tales—it's"—he floundered for a minute, then jerked her a nod—"it's . . . givin' the news about town."

Gladys snorted. "That ain't news! For heaven's sake! It ain't the first time young folks've kissed, y'know."

"This wasn't just no ordinary kiss, Gladys." He leaned his forearms on the clean pine table and smiled at his old friend. "It looked to me like the doc was tryin' to swallow that girl . . . teeth, bones, and hair!"

Gladys cleared her throat and shifted in her chair. She remembered kisses like that. And, she thought wryly, *that* was one of the hardest parts of gettin' old. Rememberin' that hunger and fire so clear and not gettin' to feel it anymore.

Oh heavens, she sighed, did she remember kisses like that. In fact, up until her husband died a few years back, she'd come close to bein' "swallowed" herself, on occasion!

And Lordy, did she miss it sometimes.

"Still," she managed to say, and forced herself to glower at August, "ain't none of your business . . . or anybody else's, either, what them two are doin'."

"I just think it's real interestin', is all," August said, stretching his turkeylike neck again. "The doc just ain't the kind to be so . . . *free*."

Gladys snorted again. "*Any* man's that kind."

"Aw, Gladie . . ."

"Don't you 'aw, Gladie' me, August Haley. You forget, I knew you back when you had hair on your head!"

His thin lips pursed slightly.

"And," she went on pointedly, "I seem to recall battin' those hands of yours away a time or two, myself!"

His eyebrows wiggled and danced over pale green eyes that suddenly seemed years younger. August reached across the table and patted her hand gently. "And *I* recall a time or two when you *didn't*!"

Gladys's cheeks puffed out and a soft pink flush crept up her neck. She wanted to smack him soundly for bringing up such delicate matters. But, as she watched his familiar smile, Gladys felt her indignation melt away. After all, once you're old, you ought to be able to talk about any damn thing you wanted to! It's little enough compensation, she told herself.

Slowly, a smile curved her lips. "I remember too. *But*," she added before he could talk about more memories best left in the past, "we ain't talkin' about old times here. We're talkin' about Leda and the doc."

"True, true," he agreed, then leaned forward and grabbed another cookie before she could stop him.

"You say it looked serious, do ya?"

"Hmmph! They was *plenty* serious, believe you me."

"Well then, mayhap we ought to help 'em out a bit."

Chewing, he asked warily, "Like how?"

"Oh, we'll think of somethin'." Gladys smiled broader, shoved the plate toward him, and offered, "Have some more cookies, August."

He reached for yet another. "You make these?"

"Surely did. Just last night."

"Thought you give up bakin', what with your hands an' all."

Rubbing one gnarled, bent hand with the other, Gladys said offhandedly, "They're feelin' some better here lately."

And Gladys knew she had Leda James to thank for that. Be it her onions, her tea, or her company . . . there was purely something magical about that girl.

Maybe, she thought, it was time to try to pay the girl back for her kindnesses. Besides, it was beginning to bother Gladys, hearing the younger woman talk about dyin' so much. Folks that young ought to be thinkin' about livin' and lovin'. Lord knew there was plenty of time for the other.

She leaned back in her chair and glanced across the table at her old friend. The man had already made quite a dent in the cookies. Another few minutes and they'd be gone. Gladys knew that August relished any chance he got for some good home cookin'. Came from bein' alone too much.

Shaking her head, Gladys thought it was a shame how August had spent his life alone. Oh, he'd been happy enough, she supposed, but folks wasn't put on this earth to live out their lives on their own. It just wasn't right. And she wouldn't let it happen to either Leda or the doc.

Besides, if what August had told her was gospel, it looked as though the two young people were already takin' a step in the right direction.

Yessir, she told herself, when a man starts takin' his kissin' as serious as August said Max was, then sometimes all it took was a little extra shove at the right time. And who better for the job than herself? she wondered silently. Hadn't she married the best catch in all of Idaho Territory when she was just seventeen?

Suddenly, she cocked her head and listened.

"What's wrong?" August asked, his mouth still full.

"Nothin', I guess." Gladys shook her head. "Thought for a minute I heard somethin'."

"Like what?"

"A scream."

"What?"

"Oh, never mind."

Tapping her index finger on the kitchen table, Gladys listened to August chew as she went back to making her plans.

"Doc!"

Maxwell leaped up, tossed the sketch Leda'd left him to the desktop, and ran to the front door.

"Doc!" Cyrus Finster shouted again just as Maxwell entered the hall.

The blacksmith, unnaturally pale, was gasping for breath as he pushed through the door and braced himself against it, propping it open.

"What? What is it?" Maxwell stared at Cyrus's sling, thinking for a moment that this had something to do with the man's earlier injury.

But even before he could ask, Cyrus shook his bushy head and blurted out, "It ain't me, Doc! It's Julius!"

The gunsmith?

"Terrible thing," Cyrus muttered thickly, "just terrible. Didn't you hear him scream?"

A scream? No. No, Maxwell hadn't heard a thing. He'd been too lost in his own preoccupation with that damned drawing.

"What happened to him?" he finally asked. "Where is he? Was he shot?" Maybe there'd been an accident with one of the guns the man crafted and repaired.

"Shot?" Cyrus shook his head again and glanced back the way he came. "No, he wasn't shot. And they're comin' now. You best get ready."

Maxwell looked past the blacksmith, following the man's gaze. Headed his way at a fast walk were three men. Two of them walked side by side, their arms linked between them. The third, Julius Lloyd, sat upright on their crossed arms, his hands on their shoulders. If his face hadn't been twisted in pain, poor Julius would have looked like some sort of ancient king with his peasants.

Immediately, Maxwell hurried back to his examining room to wait for them.

"There now, Tom," Leda said when she was finished. "That wasn't so bad, was it?"

The farmer reached up and fingered the still sensitive spot on the back of his head. "It ain't bleedin', is it?"

"Of course not."

He pulled his hand away and anxiously inspected his fingertips.

Leda hid a smile. She'd never met anyone with as weak a stomach for the sight of blood as Tom Shipley. You would think that working as he did, with animals and such, that he'd be accustomed to dealing with all kinds of wounds and unpleasant situations.

But as she recalled the day she'd had to stitch him up, she remembered just how pale he'd become as soon as he realized that he was bleeding. Even now, he looked at his fingers carefully, checking for the slightest hint that his wound still wasn't healed.

Perhaps, she told herself, this would be the perfect opportunity to take advantage of her new partnership with Max. Maybe Tom would feel better if a *real* doctor looked him over.

"Y'know, Tom," she said slowly, "the doctor is only a few doors away."

He started shaking his head even before she stopped talking. The uneven haircut she'd given him the week before flopped around his ears. "Don't want to see a doctor."

"But he would only *look*, I promise." She felt fairly safe giving her word, since she didn't see how Max could find anything more to do to the man. The wound was healing and now all that was lacking was the hair to cover it.

"What for?" The man's eyes narrowed suspiciously. "You said it was fixed."

"And it is," she assured him quickly. "It's just that, well . . . Max—Dr. Evans and I—are partners now."

"Partners?"

"Uh-huh. As a matter of fact, I'll be moving some of my things to his office this very morning."

"Hmmm."

"And I just thought that you might like to walk with me." The more she considered the idea, the more she liked it. If she could just get Tom to go along with her, she could prove to Max that their partnership was already working. But Tom Shipley didn't look the least bit pleased with the thought of having yet another person poking at his head.

A sudden idea struck her. "You could help me carry my table!"

"I got work to do, y'know."

"It will only take a minute, Tom. Really."

He thought about it for a moment, then shoved his hat back on his head, hiding his mutilated hair from sight. "Well, I s'pose I could do that, then."

"Thank you!"

Quickly, Leda lifted the crystal ball from its wooden base, then snatched up the base with her free hand. Setting both items down carefully on a nearby shelf, Leda draped the black cloth over the crystal. She'd come back for the globe when everything was set up and ready. Smiling, she told herself she couldn't risk damaging her mother's crystal.

Tom picked up her small table easily and headed for the door. She only had time to throw the man behind the counter one quick glance. "I'll be back for the rest later, Uncle Garrett."

"No hurry, girl" he said, never taking his eyes off his account ledger.

"It's a clean break," Max muttered, more to himself than the men hovering around the examining table.

"Lordy, it hurts like the devil, Doc." Julius's face was bathed in sweat.

"I should imagine," Max agreed. "The bone is sticking up right through the skin."

"Ooooh." Julius's head dropped back to the table and his eyes slid shut.

"Lookit that," Cyrus said, leaning in front of Maxwell for a better view. "I never seen a bone on the outside before. Ain't it pretty and white, though?"

Julius moaned.

"Sure is," one of the other men commented, "and would you look at all that blood?"

A strangled sob escaped the injured man.

The wagon driver stood to one side, twisting his hat brim in his hands. "He gonna be all right, Doc?"

Maxwell frowned and looked down at the backs of two heads leaning over his patient's wound. Shouldering both Cyrus and his friend aside, Maxwell shot them both a warning look then answered the man in the corner. "He'll be fine. Once I get the bone set."

"Set?" Julius whispered fearfully.

"Sure," Cyrus answered before Max could open his mouth. "Don't want to walk around with your bones on the outside, do ya, Julius?"

"Ooooh."

Maxwell ignored them all, picked up a wet, clean cloth, and began washing the open wound. Thankfully, it didn't look like any major damage had been done. Once the area had been cleaned, he'd set the bone, splint it, and Julius Lloyd would be on the road to recovery.

Concentrating on the task before him, Maxwell began to notice a peculiar odor. In fact, it smelled suspiciously like the pungent aroma that had heralded Cyrus Finster's last visit. Covertly, he leaned more toward the blacksmith and sniffed delicately. No.

Then he centered himself over his patient again and the foul scent shot up his nose. It was definitely wafting up from Julius Lloyd's prostrate body.

His gaze moved over the short gunsmith quickly and, for the first time, noted the telling stains on the man's clothing.

But how in heaven had the man come to be covered with horse manure?

Fingers moving expertly around the injured flesh, Maxwell asked casually, "Would someone mind telling me what happened?"

The wagon driver in the far corner of the office started talking. "He walked right out in back of me. I checked before I started the wagon moving, Doc. He wasn't there." The man waved his hat in the air helplessly. "Then all of a sudden, there he was. And he screamed and I pulled up and threw on the brake, but the wagon just went right on over him. I couldn't stop it. Tried. Really did."

"I'm sure." Maxwell tossed a quick glance at the man. He looked miserable. Even his red suspenders seemed to be drooping.

"Hell, Doc," Cyrus added, "you know when that manure wagon's full up, it purely weighs so much, it don't just stop all that easy."

A manure wagon.

"As it was, Bob over there dumped a lot of his load when he stopped so quick." The wounded blacksmith shrugged and pointed out unnecessarily, "Most of the dung landed on Julius. But we brushed him off good before we brung him here."

Maxwell glanced at Julius's face. Dusting the man's pallid complexion was a layer of dust, spotted with what had to be some of the spilled "cargo."

He rolled his eyes and finished cleaning the wound.

A commotion at the front door registered in the back of his mind and Maxwell found himself wondering what *else* could happen. Then he heard Leda's voice and knew that *anything* was possible.

"Just put it right there, please, Tom."

Only a moment later, she stepped into the office, and asked, "What happened?"

Maxwell opened his mouth to speak.

"It's Julius," Cyrus answered quickly.

Maxwell's jaw snapped shut again.

"Julius!" Leda came up to stand beside the injured man.

Maxwell glanced at her, saw her run her fingertips lightly across the gunsmith's forehead, then he turned back to his task.

"What happened?" she asked again.

"Was going to the mill," the injured man began.

"The mill?" the wagon driver asked. "That's the other way from where you were walking."

"Leda," Julius whispered.

Leda? Maxwell's hands stilled and his gaze rose to her face.

"Said there was danger," Julius finished on a groan.

"Oh, Julius," Leda crooned, "you mean this happened when you went the back way?"

"Sure did," Cyrus answered for the injured man. "Wagon went right over him and *snap*! There goes his leg."

The gunsmith groaned piteously.

"Julius, I'm so terribly sorry," she said, her eyes filling with sympathetic tears. "But what a blessing."

"Blessing!" Astonished, Maxwell gaped at her.

"Oh yes, Max," she said quickly, her hand still smoothing Julius's matted hair. "If he hadn't taken the back way, he would have been killed."

"Y'know," Cyrus said solemnly, "she's right. A broken leg's a helluva lot better than bein' dead."

"Amen," Cyrus's burly friend whispered.

"Sure was lucky he listened to her," the wagon driver muttered, staring at Leda.

"Amen," the anonymous man echoed again.

"But he broke his leg!" Maxwell yelped. Good God, he asked himself helplessly, was the whole town crazy?

"And it will heal," she said, smiling at him. "You're such a wonderful doctor." Looking down at Julius, she added, "Aren't you lucky, Julius?"

The gunsmith stared up at her and somehow managed to nod.

Maxwell shook his head. As he looked from one man to the other, he saw plainly that not one of them was going to argue with Leda's astonishing logic.

"Who's got a broken leg?" another voice said brusquely.

Maxwell half turned as Tom Shipley walked in. When the farmer came even with the examining table, he looked down at the wounded man. In seconds, Shipley's color drained from his face, his eyes rolled back in his head, and he crumpled to the floor in a dead faint.

"Tom!" Leda called anxiously.

Maxwell groaned.

CHAPTER 11

A blessing.

Maxwell leaned back in his desk chair and stared blankly at the wall opposite him. How in the world could he argue with a woman who called a broken leg a *blessing*?

Shaking his head, he pushed all thoughts of the injured gunsmith from his mind. It was enough to know that the man was even now resting at home, being waited on and catered to by his wife.

Hopefully, Tom Shipley was getting the same kind of treatment. The poor man had come to town to get his stitches removed and had gone home with not one new knot on his head, but *two*! Maxwell sighed heavily as he remembered Leda bringing Tom out of his faint just in time to hear Julius yell as his leg was snapped back in place.

Naturally, the burly farmer passed out again.

Now, though, the commotion was over. Cyrus and the other men had gone back to their work after carrying Julius home. Tom Shipley'd staggered out to his horse then made a quick escape. Even Leda had gone home to fix something for the boys to eat when they got home from school.

Maxwell was alone again. But he didn't find much peace

144

in the accompanying silence. His own thoughts were too busy for that.

He set one elbow on the chair's armrest and propped his head in his hand. Idly rubbing his temple, Maxwell tried to think clearly. Logically.

Instead, images of Leda rose up in front of him. Only the night before, he'd managed to convince himself that they could work together. That somehow, this partnership of theirs would be the perfect compromise.

He'd even begun to relax in her presence. To enjoy the very things about her that were so different from himself. But now. Now, he told himself, he was confronted by the plain, simple truth.

No matter his feelings for her, she was *too* different. The world she lived in had nothing at all in common with his. Why, when she'd discovered the reason behind Julius's injury, she hadn't felt in the least responsible.

And he hadn't even bothered trying to tell her that there was no runaway team in the street. That Julius wouldn't have been struck down. He'd tried that once before. She would only argue that the team hadn't been there because Julius wasn't there to be killed.

He sighed, sat up, and leaned his elbows on his desk. In front of him lay the sketch she'd left behind earlier. Maxwell looked into the drawn image of his own eyes and felt that same, strange sense of wonder that he had at first sight of the drawing.

Was it possible? he asked himself. Was it truly possible that somehow, he and Leda had been fated from the beginning? Was there some "mystical" force involved here?

Maxwell stopped, stunned. Mystical force? Good God. Where did *that* thought spring from? He pushed one hand through his hair, then rubbed his clean-shaven jaw. Shaking his head, he told himself there was nothing *mystical* about Leda James. *Or* what she did to him. He was absolutely certain—despite her protestations—that she was no more psychic than he was! And yet, he thought, there *was* something . . . special about her. A helpless smile settled on his features. How else to explain his unreasonable attraction to a woman so far removed from what he'd always considered the perfect woman?

"Attraction"? he asked himself. A mild word, indeed, for what he felt whenever he was around her. Just the memory of her kiss, the feel of her body pressed close against him was enough to send logic flying out the closest window. Even now, he felt his pulse quicken and his body tighten.

Yes, he thought wryly. "Attraction" was *much* too mild a word. He shifted in his chair, looked away from the intriguing drawing and found himself staring toward the entry hall of his office.

From his vantage point, he could only see two legs of the small table Leda had had Tom Shipley carry down from the store for her. He knew even without looking that her blasted crystal ball would be sitting in the middle of that table.

She'd already moved into his heart. Now, it seemed she was determined to move completely into his life.

"Dr. Evans? You here?"

He shook himself and practically jumped to his feet.

Gladys Fairfax.

"Whatcha doin', Leda?"

She glanced down at Denny and smiled. The boy looked better every day. Since Arthur's arrival, she hadn't once seen that sad, lost look on the child's face.

"I'm just . . ." She hesitated a moment then said, "Denny, can you keep a secret?"

"Sure I can!" He laid one hand on Arthur's massive head and the dog leaned into him, making the boy stagger slightly.

"All right, then," she whispered, "I'll tell you." Leda glanced over her shoulder at the doorway separating the kitchen from the rest of the Malone house. Satisfied that no other ears were close at hand, she continued, "I'm fixing a cure for Max."

"The doc?" Dennis's brow wrinkled. "Is he sick?"

"No, not sick, really." She took a pickle from the bowl on the counter and laid it down on a small saucer.

"Well, why's he need curin'?"

"I suppose it's not really a cure either. More of a help, I should say." She picked up a paring knife and carefully slit the pickle lengthwise and laid the two halves side by side.

"A help with what?"

With a tired grunt, Arthur dropped to the floor and stretched out across both Dennis's and Leda's feet.

She smiled at the dog, winked at Denny, and bent down closer to him before saying, "Max was a bit sour today . . . after that accident Julius had."

"Uh-huh," Denny said, even though Leda could tell from his expression he didn't understand. "What d'ya mean, sour?"

"Out of sorts. Down in the mouth. Grumpy."

"Oh." He leaned one elbow on the counter's edge and glanced down at his dog then back up to his cousin. "Well, what's a pickle got to do with it?"

"Ah." Leda grinned and reached into the cupboard for the sugar bowl. "*That's* the secret." She picked up a teaspoon, dipped it in the sugar bowl, then sprinkled the fine white granules on the pickle halves.

"Yeewww . . ." Dennis's nose wrinkled and his lips curled. "That's disgustin'." Then his face cleared and an anticipatory gleam shone in his eyes. "Ya gonna make him *eat* it?"

"No!" Leda laughed down at the little boy. "Now that it's ready, I set it out in the sun."

"Why?"

"To sweeten him up, of course," she said and picked up the plate with the pickle. "As the sun burns the sugar into the pickle, it will burn the sweetness into Max."

"Oooh." He nodded sagely. "You're puttin' a spell on him!"

"I'm not a witch, Denny," she explained with a sad shake of her head. "Though sometimes, I'll admit, it would be a lot easier if I was."

"But"— Dennis scratched his head thoughtfully—"how's the sun gonna know who to burn the sweetness into?"

"While I sprinkled the sugar," she said with a wink, "I whispered Max's name."

"Oh."

All questions answered and her "cure" ready, Leda picked up the saucer and carefully pulled her feet out from under a now snoring Arthur.

She walked out the back door and crossed the yard to the chopping block. As she set her offering down, Leda couldn't help but send an encouraging smile toward the sun.

"Mrs. Fairfax," Maxwell said and helped the older woman into his office.

Gladys slapped at his hand on her elbow. "I can still walk, young man."

"I beg your pardon." Suddenly self-conscious, Maxwell jammed his hands in his pants pockets and waited while his patient seated herself in the most comfortable chair. His. "What can I do for you today?"

"I was down at Garrett Malone's place," she began, "and he tells me that you and Leda are workin' together now."

Oh. That certainly explained her visit, he told himself. She'd come to see Leda, not him. Still, if he was to win his patients back, he would do better to at least *try* to be more cheerful, helpful.

Maxwell forced a smile. "Yes, we are, Mrs. Fairfax. But I'm afraid she went home to fix dinner for the boys. If you'd like to wait . . ."

"Not necessary," the older woman said with a quick shake of her head. "You'll do, I suppose."

High praise indeed.

"Thank you," he managed to say. "If you'll just move to the examining table."

Gray brows drew together at a dangerous slant. "I don't need to be examined, young man. There's no call to be undoin' buttons when you know very well it's my hands give me trouble."

Maxwell inhaled slowly, deeply.

"Then what exactly can I do for you, Mrs. Fairfax?" He couldn't resist adding, "I'm afraid I don't have any onions."

She looked at him from the corner of her eye. "Don't get smart, now! I come for that tea of Leda's."

He sighed. "Mrs. Fairfax, the herbal tea, while very tasty, I'm sure, has *no* medicinal qualities."

"What?"

"It's *not* medicine."

"Then how come my hands're better?"

He glanced at her obviously painful, twisted hands. "I'm sure I don't know," Maxwell finally admitted. After all, who was *he* to insist her hands were painful if *she* didn't think so!

"That's better," she said and inclined her head toward the other chair. "Why don't you set down, Doc? Lookin' up at you is givin' me a crick in my neck."

Once he was seated on the wrong side of his desk, Maxwell waited. There was an expectant air about the older woman and he was sure she'd come for more than the tea Leda prepared for her.

He didn't have to wait long.

"That Leda, she's really somethin', ain't she?"

"Yes," he agreed warily. "Yes, she is."

"Uh-huh." Gladys poked at the papers on his desktop with one finger. "Matter of fact, me and August was talkin' about that just a bit ago."

Maxwell watched as her fingertip came to rest on the sketch. His gaze locked on her arthritic hand, he didn't realize she was speaking again until she shouted at him.

"Doc! Are you listenin' to me?"

"I beg your pardon," he muttered, still trying to think of a way to get the drawing away from her without commenting on it.

"You sure do a lot of that."

"Hmmm? What? I do a lot of what?"

"Beggin' folks' pardons."

He frowned.

"Course, we sure can't fault you on your manners any, can we?"

"I suppose not." Now that she'd mentioned it, he had to admit that he *did* use that one particular phrase more often than not. Strange that it had never occurred to him before.

She lifted one corner of the drawing and Maxwell almost sat on his hands to keep from jumping up and snatching it back. Perhaps, he told himself, if he didn't bring any extra attention to the drawing, she wouldn't make anything of it.

"This is interestin'," she said quietly and picked it up for a better look.

He should've known better. "I forgot to put it away earlier," he said quickly. Deliberately, he leaned toward her, his hand outstretched.

Gladys sat back, holding the paper out of reach. "Let me get a good look at this, Doc." She studied the sketch for several long moments, then lowered it and looked at Maxwell with the same careful deliberation. "Who did it?" she finally asked.

"Leda's mother," Maxwell admitted and slumped back in his chair. There would be no stopping the woman's curiosity now.

"Her ma? But I thought the woman was dead."

"She is. She, uh . . ." There was no way to tell her *that* part of the story without drawing even *more* interest. But even as he considered ignoring her inquisitiveness, Maxwell knew that Leda would be more than happy to tell Gladys all about the psychic drawing. It really was pointless trying to hide any of this, he told himself.

"Leda's mother drew it about fifteen years ago." He blurted out the truth then clamped his mouth shut.

Gray eyebrows arched over wide blue eyes. "Didn't know you and Leda went that far back, Doc."

"We don't."

"Then how?"

"I don't know!" Maxwell suddenly shot to his feet. He began to pace back and forth along the length of the room. Damn Gladys Fairfax anyway. She'd put her finger on the one fact he'd been trying to forget! "I just don't know," he repeated, more to himself than the woman watching him. Glancing at Gladys, he pointed an accusing finger at the yellowed paper in her hand. "I've been staring at that blasted thing all morning and I'm no less confused than when I first laid eyes on it!"

"A good likeness," she acknowledged.

"A *damn*— Excuse me, Mrs. Fairfax. A *very* good likeness. And that's what I can't understand!"

"I can see it's upset you some."

Maxwell looked at her, saw her half smile, and looked away again, disgusted. "This isn't funny, Mrs. Fairfax."

"Gladys."

"What?" He paused in his furious pacing and stared at her, clearly bewildered.

"I said, my name's Gladys. You can call me that. If you want." She shrugged and her black crocheted shawl slipped off one shoulder. "Takes less time than all that 'Mrs. Fairfax' stuff."

"Thank you. Gladys." He jerked her a nod, then quickly began his pacing again as if he'd never stopped. "I've thought and thought about this, Gladys. And nothing makes any sense."

"Uh-huh."

"It's ridiculous to believe that a woman I never met could draw an accurate picture of me."

"*Very* accurate," she reminded him.

"Yes. *Very* accurate." He nodded briskly, then went on

with his statement. "Fifteen years before I even met her daughter!"

"True," Gladys chimed in and brought the sketch up closer to her eyes for a better look.

"The artist herself is dead now."

"True," she said again.

"I tell you, it's *impossible* for that sketch to exist."

Gladys waved the paper gently. "But it does."

"I know!"

"Well . . . how do you explain it, then?"

"I can't." Maxwell lifted his shoulders in an eloquent shrug. "There *is* no explanation. The drawing simply *is*. I can't deny it. I can't even call it trickery."

"Trickery!" Gladys gasped. Narrowing her eyes, she glared at him.

Maxwell held up both hands in mock surrender. "I wasn't accusing Leda of anything!"

"Then what are you sayin'?"

"I don't know what I'm saying." He pushed one hand through his hair.

"You best figure it out, Doc." Her lips thinned into a mutinous line. "I won't have you sayin' anything against that sweet child. Not to me!"

"That's not what I meant!"

"It's what you said," she reminded him.

"All I meant was I knew it *wasn't* trickery."

"You say that like you hoped it was."

"It would certainly be easier all the way around that way."

"How do ya figure?"

"Don't you see? If that drawing is real"—he shook his head and waved one hand at Gladys when he saw her temper start to rise again—"and I'm sure it is. That puts me in an awkward position."

"Don't see how."

How could she not see it? he asked himself. Crossing back to the chair, he dropped into it, braced his elbows on his knees, and said quickly, "I've been talking against these 'visions' of hers for weeks now."

"True."

"But if this is real, then maybe the rest of it is too."

"So you still don't believe it?"

"I *have* to believe it. At least *this* part of it." He reached across the desk and tapped at the drawing accusingly. "The paper is *obviously* old. The sketch itself is faded and creased deeply from the folds." Maxwell suddenly slapped both hands palm down on his desktop and leaned toward Gladys. "You can't possibly say that Leda is attempting to trick me into believing in her nonsense!"

"I didn't say anything, Doc," the old woman reminded him in a wry tone.

"Of course not. You wouldn't. How could you?" He shook his head and ran both hands through his hair.

It didn't seem to bother him that his sandy-blond hair was now standing up in wild tufts all over his head.

Gladys swallowed the bubble of laughter she felt growing in her chest. If she started chucklin' now, it'd prob'ly push the poor man right over the edge. But she had to admit, however silently, that it did her heart good to see the usually unruffled man so flummoxed.

While he ranted and raved, Gladys took the opportunity to study the portrait one more time. Whether the girl had meant to or not, Leda had really shoved a stick in the doc's spokes.

"Well," she said thoughtfully, "when you come down to it, what difference does an old drawing make to anything?"

He looked up and stared at her. "What difference?" Maxwell slumped back in his seat. "What difference?" he repeated.

"That's what I said."

"Don't you see? Since the moment I met Leda James, she's been telling me about how we were 'destined' to be together."

"Uh-huh."

"She even had the nerve to refuse a marriage proposal that I never made!"

Gladys snorted.

"But *this*!" He waved one hand at the sketch as Gladys set it down. "*This* makes everything she's said and done seem almost . . . *logical*!"

"And?"

"And?" Maxwell shook his head. For a moment, he'd thought Gladys understood. He'd thought she knew what it was that was niggling at the deepest heart of him. But she didn't.

That shouldn't surprise him, though. He'd only just identified it himself.

"Don't you see?" He propped his elbow on the arm of the chair and leaned his head on his hand. "I've been telling myself that Leda's predictions and claims of Destiny are only so much nonsense! But now . . . that . . . *drawing* sheds a new light on the whole matter."

"How so?"

"If her mother truly did have the 'gift,' " he said wearily, "and it certainly appears that she *did*—then is what she told Leda about me true? Were we destined from the start? Did I never have any say in the matter at all?"

"Ah," Gladys said and leaned back in the comfortable chair. "Then what's botherin' you is not gettin' together with Leda, but the thought that it wasn't *your* idea."

"No. Yes. Hell, excuse me." He sighed in defeat. "I don't know. I don't know anything anymore!"

"I figure, ya *do* know ya like kissin' Leda James." She looked down at her hands in her lap.

Slowly, Maxwell raised his head and looked at the old woman. "What do you mean?"

"Oh," she said on a half laugh, "I figure you know pretty much *just* what I mean. Course, if you don't want folks knowin' your business, ya ought not stand in open doorways to do your sparkin'."

Good God. He frowned and tried to remember what she'd

said earlier. That she and August had been talking together? Of course, Maxwell told himself. August Haley.

"Perhaps August should keep his nose in his telegrams," Maxwell said stiffly.

"Perhaps. But it ain't likely." Her lips quirked slightly. "Why don't you tell me what all this upset is about, Doc?"

"I already have," he muttered.

"No. I mean, why's it bother you so? Seems pretty clear that you take to Leda." Gladys shrugged and her shawl slipped down to hang around her elbows. "She's a real nice girl. Pretty. Sweet."

He nodded.

"Then blast it," she whispered, "what's wrong? What does it matter if her ma seen ya fifteen years ago?"

"It doesn't, I suppose. Not really." Maxwell stared down at his hands as if wondering why they were of no help to him in this situation. "It's . . ."

"What?"

"I . . . *care* for Leda, Gladys." Lord, he thought with a start. What *had* happened to him? He'd never spoken so openly with another living soul! A reluctant smile curved his lips briefly then slid away again. Leda. Everything came back to Leda.

"That's good." Gladys almost crowed with delight.

"No." He looked up at her and shook his head slowly. "No. It's not good."

"Why the hell not?"

"Because I don't ever intend to lo—*care* for someone."

"Seems to me it's a mite late to be thinkin' of that."

His eyebrows lifted and he nodded helplessly. How right she was.

"Mind tellin' me why?" Gladys prodded.

Why? he repeated silently. What could he say? Could he sit here calmly and tell this woman that he was too afraid to care? That he sought to spare himself pain by avoiding love?

No. She wouldn't understand that. He doubted seriously that anyone would. Hell, he hardly understood it himself anymore. But until Leda had rushed headlong into his life, it had always made perfect sense.

Hadn't he seen his own father die in pieces every time he lost a patient? Hadn't the elder Dr. Evans nearly been crushed at the death of his wife?

Maxwell'd seen it all. He'd watched helplessly as his father gave and gave of himself until there was nothing left. Not for himself, and certainly not for his son.

Determined to protect himself from the ravages of that kind of pain, Maxwell had successfully kept himself separate from people for years. Though a good doctor, he'd always managed to keep a safe distance from his patients. He would do his best for them, help them in any way he could. But in the end, there was no saving people from death and he refused to be destroyed a bit at a time by something he couldn't change.

Through the years, Maxwell'd accomplished his goal. Though others had considered him cold, uncaring, they'd never been able to fault him on his medical knowledge. Or his dedication. Merely his manner.

It was something he'd grown accustomed to. It was a quiet, safe life. Protecting his own emotions had become second nature to him.

Until Leda.

Somehow, the little gypsy had managed to slip past every safeguard he'd erected over the years. With a determination to match his own, Leda had resolutely chipped away at his detachment. She'd stormed the walls he'd built around his heart with no more effort than a casual toss of her head. Stone by stone, his fortress was crumbling. Soon, he would be left unguarded. Open to the pain and grief that would destroy him as it had his father.

But how could he tell Gladys all that?

How could he make her understand his most basic fear?

If Leda's mother's gift was genuine, wasn't there a chance,

however slight, that Leda, too—despite her many mistakes—had some sort of precognition?

Wasn't it possible that she *had* inherited at least a part of her mother's talents?

And if she had, if she was right about the two of them being destined for each other, couldn't she be right about other things as well?

The ugly fear that had begun to form in the back of his mind the moment he'd first seen that drawing rose up again. It seemed to gather strength as the seconds passed and soon he was almost choking on dread.

He pulled in a deep, shuddering breath and closed his eyes to the images swirling through his brain. But it didn't help.

Maxwell could try to ignore her predictions of love and marriage. But one of her prophecies he couldn't afford to disregard.

She'd foretold her own death.

CHAPTER 12

Montana/Idaho border
Cooter shoved another piece of wood into the fire then dropped the stove lid back into place. He set a battered tin coffeepot on the stove then turned his back on the growing heat, holding his hands out behind him.

But the tremors shaking his body had nothing to do with the temperature in the room.

He walked to the nearest window and peered out into the still afternoon. Cecelia Standish ought to be riding up any minute. And though there was no sign of life in the miles of open land that stretched out before the cabin, Cooter realized that didn't mean anything. He tossed a wary glance at the almost sheer rock wall to the right of the ramshackle building. From long experience, Cooter knew that she would approach the cabin through the notch in the cliff face.

He and Deke had stumbled on the narrow, snaking path accidentally, then discovered that it cut nearly an hour's time off the ride to the nearest town.

Cecelia used the trail regularly, but Cooter tried to avoid it. Riding that lonely passage, surrounded by nothing but mountains of stone, gave him a cold chill. The track was barely wide enough for one horse and rider, so there would be no escape should someone come after him. And it was dark. Even in broad daylight, it was dark. With the bluff so high above him, sunlight seemed to drift down the rock walls, and by the time it reached the canyon floor, it hardly had the strength left to shine.

He shook himself suddenly, dropped the rag of a curtain back over the dirty window, and walked back to the stove. He was sure she'd gotten his message telling her to come to the cabin. Hell, he'd paid that damn kid in front of the hotel fifty cents to hand it over to the woman personally.

The fire snapped suddenly and Cooter spun around as if attacked.

His nerves were shot. All this waitin' and worryin' was beginnin' to tell on him. Hell, if he'd had a choice, Cooter'd much rather be sittin' in that jail cell in Tanglewood than have to face Cecelia all on his own.

He dropped down into one of the two ladder-back chairs in the sparsely furnished cabin. Staring at the gouged-up, scarred floorboards, his mind in a jumble, he almost missed the sounds of a horse approaching.

Reluctantly, Cooter stood up, hitched his gun higher on his hip, and waited for the door to swing open.

Minutes passed like hours until Cecelia threw the door wide and stepped into the firelit cabin.

"What in heaven were you thinking? You know I've told you not to come into town and contact me directly."

"Yeah, but—"

"There is no excuse for this, Cooter." The elegant woman moved into the room and closed the door behind her, shutting out the sun. She shrugged out of her ankle-length black coat and tugged at the gray leather gloves hugging her delicate hands. When she'd tossed those items onto a chair, she faced him.

Cooter shuffled his feet uneasily.

"Well?" she prodded. "I assume there is a *reason* for this idiocy!"

"Yes, ma'am."

She shuddered delicately. "Don't 'ma'am' me, Cooter. I am *not* your elderly aunt."

"Yes, ma'am, uh, I mean, Miss Standish."

Her eyes rolled heavenward and Cooter's eye began to twitch.

She glanced around the tiny cabin, looked back at him and snapped, "Where is your cohort?"

"Well"—he hesitated—"if you mean Deke, Miss Standish . . ."

"Of course I mean Deke."

"That's what I wanted to talk to you about."

"Very well." Cecelia sighed, looked at the chairs, then held her hand out toward Cooter. "Give me your handkerchief."

He looked confused for a long minute, then jumped. "Oh! Yes, ma'am!"

Cecelia bit back the oath resting on the tip of her tongue. When he'd finally managed to scrounge his bandana out of his back pants pocket, she held it gingerly by one edge and slapped it against the chair seat.

A small cloud of dust flew into the air, but better that, she told herself, than ruining an almost new gown. She seated herself at the edge of the rickety chair, smoothed her pale lavender skirt, then tossed his bandana back to him.

"What is it?" She folded her hands in her lap and added, "I warn you, it had better be important." Glancing down at the small gold watch pinned to her bosom, she finished, "And hurry, do. I have a supper engagement tonight. *With*"—she gave him a satisfied smile—"the bank manager."

"Well, Miss Standish, we got a little problem."

Though her features gave no evidence of it, Cecelia felt her temper on the rise.

"Problem?"

"Yes, ma'am. It's Deke."

"What about him?"

"He's in jail."

"Where?" The single word came out in a low growl.

He swallowed heavily and she watched his Adam's apple bob up and down.

"Tanglewood."

Her jaw clenched, Cecelia congratulated herself on her self-control as she said softly, "Tell me. All of it."

As Cooter pulled up the other chair and sat down opposite her, she told herself that maybe she should think about retiring earlier than planned. And the longer Cooter talked, she thought later, the more she was convinced that it was time to get out of this business.

"Max?" Leda's unmistakable voice called from the hall.

He looked up, wild-eyed, at Gladys.

The old woman frowned. She hadn't gotten near the information she wanted out of him and she sure wouldn't with Leda around. Looking at the man now, she told herself, it was hard to imagine the stiff, starchy doctor they'd known so well just a few months ago.

"Gladys!" Leda said as she came into the room. "How nice to see you!"

Gladys watched Maxwell watch Leda and was pleased to see the telltale softening on his features. Whether he knew it or not, she told herself, Doc Evans was a man in love.

"Leda, I come to get my tea." She tore her gaze away from the suddenly silent doctor and pushed herself out of the chair.

"Oh. It's still at the store." Leda smiled, walked to Maxwell's side, and rested her hand gently on his shoulder.

Gladys saw the man lift one hand as if to touch the young woman, then he changed his mind and let his hand slide back to his lap. For some reason, Gladys felt a stab of disappointment. Abruptly, she looked at Leda. "Well then, let's us go and get it, shall we?"

"All right." Leda bent down and her long fall of hair swept Maxwell's lap. She planted a quick kiss on his surprised face and told him, "I'll be back in a few minutes, Max."

Gladys shook her head. The girl didn't even notice the doc's befuddled expression.

On the short walk to Malone's Mercantile, Leda slowed her steps to match Gladys's. The older woman didn't even feel a little guilty about walking even slower than usual. She wanted a few minutes alone with the girl, and this seemed like the best time to get it.

Leda's stream of conversation only vaguely distracted Gladys as she tried to get her thoughts in order. A sudden movement across the wide street caught her eye and Gladys looked in time to see Flora Lloyd dive back inside the gunsmith's shop.

Her lips quirked, Gladys told herself that it looked as though even Flora had had her fill of Leda's predictions. And small wonder. What with her five children and now having to wait on Julius until his leg was knit, well it was enough to put anybody off.

Still, the old woman thought with a sideways glance at Leda, she'd be willing to bet hard money that even Flora wouldn't say a word against the girl. Strange how the whole damn town seemed determined to keep Leda from finding out that her predictions caused more trouble than they saved.

But then, she *was* a sweet thing, and even if her fortune-telling wasn't much better than a good guess on a lucky day, Gladys knew for a fact that her teas and such were a real help. And even *that* wasn't the whole reason for the town's common, yet unspoken, goal to keep from hurting the young woman's tender feelings.

Gladys smiled to herself. From the minute Leda James arrived, she'd been better than a dose of salts for bringing new life into Tanglewood. What with her crystal ball and her strange clothes and her even stranger way of lookin' at things, Leda'd kept things hoppin' in a town that had been so settled, it was durn near asleep!

"Gladys?"

"Hmmm?" She shook herself mentally.

"Are you feeling all right?"

The older woman looked into Leda's green eyes and smiled. "Yes, child. I'm fine."

"I have your tea at the store. It's all made up and waiting for you."

"Good, good."

A halfhearted breeze snaked down Main Street and plucked at Gladys's shawl. Her fingers tightened around the worn yarn instinctively. "Leda," she started, "what's this I hear about you settin' up shop with Dr. Evans?"

"Isn't it wonderful?" She grinned, brushed her hair out of her eyes, and added, "It was Max's idea too!"

Somehow, Gladys doubted that, but she didn't say so.

"So, you figure you finally got him convinced that this was all meant to be?"

"Almost," she answered and chewed thoughtfully at her bottom lip.

"Think that drawin' of yours helped any?"

"Oh, did he show it to you?"

"In a manner of speakin'," Gladys hedged. He *had* told her about it after she'd found it for herself. "It's a fine likeness."

"Oh yes. My mother was very good at sketching." Leda nodded. "Max was nearly speechless when he saw it."

Like he'd been hit over the head with a hammer, Gladys thought.

"But if he's shown it to you already, that's a good sign."

"Of what?"

"That he believes, of course." Leda shrugged, tugged at a gold coin around her neck, and said, "It means he's really starting to believe that we were destined for each other."

"Uh-huh." Gladys stood still a moment and tried to ignore the wave of relief that crawled through her old joints. Lord, age was a nasty business. She remembered hurryin' down this very same boardwalk, chasin' after Lester time and again over the years. Now, it was all she could do to hobble from store to store with an occasional rest. "Didn't you notice that he was a mite . . ."—couldn't say "poleaxed." Even if it was the truth—"*confused* when we left him?"

"No." Leda's brow furrowed as she tried to remember. "But he did seem awfully distracted."

True enough.

"That drawin' of yours shook him to the bone, girl."

"You think so?"

"I know so." Gladys started walking again and Leda kept pace.

"I didn't mean to upset him," Leda said.

"Oh, he ain't *that* upset."

"Good." The younger woman smiled her relief. "I do so want us to be happy together for whatever time we have."

Gladys frowned. She'd hoped that the girl's feelings for the doctor might rid her of this notion about death.

"You might want to stop talkin' about dyin' and start thinkin' about livin'," she finally told her.

"That's what Uncle Garrett says."

"Always knew Garrett had a head on his shoulders."

"But if I'm going to die anyway, thinking about living will only make my Fate that much harder to bear."

At the door to the Mercantile, Gladys stopped. She stared hard at Leda before saying what she'd wanted to say since she started this conversation. "Everybody's gonna die, girl. And if we all just sit around and wait for it, nobody's gonna get any livin' done."

"Yes, but—"

"No buts." Gladys cut her off. "If you go through the next thirty years plannin' your life around your death—you might as well be dead already."

Leda's gaze shifted to the sun-washed street. But she was still listening, Gladys knew.

"Troubles come all too quick anyway, Leda. Whether you think on 'em or not. The trick is to enjoy your time here. Do your best with what you've got. Try to leave the world a little better off than when you were born." She inhaled sharply and told herself she should listen to her own advice sometimes. Then, while she still had the girl's attention, she finished, "Life's a gift, Leda."

The younger woman looked at her and Gladys saw the confusion in her eyes. "Every minute, every hour is a precious gift. And I don't believe God takes kindly to folks just tossin' His gifts away like so much trash." She laid one hand on Leda's forearm. "If you're gonna spend your time worryin' about dyin', then God just wasted space when He made you. Didn't He?"

Leda covered the older woman's arthritic hand with one of her own.

"Well, now!" Gladys announced, her tone brisk, business-like. "I ain't talked that much all at once since I caught Lester sneakin' off to go fishin' instead of goin' to Sunday school! Why don't you give me that tea you promised and I'll take these old bones home and stack 'em in a corner for a while?"

Impulsively, Leda leaned forward, gave her friend a quick hug, and planted a kiss on her lined cheek. "Thank you, Gladys."

Gladys sniffed, waved one hand in the air, and ordered, "None of that, girl. Just you get me that tea, y'hear? I got a sweater at home I mean to finish knittin' one of these years."

The bell over the front door jumped and clanged as the two women stepped into the shadowed coolness.

The minute Gladys and Leda left his office, Maxwell leaped up from his chair. Like a man trying to dance on the line between heaven and hell, he took a step first one way, then another. He had to do something. *Anything.*

Maxwell pushed one hand through his hair, trying to think. He had to talk to someone. Someone who'd understand. He snorted. Who on earth would be able to understand *any* of this?

And almost as soon as his mind screamed out the question,

a tiny voice in the back of his brain whispered the answer.
Garrett.

He hurried to the door, then stopped just as suddenly.
She was at the store. Then he remembered. It was Saturday.
Garrett always took his boys fishing on Saturday. Without
another thought, Maxwell yanked his front door open,
crossed the boardwalk, and ran past the livery on his way
to the lake.

"Hey, Doc!"

Maxwell's chest was heaving with the effort to breathe
by the time he reached the sheltered cove that was Garrett's
favorite fishing spot.

He hardly noticed the pine trees crowded around the tiny
clearing as his gaze flew unerringly to the man he'd been
looking for.

"I said, hi, Doc!"

That voice again. Maxwell turned in a slow circle. He
saw Garrett and Michael watching him, but couldn't find
Sean or Dennis anywhere.

"Up here." Laughter tinged Sean's voice and Max looked
up to see the fourteen year old straddling a limb of an
ancient pine.

"Hello, Sean," he said and looked back toward Garrett.

"Somethin' wrong, Doc?"

He glanced at Michael warily. Was the whole family
cursed with this supposed "gift"? "No. Why do you ask?"

The twelve-year-old replica of his older brother shrugged.
"I just never seen you with your shirttail out before, is all."

Maxwell glanced down at his person and saw the boy was
right. For the first time, he realized what he must have looked
like as he ran out of town. Features crazed, no jacket, and his
shirttail dragging. Good God. Then his gaze slipped farther
down and he saw with dismay that he was even wearing
mismatched shoes. One brown. One black.

How had *that* happened?

Though why should he be surprised? Just being around

Leda James for almost three weeks had nearly destroyed his complacency. Would his wardrobe really be such a difficult task?

Grumbling, he tucked his shirttail under his waistband and said, "Garrett, I have to talk to you."

" 'Bout Leda, huh?" said a voice from the tree.

He glanced up at Sean. The boy really *was* growing up, he told himself. But why does he have to do it now?

"Sure it's about Leda!" Michael crowed. "She told Dennis that the doc here *loves* her!" The boy clapped both hands over his heart, tilted his head back, and made kissing noises.

Maxwell frowned.

Sean laughed and wobbled unsteadily on his perch.

Garrett silenced them all with a gruff, "Hush now. Both of you!" Glancing at Maxwell, he waved one hand at a patch of dirt beside him. "Have a seat, Doc."

Well, Maxwell told himself, what was a little more dirt and grass to a man already disheveled beyond redemption? He plopped down alongside the other man, drew his legs up, and rested his forearms across his knees.

"So, what seems to be the trouble, Maxwell?"

Maxwell. Strange. Somehow that name sounded odd to him now. He'd grown accustomed to Max. As he'd grown accustomed to Leda.

"The boys're right, Garrett. It *is* Leda."

Laughter spilled down from the tree branch above them and Garrett warned, "Sean . . ."

"Sorry."

"She's driving me insane!"

"Aw," Michael broke in, "Leda's all right. She's fun!"

"Yeah, Doc," Sean agreed.

"The doc ain't talkin' to you two," their father reminded them. "Now get busy and catch some supper." Looking at Max, he urged, "Why don't you tell me about it?"

And Max took him at his word. He told Leda's uncle everything. When he was finished, though, he didn't get the reaction he'd expected.

Garrett grinned. "She *is* a pistol, ain't she?"

A *loaded* one, Max told himself. But all he said was, "And dangerous. Look at Cyrus. At Julius."

"Here now, you can't blame Leda for them two."

"Why the devil not?"

"Well, it was Cyrus's own fault he fell off that rotten ladder." Garrett pulled his line in, checked the bait, then tossed it back into the water. "I've been tellin' that man to buy a new one for years. But he's too blamed tightfisted."

"But he only climbed that ladder because Leda asked him to."

"He's a grown man. He makes his own decisions, Doc."

"And Julius?" Max asked, incredulous.

"If Julius was watchin' where he was goin', he'd have never been hit by that wagon."

True, Max thought. And yet . . .

"Hell, if nothin' else, he should've *smelled* it!"

"The point is," Max argued, "that Leda stuck her pretty nose in both times and disaster struck!"

"Pretty?" Michael asked and Max cringed. He'd forgotten momentarily about the boys.

"Course she's pretty," Sean said. "What's the matter with your eyes?"

"Aw, I don't look at no girls. Not even Leda." Michael cocked his head and grinned at his older brother. "Is she prettier'n Jenny Lloyd, Sean?"

Beet-red color rushed into the oldest boy's cheeks and he turned to look back at the lake.

"That'll do, Michael," Garrett warned.

"And what about the drawing, Garrett?" Max pointed out. If the man was going to side with Leda about the accidents in town, the least he could do was explain that damned drawing!

"Ah, she showed it to you, then."

"Just a while ago, yes."

"That Eileen, she was a wonder." Garrett shook his head in memory.

"Eileen?"

"My sister. Leda's mother."

Oh yes. The one with the "gift."

"How in the name of heaven did she draw that likeness of me, Garrett?" Max shook his head helplessly. "It doesn't make any sense."

"Not everything does, Maxwell."

"Max."

Garrett's eyebrows lifted but he didn't comment. "Now Eileen, she could look at a man and tell what he'd been, what he would be, and what he hoped to be."

"That's terrifying."

"To some." Garrett shrugged. "Me, I was raised by women. And on my mother's side, stretching back past anyone's memory, the women in the family had the sight."

"All of them?" Max shuddered merely at the thought of generations of women staring into his soul.

"No, not all. Most times it skipped a generation." Garrett's eyes narrowed in thought. "Eileen had it, our mother did not. Her mother did, that was Granny Doyle. And Granny's grandmother."

"Does Leda?"

A long, silent moment passed. A soft breeze rippled across the lake and lifted Max's hair before swirling around him like a phantom hand offering comfort.

"Garrett," Max said softly, "I *need* to know."

The other man looked at him long and hard before sighing, "Aye, I guess ya do."

"Does she?"

Garrett inhaled sharply before saying, "No."

Max slumped in relief.

"At least, I don't think so."

Warily, Max stared at him. "What do you mean you don't think so?"

"Well"—Garrett rubbed his chin—"she *has* been right a time or two. And she sometimes has the 'look' about her." He shrugged. "I don't know, Max. Not for sure, anyway."

"Then I know no more now than I did before."

"Does it matter?"

Max gaped at him. "Of *course* it matters! She keeps talking about dying, for God's sake!"

"Ah." The other man smiled gently. "And that bothers you, does it?"

Backing up fast, Max countered, "Naturally. I wouldn't want to see *anyone* die needlessly."

"Neither would I."

Too late, Max remembered Rachel. Garrett's wife, still young and beautiful, had died just two years before. And to this day, Max thought dismally, he had no idea *why*.

"I'm sorry, Garrett. I didn't mean to remind you of—"

"Rachel?" A soft smile touched his face. "Every time I look at our boys, I'm reminded, Max. And I'm bloody grateful for it."

"Grateful?" All too well, Max remembered the pain and grief that had ridden Garrett for months after Rachel's passing. Why would he be grateful for a constant reminder of that pain?

"Y'know," Garrett said suddenly, a wide grin on his face, "I think it was Eileen told me all about Rachel and the boys a full three years before I met the woman."

"She told you? Everything?"

"Yes, she told me about Rachel dyin' young. And me and the boys bein' alone for a time."

Max didn't understand. Most of his life he'd spent his energies trying to avoid close contact with people. He'd watched his father fade away a day at a time because he'd cared too much.

And Garrett, even *knowing* how his marriage would turn out, willingly went ahead? "Why?" he said and didn't realize he'd spoken aloud until Garrett spoke.

"Why what?"

He'd already dredged up sad memories, he told himself. Why stop now?

"Your sister told you Rachel would die young? And you

believed her, yet married Rachel anyway. Why?" Max shook his head. "When Rachel died, the pain almost killed you!"

Garrett nodded.

"Then why did you marry her anyway? Good Lord, Garrett, I saw you when Rachel died. The pain almost killed you too!"

"Aye," the other man whispered, "it nearly did." He glanced up at Max, then let his gaze slip to his sons. Both boys were quiet now, watching the two men. "But if I hadn't married Rachel, I wouldn't have my sons." He looked back at Max and finished steadily, "And the years I had with Rachel were something I wouldn't have missed if it had meant my soul."

He meant it. Max stared into his friend's eyes and saw past the flash of pain to the remembered joy. Guiltily, Max turned then and faced the boys.

Michael's small face was unnaturally solemn and Sean's lake-blue eyes glistened with the sheen of unshed tears. Max wanted to kick himself. In his haste to find answers to his own questions, he'd brought back unhappy memories to two boys who'd lost their mother.

Thank God Dennis was off somewhere. Max didn't know if he'd be able to look himself in the face if he'd brought the sadness back to that child.

A stab of shame buckled through Max and he had to look away from the boys' knowing eyes.

He stared down at the dirt and grass, and his mind conjured Leda's meadow-green eyes looking back at him.

How had this happened? How had he come to care for her when he'd strived so madly not to? And if he allowed these feelings to continue and Leda *did* die . . . what, then? Would he be strong enough to survive the pain as Garrett had?

Or would it destroy him as it had his father?

CHAPTER 13

"A gift," Leda murmured thoughtfully. It was as if Gladys were still there in the store with her. Even though the older woman had accepted her tea and gone home, her words kept echoing in Leda's mind. Over and over, bits and pieces of Gladys's advice rose up and demanded attention.

Of course life was a gift. Leda'd always felt that way herself. She'd just never considered that giving in to a death that seemed inevitable was like tossing that gift away. She sighed, leaned back on the counter behind her, and dipped into the rock-candy jar.

Leda popped the crystallized sugar into her mouth and rolled it around on her tongue. All her life, she'd listened to signs and omens. She'd stared into the depths of her mother's glass ball and read the tarot for help in determining her path. She'd believed in the forces of Fate. Destiny.

Could she really stop now?

Did she even *want* to?

Her teeth bit down on the hard candy and the sugar splintered in her mouth. Yes. Yes, she wanted to believe that no matter the signs, she could fight and win the right to be with Max for the next thirty or forty years.

She wanted to believe, but a small voice from deep inside her warned that no matter her own wants or needs, Destiny would not be denied.

"Oh, Max," Leda said softly.

"Nope. The name's Dan."

Leda jumped and looked at the front door. The tall, dark-haired lawman stood just on the threshold, leaning negligently against the doorjamb.

"Hello, Dan."

"Afternoon, Leda," he said with a smile and stepped into the store. "Who ya talkin' to?"

"Myself."

He nodded, then slapped his hat against his thigh. "What's all this I hear about you and Maxwell goin' into business together?"

"How did you know?" Leda hadn't told anyone besides Garrett. And as far as she knew, Gladys was the only other person aware of their plans.

"August Haley." Dan grinned.

She should have guessed. "But how . . . ?"

"Don't even try to figure it out. Lord knows, *I* quit tryin' some time ago." He shook his head slowly, part frustration, part admiration. "That old goat's the best I've ever seen in ferretin' out secrets."

"Well," she said, "it's really no secret."

"Good." He glanced over at her crystal ball and the chest full of teas. "Need any help?"

"No, but thank you, Dan."

"Sure." The sheriff turned back for the door. "Just poked my head in to say hello."

"You don't have to go. Would you like some coffee?"

"No, thanks, Leda." He glanced back at her. "Got to go see Hiram over at the bank."

"Trouble?"

"Hope not."

She watched him as he left, but just before he stepped outside, he looked back at her.

"Hope you don't mind my sayin' so, Leda," he said softly, "but I'm real happy how things are goin' for you and Maxwell."

"You are?"

"Sure." Dan chuckled then added, "As long as it ain't me, there's nothin' I like better than watchin' a man come all unraveled over a woman."

"Unraveled? Max?"

"Hell, excuse me, yes, ma'am." Dan winked at her. "Maxwell is no more the same man he was a few months ago than August Haley is a man who minds his own business."

A swell of happiness shot through her. It did her heart good to know that one of Max's oldest friends had noticed the changes in him. And approved.

Leda smiled then challenged, "Would you like me to look into the ball for you, Dan? I'll bet I could find a woman who just might make *you* unravel!"

His smile faded a bit before he said thoughtfully, "I'll wager you could, Leda. But I'd just as soon you didn't. I'm as unraveled as I care to be."

He nodded at her, plopped his hat down low over his eyes, and stepped into the afternoon sunlight. Briefly, Leda wondered what it was that was hiding behind Dan Nichols's level gaze. Then, just as quickly, she shrugged and pushed the notion aside. Lord knew, she had plenty of *other* things to think about.

Lifting her chin, Leda inhaled sharply, crossed the room, and picked up her chest of teas and herbs. Then she left the store, closing the door behind her.

An hour after he'd left Garrett and the boys at the lake, Max went down the stairs from his room and heard singing.

He paused on the next to last step, his fingers curled over the polished banister. He didn't recognize the tune, but he would have known Leda's voice anywhere. Soft, low, and slightly off-key, it was coming from the back of the building. From the kitchen.

Straightening his shoulders, Max smoothed his neatly combed hair, adjusted his tie, and tugged at the hang of his coat. Once back from the lake, he'd tried to pull himself together somewhat.

Now, he was looking much more like his old self. More in control. More able to face the woman who'd become so important to him. He only wished the turmoil in his brain was as easy to rectify. Max sucked in a gulp of air, nodded to himself, and descended the last two stairs. Then he made a sharp right turn toward the sound of Leda's voice.

Down the narrow hall, he stopped outside his unused kitchen and listened to her. No wonder he hadn't recognized the tune, he thought. It wasn't a song she was singing. It was merely words she made up as she went along.

An indefinite tune, matched by her unsteady voice, the words nonetheless grabbed at him.

She was singing about him. About them. About loving. And life.

He squeezed his eyes tightly shut for a moment, then opened them again and pushed through the swinging door. She didn't hear him enter. And for a heartbeat, he didn't see her either. But he followed the sound of her voice and finally noticed her, on the floor, the top half of her body stuck inside an empty cabinet.

"Leda?"

She jumped, smacked her head, and began to squirm backward out of the cupboard. "Max?" she said before she was completely out. "I didn't know you had a kitchen!"

"I don't use it."

In fact, he hardly ever thought about the room. No one ever used the back door. At least, until lately. Until his patients had taken to sneaking out of the office to avoid Leda.

His gaze moved from the soles of her red socks, up the line of her calves as her skirt hiked up around her legs. With each twist of her body, more leg was exposed and Max found it suddenly very hard to breathe.

"So I see." She laughed and, once free, turned around, sat down, and looked up at him.

Dirt on her forehead and cobwebs in her hair, Leda James was the most beautiful woman he'd ever seen. His mouth went dry as his gaze swept over her. The dusty pale blue shirt she wore had come unbuttoned with her efforts under the cupboard. A hint of lace peeked through the deep vee opening to tantalize him.

Her full breasts rose and fell with her rapid breathing, and at once, all he could think of was slipping her shirt off her smooth shoulders and cupping her flesh in his hands. Instead, his hands curled into fists at his side.

"Why do you eat at Selma's when you have this lovely big kitchen?"

Who cared about such trivial things? he wondered frantically. We're all alone here. Together.

"I'm not much of a cook," he finally forced out.

She rubbed her forehead with the back of her hand and left yet another streak of dirt behind. He wanted to wash it away for her.

"Well," she said with a grin, "*I* am. And when I get this place all cleaned up, I can cook for you."

"You don't have to do that, Leda," he said quickly, but even as he said it, he imagined her standing in his kitchen, with him beside her. He saw it all so clearly. The closeness. The heat from the stove enveloping them, and then their own heat surpassing that of the fire.

Max swallowed and forced himself to say, "You already cook for Garrett and the boys."

"Oh." She rolled onto one hip, then pushed herself upright. Her plain black skirt hugged her bottom for a moment and Max groaned quietly. "That doesn't matter," she said.

"Still . . ."

She crossed the room to stand in front of him. Looking up into his eyes, she went on. "Besides, since I'll be working here every day now with you anyway, well, I'll just cook one meal for everyone and use this kitchen!"

His fantasies of their time alone splintered and another image rose up to replace it. The entire Malone family seated around his small table, staring at him. He could almost hear Michael's chuckles, see Sean's telltale blush, and Garrett's knowing eyes.

"I don't know . . ." It wasn't that he didn't like her family. He did. But Garrett wasn't a stupid man. And children always saw more than they should.

Surely, one of them would notice what he was having a hard time concealing. Especially after that talk he'd had with her uncle just a while ago. They probably already guessed that he wanted Leda more than he'd ever wanted anything or anyone in his life. His whole body ached for her.

"Oh, it'll be wonderful, Max. You'll see. And I can mix up my teas and store my herbs in here and . . ." Her voice faded away and still she stood stock-still in front of him, her eyes half shut.

"What is it?" he asked, his voice choked. "Are you feeling all right?"

"Uh-huh." She nodded then opened her eyes and looked at him again. "It's just that when you touch me, I can't hardly think."

"What?" Max looked down. His right hand had moved of its own accord to her hair and was twisting one of the soft coppery curls around his finger.

A hesitant smile curved his lips. Instead of releasing her, Max ran his thumb over the silky red strand. Her hair was every bit as soft as he'd always imagined it would be.

He didn't remember reaching out to her. He didn't recall touching her hair. A hard truth hit him in an unexpected revelation. One part of his mind, however deeply buried, was smarter than he was.

Despite his efforts to ignore the impact that Leda had on him, something deep inside him *knew* how much he wanted her. How much he needed her.

Startled, he questioned that silent declaration. Yes, Max acknowledged after a moment. He needed her. And even though the thought of needing this woman scared the hell out of him—the thought of living without her, he realized, was terrifying.

For the first time in years, Max made a sudden, impulsive decision.

"Leda," he said, his fingers still wrapped in a curl of her hair, "will you marry me?"

Her jaw dropped. Max noted with a silent chuckle that it was the only time he'd seen her speechless. He stared down into her eyes and marveled anew at the slight upward tilt that gave her such an elfin look.

While she sputtered and stared, he told himself that marriage was the one answer open to him. If his fears were well-founded, and she really *was* in danger of dying, then the closer he was to her, the better able he'd be to protect her.

And he knew that he would do everything in his power to see that her prediction of doom didn't come true.

"Max, I . . ."

"Surely you're not surprised," he said quickly. "It *was* you who predicted this the day we first met."

"Yes." Leda smiled, reached up and laid the palm of her hand against his cheek. When he turned his face into her touch, it almost broke her heart. "But I also told you that I couldn't marry you, Max."

"I know," he said, cutting her off. "And don't say it again."

"I have to." She shook her head gently and felt her eyes well up with tears. What should have been the happiest moment of her life was, instead, the saddest. "Max, I'm going to die soon. I'm not sure when. But I know it's coming."

"We're all going to die, Leda."

His hands cupped her shoulders and she felt the warmth of him seep into every corner of her body.

"But, Max—"

"No buts."

"I do love you, Max," she said quickly, before he could interrupt again, "but I won't marry you and leave you a widower tied to a memory."

"You don't *know* that's what will happen."

"Dear Max." Her hand slipped from his cheek to his shoulder. Leaning into him, she laid her head on his chest and listened to the steady beat of his heart. All her life she'd dreamed of this moment. Longed for it. And now that it was here, she was forced to turn her back on it.

Despite everything Gladys had said and every conclusion she'd reached on her own such a short time ago, Leda wasn't willing to risk Max's future happiness on what might well be a futile hope. Oh, she would fight. She would hold on to life with everything in her, but that still might not be enough. Destiny was a formidable opponent.

However, she told herself as her brain began to whirl with a new, exciting idea, there may still be an answer.

She snuggled in closer. Resting his chin on the top of her head, he snaked his arms around her and tightened. Grasping her to him, Max told himself he wouldn't let go. He wouldn't release her until she'd promised to marry him.

He stared blankly at the dingy wall opposite him. Nothing had changed. His abandoned kitchen looked no different. The sounds of Tanglewood, drifting in through the partially opened back door, were uninterrupted. And yet he knew that nothing would be the same again.

Max couldn't believe that she'd turned him down. Despite her protestations, he'd really thought that when faced with his proposal, she'd accept wholeheartedly. And as he held her, another realization crept through him slowly, stubbornly.

Without Leda, he would be alone again. Only now, that loneliness would be tinged with echoes of what might have been and his self-imposed seclusion would be more desolate, more all-encompassing than anything he'd ever known.

Instinctively, his hold on her tightened. As if his strength would be more convincing than his words had been.

"Max?" she whispered, her breath warm against his shirtfront.

"What?"

"I have a proposal for you," she said and he heard the smile in her voice.

"I accept," he said, squeezing her even harder and she gasped. "Sorry," he said and loosened his hold a bit.

Leda tilted her head back and looked up at him. "Don't you want to know what the proposal *is* before you say yes?"

"Doesn't matter." Nothing mattered except how right it felt to hold her.

Her mouth twitched.

He bent and kissed her gently, briefly.

She pulled in a shuddering breath and then spoke in a rush. "I want a compromise."

"Compromise?"

"Yes."

"What kind of compromise?" All right, he told himself. It *does* matter. A little.

"Well." She moved one of her hands to the back of his neck and let her fingertips slide into his hair. "I can't marry you, Max—"

"Yes you can, Leda. We'll—"

"Let me finish." She shook her head and slid her fingers to his earlobe.

Good God. His eyes snapped shut and every nerve in his body leaped to attention. With the last of his quickly dissolving control, Max somehow managed to look at her again as she went on.

"I can't marry you, *but*"— she added quickly—"I would like for us to . . ." She lowered her gaze and he saw a faint flood of color rush into her cheeks.

Intrigued, he asked, "What?"

"Well"—she shrugged helplessly—"to be lovers."

A hammerlike blow struck him full in the chest. Max's heart stopped, his breath caught, and it seemed like several minutes before his lungs began to work again.

"Lovers?"

"Yes." She studied the lapels on his jacket with concentration.

"Do you know what you're saying, Leda? What you're asking?"

"No, I don't," she whispered, her fingertips following the line of his ear. "And that's just it, Max." She raised her gaze and looked deeply into his eyes. "I *want* to know."

"But—"

She shook her head. "Don't say no yet," she pleaded. "If I have to die, I would hate to leave this world never knowing what it was like to be loved by you."

"Leda." It was more of a groan than a whispered plea.

"Please, Max." She raised up on her toes, cupped the back of his head, and drew him down to her. Her lips teased his, tugging and pulling gently. "Don't let me die a virgin. Love me for however long we have left."

Her last words came in a breathy rush and he swallowed them as he slanted his mouth over hers. When his tongue plunged inside her warmth, he tried to give her everything he had to give.

She pressed herself against him and he felt the line of her body along his. Max dipped one hand to her behind and pulled her hips to him, sure she could feel his body's reaction. In response, she swiveled her hips in a desperate effort to get even closer.

He was lost.

In moments, he pulled away, and as he struggled for air, he looked down at her flushed face and knew that he would accept her compromise. He would do anything he could to be as close to her as possible.

Besides, a voice in the back of his mind whispered, if he was lucky, she would conceive. And once pregnant, Max knew he could convince her to marry him.

Threat of Doom or not.

"Well, Max?" Her hands smoothed over his shirtfront and slid under his jacket. "Will you be my lover? My teacher?"

He clenched his jaw tightly as her hands moved around to his back and slipped along the edge of his waistband. Jerking her a nod, he said, "Yes, Leda. For however long you want me, I'll be your lover."

A shadow of sadness crossed her features and was gone again in the next moment. "I'll want you forever, Max. I just don't know how long the Fates will let me have you."

He wanted to argue with her. To tell her that the Fates had nothing to do with him. With them. But he thought better of it. Why tell her with words, when his body could say everything he wanted her to know?

He dipped his head toward hers again, thinking that he would never be able to taste enough of her, when a shout from outside stopped him.

"Doc! Doc! Are ya in there?"

"Denny," she whispered and stepped toward the back door just as it swung wide.

Sunshine splashed across the dusty floor and the neglected walls, showing the room for the shabby, forgotten place it was.

"Doc!" Dennis ran into the room, followed close on his heels by Arthur. The boy glanced quickly around the room, wrinkled his nose, then fastened his gaze on Max. "Doc, I think Arthur's gonna be bad sick!"

"You think he's *going* to be sick?" Desire faded quickly in the presence of the frightened child.

"Yeah. Anytime now."

Max glanced at the slobbering animal now seated at Dennis's feet, throwing the boy a look of adoration. "What makes you think so? He looks fine to me." At any rate, he added silently, as fine as the dog *could* look.

"It's somethin' he ate, Doc." Dennis glanced at his cousin, then let his gaze drop to the floor.

Leda took a step toward the boy. "Denny, what is it? What's happened?"

"I tried to stop him, Leda. Honest." The child raised his head and looked at her. A sheen of tears glazed his blue eyes and he added, "I yelled and yelled, but he ate it before I could get to him."

"Ate what?" Max tossed in.

"Oh," Leda said with sudden understanding.

"Yeah." Denny nodded. "And he ate every bite too. I just know it'll make him sick. Don'cha think?"

Max glanced from the boy to Leda and back again. Obviously, they both knew something that neither of them was telling.

"Would one of you mind letting me know what is going on?"

"Now, Denny," Leda said with a quick look at the dog, "I'm sure it won't do him any harm at all."

"I better ask the doc, though, to be sure."

"Ask the doc *what*?" Max was getting further and further behind in the conversation and it was starting to bother him.

Denny turned to look at the man. "I wasn't s'posed to say, but Arthur ate up Leda's spell!"

"Denny . . ."

"I know it was a secret," he said, looking at her briefly, "but Arthur might be bad sick."

"Spell?" Max asked.

"It won't make him sick, Denny. Really." Leda smiled at the boy and ruffled his already windblown hair. "And don't you worry about the secret, all right? It doesn't matter now anyway."

"Secret?" Max questioned.

"Ya mean it already worked?" Denny grinned at her.

"I think so," she said, returning the smile.

"*What* worked?" Max shouted and threw his arms wide, demanding they notice him.

Dennis shot Leda a questioning glance and, at her nod, turned back to the doctor.

"Leda fixed up a spell."

"A cure," she corrected.

"And set it out in the sun," Denny went on, "but Arthur didn't know it was a spell and he ate it. And I was worried 'cause I don't want him to get sick and I figured that even if you're a people doctor, you could prob'ly fix him, so I brought him here."

When the boy shrugged, and paused for breath, Max shook his head. He *still* didn't understand what was going on. And what exactly was this "spell" that Arthur ate?

His confusion must have been written on his face because Leda laughed and told him, "It was a pickle, Max. A pickle with sugar on it."

"That sounds disgusting."

"That's what *I* said." Denny nodded. "But Leda said it wasn't for eatin'. That's why I was scared when Arthur just gobbled it up."

"If it wasn't for eating," Max asked slowly, "what was it for?"

One corner of her mouth lifted in a half smile. "It's a cure for sour-tempered people."

"Ah." He nodded. Of course. He wasn't even surprised by her explanation. It even made a strange kind of sense.

Then, the way she was watching him and her spreading grin betrayed her.

"It was for me, wasn't it?" he accused. "This 'cure' of yours was for me?"

"Uh-huh." Leda grinned.

Index finger poking himself in the chest, he said, "Sour? You think I'm a sour person?"

"Not anymore," she conceded.

"It works fast, huh?" Denny asked.

"Oh, very fast," his cousin agreed.

It was impossible to maintain his offended air while faced with the gleam in her eyes. Max shook his head and smiled back at her.

"Boy, Doc," Denny suddenly observed, "this place is a mess!"

No one answered him.

"Y'know," the boy went on, "it's gonna take you a heck of a long time to clean up around here." He ran one finger along the plank counter, looked at the grime he'd collected and grimaced.

Max watched her and noticed that she didn't even glance at her cousin when she said, "Denny, will you tell your father that I won't be home until late?"

"How come?"

"I'm going to stay here and clean up this kitchen." Her tongue darted out to move over dry lips.

Invitation glistened on her delectable mouth and promises shined in her eyes. He groaned inwardly and tried to remind himself of Dennis's presence. But it was all Max could do to keep from grabbing her, clutching her to him, and kissing her until neither of them could breathe.

"What about supper?" Denny whined.

"Your father can handle it tonight," she countered quickly, her voice strained.

"Aw, Leda."

Arthur's tail began to thump wildly against the floor.

Max followed her hand with his eyes as she reached up and pushed her fingers through her glorious hair. His own hands clenched at his sides.

"Go on now, Denny," she coaxed the boy, her eyes fixed on Max. "I've got to get busy."

"Cleanin' this place could take ya all night," he warned.

Leda's lips curved in a slow, tantalizing smile that stopped Max's heart as she said, "You know Denny, you're right. It just *might* take all night at that."

CHAPTER 14

The back door banged shut behind Dennis and the kitchen seemed to shrink in size.

Max crossed the floor quickly, turned the lock, then swiveled his head to look at her. The sharp sound of the lock slamming home echoed within her and Leda knew there would be no turning back.

She *was* doing the right thing. She felt it. If she was to fight for her life, then wasn't it best to have every advantage? To know everything that she would lose if the Fates had their way? Wouldn't that strengthen her sense of purpose?

Good reasons, all of them, she thought. And yet, none of them the one overpowering reason behind her decision. Leda wanted to be a part of him. More than anything, she wanted to know, in case she lost her battle with Destiny, what it was she would be missing for all eternity.

Suddenly, a swarm of butterflies filled her stomach, their fluttering wings keeping in perfect rhythm with her frantically beating heart. A bit flustered now that the moment she'd longed for was at hand, Leda raised her gaze to meet Max's and found his pale blue eyes fixed on her. Warmth blossomed inside her, immediately quieting her nerves.

"I'd like to wash up," she said softly and held out her dust-streaked hands.

He nodded, crossed the room, and quietly stepped around her to the counter. Lifting an old cream-colored water pitcher, Max turned for the pump. The screech of metal on metal scraped the air just before a gush of water spilled into the waiting jug.

In the thundering silence that followed, he said, "I really only use this kitchen when I need water." He shrugged and added, "That's why it's so dusty in here."

"Uh-huh." Leda understood why he was talking about such trivial things. She, too, was feeling a bit awkward.

"I'll get you a cloth," he offered and left the room almost before he'd finished speaking.

She swallowed heavily and walked to the sink. Slowly, she unbuttoned her shirt and pulled the tail from her waistband. Staring blindly at the curtains above the sink, Leda shrugged and felt the soft, worn fabric slide down the length of her arms.

Suddenly alone, Leda asked herself why she was feeling so . . . *skittish*? She'd been longing for and dreaming of this moment for years. And since finally finding Max just a few weeks ago, she'd thought of nothing else except being in his arms, kissing him. Touching him.

The hall door opened again and his footsteps sounded against the floorboards as he moved to stand behind her. She inhaled slowly, deeply as once again his presence put to rest any lingering misgivings.

From the corner of her eye, Leda saw him lay a fresh towel and a bar of soap on the counter. She held her breath as he reached past her. He'd taken his jacket off and his shirtsleeves were rolled back to the elbow. The fingers of his left hand slid up and down her spine and the thin fabric of her plain white chemise did nothing to disguise the feel of his flesh on hers.

She lifted her mass of necklaces, to take them off, but Max stilled her hand. Immediately, Leda let the ropes of beads drop back into the hollow between her breasts.

Slowly, Max dipped a clean cloth into the pitcher of cool water, then squeezed out the excess.

His left arm suddenly reached around her for the soap, and she was cradled by the strength of him. Without a word, he worked up a rich lather. Then, the cloth held in his right hand, he drew the cool, soapy dampness up the length of her arm.

Leda shivered and leaned back into him. Her head against his chest, she closed her eyes and concentrated on the sensations rocketing through her.

He bent his head and his breath whispered against her neck. Slowly, tenderly, he stroked her hands, her arms. With a lover's touch, Max smoothed the chilled cloth over her body. He washed away the layer of dust and at the same time created a path of fire that raged in her blood.

Max turned her then and she felt the edge of the counter bite into the small of her back. Eyes closed, she gave herself over to him and the wonder of his caresses. The cloth skimmed lightly across her face, down the line of her throat, and came to rest on her chest. As he gently dragged the coolness over her flesh, tiny beads of water dripped from the edge of the material and trickled down beyond the lace-edged fabric covering her into the valley between her breasts.

She heard his quick intake of breath, then felt him tug on the ribbons at the front of her chemise. Leda let her head fall back as the pale pink strands slipped free, baring her breasts to him. The ropes of beads and charms about her neck now lay cold against her heat and Leda felt the weight of each individual strand on her sensitive skin.

His hand splashed back into the water jug. Leda heard him rinse the cloth just before he lifted her arms, one after the other, and smoothed the clean water over her soapy skin again and again. Droplets of water clung to her, soaking into her chemise, leaving it to hug her body with a thin, fine grasp.

Once more, he lifted the clean cloth to wipe away the soap from her face, her neck, her chest. Leda's breath came heavy as he slid the cool, damp material under her chemise and stroked her breasts, each in turn. The cloth moved across her hardened, tender nipples and she groaned at the unexpected jolt of awareness.

Her fingers curled over the edge of the counter and tightened. Spasms of pleasure started low in her belly and snaked down the length of her legs. A soft smile curved her lips as Max pulled the edges of her chemise farther apart. She heard him discard the cloth he'd wielded with such incredible talent and then she waited, breath held for what he would show her next.

His hands grasped her waist and lifted. Gently, he sat her down on the counter and moved to stand between her legs. Leda shifted to accommodate him. Raising her head, she opened her eyes and watched him.

Max's gaze locked with hers as he reached to trail his fingertips around the curve of her breasts. She saw her own passion-glazed reflection in his eyes and watched him smile gently when she gasped at the intimacy of his touch. When his thumbs began to circle her nipples, though, she had to close her eyes again and force herself to remember to breathe.

His featherweight caresses inflamed her until Leda was sure she would die with the pleasure of it. Then he bent down, covered one hardened bud with his mouth, and a luscious, mind-numbing delight filled her. Heat coursed through her body and centered itself exactly where Max's body leaned against her. With each touch of his tongue to her nipple, the indescribable fire burned brighter. Instinctively, Leda's hand cupped the back of his head, holding his mouth to her breast, telling him without words that she never wanted him to stop.

She opened her eyes slowly and looked down to watch him as he tasted her body.

"Oh, Max," she whispered, "my love."

He suckled her and she jumped, startled at the overpowering sensation. It felt as though he were drawing her into himself. A strangled groan shot from her throat and she threaded her fingers through his hair. As his mouth and tongue worked their magic, Leda's other hand reached for him. Her fingers touched the place where his mouth joined her breast, then she ran her fingertip over his jaw and across his neck.

The image of Max at her breast would remain with her through eternity, she knew.

Sharp stabs of delight streaked from her nipple to one spot between her thighs that now tingled and burned for his attentions. Aware of a need she couldn't name, Leda twisted on the counter, swiveling her hips against him.

Immediately, Max lifted his head and turned to her other breast as he snaked one arm out to wrap around her behind and hold her firmly in place. As his lips tugged at her nipple, his free hand flipped up the hem of her skirt and began to slide up her leg. His every touch was like fire. Leda didn't know what to do. Which way to move.

When his fingers passed her knee and began to stroke the inside of her thigh, she simply held on to him. His mouth released her and he straightened up. Leda looked into his eyes and saw raw, undisguised desire shining in the pale blue depths. Then his fingers entered her body and she lost all thought.

Her hips writhed in response and Max swallowed her gasp of pleasure when he covered her mouth with his. His tongue claimed hers even as his fingers moved in and out of her slick heat. Leda moaned and lost herself in his kiss. Stroke for stroke, her tongue moved with his, caressing him, teasing him. Her breathing ragged, she clung to him and tried to press herself close enough to become a part of him.

Max moved his thumb over a deliciously sensitive piece of flesh and Leda gasped, tearing her mouth from his. She shivered, closed her eyes, and moved against his hand, wanting more of him. She'd never known anything like this. To actually *feel* Max inside her body was almost more than she could bear. Yet at the same time, Leda knew she wanted more than his hand to fill her. She wanted to know everything. To feel everything. To become so much a part of him that even when they weren't together, they would never be separate.

Leda buried her head in the curve of his neck and arched her hips against his hand. Max moved to trace whisper-light kisses along her shoulder and she clutched at him desperately.

Lifting her knees, she spread her thighs wider, hoping he would see her distress and ease the building tension gripping her.

"Max," she said helplessly between gasps of air, "something's happening to me. I need to—" Her hips twisted again.

"I know, Leda. I know what you need," he assured her and tightened his grasp on her bottom.

Her fingers moved through his hair frantically. Her legs trembling, she arched once more, but he held her still.

"Please, Max," she said in a rush, "be inside me."

"Not yet, Leda," he whispered against her throat and his tongue flicked against her neck. "Not yet." His fingers dipped into her warmth again, promising an end to the quest she'd begun what seemed like centuries ago.

Deliberately, his thumb moved even more slowly over the bud of flesh that throbbed with her every pulse beat.

As he caressed her with her own heat, Leda felt his strength flow into her. She braced the soles of her feet on the cabinet beneath her and leaned back, her clutching hold on Max's shoulders the only stable thing left in her world.

Teasingly, he covered her throat with kisses and moved up until his mouth hovered just above hers. "Let it happen, Leda. Feel my touch and let it happen."

Almost at once the incredible tightness clamping down on her chest began to strangle her. "Max?" she whispered, and then her world exploded. Leda cried out, her fingers digging into his shoulders as her body trembled uncontrollably.

And when the shaking stopped, she looked up into his smile.

He pulled the hem of her skirt down over her legs and drew her into the circle of his arms. Max's heart was pounding and he was as short of breath as if he'd been running for hours. As he cradled her limp form close against his chest, Max realized that even though his own body still screamed out for release, he'd never felt so . . . satisfied.

Just bringing her pleasure, watching her reaction to his touch had left him stunned. He smoothed her hair back but couldn't resist sliding his hand over the edge of her breast. She shuddered slightly and leaned further into him.

He'd never experienced anything like this. How could he feel such a sense of completion even while aching for relief?

"Max?" she said softly.

"What?"

"That was wonderful."

He smiled into her hair and kissed the top of her head.

"Max?"

"What?" he chuckled. Leave it to Leda, he told himself. Not even a shattering climax was enough to keep her quiet for long.

Her fingers worked the buttons of his shirt free and Max stopped laughing.

"We're not finished, are we?" she asked and pressed her lips to his chest.

"No." His throat tight, he barely managed to force out the word.

"Good." Leda ran her palms across his chest and he inhaled sharply.

"Leda . . ."

"I want to feel your skin against mine."

He bit back a groan as his body tightened.

She lifted her legs and locked them around his waist, drawing him in close.

Max struggled for air.

Leda pulled the edges of his shirt wide and pressed her breasts to him. She gasped, sighed, then gently began to brush herself against him.

His eyes closed.

"Don't you think we should go upstairs now, Max?" she said, flicking her tongue across one flat nipple.

"Yeah." He groaned and held her head between his hands. "Yeah, I guess we'd better."

"Now, Max," she said urgently, her hands skimming around his waist, "let's go now."

Quickly, he stepped back from her, scooped her up in his arms, and started walking. One of her hands curled through the hair at his nape and the other scraped across his abdomen, her thumb sliding beneath the waistband of his pants.

Mouth dry, heart pounding, Max practically raced through the hall and up the stairs.

"Aren't you going to lock the front door too?" she whispered, her tongue smoothing over his flesh.

"Uh, no," he answered, intent on reaching his room and the bed before his legs gave out. "If someone needs me, they'll wait in the office. No one comes up the stairs, Leda."

She nodded against him and murmured, "Then hurry, Max."

He held her tighter, closer, and cursed the fact that he had to let her go even for the moment it took to open the door at the head of the stairs. When they stepped into the shadowy twilight of the room, Max paused only to turn the key in the lock.

Then he picked her up again and marched the short distance to his bed. With one hand, he reached down and tossed the quilt to the foot of the mattress, then laid her down gently. He stood alongside her, willing himself to patience as she sat up and pulled her open chemise over her shoulders and down to her waist.

Her breasts, high and full, had the pale sheen of ivory in the dim light. As he watched, she slowly unbuttoned her skirt and, wiggling on her behind, pushed the yards of fabric down the length of her legs. Lastly, Leda removed the red socks he'd become so accustomed to and then lay down again.

His hungry gaze swept over her lush body, as she lay naked against the cool white sheets. Leda's necklaces lay across her body like jeweled offerings to an ancient queen. Her breasts, her narrow waist and rounded hips enflamed him. The thatch of red curls that guarded the warmth of her seemed to beg for his touch.

When she held her arms out to him, Max couldn't wait another moment to feel her flesh against his. In seconds, his clothes lay scattered on the floor and he was stretched out alongside her.

One strand at a time, Max lifted the ropes of beads and charms from around her neck. He left a kiss in place of each necklace and carefully set her treasures on the table beside the bed.

His task complete, Leda's hands moved over him until he thought he would go mad with need. Her fingers skimmed through the pale dusting of curls on his chest then slipped farther down, her every touch sending him closer to the edge. Over his ribs, across his abdomen, she explored him lovingly. Max thought he could lie there forever until he felt her fingers close around him and his heart stopped.

A groan from deep in his throat accompanied her touch as her fingers claimed him. She stroked the length of him with soft, tender caresses. An overwhelming heat seemed to engulf him and Max wouldn't have been surprised to find flames licking at the bedframe.

"Max," she said and he heard the pride in her voice, "you're so beautiful."

He watched her as she raised herself up on one elbow to

look down into his eyes. Her hair rained down on either side of his face, sheltering them in a canopy of red darkness. She dipped her head to kiss him and he clutched at her, but she pulled away, shaking her head.

"It's my turn," she said and moved her hand still lower to cup him tenderly.

Good God. He clenched his jaw and tried to hold himself in check. Max felt as though he were going to burst, and dammit, he thought, he wanted to be buried deep inside her when that happened. She could have "her turn" another time.

Whenever she wanted to.

Abruptly, he moved, shifted position, and almost before she knew it, had Leda flat on her back. He ran his hands over her thighs as he moved to kneel between her legs. Leda closed her eyes, planted her feet, and rocked her hips in silent invitation.

Max groaned again, then fought for control. His body aching to enter her, he took another moment to make certain she was still ready for him. Gently, he rubbed at the heart of her and her body jerked as she tossed her head from side to side on the pillow.

He slipped his fingers into her body and felt the strength of her damp warmth encircle him. Leda moaned his name and lifted her hips from the bed.

His breathing ragged, Max reluctantly pulled his hand back. She gasped when his touch left her but he promised her silently it wouldn't be for long.

It had already been far *too* long. He felt as though he'd been waiting for this moment for years. For centuries. Max's hands cupped her bottom and lifted her slightly for his entry.

Leda's eyes opened and their eyes met as his body became a part of her.

She flinched for a heartbeat and then the brief sign of discomfort was gone, replaced by the passion he'd witnessed such a short time ago.

Inside her warmth, Max felt the *rightness* of it. In that one moment, he realized he'd found something he hadn't known he was looking for. And as he began to move inside her and Leda's legs locked around his hips, drawing him deeper, he knew he never wanted to lose this.

Max leaned over her, claiming her mouth with his and plunged in and out of her heat until tremors again shook through Leda.

And this time, she took him with her.

He collapsed and lay atop her, his weight pressing her down into the mattress. Yet she didn't want him to move. Leda wrapped her arms around him and smoothed the palms of her hands over his back. As his heartbeat slowed and his breathing became more regular, she felt him relax completely.

She smiled to herself as she realized that unlike Max, she wasn't exhausted at all. In fact, she'd never felt more awake. More alive. She wanted to tell him everything she was feeling. She wanted to know that what had just happened between them meant as much to him as it had to her.

Groaning quietly, Max rolled to one side, pulled her up against him, and buried her head in his shoulder. Leda cuddled in close and told herself that they would talk later. For now, maybe it was enough to hold and be held.

Beneath her ear, Max's heartbeat drummed steadily and she matched her breaths to his. She closed her eyes, thinking to rest for only a moment.

Then she would wake him up for another lesson.

Leda lay nestled against his side, sound asleep, her head on his chest. Max let his hand slide up and down her arm, reveling in the simple joy of holding her.

He folded his free arm behind his head and glanced around his spartan room. For the first time, he noticed just how little he had to show for his thirty-five years of living.

A few suits of clothes, even fewer pieces of furniture. A

medical degree but very few patients and only one or two friends. No home. No family.

In fact, he'd achieved what he'd always thought he'd wanted. He frowned at the whitewashed ceiling overhead. Hadn't he?

Leda stirred slightly, slid her arm across his chest and settled down again, one of her legs draped over his thighs. He grinned suddenly and promised himself he'd never complain about his "too narrow" bed again.

She sighed against his chest and mumbled something he couldn't quite catch. When she smiled, he found himself wondering what she was dreaming about.

Lord! he thought unexpectedly, how close he'd come to living his life as an empty man.

Max tightened his hold on her. In little more than three weeks, she'd come to mean so much to him. She'd dragged him, kicking and screaming, into the society of Tanglewood. He'd talked to more people since he'd met her than he had in the entire five years he'd been in town.

She assumed only the best about him and he found himself striving to prove her right. Even when she infuriated him with her convoluted logic and cockeyed way of looking at life, she entranced him. He'd never known anyone who *lived* as much as she did. Or as well.

He chuckled and ruefully acknowledged that she'd completely shattered his safe, quiet little world. And now that he'd seen what was outside, he wasn't at all sure that he wanted to be shut away again.

Leda had poured her love over him, paying no attention when he wasn't smart enough to see what she was offering. She savored every minute of every day as if it were her last.

Max frowned suddenly and wrapped his arms around her as that thought echoed in his mind. She lived that way because she truly *believed* that her days were numbered. He felt her heart beating steadily, her breath on his chest, and fought down the urge to panic.

What if she was right? What if she was going to die? Soon?

How would he live without her?

But what could he do about it? He'd asked her to marry him and she refused! He shook his head slowly. Max *still* couldn't believe it. He never would have thought that a "good" woman—no matter how unconventional—would prefer being a mistress to a wife! Especially after all her talk of Fate and Destiny.

Somehow, he told himself, he had to find a way to make her change her mind. Now that they'd found each other, he wasn't about to lose her. Not to her own strange sense of rightness. Not to death.

"Max?"

He looked down and returned her dreamy smile.

"You shouldn't have let me sleep," she said.

"It hasn't been long."

"But I didn't mean to sleep at all," she said softly. "I can do that when I'm not with you."

Max frowned, knowing that he wouldn't sleep a wink as soon as she left him for her own bed. In fact, he didn't know if he'd be able to stand the silence of his room once she'd gone.

"Leda," he said, smoothing her hair back, "I want to talk to you about that."

"What?"

"About being apart." He raised up on one elbow and looked down at her. Somehow, he had to convince her. "I don't want you to leave tonight."

"Oh, Max." Leda reached up and cupped his cheek. "I *have* to go home. What would Uncle Garrett think?"

"I don't just mean tonight," he said quickly, "I mean I don't want you to go back to Garrett's *ever*."

She shook her head. "That wouldn't be right, Max. No one in town would speak to us. You'd never have another patient."

"What are you talking about?"

"Max, two people just don't stay together if they're not married. It just wouldn't be proper."

Proper! He couldn't believe it! Here she was, lying naked in his arms, and she was blushing over what was and wasn't proper.

"I'm not talking about just keeping house together, Leda," he told her, impatience creeping into his tone. "I'm talking about getting married. Tonight. With the preacher out on his circuit, Dan could marry us. He's not just a sheriff. He's a justice of the peace, too, you know."

Max was talking so fast, so busy outlining his plan, he didn't notice that Leda looked close to tears. When he finally slowed down, he stared at her, stunned. "What is it? What's wrong?"

"Max," she said and slipped out of his grasp to sit up at the foot of the bed, "I've already told you, I can't marry you."

"But why not?" In the twilight of the room, he couldn't see her expression clearly. But with her shoulders slumped and her head hanging, she looked so small—so *sad*—Max wanted to hold her and soothe her, to give her back the smile she'd awakened with.

"Because I'm going to die," she whispered brokenly. She folded her legs beneath her Indian style and looked at him through eyes he knew were filled with tears. "Max, I won't do that to you. I won't leave you a widower, tied to the memory of me and what we had."

A small burst of anger began to work its way through Max as he pushed himself to a sitting position opposite her. Now he didn't just want to hold her. He wanted to shake her until she promised to stop talking about dying. At the same time, he knew he had no right to be surprised by her statement. Had he *really* imagined that making love would change her mind?

Trying to keep his voice level, he asked, "And you don't think I'll have any memories of you now?" He snorted his disgust. "What are you saying here?" He leaped up and started pacing back and forth around the bed. "Do you *really* believe that because we're not married, *this*"—he waved his arms, encompassing both her and the rumpled bedclothes—"meant *nothing*?"

"No, but—"

"And because we're not married, I won't feel a damned thing if you die?"

"No, Max. I didn't mean—"

He felt like a lawyer, pleading a case in court. And suddenly, he knew he'd feel more in control if he weren't stark naked.

"Because," Max said, his voice stony, "if you're so interested in protecting me, why did you come up here in the first place? Why did you make love with me at all?"

He was standing right alongside her. In the dim light, he watched her. She chewed at her bottom lip and Max's anger dropped away when a solitary tear trickled down her cheek. Helplessly, he plopped down onto the bed and pulled her into his arms. While she cried, he held her, wishing he knew what to do. What to say, to convince her that he wasn't going to allow her to die.

But most of all, right now, he wanted her to stop crying. He hadn't meant to ruin their afternoon together. He'd only wanted to ensure that they would have more of them.

Seated on his lap, Leda scooted closer to him and he felt himself harden in response to her movements.

Trying to take his mind off the unbelievably tempting fact of her nudity, Max searched for something to say. Something to make her smile again. Something that would bring back that special feeling of oneness they'd shared until he'd unthinkingly shattered it.

His wandering gaze settled on her discarded socks and he heard himself ask, "Leda? Would you mind telling me why you always wear red socks?"

"What?" She hiccuped, sniffed, and pulled back slightly. As she stared up at him, the beginnings of a smile hovered on her lips.

"The socks." He nodded at them, inwardly pleased that he'd managed to shift the conversation. Even if only temporarily. "Why socks? Why not shoes like everyone else?"

Her lips twitched.

"And if it *must* be socks . . . why red?"

She wiped her eyes with the back of her hand and impulsively planted a quick kiss at the corner of his mouth. Shrugging, she said, "Shoes hurt my feet."

"Naturally." Knowing Leda, that answer made perfect sense.

"But my feet get cold when I'm barefoot," she continued, "so I wear socks."

"Eminently logical." He nodded, surprised he hadn't thought of the simple explanation himself. "But why *red* socks?"

"Every color has a different meaning, Max." She pushed a stray lock of hair back from his forehead. "Like I told you about the gemstones?"

Max nodded again. While he waited for her to continue, he brushed the tears from her cheeks with the pad of his thumb.

"Well, red is for"—she dipped her head, nestled into the crook of his neck and finished in a small voice— "Strength and Courage." Leda took a small, shuddering breath before adding, "When my time comes, I don't want to be afraid."

Something hard and cold settled in Max's chest. His arms closed around her, pulling her tight against him.

Strength.

Courage.

She already possessed those qualities, even if she wasn't aware of it. But Max was no longer as sure about himself. He told himself that first thing in the morning, he would go buy himself a pair or two of red socks. If her time *did* come, Max wanted the strength and the courage to pull her back to safety.

Back to him.

CHAPTER 15

"So," August asked, avid curiosity gleaming in his eyes, "did ya find out anythin' interestin' when ya talked to the doc?"

Gladys frowned. Keeping her eyes downcast, she let him think she was counting stitches on the hopelessly tangled hank of yarn she'd intended to be a sweater.

Sure, she'd found out a few things. Most important being that she and August weren't gonna have to do much of anything to get the doc and Leda together. By the looks of Max Evans, she told herself, he wouldn't be a bachelor much longer.

But she didn't want to talk about that. Not yet, anyway. It would do August good to stew a bit. Besides, there was somethin' else botherin' her, and she knew better than to talk about it with August Haley.

She had to have some time to think. And to do that, she had to get rid of her nosy visitor.

"No," she lied and lifted her gaze to his. "I didn't find out a blasted thing."

Her old friend looked at her thoughtfully for a long moment, then shook his head, clearly disappointed. "You mean to tell me you had him all to yourself in that office and didn't find out *anything*?"

"That's right."

"Well, then," August whined and pushed himself from the chair. "Reckon it's up to me."

"What are you up to, you old goat?"

"Who's callin' who *old*?"

"August . . ."

"Aw, calm down, Gladie," he said, shrugging his narrow shoulders. "I just got me a little hitch in my get-along." He rubbed his right hip meaningfully. "Think I'll let the doc take a look at it."

Gladys remembered the sorry shape Max was in when she'd seen him last and quickly ordered, "You do no such thing. You leave the man alone, y'hear?"

He looked at her slyly. "You *do* know somethin'," he crowed. "Ya just don't want to tell me!"

"That ain't it."

"No matter." He sniffed imperiously and turned for the door. "I'll just find out for my ownself."

"August, the man's prob'ly havin' his supper."

He opened the door and glanced out at the lowering darkness. "Then I best catch him quick."

"I'm tellin' ya," Gladys said again, her temper rising, "leave the man be."

"Just to show there's no hard feelin's, I'll let ya know if I find out anything!"

"August!"

The skinny man stepped over the threshold, but before he left, he asked, "Gladie?" One long finger pointed at the mess of yarn in her lap. "That the sweater you started in makin' last winter?"

"Yeah," she said, thrown off stride by the change in subject. As he stared at her handiwork, Gladys had the unreasonable desire to stuff the would-be sweater down under the cushion of her chair.

"The one Geraldine offered to finish for ya?"

"Yeah," Gladys ground out, fighting back the memory of her interfering daughter-in-law's "helpful" suggestions. "Why?"

"No reason"—he shrugged again—"just seems to me that you used to knit them things a helluva lot faster."

She gritted her teeth. "Don't you have somethin' else to do?"

"Yep." He grinned and that long nose of his twitched expectantly. "Got to get on over to the doc's!"

He slammed the door before she could say another word. Gladys fumed silently, glared at the snarled brown wool in her lap for a long minute, then curled her fingers into the mess, and threw it across the room. Her knitting needles clattered against the wall, then dropped to the floor.

"Hiram," Dan Nichols said for the third time, "all I'm askin' is that you take special care for a while. That's all."

The bank was empty. Even the teller had gone home a few minutes before. In the soft glow of lamplight, Dan looked around the small building and told himself that any thief worth his salt wouldn't have a bit of trouble taking every last cent from the place.

He frowned, crossed his right foot over his left knee, and rested his hat on his scuffed brown boot. Since that telegram he'd received from Mike Connor, Dan had done some checking. What he'd discovered hadn't eased his mind any.

Someone, or a group of someones, had hit almost every bank in the general area. And always, the robbery took place right after a big shipment. Almost as though the thieves had a source of information telling them when to strike.

He glanced at the bald man across the desk from him. Hiram Adams was a pompous fool with a too high opinion of himself. He considered himself a ladies' man despite the fact that he lived alone and even the women at the Red Dog shuddered when they saw him comin'. His somber brown suits were always offset by a garishly colored vest that strained to cover the man's formidable stomach. His cool gray eyes were the exact color of the neatly trimmed beard that was the banker's pride and joy.

Right now, those eyes were staring at Dan and the sheriff met them unblinkingly.

"Hiram, I believe that somebody's gonna be tryin' to make off with that gold when it comes."

"Nonsense!" The banker shuffled a stack of papers, slid them into his black leather case, and stood up. "No one would be foolish enough to try that here."

"Why not here?"

"Well"—he blustered for a minute—"we never *have* been robbed. I presume it's because any would-be thieves know that it would not be wise."

"Hiram—"

"Not only am *I* a proficient shot"—he puffed up measurably—"but you *have* attained a certain . . . reputation, shall we say, as a lawman."

"Dammit, Hiram." Dan grabbed his hat, leaned toward the desk, and pinned the other man with a steely gaze. "Mike Connor is one of the best lawmen I've ever met. Smart, good with a gun, and not much gets past him, I can tell you."

Hiram smirked.

"And the bank in Short Hill got robbed anyhow."

Hiram sniffed. "Short Hill! In a town that small? How much could they possibly have gotten?"

"About twenty thousand."

"Dollars?"

Dan jerked him a nod. "There was a special shipment. The guards spent the night in Short Hill. Didn't expect any trouble. Nobody was supposed to know about the gold." He pushed himself to his feet and stood towering over the banker. "But somebody knew. And that somebody took it right out from under 'em."

"That won't happen here, I can assure you, Sheriff."

"How can you be so damn sure?"

"Because *I* am the only person who knows the exact arrival date of that shipment." He, too, stood up and almost raised up onto his toes in an effort to meet Dan's gaze squarely. "And I'm hardly likely to tell . . . am I?"

He scooted out from behind his desk, took several rapid, small steps to the door, and turned the knob. "Now, Sheriff. If you'll excuse me, I'd like to get to Selma Tyler's for my supper."

Dan inhaled slowly. Shaking his head, he walked to the door and jammed his hat down over his too long hair. One last glance at the shorter man told him that Hiram hadn't paid a bit of attention to any of his warnings. Not that he'd expected him to.

But it would make his job a helluva lot easier if folks would just *listen*.

"Listen!" Leda jumped from Max's lap and pulled the blanket out from under him. Throwing it around her shoulders she stood, head cocked, finger across her lips.

"What?" Max whispered, reaching out to run the palm of his hand over her hip.

She shook her head fiercely, sending long red curls flying about her. "Listen, Max. I heard something."

He paused for a long moment, then said, "There's nothing, Leda. Now, come back over here."

"Yoooo-hoooo!"

"See!" Leda whispered frantically and clutched the blanket even tighter. "Someone's downstairs!"

"All right, I'll go see," Max grumbled. He'd hardly had a patient to his name for three weeks, and the one time he *didn't* want one . . . He brushed the necklaces that had fallen to the floor aside and snatched up his pants. He dressed quickly, eager to see to whoever it was and get back to Leda.

"What should I do?" Her voice was so hushed he could hardly hear her. "I can't leave by the back stairs. Someone would see me."

"Don't do anything. Just stay here and I'll take care of whoever's down there."

"Anybody here?" the mystery patient called.

"Curses and swears," Leda mumbled and kicked the blanket away from her feet.

Max stomped his feet into his shoes and crossed the floor. As he stepped out onto the landing, he threw her a quick smile. "I'll be right back."

She nodded grimly and drew the blanket up under her chin.

He closed the door behind him, took another step and heard a rattle of some kind. Glancing down, he saw that one of Leda's necklaces had somehow attached itself to the heel of his shoe. Grumbling, Max grabbed the rope of sky-blue beads and stuffed it into his pants pocket as he went downstairs.

August Haley stood in the entry hall craning his turkey neck this way and that in his efforts to see everything. Max sighed. Naturally, it *would* be August.

"Hey, Doc!"

"August." Max nodded and thought of Leda, dressed only in that quilt, just upstairs. "What is it?"

The older man's eyebrows lifted. "Bit snappish this evenin', ain't we?"

If you only knew, Max thought and shoved his hand in his pocket to finger Leda's beads. "Is there something you need, August?"

"Who, me?" He shook his head and gray wisps stood out around his mostly bald skull. "Nope. Just dropped in to say hey."

Max clamped his mouth shut. It wouldn't do the slightest bit of good to get angry. August wouldn't care anyway. The best thing to do, he told himself, was to be polite, get rid of him, and get back to Leda.

"Well," he said, "I'm a little busy right now and—"

"Seen Leda lately?"

"I beg your pardon?"

"Leda. Your new partner. Ya seen her?"

"Why?"

"Oh, just wonderin', is all." He opened the hall closet and peeked inside.

Max scowled as August quietly closed the door again, a frown of disappointment on his face. The old gossip was looking for news.

"Hear tell," the man whined, "you and her is gettin' thick as honey."

If the old coot knew that Leda was upstairs right now, Max thought, his teeth would probably fall from his head.

"Yessir, think it's right interestin'." August peered into the examining room.

"What is?" Max's foot tapped on the floor.

"Well, how you two is hittin' it off, so to speak."

"Why's that?"

"Well"— August glanced at Max—"seems like you spend all your time fixin' up the folks she breaks!" His dry cackle of a laugh sounded like shingles sliding off an old roof. "S'pose you two'll make quite a team!"

We might have, Max told himself. If she had agreed to marry him. The old man's voice whined on but Max hardly heard him. Instead, he was remembering Leda's nervous reaction when she'd heard August's arrival.

The frantic look on her face, the blanket she held to her like a suit of armor . . . she really *was* afraid of a scandal and the ruin of his practice. Max frowned thoughtfully. Leda was determined that no one in town learn about the two of them.

But, he told himself as August stepped past him to snoop into the kitchen, if someone *did* find out—*and* if that someone just happened to be the town busybody . . .

Max smiled.

He glanced back at August, then quickly pulled Leda's necklace from his pocket. Taking a half step toward the staircase, Max laid the gleaming blue beads across the fourth step. Briefly, he admired his handiwork, then turned and leaned on the newel post as August walked back to join him.

The old man scratched his head, looked at Max from the corner of his eye, and said, "So. Anything interestin' happen around here 'ceptin' Julius?"

"Wouldn't you know if it had?"

"Well, I don't get around as good as I used to, y'know."

Max shifted position a bit so August would be facing him—and the stairs—squarely.

"Stopped by to see Julius," the man said.

"Uh-huh." What's wrong with him? Max wondered frantically. Why doesn't he notice the necklace?

"Seems fine. Bit crotchety"— he sniffed—"like some others I could name."

He should have seen it by now. And once seen, he would figure out quickly that Leda had gone up those stairs to Max's room. Recently.

"Course, Flora's all tuckered out, what with fetchin' and carryin' for him."

"Uh-huh." Maybe if he sat on the second step, Max thought and lowered himself slowly.

"An' then, too, Flora's prob'ly worryin' over young Jenny."

"Huh?"

August bent his head low and whispered in a tone loud enough to carry across the street, "Young Jenny's got herself a beau!"

"Really?" Was the man blind? Did he need glasses?

"Yup. An' you won't never guess who!"

"Sean Malone?"

August's satisfied smile drooped from his lined cheeks. "You see 'em too?"

"See who?" For heaven's sake! He had to be looking right *at* the damn thing!

"Jenny and Sean, o'course!" August leaned even closer. "Seen 'em myself, not twenty minutes ago. Cuddled up so close you couldn't have slipped a moonbeam between 'em!"

That rattling laugh sounded again and his narrow chest shook.

"Yessir, they was kissin' and whisperin' and kissin' some more for nigh on fifteen minutes or so 'fore ol' Flora come out to use the necessary and caught 'em!"

Max spared a moment's sympathy for Sean, facing an outraged mother. The fact that August Haley had watched the young couple for at least fifteen minutes didn't surprise him in the least.

August grinned. "Flora chased Sean off then Jenny run cryin' to the house and then . . ."

The old man's voice faded off and it was a full minute before Max noticed that August wasn't looking at him. Instead, his sharp, pale green gaze was locked on a spot just behind Max.

The necklace.

At last.

"Hmmm . . ."

With a great effort, Max kept his features blank.

August straightened up slowly as if giving his creaky bones a chance to get used to the idea. His gaze flicked from Max to the necklace and back again. Then, Max watched as the town snoop thoughtfully glanced toward the head of the stairs.

Max could almost *see* wheels turning in the old man's mind. August's nose twitched, bushy gray eyebrows arched, and his lips pursed around a low whistle.

"Well," he finally said and started backing toward the door, his eyes still on the staircase. "I best get goin', Doc. Telegrams to send, y'know." His eyes rolled up as if he could see through the ceiling to the room above. He stumbled when he backed into the wall, said, "See ya tomorrow, Doc!" opened the door and fled into the growing darkness.

By tomorrow afternoon at the latest, Max told himself, everyone in Tanglewood would know about Leda being in his bedroom. He grinned, jumped up, snatched the necklace, then ran up the stairs to the woman waiting for him.

* * *

Two days later, August *still* hadn't talked and it was driving Max crazy.

What was the old fool waiting for? Why hadn't he done any gossiping? Had he suddenly experienced a surge of conscience? And if he had, why *now* for God's sake?

Max crossed his office floor and stopped beside the front window. Staring out at Main Street, he watched the shadows lengthen and, one by one, the flame of oil lamps appear behind curtains. Sundown. Soon it would be full dark and Leda would come to him.

On one pretense or another, she'd managed to be with him both evenings since their first night together. Max smiled, laid his palm against the cold, clean windowpane, and told himself he should stop worrying and simply enjoy what they'd found in each other's arms.

But it wasn't enough. He didn't want to sneak around in the darkness, hiding from people. He didn't want a few stolen hours, here and there. He didn't want to have to remember to speak in whispers so no one would hear them. Max suddenly turned from the window and leaned back against the wall, staring at the emptiness of his office.

He wanted *all* of her. He wanted to walk down Main Street with her hand tucked through the crook of his arm. He wanted to live to be an old man and watch the lines of loving etch themselves into her features.

Dammit. He wanted more. And if August Haley didn't start talking soon, Max had no idea how he would convince Leda to marry him.

"You just keep your nose out of it and your big mouth shut for a change!"

"But, Gladie . . . she was up there. In his *room*."

Gladys scowled at him. He'd been saying the same damn thing for two days now and she was beginning to wear down. Oh, she'd find a way to keep the old buzzard quiet, but that

whinin' voice of his was startin' to pound on her head like
a blacksmith's hammer.

"That ain't none of your concern," she told him.

"But, Gladie . . ."

"No." Gladys stood up, walked to the kitchen, and grabbed
an onion from the nearest shelf. She picked up a knife and
waved it at the man across the room. "You start flappin'
your lips about Leda and so help me, August—"

He shifted from foot to foot in a frenzied dance of
anticipation. "But this here's big news! Folks'd be mighty
interested."

She frowned thoughtfully. He was right, of course. She
knew darn well that most folks jumped on a good piece
of gossip faster than a duck on a bug. And gossip about
the town doctor and Leda . . . well, it would be big news
indeed.

But she wasn't gonna have anybody talkin' about Leda.
Not like that. Why, the girl had been as good to Gladys as
if she were her daughter. Hmmph! she thought suddenly.
Leda'd been better than blood. Hadn't Lester, her very own
son, up and moved to San Francisco without givin' a thought
to his mother?

With the thought of Lester came memories of Geraldine.
His wife. Gladys gritted her teeth. That female may have
Tanglewood fooled, but she didn't fool her mother-in-law.
The only reason that woman had talked Lester into moving
to San Francisco was to get away from Gladys. She didn't
want an old woman hangin' around.

Gladys sniffed and pushed troubling thoughts of her family to one side. There'd be plenty of time to think about *them*
two in the years to come. Right now, the most important
thing she had to do was find a way to keep August quiet.

"Gladie, folks're gonna find out anyhow," he argued.

"Not from you."

"Well, why not me?" He slid his thumbs under his suspenders and snapped them against his narrow chest. "It was
me that found out! Only right that I be the one to tell the

story." August's bottom lip curled into a pout. "I got me a reputation. Folks kinda *expect* me to know what's goin' on and if I don't tell, well . . . *somebody's* gonna find out sometime!"

Deliberately, Gladys set the razor-sharp knife edge on the onion, then sliced through it, the knife slamming home onto the wooden table.

August flinched.

"You open that durn mouth of yours, August, and I'll tell every livin' soul in town about the time you stole that horse."

He paled visibly. "Gladie, you wouldn't do that to me."

"You just see if I won't." She stared at him long and hard. "Let's see now, it was on that ride you and me, my mister, and Jack took to Texas that time on a buyin' trip. I remember Jack's wife, Minnie, was s'posed to go, too, but she come up expectin' and couldn't leave home."

"But that was twenty years ago!" He shuffled his feet nervously and turned his wide green eyes on her in appeal.

"Sure was"—she nodded—"but I remember it all like it was last night."

"Nobody around here knows nothin' about that, Gladie!" He shot a nervous look about the empty room.

"Course not. Me and my man promised to be quiet and Jack sure as hell didn't want Minnie findin' out that he was drinkin'. But with Jack and Minnie both gone now, folks in town *could* find out."

"*Twenty* years ago!" he whined. "That whole horse thing is long since over."

"Don't matter, stealin's stealin'."

"Didn't steal that durn horse." He straightened up and squared his shoulders. "I *borrowed* it."

"That ain't what Jack Sholter said when they caught up to ya."

"Jack was drunk." August shifted uneasily. "He didn't remember tellin' me I could use that animal."

"That's what ol' Sheriff Johnson figured," she agreed. "Course, if you *didn't* steal it, how come you went and hid out? *And,* there was still what happened to that cathouse you was hidin' in."

"Gladie!" he snapped, clearly surprised that she would even *mention* a place like that. "I didn't start that fire!"

"Says you."

"I was there." He lifted his pointed chin just a bit. "I ought to know."

"Yeah." Gladys smiled without a trace of humor on her face. "That's what *she* said too. That you was there. As I recall, she said a few other things too."

August flinched again.

"What was her name, now?" Gladys tapped the flat of the knife against her chin thoughtfully and rolled her eyes heavenward. "Oh yes. *Now* I remember."

August stretched his neck and pulled at his shirt collar.

"Sadie. Saddle Sadie." Gladys looked at him from the corner of one eye and enjoyed the discomfort she saw written all over him. She never would have guessed that August Haley was the blushin' kind of man. "Now, I wonder how she come to be called *Saddle* Sadie . . ."

"That don't matter any," he said quickly.

"True," she answered, though truth to tell, she *had* always wondered about it. Whatever could the woman have used a saddle for? Gladys shook her head, narrowed her eyes, and stared at him. "What matters is you burned that cathouse to the ground."

"Gladie—"

"The way I recall it happenin' "—she tilted her head back as if lost in thought—"Sadie's place went up in just a few minutes."

"Gladie—"

"All that wood, y'know. Like a tinderbox, it was."

"Ah, Lordy—"

"Why, Sadie's girls was runnin' all over that town, screamin' for help. And hardly a one of 'em was wearin' more than lip rouge."

August grimaced slightly at the still fresh memory.

"What was it Sadie said that night . . ."—she paused dramatically—"*before* she come into all that money and left town?"

August groaned.

"Oh yeah, she was sayin' somethin' about how you rode that horse right through her front door and up the stairs." Gladys grinned. "Said you was so drunk you didn't even know you was still on that horse when you started shoutin' how you needed a place to hide."

"I was, uh . . . just funnin' with 'em."

"Uh-huh." Gladys picked up the two halves of onion, set them on two different plates, and walked back to the main room. She set the onion halves at opposite ends of the room, then turned to look at him again. "S'pose you was still funnin' when you knocked over that oil lamp and Sadie's girls run for their lives?"

"I never saw that oil lamp."

"Don't reckon not. As I recall, it was a pure wonder that you could see the horse!"

"Gladie," August pleaded, "that there was a long time ago. I'm a telegraph man now. I got responsibilities. Folks look up to me."

She rolled her eyes.

"You can't tell the town all that. Not now. I'm an old man!" He tried desperately to look pitiful.

Slowly, Gladys walked across the room to stand right in front of him. She waited until he looked her in the eye, then she said softly, "You an' me are the only two left who know about that night, August."

He scowled.

"An' you got my word on it that I'll keep quiet."

He sighed heavily.

"As long as *you* keep quiet about the doc and Leda."

August inhaled deeply, frowned then gave her a brief nod. "All right. I'll do it." He shot her a quick glare. "But it ain't fair, Gladie. It just ain't fair."

Gladys allowed herself a small smile.

CHAPTER 16

"There y'are, Sheriff," Cooter said and tossed the wadded-up bills to the desktop. "You can cut Deke loose now."

After looking at the pile of crumpled money, Dan glanced at the younger man warily. It was much too early in the morning to have to deal with this. He hadn't even had his first cup of coffee yet. Hell. The *sun* was hardly up. His gaze shifted to the front window, and in the distance, he could just make out the stirrings of light. Deep lavender touched the sky with only the barest hint of dawn.

Sighing tiredly, Dan looked at the stove in the far corner of his office and the blackened coffeepot sitting atop it. Damn. Coffee still wouldn't be ready yet.

"Sheriff?"

"I heard ya." One by one, Dan smoothed each crinkled bill and stacked them neatly before looking up again. The younger man seemed nervous. The twitch in his right eye was as bad as ever. But this morning, the man's whole body seemed to jerk in time with his eyelid. The man was obviously jumpier than a fish on a line.

Slapping his palm down on the stack of cash, Dan suddenly found himself wondering where the fella'd come by it. When he left town a few days ago, he'd said he was broke.

And it was mighty unusual for a busted, down-at-the-heel man to find the amount of money *this* one had.

The silence lengthened, and with every passing minute, the kid got more jittery. As if he were expecting trouble. Dan leaned back in his chair and glanced at the far wall, papered with Wanted posters. No help there, Dan already knew. He'd spent the better part of a day going through them and the dozens more in his desk. Nothing. Either this fella and his partner weren't wanted for anything—or most likely, there just wasn't any paper out on them yet.

"C'mon, Sheriff," Cooter said, clearly skittish with Dan's silence, "you gonna let Deke out or not?"

Dan tilted his head and studied the nervous man. There was something about this Cooter fella and his partner that bothered him. Something . . . *wrong*. He couldn't put a finger on it. But there was something.

In the few days he'd had Deke in jail, though, the man hadn't said more than a word or two. Almost as though he was afraid to talk. Curious.

But with no Wanted posters on them, and no more reason to hold either one of them, he had to let them go.

"Yeah." Dan pushed himself to his feet, snatched up the key ring from his desk, and walked back to the cells. He heard Cooter following him and immediately wished he'd had ol' Eye-twitch go first. Even in the best of times, Dan didn't like folks being behind him. And he was especially uneasy now. There was a strange itch between his shoulderblades, like he was bracin' for a bullet. Or a knife.

Mentally, he snorted at his own fancies. It was *much* too early in the morning to be dealing with this bunch.

"Cooter!" the prisoner yelled and Dan winced. He wouldn't be sorry to see Deke go, that was for sure. The old bastard might not say much—but everything he *did* say he said at the top of his lungs.

"How ya doin', Deke?" his partner called.

"Doin'? What the hell do ya *think* I'm doin'?" The man jumped up from his cot and stomped to the cell door where his fingers gripped the iron bars fiercely. "I'm settin' in here *rottin'* waitin' on you!"

Deaf as a post, Dan told himself.

"Quit standin' there, then," Cooter urged him as the cell door swung open.

"*Standish?*" Deke yelled back. "She here too?"

Dan glanced at Cooter and saw the man pale.

"I *said,*" Eye-twitch yelled, "don't stand there. C'mon!"

"I'm comin'," Deke shouted. "No need to yell!"

"Stay out of trouble, y'hear?" Dan said as the bigger man passed him.

"I hear just dandy," Deke countered.

Dan snorted.

"We ain't lookin' for trouble," Cooter added.

Dan motioned for the two of them to go first out of the cells. He followed close behind. "You two leavin' town now?"

"Any reason we should?" Cooter asked.

Dan reached into the bottom drawer of his desk, pulled out Deke's pistol and holster and returned it to him. "No," he said calmly, then asked, "Any reason why you want to stay?"

That right eye started twitching at an alarming rate. Dan stared at it, fascinated.

"It's a nice little town." Cooter shrugged, not even sparing a glance at his partner as he threw his holster around his hips. "Why not?"

Dan rested his right hand on his own pistol negligently. "No reason, just figured you boys'd have a higher time someplace else."

"No hurry." Cooter shrugged again.

"Worry?" Deke yelled, his brow furrowed. "What'cha worried about, Cooter?"

"I ain't worried," he shouted back.

Yes you are, Dan thought absently. But about what?

"Anyway," Cooter said, "we best be goin'. So thanks, Sheriff."

"What about the bank?" Deke yelled.

"I didn't say 'bank.' I said 'thanks'!"

Dan's head began to pound.

"All right, all right," Deke called out. "Just wonderin' why you was askin' the sheriff about the *bank*."

Cooter's right hand curled into a fist tight enough to make his knuckles white. What's goin' on here, Dan wondered, that he didn't know about?

"C'mon, Deke," Cooter said angrily and pulled his partner toward the door. "Let's go get somethin' to eat. It'll make ya feel a lot better."

"Well, all right," Deke yelled, "but can't we get somethin' to eat before we talk to Cecelia?"

Eye-twitch about jumped out of his boots. Quickly, he shoved the other man out the jailhouse door and into the street. Dan wandered slowly to the open doorway and watched the two men as they moved down Main Street toward the rooming house.

Now just who in the hell was Cecelia? And what about this Standish? And why was Cooter so afraid of them?

Cecelia accepted the stage driver's hand, lifted the hem of her deep blue day gown, and climbed into the coach. She took a seat against the driver's side of the stage and smoothed her skirt unnecessarily. Though she didn't much care for facing the wrong way while traveling, she knew from experience that those unfortunate people sitting opposite her would spend most of the trip enveloped in a cloud of dust.

Nodding politely to the woman directly across from her, Cecelia Standish mentally dismissed her.

Well past the first bloom of youth, the woman's timid smile displayed a crooked front tooth. She wore an obviously homemade gown, and what was worse, she wore it badly. Dirt-brown hair escaped a limp bonnet untidily and her wide-set, huge brown eyes reminded Cecelia of a cow.

The man beside "Bossie" made a deliberate effort to distance himself from his seat companion, then gave Cecelia what she supposed he must consider a promising smile. Absently, she told herself that he should refrain from smiling at all, considering the state of his yellowed teeth. She turned away when he began to tug at his hopelessly vulgar checked vest.

Cecelia sighed and gazed pointedly out the open window frame. Apparently, she wouldn't have any diversions on the short trip to Tanglewood. Ah well, she told herself, perhaps it was best that way. Now, she could concentrate solely on the task at hand.

She glanced up at the vivid, deep blue morning sky. The sun's arrival streaked the undersides of the few clouds in shades of pink and violet. A soft, cool wind brushed past her and caressed her cheeks. If only she wasn't trapped on this bloody stage.

And if not for Cooter and his dim-witted cohort, she wouldn't be. At least not yet. She hadn't planned on being in Tanglewood for another few days yet. But it was too late to think about that now, she told herself. And too much worrying would only create more of those nasty little lines in her face. Besides, a bit more time in town certainly couldn't hurt.

Cecelia knew that Cooter would have Deke out of jail by this time and the two of them should be busy looking over the lay of the town. It still irked her that she'd had to pay good money to settle Deke's debts. But whether she liked it or not, she needed both men if she was to carry out her final job.

And the Tanglewood bank *would* be the last. She'd decided only the night before that it was time to retire to Europe. She'd had more than enough of having to socialize with the coarse, ill-bred inhabitants of backwater towns. It was time she found a place where she would be appreciated for the woman she was.

"Excuse me," a deep voice said and Cecelia was startled out of her thoughts.

An absolutely exquisite man had opened the stage door and was now poised, ready to climb inside.

Cecelia's quick gaze took in the stranger's night-black hair, strong jaw, and deep brown eyes. He wore a flat-crowned black hat, a white shirt, and a dove-gray vest under a freshly pressed black jacket. What she could see of him looked to be tall and lean.

"I beg your pardon?" she said softly.

He grinned and Cecelia's mouth went dry. Dimples.

"I said excuse me, ma'am."

"Miss," she corrected quickly.

"Miss." His eyes touched her more thoroughly then and she sat up a little straighter. Prouder. The stranger nodded toward the seat beside her. "I'd appreciate it if you could tuck in a bit of that lovely dress of yours, so's I could get by without damaging it."

At last, Cecelia thought with delight. A man worthy of notice. And a pleasant diversion, indeed, during the trip to Tanglewood. Obligingly, she swept the hem of her gown out of his way and he climbed inside.

The stage swayed as he entered, and when he sat beside her, it was all Cecelia could do to keep her hands to herself. She watched him from the corner of her eye as he smiled politely at "Bossie," then nodded at the other man.

Finally he turned to her, an admiring gleam in his brown eyes. Cecelia inclined her head graciously and gave him what she hoped he recognized as a smile of interest.

"If you'll forgive me for sayin' so, miss," he said, and his deep voice was low-pitched. Intimate. "You are beautiful enough to shame the dawn."

She folded her hands demurely in her lap before saying, "You're forgiven. And thank you."

"Not at all." He stretched out his long legs and the black fabric of his pants clung to his muscular thighs. "I'm pleased to have the honor of your company on this little trip. Will you be riding with us for long?"

Cecelia suddenly wished that she were riding that stage for the next few days at least. Unfortunately, they would reach her destination by the next morning.

"Actually," she answered, "I'm only traveling as far as Tanglewood."

"Really?" His grin spread wider across his too handsome face. "Well, that's where I'm headed myself. Going to visit an old friend."

"Isn't that a coincidence?" Perhaps, she told herself, since she would have a few extra days in town, she could amuse herself with this delightful male. Cecelia was beginning to feel very forgiving toward Deke for having caused all of this.

"Maybe you would allow me to buy you supper one night?"

She swallowed her smile and said playfully, "But we haven't been introduced."

"I *am* sorry, Miss . . ."

"Standish," she replied, holding her hand out toward him. "Cecelia Standish."

He took her hand gently in his and rubbed his thumb across her knuckles. "My pleasure indeed, miss. My name is Connor. Mike Connor."

Leda walked through the early-morning hush, breathing deeply of the still damp, cool air. Under her bare feet, meadow grass wet with dew cushioned her steps. She pulled her black shawl tighter about her shoulders and lifted her face into the gentle wind that teased at her hair.

Even though she'd been getting very little sleep in the last few days, she'd found that she still woke long before dawn. And for that, Leda was thankful. She would never tire of the mornings, she knew. Before people woke up and brought their own sounds and noises to life, there was a magic, a certain quiet about the world.

Leda bent down and picked up a small fallen pine branch. Lifting it to her nose, she inhaled the fresh, clean scent and let the perfume of it seep through her.

So much beauty, she thought as her gaze moved over the now familiar countryside. So many things to wonder at and enjoy. And so few who took the time to notice.

She glanced back at the town, just down the slight hill. Tanglewood was beginning to stir to life. Soon, the children would be going to school, Garrett would open the store, and another day would start. How lucky she was to have been given so many of these days when she'd expected so few.

Leda smiled, tossed the pine branch back to the ground, and began a slow walk toward town. Max would be awake by now, she thought. Max. A tingle stretched up her spine and she felt the warmth of it snake throughout her body.

Absently, she rubbed her good-luck coin between her thumb and forefinger. How she hated to leave him in the dead of night, to sneak back to her own home like a thief. Tearing herself from his side was becoming more and more difficult. She wanted to lie beside him all night long, listening to the pattern of his breathing and the steady beat of his heart. She wanted to awaken in his arms and tease him into joining her on her predawn walks.

Leda stared down the hillside at the doctor's office and saw her beloved open the door. A soft smile curved her lips as she watched him step out onto the boardwalk. Her heartbeat leaped merely at the sight of him. And even at a distance, she felt the strength of her love blossom and grow deep within her.

Throwing his arms wide, he stretched lazily and a warm curl of desire sparked in her belly. His movements were now so familiar to her, such a part of her, she sometimes felt as though she were drowning in him. Max glanced up at the sky, then looked around Main Street as if searching for someone. Leda held her breath, willing him to turn his gaze to the hillside. She knew he was looking for her. She felt it as surely as she did her own heart-beat.

As he turned to go back inside, Leda grinned and lifted the hem of her skirt. A quick run down the hill and she would be in his arms again.

She took a half step and stopped when a sudden gust of wind caught at her. Her hair whipped up into her eyes, her striped skirt lay flattened against her legs, and the cold air seeped into her bones.

Leda shuddered and threw a quick glance at the sky. No sign of a coming storm. The same few, lazy clouds wandered across a wide expanse of blue. And yet a chill grabbed her and she felt in her bones that a storm was, indeed, headed their way. All at once, though, just as suddenly as it had appeared, the wind faded away again, leaving nothing behind to mark its existence expect the goosebumps on Leda's flesh.

Instinctively, she ran. She didn't feel the pebbles and sticks bruising her feet as she raced out of the meadow and across the narrow path snaking down the hillside.

Her only thought was to get to Max. To feel his arms around her. To forget the chill in her bones by burying herself in his warmth.

"Don't see why she couldn't feed us anyhow," Deke yelled, making Cooter wince.

Pulling away from his partner, Cooter glared at him and said, "Ya don't have to yell! I ain't deaf. *You* are!"

"Deaf?" Offended, Deke raised his voice to new heights. "I ain't deaf! I can hear ya fine."

"Then stop shoutin'. My head's about to bust!"

"Cuss? I didn't cuss at ya! What're ya talkin' about?"

"Shit." Cooter shook his head in disgust. A day startin' out as bad as this one was bound to get worse. He looked up at the man he'd been traveling with for four years. Ol' Deke was really somethin' when they first started ridin' together. And, Cooter told himself with a burst of loyalty, bad ears or not, Deke was still the fella he wanted alongside him if shootin' started.

A man didn't have to hear good to shoot good.

But Lordy, he wished his partner would just shut up now and again. Not only had Deke shouted out Cecelia's name in front of the sheriff, but now he was drawin' all sorts of attention to them. Cooter could feel the interested stares directed at them from behind closed curtains.

If the damn female who ran the rooming house would just open up and serve them breakfast, Cooter'd feel a lot better. With his mouth full of food, Deke wouldn't be able to talk! And they'd be off the street for a while. Then, once the whole town was up and movin' around, him and Deke could look the place over. With folks out doin' their daily business, nobody was likely to notice a couple of strangers wanderin' around.

He just felt so dang . . . *naked* standin' out in the open like they were now. Especially with Deke bellowin' loud enough to wake the dead! Cooter glared at the still closed door behind them. Surely fifteen minutes had gone by! Why wasn't she openin' up?

"Say, Cooter," Deke shouted, "looka there!"

He followed the direction Deke's pointing finger indicated and saw a young woman, red hair flying out behind her, running down the hill toward town. Briefly, Cooter admired the sight of her milky-white legs and bare feet, telling himself she must be in some kind of hurry to be showin' herself off like that. Why, she had the hem of her dress pulled up almost to her thighs!

He grinned, rubbed his jaw, and looked up at Deke.

"Pretty, ain't she?" his partner shouted.

"She surely is a sight," Cooter agreed and glanced back at the approaching woman. Instinctively, he hitched his baggy pants a little higher, tugged at his coat, and prepared to give the little lady his best "pleased to meet ya" smile.

As she came nearer, though, Cooter's smile began to fade. Slowly at first, a creeping realization wormed its way through him. A knot formed in the pit of his stomach and the weight of it grew heavier with every passing second.

Something niggled at the back of his mind. Poking at him. Taunting him.

Her nicely shaped legs were bringing her ever closer and Cooter spared a quick glance up at his partner. But Deke's features hadn't changed one whit. The older man's gray whisker-stubbled cheeks were split in a wide, admiring smile.

Looking back at the woman, Cooter saw that she'd neared the edge of the livery stable and still hadn't slowed down. Then he noticed the ropes of beads and charms around her neck that bounced and swayed with her movements.

Red hair. Necklaces. Like a gypsy.

Sweet Jesus!

"It's her," he whispered and felt his throat tighten. "Damned if it ain't the woman from Red Deer."

"I don't need to hear nothin'," Deke assured him, his smile still in place. "And my eyes work just fine."

She ran past them without a glance in their direction and Cooter watched openmouthed as she leaped up on the boardwalk and entered the doctor's office right next door. When the door slammed behind her, Cooter punched Deke's shoulder.

"What?"

"Don't you know who that is?"

"Huh?"

"That woman!" Cooter leaned over and got right in the older man's face. With a quick look around, to make sure no one was in hearing range, Cooter said clearly, "It's that damn female from Red Deer."

"Huh?"

"The one we was supposed to take care of?" Jesus! Did he have to say it aloud? Had the man's memory gone the same place as his hearing? "The one"—he paused and looked over his shoulder furtively—"the one *Cecelia* told us to take care of?"

Cooter watched his partner as recognition finally dawned. The older man's features creased in worry lines and he looked over his shoulder at the door where the redheaded woman'd disappeared before turning back to Cooter.

"What d'ya figure we ought to do?"

Amazed, but grateful that Deke had whispered his question, Cooter said, "What the hell do ya think? We got to get rid of her."

"I don't know."

"Deke." Cooter grabbed his partner's shirtfront and brought the man's bad ear close. "If Cecelia finds out that female's here, in Tanglewood, what do you figure she's gonna do?"

Deke grimaced. "She surely won't be pleased."

"Yeah, I think that's safe to say. But if we get rid of her before Cecelia gets here . . ."

"Shit, Cooter. Her stage'll be here by tomorrow."

"I know, dammit." Hell. He didn't even know if he could do it. Bein' a thief was one thing. Didn't seem so bad, takin' from those that already had more than their fair share. But bein' a killer . . . that was somethin' else again. So far, workin' for Cecelia, all he'd had to do was tap a body on the head with his gun barrel. Even ol' Queenie didn't know that him and Deke had never killed anybody before!

But what other choice did they have? If they didn't get rid of that girl, Cecelia would sure as hell get rid of them. He'd seen it in her eyes before. That was a cold woman. And he was damn sure she wouldn't have no trouble at all pullin' a trigger.

"So we ain't got much time, do we?" he finally said, regret and worry tinging his voice.

"No, but how you gonna . . ." Deke rubbed his whisker-stubbled cheek hard.

"I ain't figured that out yet. But it better look like a accident," Cooter mumbled, "else the law'll be up in arms right when ol' Queenie hits town." Besides, the thought of havin' to tell the boss about stumblin' onto the woman was enough to give Cooter cold chills.

"All right, you two!"

Cooter jumped and spun about. He hadn't even heard the rooming-house door open. But the woman who ran the place was standin' in the doorway, hands at her hips, staring at them.

"You can come on in now," Selma Tyler said grudgingly. "Breakfast'll be ready in a few shakes." She shook one finger at them in warning. "But you keep it down, now. Y'hear me? It's too durn early for any noise."

As she turned to go back inside, Deke followed her. Cooter, though, stood where he was. Suddenly, inexplicably, he wasn't hungry anymore.

"Max?" Leda shouted as she came through the front door and slammed it shut behind her. "Max?"

"Back here."

His voice came from the kitchen and Leda hurried down the hall. She stepped into the room and stopped. Max was standing with his back to her, pouring a cup of coffee. Her gaze slipped over his broad back as she remembered the feel of his strength beneath her fingers. He reached into the cabinet to his right and pulled down another cup and Leda watched the sunlight play on his hair.

The kitchen fairly glowed in the early morning sun. Rays of light streamed through shining windowpanes and painted bright patterns on the freshly scrubbed floorboards. Brand-new, bright red curtains fluttered in the breeze and the gleaming bottoms of the pans hanging on the opposite wall reflected her own image back at her a dozen times. The whole room smelled of soap and polish and Leda couldn't help but remember the night the kitchen had been put to rights.

After that first glorious joining in Max's bed, they'd come downstairs, knowing that they'd better have a clean kitchen to show her uncle the following morning. She smiled inwardly at the memory. Heaven knew, she'd never had such a good time cleaning.

And when the room was sparkling, in the soft, pale yellow light of an oil lamp, Max had laid her down on the still damp floor. Now, she could almost feel his mouth on hers. The warmth of his hands, the surrounding scent of soap, the cool touch of the towel-draped wood floor against her back.

Hot color flooded Leda's cheeks as she stared at the floor, her mind's eye creating an image of her and Max together.

A low, deep-throated chuckle sounded close to her ear. Leda jumped, startled to find Max standing beside her.

He held out a cup of coffee toward her, bent down and placed a gentle kiss on her forehead. "Good morning, Leda."

"Good morning, my love."

Max smiled at the endearment and Leda's heartbeat staggered.

"I know what you're thinking," he whispered, "because I haven't been able to step into this kitchen without thinking the same thing."

She leaned into him and laid her head on his chest.

"Leda?" Max asked as he set his coffee cup down on the table beside them. "Are you all right?" His hands curled over her shoulders and pulled her far enough back from him so that he could look into her eyes.

Leda nodded, her fingers tight around the handle of her cup. Now that she was here, with Max, she was fine. It was almost hard to remember exactly why that cold wind had frightened her so.

Down the hall, the front door opened and they heard a voice call, "Doc? Leda? Anybody here?"

Walter Bunch, the barber. Leda's lips quirked slightly. She knew from experience that Walter's only problem was that he enjoyed being sick. In the last three days, the man had been to the office first thing every morning. After a long talk with Max, Walter always insisted on Leda preparing a special tea for him. Something to soothe his "nerves."

And no matter how silly the man's complaints sounded, Leda'd noticed that Max took the time to listen carefully. He didn't seem to be as abrupt as he once was.

"Our first patient." Max chuckled and bent to slant his mouth across hers. When he reluctantly pulled away again, he said, "Drink your coffee, partner. I'll go deal with Walter."

He hadn't taken more than a step or two when Leda stopped him with a hand on his arm. For some reason, she didn't want to be alone. Not yet. That indefinable sense of dread she'd experienced when the wind sprang to life around her had begun to creep back. "We'll go together," she told him softly.

He held out his hand, waiting.

Leda set her coffee cup down and laid her palm in his.

Max's fingers closed around hers and the two of them walked down the hall to greet Walter.

CHAPTER 17

Max ducked as he left his office. Congratulating himself on avoiding the too-low bunches of herbs hanging from the ceiling to dry, he grinned. He must be getting used to dealing with Leda, he told himself. Of course, he'd already been slapped in the face by the damned things three times that day.

But it was a small price to pay, he thought, for the pleasure he'd found in having Leda's company. And as he recalled the stream of patients he'd seen in the last few days, he had to admit they *did* work well together. Between his medicines and her warm compassion, they made quite a team.

He stood for a moment in his hall and looked at the changes she'd wrought in just a few days. The herbs, of course. And wildflowers in several different types of containers were scattered about the entry—no, he corrected himself with a grin, not the entry. Leda's office. And indeed, it certainly was more her than him these days. From the horseshoe over the door to the cobalt-blue bottle that held her rosewater cologne, right down to the table supporting her crystal ball.

The smile dropped from his face as he stared at the glass globe. Max knew he would never be comfortable with that symbol of Leda's belief in Fate—Destiny. Although, he acknowledged silently with a glance at his feet, even now he was wearing one of several pairs of red socks he'd purchased from Garrett. But he shrugged off his concession by telling himself there was no sense in taking chances.

And he'd feel a lot better about his ability to keep her safe if they were married and able to be together openly all the time. Frowning, Max admitted that he was no closer to convincing Leda to marry him than he'd been before she'd come to his bed. And he was getting desperate. If August didn't start talking soon, Max was going to have to start the rumors himself.

"What are you thinking?"

Startled, Max blinked, looked down into Leda's smiling face, and lied. "I was thinking about how beautiful you are."

She moved into the welcoming circle of his arms and tilted her head back to look at him. "You should have been thinkin' about coming back to the kitchen to help with supper."

"Oh." He grinned. "Is it that time already? I hadn't even noticed." Another lie. Since she'd been coming to him at night, that was all Max thought about. He'd found himself *willing* the sun to set.

Leda's eyes glazed over and she sighed softly.

"What is it?"

"You're doing it again," she said.

"Hmmm?"

"Touching me."

"Oh." He shook his head as he noticed that his hand had indeed moved from the small of her back to caress her breast. It was almost as if his body had a mind of its own. And he was grateful for it.

"Max," she breathed and stilled his restless hands with her own. "We'll never get supper cooked if you keep that up."

"I'm not hungry anyway."

She chuckled and stepped back from him. "Maybe not. But I'll wager Uncle Garrett and the boys are."

True. And even though Max had enjoyed taking most of his meals with the Malones, tonight he wished they'd fix their own supper. All he wanted right that minute was to carry her up the stairs to his room and close the door on the rest of the world.

Leda turned and started for the kitchen. Over her shoulder she told him, "I only wish I had an orange to give you."

"An orange?" What on earth?

"Oh, they're wonderful, Max. Haven't you ever had one?"

"Of course I have." He started following her and couldn't help but admire the sway of her hips. Deliberately, though, he tried to keep up with her conversation. "But why would you give me one now?"

She stopped, half turned to face him, and grinned. "Because oranges are love fruit. And eating an orange hinders *lust*."

Max leaped across the few feet of space separating them and swept her up in his arms. "In *that* case, Miss James, I will *never* eat another orange!" Her hands on his shoulders, he held her high overhead and let her laughter pour over him. Greedily, he drank it in, relishing the warmth that filled him whenever she was near.

Maybe, he told himself, he shouldn't have been so quick to dismiss Leda's brand of "magic." Certainly, she'd touched and changed him in a way that was nothing less than magical. All the dark, lonely spots in his soul were banished each time she smiled at him. And with every kiss, she was drawn deeper into his being until he could hardly remember his life without her.

"Max?"

"Shhh . . ." He lowered her slowly, brushing their bodies together until her lips were only a whisper from his. He watched her eyes soften with the same desire that coursed through him. She snaked her hands around his neck and leaned into him. Max's arms encircled her waist, holding her tightly, and then he kissed her. His mouth moved over hers with a familiar hunger. And when he dipped his tongue inside her mouth, she met each of his caresses with an eager abandon.

Her fingers slid into his hair and Max groaned at her touch. The fire she created in his blood never seemed to diminish. It only burned brighter, hotter. His blood raced through his veins and he felt his body tighten in anticipation. He shifted position slightly and leaned back against the doorjamb. His hands moved up and down her back, and when tremors rocked her, Max felt them move through him as well.

"Doc!"

The front door slammed open, crashing into the wall behind it.

Max tore himself away from Leda and set her on her feet. He gasped for air like a drowning man and steadied Leda as she wobbled at his side.

"Doc!"

His gaze flew to the frightened woman standing silhouetted in the open doorway at the end of the hall. Trying to clear his head, Max gave himself a shake and started walking. He heard Leda right behind him, but his concentration never wavered from the woman wailing at him.

"Doc, she's not any better." Flora Lloyd's voice was high, strained, and quaking with a fear that seemed to have a life of its own.

"Flora, calm down," he said in a practiced, even tone. "What is it? Who's not any better?" Flora's usually neat topknot had slipped to one side of her head and wisps of hair straggled down along her cheeks, framing her face. Her eyes were awash with unshed tears, and even in the dim lamplight, Max could see the woman was pale and shaky.

Immediately, he grabbed her arm and tried to pull her to the nearby chair, but she wouldn't be budged.

"It's Jenny. My Jenny," she groaned. Her hand was clutched around her throat as if she could drag the words out. "She's layin' in her bed all curled up with the pain."

"Pain?" he asked, already moving to the office for his medical bag.

"Leda," the woman said anxiously, grabbing at the younger woman's hands, "*you* remember. I had her here earlier. Her belly was botherin' her and you said it was prob'ly just somethin' she ate. Remember?"

Max came back into the hall in time to see Leda nod.

"Well, it's worse now. *Much* worse." Flora dropped Leda's hands and turned to the doctor. "I don't know what to do, she keeps cryin', and if I try to touch her, she about screams." Her voice shot up another octave. "Doc, you gotta come." She grabbed at him and started to drag him out the door.

Max glanced over his shoulder as Flora pulled him across the boardwalk. Leda's face was chalky-white and her lips were pressed firmly together. Something was terribly wrong.

Hands clenched in front of her, she said only, "I'll wait right here, Max."

He didn't have time to wonder why her voice sounded so odd, or even why she looked suddenly so . . . desolate. Shaking Flora's hand off, Max started running. With Jenny's terrified mother falling far behind him, he reached the Lloyd house behind the gunsmith shop in a matter of seconds.

Dan Nichols propped one foot on the brass rail, leaned his elbows on the plank bartop, and nodded at the bartender. "Evenin', J.T."

"Sheriff."

"Get me a beer, will ya?"

"Sure thing," the man answered and grabbed a tall mug before moving to the keg at the far end of the bar.

Dan closed his mind to the distractions surrounding him. He paid no attention to the other customers at the bar, the tinny piano music drifting out over the jostling crowd of cowhands and drifters, or the raucous laughter and stomping coming from upstairs.

J.T.'s girls knew better than to bother him when he stopped by. They'd discovered long ago that the sheriff plain wasn't interested. The only woman Dan wanted in his life was out of his reach and he refused to console himself with tawdry substitutes.

He shook himself deliberately, pushing away old, painful memories that had nothing to do with his present life and problems.

Besides, all he really wanted was a couple of minutes to drink his beer and try to figure out why Mike Connor was on his way to Tanglewood.

J.T. slid a mug of cold beer under his nose and Dan immediately lifted it and took a long drink. When he set the glass back down, he let himself recall the latest telegram he'd received just a couple of hours ago.

BE IN TOWN TOMORROW MORNING STOP HAVE
MORE INFORMATION STOP THINK YOU SHOULD KNOW
ABOUT IT STOP SIGNED MIKE

What kind of information? And why couldn't he just send it in the telegram? Dan shook his head, drained the last of his beer, flipped a coin onto the bar, and turned to leave when a voice in the crowd stopped him.

Deke. There was no mistakin' *that* voice, he told himself wryly. Covertly, the sheriff looked around the room until he found the man he was looking for. Deke was in a corner, clearly enjoying himself with the blonde on his lap. The girl laughed and Deke shouted something into her ear just before she stood up and began to tug him toward the stairs.

Dan watched them climb the steps to the rooms above, then he left the saloon. Standing on the wide porch, he leaned against a post and stared thoughtfully at the back sides of the stores lining Main Street.

If Deke was upstairs with Molly, he asked himself, just where in hell was Cooter? And what was he up to?

*   *   *

Cooter stifled a sneeze, glared at the bush he was hiding behind, and tried to stretch his cramped legs one after the other. He'd been waitin' for what seemed hours and there was still no sign of her.

Wasn't that damned woman *never* gonna go home?

Glancing up at the black sky overhead, Cooter frowned and told himself time was wastin'. Queenie was due in town the next morning and if she found the gypsy girl alive and well—him and Deke sure wouldn't be for long!

He snorted, rubbed at his nose, and silently admitted that even if the girl stepped off the back porch this very minute, he still wasn't sure just what it was he could do to her. Aside from shootin' her, that is. And Lord knew, he couldn't do that. With a bank robbery comin' in the next few days, the last thing Cecelia would want is a murder to rile up the town.

His nose began to itch again and this time he couldn't stop the resulting sneeze. Following the explosion of sound, Cooter clapped his hands over his nose and mouth as though he could undo the damage.

Immediately, the back door of the doctor's office flew open and Leda James was standing there in a patch of lantern light.

"Max?" she called.

Cooter stared at her and couldn't help but admire the way she filled out her clothes. Course, he told himself, she couldn't be none too bright. The doc had left by the front door about fifteen minutes ago. Why in tarnation would he come around to the back now?

Females. He snorted. Damn women. First Queenie, now this gypsy. Nothin' but trouble.

Leda went back inside and Cooter let go of his mouth and changed positions behind the bush. It looked like it was gonna be quite a while before she headed home. Might as well be comfortable, he told himself. Going onto all fours, he at least gave his legs a bit of a rest from squattin'.

He tensed suddenly and cocked his head, straining to listen. Pebbles and pine needles bit into the palms of his hands and he was kneeling on what felt like a boulder. He held his breath, waiting. After a long moment or two, he began to relax. Huh, he laughed silently. For a minute there, he'd thought he'd heard . . .

There it was again. Louder this time. Closer. *Deeper.*

A dog.

And by the sound of it, a *big* dog.

Cooter dropped to the dirt, curled into a tight ball, and wedged himself even farther beneath the bush's concealing branches. Every few seconds now, he heard a *woof!* It was a sound that was deep, angry. Maybe, he told himself . . . *hungry.*

Dammit!

Anxious snuffling came within a few feet of his face and Cooter knew it would all be over soon unless he could stay hidden. Hopefully, he thought, the dog's sense of smell wasn't any too good. Carefully, he lifted the edge of a leafy branch to sneak a peek at the animal. He stifled a groan when he saw four shaggy white feet the size of bear traps.

As if that wasn't bad enough, Cooter felt his nose begin to itch again. His fingers shot up to curl over his nose, desperately trying to quell the urge to sneeze.

Leaves over his head trembled with his movement and he prayed like he hadn't in years, as the itch in his nose began to grow and blossom. Tingles spread from his nose to his cheeks and up into his brain. He pulled in a staggering breath and clenched his teeth. His features twisted with his efforts, Cooter squeezed his eyes tightly closed and lost his battle.

"AH-*CHOOO!*"

The sneeze of a lifetime shot from his throat and nose. Sound seemed to echo around him, going on and on. His heart sank and Cooter tensed, sure what would happen next.

Just inches from his face, the leaves parted and he was eyeball to eyeball with the biggest dog he'd ever seen in his life. The animal growled and the noise rumbled through its massive chest before scraping along Cooter's spine. Eyes wide, he let loose a panicked scream that sliced through the air just before he jumped to his feet and began to run.

But his cramped legs would barely support him. He moved across the expanse of grass and dirt like a drunken spider and he was no match at all for the four very large, very strong legs chasing him. And still he ran. *Anything* was better than surrendering to the beast snapping at his heels.

Just as he rounded the corner of the gypsy's house, Cooter felt teeth sink into his backside. Pain shot through his cramped body and somehow lent strength to his wobbly legs. He yelled again, found a last burst of power somewhere deep inside him, and yanked himself free from the slobbering animal.

Vaguely, Cooter heard a child's voice calling, "Arthur?"

The dog halted immediately and Cooter spared it only a quick glance as he kept running. He wasn't surprised in the least to see a tattered piece of his trousers hanging from Arthur's jaws.

Cooter was sure he could still hear the dog's snarls as he sprinted toward the millpond and the cool water that would feel so good on his behind.

Max raced through the open office door, Jenny Lloyd cradled in his arms.

Leda stood by helplessly as she watched him lay the young girl on his examining table. Poor Jenny's features were taut with pain and every groan that escaped her lips felt like a knife slicing into Leda's heart.

"Leda?"

She shook herself as Max came up to stand in front of her.

"Leda, it's her appendix." He laid his hands on her shoulders, and briefly, she felt his calm confidence seep into her. His pale blue eyes looked down at her with a gentle urgency. "I have to operate and I'll need your help."

"Operate?"

They turned as one to see Flora Lloyd in the doorway, clutching the bag she'd carried for Max. Just behind her stood Sean Malone. Leda thought of all the times she'd heard Dennis and Michael teasing their older brother about his feelings for Jenny. And tonight, she told herself, the depth of those feelings were clear in his grim features and his frightened eyes.

"Yes, operate," Max repeated. "And as quickly as possible."

"Ooooh . . ." Flora swayed and Sean caught her.

"Sean," Max ordered, "you stay with Flora. Leda, you come with me." He grabbed her hand and pulled her into the examining room.

As he moved to close the door, Sean's tight voice stopped him. "Is she gonna be all right, Doc?"

"I hope so, Sean." He reached out and took his bag from the girl's terrified mother. "I'll do my best."

Leda watched her young cousin and swore she saw him age and mature in the flash of an eye. Sean nodded stiffly, swallowed back any other questions he might have had, wrapped one lanky arm around Flora and guided her back to the kitchen. Leda heard him whispering, "I'll make you a cup of tea, Mrs. Lloyd."

When the door closed, Max clutched his bag and immediately set to work. He crossed the room, opened one of his glass-fronted cabinets, and began to rummage inside.

As if from a distance, Leda watched him. Jenny's moans of distress seemed to swell until they enveloped the room, crowding out any other sound. Leda stared at the girl, lying so helplessly, and listened to the accusing voice in the back of her mind as it raged at her.

Why didn't you see that the girl was ill? Why did you send her home with some raspberry tea? Why didn't you have Max look at her?

Desperately, she longed to have the afternoon back. She wanted to live the day over. To pay more attention. To *see* what she'd obviously overlooked.

Leda pushed her hands through her hair and gripped each side of her skull as if it were about to explode. She had no answers. Not to any of the accusations running through her brain and not to the fear gripping her now. She didn't *know* why she hadn't sensed Jenny's illness was serious.

She *should* have. She should have *felt* it. What was wrong with her? Where was her "gift" when she'd really needed it? Was it gone? Had she ever really *had* it?

Jenny cried out and Leda gasped with the pain. If Jenny died, how would she ever live with herself?

"Leda!"

Leda couldn't hear him. She couldn't even hear the questions in her mind anymore. All she heard was Jenny's pain. All she could see was Sean's fear and Flora's terror.

"Leda!"

Max, she thought numbly. What must he think of her?

"Leda, I need you!"

"Oh God, Max." A low, miserable groan wracked her. Leda's words came pouring out as her gaze locked on the girl across the room. "Jenny's sick. And I didn't see it. I didn't feel it." She looked up at him and found no comfort in his stern, no-nonsense features. "Why not, Max? Why couldn't I help her?"

He grabbed her and gave her a little shake before pulling her into his arms for a brief, hard squeeze. Then, setting her back from him again, Max spoke in a harsh tone that demanded her attention.

"Stop it. We don't have time for you to feel sorry for yourself *or* Jenny. Do you understand?"

Sorry for herself. Is that what she was doing? Leda thought frantically. Jenny writhed on the table, her knees drawing up to her chest. Leda's stomach turned to water and she forced air into her lungs. Max was right. There would be

time enough later to deal with the doubts and questions
plaguing her.

Squaring her shoulders, Leda lifted her chin, met Max's
eyes, and nodded. "What do you want me to do?"

"Good." While he watched Jenny, he whispered, "If you
think you can do it, I'd like you to give her the chloroform
while I operate."

She bit back the protest she wanted to scream at him.
The thought of witnessing an operation was enough to send
fingers of dread crawling up her spine. But there was no
one else and she knew it.

"I can do it."

"You're sure?" he asked.

He watched her and Leda made a frantic attempt to look
more confident than she felt.

"You won't faint in the middle of things?" he whispered.

"I'm sure." Leda inhaled sharply. "And no. I won't faint."
Not if she had to prop herself up. She owed Jenny that much
at least. She willed the fluttering in her stomach to ease. "Just
tell me what to do."

Quickly, Max outlined the procedure for her. He handed
her a small cone-shaped object and a bottle of chloroform with instructions to be careful not to breathe it in
herself.

As Leda took up her position at the head of the table, she
concentrated solely on Jenny's face. Though she could hear
Max setting out his instruments and washing his hands, Leda
paid no attention. Instead, she whispered encouragement to
the frightened girl.

"It's all right now, Jenny."

"I hurt, Leda." Her lips quivered and her chest rose and
fell rapidly with the gasping breaths shaking her. "Really bad."

"I know, honey." Leda's fingers moved gently across the
girl's brow, smoothing back her long chocolate-brown hair.
She fought back the urge to cry, knowing it wouldn't help.

"But Dr. Max is going to help you. Soon you'll feel so much better. I promise."

"I heard him. He's going to . . . *operate*."

Leda glanced up at Max and he nodded, telling her silently not to lie to the girl. He needn't have bothered, because Leda never considered lying in the first place.

"Yes, he is"—she bent close and looked into the girl's warm brown eyes—"and you're a very lucky girl, Jenny."

"Why?" She bit down hard on her bottom lip.

"Because Max is a wonderful doctor. In a week or so, you'll be out walking with your beau again."

"Can you *see* it?" the girl asked quietly.

Do hopes and wishes count as visions? Leda wondered frantically. Her fear mounting with every moment, Leda hesitated. "Yes," she said firmly. "I see it." It's not a lie, she insisted to herself as her mind dredged up an image of Jenny and Sean, arm in arm.

She laid her fingertips on Jenny's brow. "And I'll stay right here with you the whole time."

"Promise?"

"I promise."

"All right, Leda, you can start now."

She looked up then and saw that Max had aligned several oil lamps, their wicks turned as high as possible, so that the light would fall on the table. He stood opposite her, a fresh white apron over his clothes. His sleeves were rolled up back over his elbows, his face was calm, his hands steady. She tried not to look at the small silver knife his fingers held so easily.

"All you have to do, Jenny," she said, slipping the cone over the girl's nose and mouth, "is breathe normally."

"What'll happen?"

"You'll fall asleep and dream"—Leda's voice dropped to a crooning whisper—"and when you wake up, it will all be over."

"Sleep?" Jenny mumbled as the first drops of chloroform fell onto the cone.

"Yes, honey. Sleep." Her voice caught on the knot in her throat. "Dream about my cousin. That handsome young man of yours," she urged.

"Sean," Jenny sighed and slipped quietly into a deep, even sleep.

"Are you ready?" Max asked. "I may need you to hand me the instruments."

"I'm ready, Max."

He nodded briefly, bent his head and began.

Leda watched his every move, and despite her fears that her stomach would betray her when she could least afford it, she was far too fascinated to think of being ill.

Max's hands were magic. *Real* magic. He moved so swiftly, so surely. Every movement was perfect, like a well-rehearsed dance. His eyes seemed to see everything at once and he never faltered or hesitated.

In the rush of pride she felt in his skill, Leda was spellbound. She moved only when his deep, commanding voice requested an instrument or a square of linen to mop sweat from his brow.

What she'd thought would be the longest hours of her life instead passed so quickly, she scarcely noticed her own weariness. Until, after taking the final stitch in Jenny's flesh, Max announced, "It's over, Leda. She's going to be fine." He sighed tiredly as he shook out a sheet, drew it up over his patient, and tucked it under her chin.

Relief was almost painful. Leda pulled in a deep breath, set the cone and bottle down on the table behind her, and looked at the peacefully sleeping girl. Jenny was fine. In a few weeks, or maybe even days, she would be feeling like her old self again.

Because of Max.

She glanced up and saw him moving around the small room, cleaning up his equipment and washing his hands again. He acted as though he'd done nothing special. As if the . . . *miracle* he'd just performed were nothing more wondrous than pulling a sliver from a child's hand.

But she knew better.

What must it feel like, she wondered, to be able to do what Max had done?

Leda looked down at her own hands and wasn't surprised to find them shaking. She felt as though everything inside her were breaking up. Splintering into a million pieces. She looked up at the man now standing beside her and told herself that he was the real magic. *He* was the one with the true gift.

All of her herbs and teas and potions made little difference in the world. Her "visions" and her crystal ball suddenly seemed like nothing more than parlor tricks. But Max . . . Max could save a child from death. He could give young Jenny the opportunity to grow old enough to watch her great-grandchildren playing at her knees.

"Leda?" he asked. "Are you all right?"

"Yes." She forced the word out despite the fact that she thought she might never really be all right ever again.

"I have to go tell Flora the good news," he whispered with a glance at Jenny. "But first, I want to say thank you. I've never had a better nurse."

"Thank you?" She shook her head. "I didn't do anything, Max. Nothing."

"You took away Jenny's fear." He cupped Leda's cheek with one hand and turned her to face him.

It wasn't enough, she screamed silently.

"Max." Her chin trembled as she fought a silent battle against the tears threatening to burst from her. "Flora brought Jenny in earlier today. Her stomach hurt. You were busy with someone else. And I gave her raspberry tea and sent her home."

"But Leda, sweetheart, you couldn't know."

"I *should* have known. Don't you see? I *should* have sensed that she was in trouble."

"Leda . . . without you—" Max pulled her into his arms and gave her a brief hug. His strong, talented hands pushed through her hair, his fingers moving gently along her scalp. "You made it possible for me to help her."

He was being kind. Leda closed her eyes tightly and told herself that it didn't matter what he said. She knew the truth.

And as much as she craved the feel of his arms around her, Leda stepped back after only a moment. He had more important things to do than hold her hand and offer her sweet words that couldn't possibly fill the emptiness building inside her.

"I'm all right, Max. Why don't you go tell Flora and Sean?" Her light tone was forced, but she prayed he wouldn't notice. "I'll stay with Jenny."

He nodded and walked to the door. But before he stepped through it, he turned for another look at Leda. "I'll be right back. Don't go away."

She didn't even wonder how he'd known that all she wanted to do was run blindly into the darkness.

CHAPTER 18

"That ain't news," Gladys snorted. "Everybody knows about last night and Jenny's operation."

"Don't ya think I *know* that?" August complained and plopped himself down beside a freshly frosted chocolate cake. As he picked up the knife and carved himself a huge slice, he went on. "I'm talkin' about what Flora Lloyd saw when she went to get the doc."

"What're you talkin' about, old man?"

"I'm talkin' about . . . she seen 'em too!"

"Seen who?"

"The doc and Leda—with their lips stuck together like they was nailed shut."

"Oh." Gladys frowned. "I hadn't heard."

"Course you hadn't. You ain't hardly left the house for three days." August dipped his finger into the frosting appreciatively, stuck his finger in his mouth, and rolled his eyes like a man bound for heaven. "Natur'ly, Flora was too upset last night to think on what she saw right off— but once the doc told her Jenny was fine and dandy . . . well! Ol' Flora started talkin' and she ain't stopped yet!" He glanced at the brown wool in Gladys's lap. "Still tryin' to get that sweater knit, are ya?"

She balled it up in her gnarled fingers. "None of your business."

"Hmmph!" August forked up a huge bite of cake, shoved it in his mouth, and talked around it. "I only come to warn ya that you can't be tellin' that horse-stealin' story against me now."

"I will if you start talkin'."

"Gladie, that ain't right." Offended, he swallowed, took another bite, and said, "It ain't like I spilled the beans. Flora's already done that." He leaned toward her, leering. "Folks is just buzzin' with the news too." A short, wheezing laugh shuddered through his chest. "That operation of Jenny's is just gettin' tucked under a rug. And when they hear what *I* seen for myself—hell. Folks'd much rather talk about sin than savin'."

That was true enough, Gladys told herself. Though if there weren't so many sinners, she doubted there'd be much use for church or the Good Lord, either, for that matter.

"Anyhow," August said, pushing the last two bites of cake into his mouth and standing up, "I only come to tell ya that the doc and Leda is fair game now. So don't you go ruinin' my reputation none with tall tales out of a past best forgotten."

Gladys glared at him. "Oh, take yourself off, you old goat. Go bother somebody else for a change."

"Well, now. That's a fine thing, I must say. Insultin' your old friends!"

She picked up the yarn again and methodically began to pull the last few, uneven stitches out.

"Oh say, that yarn there reminds me."

"What?"

"Garrett says there's a package for ya down at the store. Come all the way from San Francisco."

"And just what is it about my wool here that reminds you of a package from Lester?"

"Not from Lester. From Geraldine." He grinned when she frowned. "Anyhow, it's that durn sweater you're forever

messin' with. I recall Geraldine tryin' to figure out how to
help ya with it and you layin' in to her."

Gladys fumed silently. It was hard enough admitting she
wasn't the knitter she used to be. She didn't need August
remindin' her about Geraldine's clumsy attempts to help.

Dammit! Her hands couldn't hardly hold a knitting nee-
dle anymore—and her "too rich to work," fancy, city-girl
daughter-in-law never bothered to learn! Just wasn't fair
any way a body looked at it.

"Whatcha s'pose Geraldine's sendin' ya?" August's eyebrows wiggled with interest.

"How in tarnation would I know that?" she snapped. "And
if I *did* know, I wouldn't be tellin' *you*! Now git!"

The old man's laughter hung in the still air and seemed
to taunt her even after he'd shut the door behind him.

Geraldine? Sendin' a package?

Tiredly, Gladys pushed herself out of the chair and reached
for her shawl. Might as well go collect it now, she told
herself. Get it over with. Besides, maybe she could have a
little talk with Leda, too, while she was at it.

Prepare the girl for the gossips' waggin' tongues.

The stage rolled up right on time and came to a stop
outside Malone's Mercantile. Cooter and Deke plastered
themselves against the side wall of the store and peeked
around the corner of the building.

"Don't see why we're hidin'," Deke complained, much
too loudly.

"Course you don't," Cooter snapped. "I swear, if you
didn't have me around, you'd be in prison full-time by
now."

"How the hell d'ya expect me to know the time? I ain't
got a watch and you damn sure know it."

Cooter's eyes rolled heavenward, and when he inched
closer to the edge of the building, he winced as renewed
pain shot through his butt.

"Still smartin' some?"

"It hurts like hell."

"An' ya say a *dog* bit ya?"

"That's right."

"In the ass." Deke muffled his snort of laughter. Barely.

"It ain't funny, you halfwit."

"Don't see why you want to sit, if it hurts that bad."

"Shut up!" Cooter ignored his partner and stared at the passengers as they stepped down from the coach. First some woman he'd never seen before. Next, an oldish fella with an ugly vest. Then a well-set-up man dressed in black climbed out and reached his hand back into the coach.

Cooter swallowed heavily.

Cecelia stepped out and his breath caught. No matter what else she was, Cecelia was a right handsome woman. No two ways about it. From behind him, he heard Deke sigh and knew his partner was thinkin' the same thing.

Ol' Queenie smiled up at the big man, then looked around at the town. Instinctively, Cooter jerked back, unwilling to be seen just yet. Deke was too close and the man's hip slammed into Cooter's backside.

He bit down hard on his lip to keep from yelping. The gash was almighty sore and likely to stay that way for quite a while yet. Course, he told himself, pourin' good whiskey on it prob'ly hadn't helped the pain any. Waving one hand at Deke, he managed to get the man to back up.

"Ain't we gonna talk to her?"

"Not now. Why d'ya think we was hidin'?"

"Hell, I don't know."

"So's folks won't know we know her, that's why!" He started limping along the side of the store, toward the back. There was only one place in town where the boss could stay. The rooming house. All him and Deke had to do was go there for breakfast and let Cecelia see them. *She'd* find a way for them to meet.

"Ain't this about where you were when that dog bit ya?"

"Yeah," Cooter muttered, his gaze flicking this way and that nervously.

"Think it's out and about now?"

"Maybe." Cooter tried to hurry a bit. Truth was, he didn't want to risk a shot, but if that damned hound showed up to finish him off . . . he swore that he'd shoot it dead.

Dan reached Mike just as the other man was nodding a goodbye to a beautiful blond woman. "See you didn't mind your stage ride any," he said and held out one hand when his friend spun around.

Mike grasped the outstretched hand with his own and grinned. "Good to see ya, Dan. And no, I didn't mind it one little bit. Matter of fact, I'm takin' that lady to tea this afternoon."

"Tea?" Dan laughed. "In Tanglewood?"

"Jealousy's an ugly thing, my friend."

"What's her name?"

"Oh no," Mike countered and caught his bag as the driver tossed it down. "I'll not make it *that* easy for you."

Dan shook his head. Mike Connor could find a good-lookin' woman in the middle of the desert. But no matter *how* pretty they were, he never paid them more than passing attention.

"What brings you here, Mike?"

His friend's smile faded and his brown eyes narrowed thoughtfully. "Why don't we go over to your office, Dan? This might take us a while."

Leda hadn't been in all morning.

Max scowled, tossed the dregs of his coffee into the sink, and stared out the kitchen window at the Malone house. He didn't know *why* she was staying away, but he had a sinking feeling that she wouldn't be coming back on her own. And now that Flora had arrived to sit with Jenny, Max told himself, maybe it was time *he* went to *her*.

But first, he thought with sudden inspiration, first he'd go by the Mercantile. Maybe Garrett had an idea of what was wrong.

He marched down the hall toward the front door and snatched his jacket off the peg as he went. Glancing in the room where Jenny lay, Max called out, "I'll be back soon, Flora."

A quickly strangled twitter reached him just before the woman sang out, "Goin' callin' on Leda, are ya, Doc?"

"Yes," he said slowly, "as a matter of fact, I am."

Another muffled laugh floated out to him.

"Not surprised," Flora singsonged.

"Flora?"

"Uh-huh?"

"Are you all right?"

This time, he was *positive* he heard Jenny chuckling.

"Sure thing, Doc. Right as rain. You go on about your . . . *business* now, y'hear?"

He had the strangest feeling that Flora and Jenny knew something he didn't. Turning back for the door, Max decided to ignore Flora's behavior. After all, the woman had had quite a fright just the night before. It was only natural that she should be . . . He shook his head and went outside.

A busy day in town, he told himself. More than half of Tanglewood seemed to be dawdling in front of his office. Max noticed more than a fair share of smiles from the women and knowing smirks from the men directed at him.

Strange. Nonetheless, he nodded a brief greeting at those he hurried past. He barely glanced in the bank window and paid no particular attention at all to the lovely woman sitting at Hiram Adams's desk. Instead, Max's attentions were centered on Garrett's store. And seeing Leda.

He stepped into the Mercantile and breathed deeply of the warm, familiar scents that seemed to welcome him. From out of nowhere, Arthur rushed forward, leaped up, and planted his hairy forefeet on Max's chest. The dog's tongue lolled out one side of its mouth and shaggy white hair almost completely hid its eyes.

"Morning, Arthur," Max said and dutifully rubbed his hand through the dog's matted fur.

Arthur *woofed* and curled his upper lip as if it were stuck on something.

Pulling the dog's strong jaws open, Max looked closer. "Hold still, Arthur," he commanded futilely as the animal began to dance back and forth on its hind legs. Determined, Max craned his head to one side, stuck his finger under the dog's lip, and felt around blindly. When he touched what felt like soggy fabric jammed between the animal's teeth, Max pinched it between his fingers and pulled. When it came free, Arthur jumped straight up and swiped his tongue across Max's cheek.

"You're welcome," he assured the beast and pushed Arthur down. Squinting at the fabric, Max told himself that it looked like the kind of material used to make men's pants. "Now, how did you . . ." he started, then shook his head as Arthur rolled to his back excitedly, inviting Max to rub his stomach. "Good God! You took a bite out of somebody, didn't you?"

His tone, if not his words, convinced Arthur that he wasn't being praised. The dog quickly flipped over, pressed his belly to the floor, and slunk off into a corner.

Still staring at the cowering dog, Max jumped when a voice said, "Morning, Maxwell."

"Garrett!" he said and turned to face the man who'd just stepped out of the storeroom. "I pulled this piece of cloth"— he held it up as evidence—"from Arthur's teeth! That beast *bit* someone!"

Garrett's arms were crossed over his chest and his features were set in an unreadable mask. Lifting his shoulders in a careless shrug, he said only, "Whoever it was, I expect they deserved it."

"But—"

"Never mind the dog, Maxwell. You and me got somethin' more important than *him* to talk about."

For the first time, Max noticed that Garrett wasn't smiling. *And* he'd called him Maxwell in a none too friendly tone.

"Is something wrong?" Good God. Leda. He took three quick steps to stand just opposite Garrett on the other side of the counter. "Is it Leda? Is she all right? Is she sick?"

Nothing.

"Garrett, dammit! *Talk* to me. What's going on?"

For answer, Garrett unfolded his arms and waved one hand toward the front windows behind Max. "Look at that bunch. Like they got nothin' better to do!"

Max glanced over his shoulder and realized that the crowd he'd already encountered had followed him to the Mercantile. Most of them were standing idly in the street, but a few of the less timid souls had their noses pressed against the windowpanes.

What the devil was going on?

"Where's Leda?" he demanded suddenly, determined to get to the bottom of all this. Her disappearance the night before without so much as a goodbye, her absence this morning, Garrett's cold behavior, and that damned crowd.

"Home."

Max spun about, and took two steps toward the door before Garrett's harsh command stopped him cold.

"One damn minute, *Doctor*."

He swiveled his head slowly, warily, and watched Garrett step out from behind his counter and walk toward him.

"Just where d'ya think you're goin'?"

"To see Leda."

"Not just yet, I'm thinkin'."

Good God. "*What* is going on around here today, Garrett?"

"I think you know more about that than me, Maxwell."

"Max."

"Flora Lloyd's been tellin' everybody in town how you were all over Leda like hair on Arthur."

At the mention of his name, the dog's tail started thumping madly against the wood floor.

Max's mind leaped back to the night before. Instantly, he realized what Flora had seen when she'd come bursting into the office. But for God's sake! Even if it was a rather . . . energetic kiss, it was still just a kiss!

But judging from the expression on Garrett's face, the man didn't see it quite that way.

"Garrett, we were only kissing. That's all." Lord. He felt like he was ten years old again, trying to convince his father that the only reason he was looking under Lizzie Jane MacKenzie's dress was because he wanted to be a doctor, just like his father before him.

Garrett looked no more believing than the elder Dr. Evans had been at the time.

"That's not what Flora's saying." The big man's voice dropped like a heavy stone.

"Flora was upset."

"Uh-huh . . . and what about *August*?"

"What?" Perfect. August Haley had finally decided to start talking. Marvelous timing.

"August at least come to me before tellin' God and everybody else that he saw one of Leda's necklaces on the steps to your room."

"Oh." Well. What could he say to that? Since he'd never wanted to deny it, Max hadn't bothered to come up with a plausible excuse for Leda being in his room.

Garrett's chest expanded to a ferocious size as he inhaled. "That's all you've got to say? 'Oh'?"

"No, dammit," Max shouted. Why should he be so damned apologetic? He'd practically *begged* Leda to marry him. "That's not all. But what I've got to say, I'll say to Leda."

"You'll say it to me first, boy-o." The big man glared at Max. "Haley didn't stop his talkin' after me, y'know. And *them*"—he waved one beefy hand at the people outside— "they've already started whisperin'. In a couple of days, my girl's name won't be worth a liar's truth in this town."

Max fumed silently. Everything the man said was true. And he felt even worse about the whole mess when he remembered how he'd been wishing for the razor-tongued gossip to get started.

But Leda hadn't exactly given him a choice, had she?

"I'll straighten everything out, Garrett."

"Not before I know one thing."

"What?"

"Are you plannin' on marryin' my niece . . . or not?"

Max thought about not answering. But it wouldn't do him the slightest bit of good to be unreasonably stubborn. Besides, he supposed Garrett *did* have the right to ask. And if he had his way, Garrett Malone would soon be family.

Deliberately, he looked the man straight in the eye and calmly said, "Yes. I *do* plan to marry Leda."

Garrett's demeanor relaxed just a bit.

"In fact," Max added as he took another step toward the door, "I already *asked* her."

"That's good, though you might've come to me first."

"I didn't have the chance. She turned me down."

"What?"

"Don't concern yourself with that," Max soothed him, "because I don't intend to let her get away with it any longer either." Then he yanked open the front door and began to push his way through the fascinated crowd.

"Wonder what's goin' on over there?" Mike mumbled.

Dan glanced out at the still growing crowd and grinned. He'd already heard all the talk floating around town and he was only surprised that the crowd was still as small as it was. Ah well, he told himself. It's early yet.

Aloud, he said, "I do believe that's a weddin' party shapin' up."

"Poor fool," Mike muttered and turned his back on the scene.

"So, Mike. Why're you here?" Dan poured out two cups of coffee and set the pot down on the edge of his desk, right over an old scorch mark. "And while you're at it, where's your gun? And your badge?"

The other lawman picked up his coffee, sat down across from Dan, and started talking.

"My gun's right here." He reached around to the small of his back and pulled a revolver from his waistband. "My badge is in my bag."

"Why not wear it?"

Mike shrugged. "Thought it better not to announce my arrival."

"All right," Dan sighed and leaned back in his chair. "Let's hear it."

"Not too much to tell. When Short Hill's bank was hit, I wasn't there. Out roundin' up an escaped prisoner."

"Too bad."

"Yeah." He shook his head. "My deputy isn't worth the wind to blow him out of the territory, an' no one in town is sure of anything. Nobody but the banker saw anybody. And all *he* knows is some fella hit him over the back of the head and when he woke up the bank's gold was gone."

"So? That doesn't tell me why you're here."

"After the holdup, I asked around. It seems the only places being robbed were the towns gettin' in an extra big shipment of gold."

"And?"

He shrugged. "And I did some more checking and found out that Tanglewood was the next town in the general area that would be gettin' a shipment like that. So I figured I'd come down and offer my help."

"Lord knows," Dan said, "I ain't too proud to accept it. But what makes you so sure they'll hit us too? Maybe they've got enough. Maybe they left the territory."

"Maybe." Mike sat up and leaned toward the desk. "But I don't think so. I think whoever's doin' this is greedy enough to stick around and try to suck everybody dry. And I think this thief has some kind of inside information. How the hell else would they know where to strike?"

"Yeah, that thought did come to me a time or two."

"I'm a lawman and I had a helluva time findin' out about shipment schedules and such. Whoever's doin' this is real slick, Dan." He sat back in his chair. "So anyway, I reckon with both of us keepin' a sharp eye out, we might just catch this ol' boy red-handed."

"We might just at that." Dan grinned and lifted his cup in a silent toast. "And now that we got *that* settled . . . you gonna invite me to tea with you and your new 'friend'?"

"Not likely."

Cecelia bent double to see herself in the warped mirror hanging opposite her bed. Muttering oaths under her breath, she swore to herself that once free of this miserable wasteland, she would never again travel any farther away from New York than perhaps . . . Paris.

Her lips curved in anticipation of the marvelous life ahead of her once this last job was completed. And, according to the self-important peacock of a bank president, that gold shipment would be arriving in just two days.

It was difficult to keep from telling the odious little man that she already knew about the gold and when it would arrive. Cecelia smiled softly. The banker in the last town they'd hit had been so eager to impress her, he'd told her all about Tanglewood's coming prize.

And at least *that* man had been presentable. Not like Hiram Adams today.

Hmmph! She could still see the man, trying to maneuver her into opening an account with his establishment by telling her all about the shipment of gold he was being entrusted with. Fool. A smile, a fluttered eyelash, a demure chuckle —*those* were the weapons men were unable to defend against.

However had men come to the conclusion that *they* were the superior gender?

A tap at her window caught her attention and she scowled. How, indeed? she repeated silently as she frowned at Cooter, trying to hide his presence in the shadow of low-hanging pine branches.

Quickly, she crossed her room and lifted the window sash.

"Mornin', boss," he said softly.

"You imbecile!" Cecelia snapped. "What are you thinking, standing outside my room this way?"

"Nobody saw me, boss. And this tree here is almighty thick. Good place to hide."

"And where is your thick-skulled partner lurking?"

"Deke's down to the livery. Waitin' on me."

"Fine. Now what do you want? I've told you repeatedly not to contact me once we're in town!"

"Yeah, I know." Cooter shifted his weight to one leg, winced, and leaned closer to her.

Cecelia drew back a bit.

"Trouble is, you recall that little gypsy back in Red Deer?"

"Yeeesss . . ." She watched him warily.

"Well, the thing is, boss, she's here. In town."

"What?"

"Yes, ma'am, I mean, miss." He nodded his shaggy head like a drunken donkey. "Her uncle is the storekeep."

"Marvelous." What else could possibly go wrong, she wondered silently. Cecelia told herself that if the girl should happen to see her before the robbery, all of her plans would be ruined.

Cooter started talking again and she forced herself to listen.

"Well, now." He lifted his chin. "Deke, he wanted to just do away with her right off. But *I* told him we best wait to talk to you first."

"Did you?" Even *she* was amazed at the man's incredible stupidity. "Well, then, this is *your* fault."

"Huh?"

"Deke was right. You should have gotten rid of her before I arrived. You fool!" Quickly, her mind raced with possibilities, discarding one, considering another. She felt Cooter's vacant eyes on her and she had to curl her fingers into fists to keep from striking him. Finally, she simply said, "Cause an accident. However you want to handle it. Just make sure she doesn't see *me*!"

"Yes, ma'—"

She cut him off by slamming the window sash back down. The fact that she smashed his fingers in the doing gave her only a small sample of satisfaction.

CHAPTER 19

Max stormed around the corner of the Mercantile, took a few more steps, and stopped. Behind him, the crowd murmured anxiously as a dozen or more people tried to figure out what he was doing. He paid no attention to them, though. Instead, his gaze was locked on the Malone house, not more than fifty yards away.

Had Leda heard all the gossip circulating through town? Was she hiding from him because she was embarrassed? Ashamed of what they'd done together?

No. Immediately, his brain pushed those notions aside. Leda James was *not* the kind of woman to hide cowering in a house because of her behavior. The Leda *he* knew would walk proudly down Main Street—barefoot, no doubt—and dare anyone to say something to her.

Of course, she had been worried about what a scandal would do to his practice, he reminded himself. Max stuffed his hands into his pants pockets and took another couple of steps. The crowd moved with him.

He smirked quietly. Apparently, the only thing the town was interested in was seeing the conclusion to all this. It didn't seem to have struck anyone as *scandalous*.

Across the grassy expanse, the Malone front door opened

and Dennis stepped out onto the porch. The boy climbed onto the railing and sat straddling the wide wooden beam, his legs dangling on either side.

"Hi, Doc!" the boy called. "You comin' to see Leda?"

Max tossed a quick glance over his shoulder at the crowd. They all seemed to be holding their breath, waiting for his answer. Dammit. This was going to be hard enough, without being watched by an audience!

Hurriedly, he crossed the yard and came within a few feet of the porch. "Is she inside, Denny?"

"Nope." The boy shook his head.

"No?" Max looked past him as if expecting to find Leda peeking from behind the front-room curtains. "Well, where is she?"

"You remember where me and the boys and Pa go fishin'?"

"Yes." He thought of the sheltered cove. "I remember."

"That's where she is."

She was certainly going to great lengths to avoid him, Max thought irritably. And it wasn't going to work. If he had to follow her all the way to Montana . . . they were *going* to talk.

Suiting action to the thought, Max started off at a brisk pace.

"You goin' to find her?" Denny called.

"Yes."

Behind him, the crowd shifted as one and Max whirled around to face them. "All right," he said, with more calm than he felt. "If you're all so blasted interested in what happens between Leda James and myself, the least you can do is wait here and give me a few moments alone with her."

"We wouldn't never find out nothin' that way," August chimed in from the back of the group.

Max frowned and pushed one hand through his rumpled hair. How in the hell could he talk to her—*propose* to her— with half the town watching?

"If you don't leave us alone," he countered, "there won't be anything *to* find out!"

A murmur of disappointment rose up briefly then faded away.

"Reckon he's right," Walter Bunch grumbled.

Max watched the reluctant nods and disregarded the scowls directed at him. Immediately, he turned and ran toward the lake. He couldn't be sure they wouldn't change their minds and start after him again.

She'd been there since before dawn. Leda'd watched the sky's transformation from black to deep lavender to pink, and saw each color echoed on the water's surface. She stood at the lake's edge, staring out at the wide expanse of the deep blue pool. Occasional winds rippled the water, sending it in a race for shore where it lapped at the toes of her red wool socks.

She shivered slightly and drew her shawl tighter about her shoulders. With her free hand, she rubbed her good-luck coin and tried to understand what had happened the night before.

Everything she'd ever believed in was gone. Her faith in herself, her gift . . . everything. And in its place was an emptiness she'd never known before. What had happened to Jenny was proof enough that she had no "sight." And if she'd been wrong about that, she must also have been wrong about Max.

Leda blinked back a sheen of tears that blurred her vision. From the moment they'd met, she been so sure. So positive that they were meant to be together. She'd done everything on the strength of her gift. Her visions. She'd pursued Max with a single-minded dedication born of her belief in the rightness of their being together. But without those visions, she'd had to admit that perhaps she'd been wrong. Perhaps Max and she were no more suited than he'd claimed from the very beginning.

A brief gust of wind blew up from nowhere and shook

down pine needles from the tree branch overhead. They settled on her gently and Leda didn't even notice.

"What're we gonna do?" Deke whispered and Cooter stared at him, amazed. Even *whisperin'*, the man talked louder than anybody Cooter'd ever heard.

Lucky for them, the gypsy girl was far enough away to have missed it. He stared down the rocky incline at her as she stood at the edge of the lake. She'd been standin' like a statue for nigh onto half an hour and it was beginnin' to give Cooter the shivers.

Course, knowin' he was s'posed to kill her didn't help any either.

Ah hell! He cussed silently as he caught sight of the town doctor runnin' up the shore to the gypsy girl. Now they'd have to wait some more. Couldn't hardly have a accident that killed off *two* folks, could they? .

He didn't want to think too much about the surge of relief he felt at havin' to wait.

"Leda!"

She turned toward him and even her obvious dismay at his sudden appearance did nothing to stifle the surge of pleasure he felt simply at the sight of her.

When he reached her side, Max grabbed her shoulders and pulled her close against him. His hands moved over her back, and for the first time since after Jenny's operation, he felt whole again. After only a moment, though, he realized she was struggling to get free.

"What is it?" he asked and released his hold on her.

Leda stepped back away from him, wrapped her arms about her waist, and said softly, "Please go away, Max."

"No." Go away? Not a chance.

"Please," she repeated and turned her gaze back out on the lake. "I don't want to talk to you right now."

"You don't want to talk to me right now?" Incredulous, Max just stared at her. He saw the film of unshed tears in her eyes, the lift of her chin, and the rigidity in her shoulders. He'd been right. Something was drastically wrong. And she didn't want to talk about it. "Well, that's a damn shame," he said aloud and Leda's head snapped around toward him.

"What?"

"I said, that's a damn shame." Max reached out, grabbed her shoulders again, and turned her to face him. He felt her tension, but ignored it. By God, he was going to have his say!

"You don't want to talk?" he snapped. "Fine. You listen, I'll talk."

"Max—"

"No!" He shook his head and his hair fell into his eyes. "You disappeared on me last night, and I didn't go after you. I thought maybe you were just tired. My mistake." She lowered her eyes a bit and he wanted to shake her. "I waited for you this morning and you didn't come to the office. I listened to Flora's and Jenny's giggles *alone*." She looked up, startled, and he nodded. "Then I went to the Mercantile where Garrett could hardly speak to me without growling. And when I went looking for you, half of Tanglewood was following me."

"What?"

A cool breeze drifted in off the lake and lifted her hair. Max reached up, smoothed it back down, and inhaled the scent of roses.

"Oh yes," he said with a wry smile, "it seems that as soon as Flora got over her nerves about Jenny, she remembered seeing us kissing in the hall."

Leda groaned.

"Uh-huh." His fingers traced the line of her cheek and he was relieved when she turned her face into his touch. "And naturally, she couldn't let an opportunity to outshine August slip past her."

"She told people?"

"Everybody." He nodded and let his hands fall to his sides.

"And then *August,* plainly fighting to hold on to his crown, finally decided to tell about finding one of your necklaces on the steps to my room!"

"My necklace?"

Uh-oh. He'd forgotten she didn't know about that. "Never mind about that now," he said quickly. "The point is that all of Tanglewood is talking about us."

"I'm sorry, Max. Is that what you came here to tell me?" She shook her head slowly. "It's just what I thought would happen. Scandal. Now you'll lose your patients because of me." Leda paused a moment, turned her face into the wind, and added quietly, "Don't worry, I'll leave Tanglewood. That should bring your patients back."

"What?"

"Well, without me around to remind folks, they'll soon forget about all this. And you're such a wonderful doctor, your patients will forgive you the slip."

"Damn my patients!" Good God! Did she really believe all this nonsense she was spouting? Did she really think he would *ever* let her go?

"Max!"

"And damn you, too, if you think I'd let you leave me so I could keep a practice!"

"Max, I didn't mean—"

"I told you already, Leda," he said after sucking in a deep breath in an effort to calm himself. "*I'm* talking. You're listening."

Her lips clamped together tightly.

He jerked her a nod, took a few steps past her, then snapped around and came back again. Shaking one finger in her face, he shouted, "I *love* you!"

"Max!" She stared at him, eyes wide.

"That's right!" He shrugged and lifted his hands helplessly. "I love you. I don't know when it happened. Or even how. God knows I had no intention of loving you. Or *anyone* for that matter."

Leda's lips twisted together and he could see she was

trying desperately not to cry. Frustration left him in a rush and his whole body seemed to sag.

"See," he said quietly, "I decided a long time ago not to love anyone."

"Max—"

He held up one hand. "My father was a doctor. A good one. But I thought he cared too much. Every time he lost a patient, a part of him died too." Max shifted his gaze out to the lake and stared blankly until an image of the elder Dr. Evans formed in his mind. "I even traveled halfway across the country to set up my practice, because I could see my father was getting older. Weaker." He swallowed heavily. "I thought that if I was far enough away, the pain of losing him wouldn't be as sharp—as painful—as it would if I saw him every day."

"Oh, my love."

He shook his head. As hard as this was, he wanted to get it said at last. Turning back to look at her, he finished. "But it didn't help. He died and the pain was every bit as fierce. All I'd succeeded in doing was robbing myself of those last few years with him."

"I'm so sorry, Max," Leda whispered and laid one hand on his arm.

He jerked at her touch, but quickly covered her hand with one of his. Max's thumb moved over her knuckles gently as he went on. "When I met you"—he snorted a laugh— "to say I was surprised, wouldn't be quite covering it. But the longer I knew you, and watched you, the more I saw that you had something most of us lacked."

He looked at her and saw she didn't understand what he was trying to say.

"You *live* every moment, Leda. You see everything around you. You *love* with all your heart, holding nothing back."

One tear rolled down her cheek and Max reached up to brush it away with his thumb.

"When I first suggested we marry, I told myself it was

more to protect you than anything else. I couldn't admit—
even to myself—that I loved you." Max's bottom lip trembled slightly and he cleared his throat. "But as God is my
witness, Leda, I *do* love you. And if you leave, I'll follow
you. Because without you"—he sucked in a gulp of air and
felt the cold bite of it deep inside him—"I don't know what
I'd do."

She came into his arms and Max's chest heaved with the
force of his relief. It would be all right. She believed him.
She still loved him.

"Max," Leda whispered and placed a kiss on his throat. "I
love you so." He squeezed her tightly and she told her brain
to remember the feel of him pressed close against her. In the
years to come, she would want to remember. "But I can't
marry you."

He went deathly still. Leda tried to draw away, but he
wouldn't let her. His arms still wrapped around her body,
she could only tilt her head back to stare up into his wounded
blue eyes.

"Why not?" His demand was no less strong for the broken
whisper.

"Because I don't even know who I am anymore."

"You're Leda James. The woman I love."

"No I'm not."

Confusion written in his eyes, he simply stared at her.
Leda sighed, rested her forehead on his chest for a moment,
then pulled back and said, "The Leda James you love doesn't
exist anymore."

"What are you talking about?"

"My gift. It's gone. I don't even know if I ever had it."

He groaned and smiled. "Is that all?"

"All?" Leda pushed at his chest and took a staggering step
when she was suddenly freed of his grasp. "It's everything.
It's who I am. It's what I've believed my whole life."

"Leda—"

"No. Don't you see? I *believed* you and I belonged
together. I *believed* my teas helped people. I *believed* that

my visions were true. And now I don't have that anymore."
She shook her head. "Jenny could have died."

"She didn't."

"But I didn't *see* that she was in trouble."

"No one did. Not Jenny. Not her mother. Not me."

"But I should have."

"Good Lord, Leda!" Max shouted at her. "Do you think
you have to play God? That no one on earth should make
a move without first consulting you?"

"No, but—"

"But nothing! Why do you expect so much more from
yourself than you do from anyone else? Your visions—"
He cocked his head and glared at her. "You've been right
sometimes, haven't you?"

"Yes, but—"

"And as for Jenny, were you there, helping her? Holding
her? Did you take away her fear—or was that someone else?"

"It was me, but anyone could have—"

"No! Not just anyone. *You.*" He cupped her face with his
hands and Leda felt the strong warmth of him right down
to her bones. "You *do* have a gift, Leda. A gift for caring,
loving, *healing.*"

She shook her head, but Max determinedly went on.

"It's true. I've been here five years. In all that time,
Gladys Fairfax never once said her arthritis was better."
He shrugged. "All my medicines didn't do a damn thing,
because I forgot something very important. Something you
knew all along."

He bent and kissed her forehead gently.

"I didn't treat her soul. I gave her medicines for the pain
in her hands and thought it was enough. *You* gave her tea.
And friendship. And love." He shrugged again and smiled
at her. "And she felt better."

"Max, I—"

Taking a deep breath, he said swiftly, "As for us not
belonging together . . . what about that drawing your mother
made of me?"

"Huh?"

"The sketch?" His head tilted, he raised one eyebrow confidently and said, "You and Garrett both have talked about Eileen's gift. How she was never wrong."

"Yeesss . . ."

"Well, then." He waited.

Leda's brain raced with everything he'd been saying. She wanted to believe him. More than anything she wanted to believe. And he was right about the drawing. Her mother'd been the one to predict her and Max's future.

"And one more thing," he pointed out. "If you're so sure that you don't have the 'gift,' then you'll have to admit that you're not destined to die anytime soon. Right?"

She hadn't thought of that. Strange. The thought of her approaching death had been with her for more than two months. She should feel relieved now that that worry was gone. Instead, though, any solace she might have found was now muddled up with her dismay at realizing that she'd lost something precious to her.

Would she be able to live without her crystal ball and her visions?

"Leda"—Max's voice caressed her ears—"you shouldn't stop believing in yourself. In what you do for people."

She looked up at him.

"There's so much we could do . . . together."

Leda stared into his pale blue eyes and felt his strength reach out to her. If her life would be different from now on, she told herself, that didn't necessarily mean it would be bad. Maybe he was right. Maybe she *did* still have a gift of sorts. And with him beside her, she thought, she could do anything.

He loved her.

As if reading her mind, he said, "I love you, Leda. And I love your family. I'd like to be a part of that family. Hell, I think I even love that damned dog—" He held up one finger and added, "Who, by the way, *bit* somebody around here last night."

"Arthur?"

"Forget Arthur for a minute. In fact . . . forget *everything* for a minute. Everything except us." He caught her chin with his thumb and forefinger. Smoothing his thumb over her bottom lip, he asked, "Do you love me?"

"Yes."

He sighed and grinned. "Good. Now." Max sucked in a gulp of air and blew it out again. "Will you marry me?"

She hesitated only a moment. Long enough to make a silent wish that she was doing the right thing. Then she said, "Yes."

"What?"

"Yes." Leda laughed. "I said yes, I'll marry you." And as if in answer to her silent hopes, a sense of rightness filled her.

Stunned, Max gaped at her.

"Changing your mind?" Leda asked with a smile.

"Not a chance."

He dipped his head and covered her mouth with his and Leda leaned into the strength of him. She parted her lips and took his breath for her own.

"Cooter?" Deke "whispered" in his ear and Cooter jumped.

"We gonna sit here all day?"

"If I say so . . . yeah."

"Just askin'."

The older man's features crumpled. Durn it, Cooter thought, him and Deke never used to argue. Not until they started takin' orders from ol' Queenie. Even the money they'd made hadn't made up for havin' to listen to her and do whatever she said.

An' now, he told himself, she wants 'em to kill a *woman*. Hell, everybody knew what happened to a woman-killer if a posse ever caught up to him. He glanced down at the gypsy and the doc again, then over at his partner, now leaning back on a huge boulder, his hat over his eyes.

Deke wasn't no killer. And blast it, neither was he. Quickly, his brain started to work. With the money they had in their pockets and the little stash of hidey-hole money tucked away in their bedrolls, they could make it. Sure, cash'd be hard to come by after a while . . . but they wouldn't have no durn posse on their heels either.

Besides, if it come down to it, they could always . . . *work.* Cooter shuddered at the thought, but then again, it beat the hell out of hangin'.

As he stared down at the couple below him, the doctor kissed the little gypsy and Cooter sighed. There for a while, he figured they was gonna start in on sluggin' each other. But it appeared they got their differences settled.

They looked real good together, Cooter told himself wistfully.

"Lookit there," he said to Deke.

His partner turned, lifted his hat, and glanced down at the couple below. "That's nice, ain't it?" Deke smiled then turned back to leaning against the boulder. He slanted his hat brim firmly across his eyes.

"Yeah." Cooter watched the couple for another moment or two before reaching a decision. "C'mon, Deke," he said, his voice low, urgent.

The other man didn't stir.

"Deke!" he punched his partner's shoulder.

The older man lifted the edge of his hat and peeked out at Cooter from under the brim. "What? You think of a way to kill her accidental like?"

"Nah. I'm thinkin' we ought to get shut of this place."

Deke brushed frantically at his cheeks with the palms of his hands. "What? What's on my face?"

Cooter sighed, reached out and grabbed the man's hands. "Nothin'." He got down close to the man's ear and said again, "I think we should just go on and go."

"Go? Go where?"

"Anywhere but here."

"But what about Cecelia?"

"I've had about enough of her. How 'bout you?"

"Well"—Deke chewed at his lip for a long moment—"I guess I have too. What about the girl?"

"What about her?"

"Cecelia wants her dead."

"Then let Cecelia kill her." Cooter's mouth twisted mutinously. "I ain't no murderer, Deke, and I don't intend to start now."

Slowly, the other man grinned. "Me neither. 'Sides, she's too durned pretty to kill."

Cooter glanced back at the gypsy and her man, still locked together in a hungry kiss. "Yeah," he said finally, "reckon she is at that." Someday, he added silently, he'd like to find a woman like that for himself.

"We gonna tell the boss we're leavin'?"

"Hell, no!" Cooter slowly stood up and groaned as his sore behind punished him. "Just 'cause I don't wanna be a killer, don't mean I'm anxious to get killed myself!" He waved one hand at Deke. "C'mon. Let's get outa here."

"I'm with ya, partner," Deke said and pushed against the boulder as he clumsily got to his feet. The huge rock tilted a bit, but Deke kept on anyway. The older a man got, the more help he needed gettin' up from the ground. With a last, hearty shove, he reached his feet and moaned as he stretched his tired muscles.

The boulder rolled an inch or two and seemed to stop.

Thinking no more about it, Deke turned to go.

Cooter was about to follow him, when out of the corner of his eye he saw that rock start movin'. Slow at first, as if showin' its age, the stone picked up speed as it tumbled down the hillside. Mouth open, eyes wide, Cooter saw that the damn thing was headed right for the oblivious couple below.

Were they finally gonna succeed in killin' her just when they decided not to?

No.

Cooter jumped up and down, snatched his hat from his head, and shouted, "Hey, you two! RUN!"

Smaller stones and pebbles, scattered by the boulder's fall, rained down the incline, heralding its arrival. It seemed to take forever, but at last the couple broke apart and glanced up at the hill.

Even from a distance, Cooter saw their shocked expressions as they watched the rock plunging toward them.

"Jump!" he yelled again and this time Deke's voice joined his.

When they were almost out of time and prob'ly close enough to the boulder to spit, the doc took hold of the gypsy and made a flying leap to one side. His arms locked around her, they hit the ground and rolled to safety. The stone thundered on past them and finally came to a stop in the lake.

Cooter's pent-up breath rushed from him, and he turned to Deke and returned the man's wide grin. Then he glanced back to the bottom of the incline and saw the doc picking her up and squeezing her tight. Impulsively, Cooter lifted one arm and waved.

When the doc waved back and the gypsy shouted "Thank you!" an unfamiliar spark of pleasure flared up in his chest.

It felt good.

"You ready?" Deke shouted.

"Hell, yes. Let's get the horses and go."

"I'll show *you* who's slow!" the older man called out and started to half run back to town.

Cooter paused only a heartbeat before he took off after him.

"Well, if that doesn't prove we were meant to live together forever," Max said with a shuddering glance at the boulder, "nothing will."

Leda's arms snaked around his waist gratefully. Her breathing was a little ragged and her bones ached from being tossed to the ground. "I do believe you're right, my love." She snuggled in closer. "It must be Destiny."

He looked at her warily.

Leda grinned and hugged him. "There is one thing, though, Max."

"What?"

"Those men. On the hill."

"What about them?"

"They looked awfully familiar."

CHAPTER 20

Gladys didn't actually get to the Mercantile until the following afternoon. On her way to pick up the mysterious package, Flora Lloyd had poked her head out the doctor's office and asked Gladys to sit with Jenny while she went home to look after Julius.

And for the next few hours, Gladys heard not only the story of the doc and Leda . . . but she also listened to Jenny describe Sean Malone's devotion in glowing terms.

By the time Flora returned, Gladys was simply too worn out to bother with claiming the package waiting for her. And truth to tell, she'd heard enough about *love* to last for quite a while. She wasn't sure she was up to listening to Leda go on about Max.

But, she sighed as she pushed the Mercantile door open, she'd waited as long as she could.

"Afternoon, Gladys!" Garrett called out from across the room. "Come for that package?"

"That's right," she muttered, still only half interested in whatever Geraldine might be sending her. Something heavy leaned against her right leg and she looked down into Arthur's hair-covered eyes. Frowning, she leaned right back until the dog staggered, and she snapped, "Get off me, you good-for-nothin' flea hotel!"

"He's only sayin' hi, Mrs. Fairfax," a young voice said defensively.

She turned and watched Dennis walk up and stand along-side his dog. Her features softened and she told herself to stop takin' her own short temper out on everybody else. "I know, boy."

Denny and the huge animal moved off and she watched them leave the store for the wide porch outside. Shaking her head, she swung back around when Garrett laid a large brown paper-wrapped parcel on the counter.

"Did ya hear about my Leda and the doc?" he asked, a satisfied smile on his face.

"Have to be deaf not to," she shot back. Garrett shrugged and walked away, leaving Gladys to question exactly why she was feelin' so surly. After all, the wedding was some-thing she'd wanted all along. It was, she supposed, simply hard to admit that they hadn't needed *her* to put them-selves right.

She sighed heavily and pulled at the knotted string on her parcel. It was a hard thing, gettin' old. Knowin' that folks could get along just fine without ya.

When the string finally pulled off and the brown paper fell open, she stared at the contents, her mouth open in surprise.

"Gladys?" Leda asked as she stepped out of the storeroom and stopped on the other side of the counter, just opposite the older woman. "Is something wrong?"

Shaking her head dumbly, Gladys didn't even look up. Though she knew she should congratulate the younger wom-an, she couldn't seem to tear her gaze from the parcel's contents. Carefully, Gladys lifted the beautiful brown wool sweater from its wrappings and held it up high. Her sharp eyes swept over the precise workmanship in admiration. Silently, she admitted that the knitting was even better than she could have done in her prime.

"Gladys?" Leda said softly. "There's something else here too."

Reluctantly, she lowered the sweater and looked back at the now much smaller package. Under a sheet of white paper lay another knitted garment. This one smaller. And done in a soft baby-blue yarn.

Gladys's breath caught as she lifted the piece of paper and saw that the blue sweater and hood had been made for a baby. A curl of cautious excitement spread through her body, erasing the aches and pains she'd been so aware of. Glancing at the heavy notepaper in her hand, she saw that the elegant script covering the sheet was Geraldine's. But with her eyes suddenly watering, Gladys couldn't make out the words. She handed the paper to Leda. "Read it for me, child."

In a soft voice, the younger woman began: " *'Dear Mother.'* " She looked up at Gladys for a moment before continuing. " *'I'm sorry it has taken me so long to finish this sweater. I had hoped to have it to you last winter, but my efforts then were simply not good enough. I have been taking lessons in knitting, and as you can see, I've improved since I last tried to offer my assistance to you.'* " Leda glanced up again, but Gladys waved her on, her fingers still moving over the two sweaters. " *'I'm also enclosing a sweater that I've made for our coming baby. Would you tell me what you think of it?'* "

Gladys gasped and wrapped one work-worn hand around her throat. "A *baby!*" Even with that tiny garment in hand, she'd been afraid to hope. But it was true. She was going to be a grandma at long last! Gladys said hurriedly, "Go on girl. Read it."

" *'Mother, I know you've said many times you have no wish to move to San Francisco. But I do wish you'd change your mind. With the baby coming, we need you more than ever. Lester doesn't understand a woman's fears, though he does try. And with my parents gone now, I sorely need your comfort and advice. If you would come to us, Lester will travel to Tanglewood and accompany you home. Please,*

Mother. Sometimes I get so afraid. Love, Geraldine.' "

A solitary tear rolled down Gladys's weathered cheek and her fingers smoothed across the brown sweater lying on the counter. "Well," she said softly, more to herself than to Leda.

"There's more," the younger woman said quietly.

"What?" Gladys rubbed her eyes. "Does she say when the baby's coming?"

"No. It says, *'P.S. Please say you'll come, Ma. Geraldine's not herself lately. Love, Lester.' "*

Gladys snorted. "Not herself! Of course she ain't herself! If that ain't just like a man!" Sniffing loudly, she gathered up her precious gifts, still stunned that her daughter-in-law had gone to all the trouble to learn to knit. Just to please a cranky old lady.

"What do you mean, Gladys?" Leda asked.

"Men! Get ya in the family way and then act surprised when ya act a little different!" Clutching her things to her chest, Gladys turned for the door. "Poor Geraldine, alone in that big ol' house with that idiot son of mine!"

"But where are you going?"

She stopped at the door and looked back. A thrilling surge of new energy rushed through her veins. "I'm goin' to find that lazy no-account August Haley! I got to send a telegram to San Francisco. Tell that worthless son of mine to come get me. Geraldine *needs* me!"

This was all *her* fault! That ridiculous woman who insisted on masquerading as a gypsy!

Impotent rage gripped Cecelia and she ground her teeth together until she thought her jaw would snap. Through narrowed eyes, she looked over the town that had beaten her. Slowly, she walked across the street, her mind racing. No, she corrected herself silently. The town hadn't beaten her. It was worse than that. She'd been bested by two cretins!

Incredible, she told herself, fanning the fire of her wrath. She'd offered those two more wealth than they'd ever dreamed of. Included them in the most finely executed bank robberies the West had ever seen. And *this* was her thanks.

The fact that Cecelia had planned to rid herself of their presence shortly was neither here nor there. That would have been *her* decision. In *her* good time. This . . . *betrayal* was quite another thing entirely.

She lifted the hem of her gown and stepped up on the boardwalk outside the Mercantile. Even in her anger, Cecelia remembered to turn her head slightly from the wide front window. The final insult would be if the miserable woman were to remember Cecelia before she could leave town on the morning stage. And leave town she must. There was no point in staying now. Without the help of the two traitors, she would never be able to carry off the gold.

All her careful plans! For *nothing*!

Cecelia tripped, her arms flailing wildly for purchase. Seemingly at the last moment, her right hand connected with something solid and her fingers curled around the porch post, successfully halting her fall. When she'd regained her balance, she looked down and noticed, for the first time, a young boy and an unbelievably unkempt dog.

In a burst of frustrated fury, Cecelia leaned down and slapped the boy across the face.

The animal instantly leaped to its feet, teeth bared and a low growl rumbling in its massive chest. The child immediately laid one hand on his dog and with the other rubbed his reddened cheek. Tears filled his eyes, but he blinked them back.

"Stupid boy!" Cecelia hissed with only a moment's pause for the dog. "How *dare* you stretch across a public walkway, tripping unsuspecting passersby!"

"I didn't mean to, lady," he said, "I'm sorry."

From the corner of her eye, Cecelia noticed that people in the street had stopped to watch her. Most of their faces held disapproving frowns. With a herculean effort, she forced herself to calm down. Though she wanted more than anything to snatch up the boy and shake him until his teeth rattled, instead Cecelia *willed* the corners of her mouth to lift slightly. In a stilted voice, she ground out, "Be more careful in the future."

The boy nodded and the door behind her opened. Cecelia swung around to leave quickly, hoping to avoid any further scenes. But the woman leaving the store was moving much too quickly and they collided. Cecelia's string bag dropped to the wooden planks. It landed with a thud, the derringer she kept in her purse making the bag much heavier than it should have been.

Leda bent down, picked up the woman's bag, and handed it back to her. As she looked into the woman's furious blue eyes, a strange sense of familiarity struck Leda. There was something . . .

"Thank you." The woman kept her face averted carefully. "If you'll excuse me," she said and began to walk off toward the rooming house.

Arthur growled again and Leda reached down to soothe the animal. The frantic impulse to defend Denny had faded now, seeing the boy was all right. But in its place, Leda felt an almost overwhelming urge to chase after the woman. What was it about her? she asked herself.

"Leda?" Denny said.

"Hmmm?" Shaken, she turned and looked down at her cousin. "Are you all right now, Denny?"

"Yeah," he said, still rubbing his cheek. "But she was mean. Arthur doesn't like her."

"I can see that," she murmured and looked back thoughtfully at the woman's retreating figure. She'd passed the rooming house entirely and was headed along the path through the trees to the lake. Leda's fingers moved over the cold surface of her good-luck coin as she watched the woman until she disappeared from sight.

All at once, though, a vivid memory sprang to life in her brain. Red Deer, Montana. Early morning. The stage leaving. A woman passenger. Beautiful. Blond. Elegant. Coldly furious. Leda saw herself wave as the stage pulled away. She watched herself pick up the coin from the dirt. Saw the bank manager stumble outside for help, blood streaming from a head wound. Heard him shout that he'd been robbed.

Of course, she thought, her hand closing around the lucky coin convulsively. *That* woman was the early-morning passenger. She looked down, unfurled her fingers, and stared blankly at the gold coin in her palm. The robbery in Red Deer. The woman in such a hurry to leave. Dropping her bag. A gold coin in the dirt.

Was it possible?

Even as she asked herself that question, her mind raced on. Images of the men at the lake the day before. She frowned. The shorter of the two . . . wasn't *he* the poor soul who'd fallen in the empty grave in Red Deer? She shook her head. No. She couldn't be sure about that. She hadn't seen him *that* closely.

But the woman . . . her gaze snapped back to the edge of the trees where the woman had gone only moments before. Leda tried to think clearly, quickly. Hadn't she heard August Haley talking about a gold shipment due in Tanglewood sometime soon? She bit at her lip. Leaping off the boardwalk, Leda ran across the street. She had to talk to Dan.

"Now, Leda," the sheriff said slowly. "That woman hardly looks the part of a bank robber."

"I'm not saying she is, Dan." Leda frowned, lifted the gold coin and its chain from around her neck, and handed it to the man seated behind his desk. "But I *did* find this lying in the street after she dropped her bag in Red Deer. And there wasn't anybody else around."

Leda waited impatiently as the man studied the coin closely. She couldn't understand why the sheriff was so reluctant to believe her. And every moment that passed only strengthened Leda's feeling that she should be *doing* something. She shifted from foot to foot in her anxiety, her red socks barely making a whisper of sound on the dusty floor.

Dan held the gold coin gingerly, letting the golden chain drape itself across his fingers. Shaking his head, Dan finally said, "This doesn't prove anything, Leda. It could have been dropped the night before, by anybody."

"But it looks new," she insisted. Surely *that* was important.

"They're *all* new at first." He dropped the coin to the cluttered desktop and shook his head. "Just 'cause it's a fresh coin, don't mean it was stolen." An easy, kind smile creased his face and he added, "Why don't you go on home, Leda. I hear you've got plenty of things to be doin' with a weddin' only a few days off."

Instinctively, she smiled at the mention of her coming wedding, but her lips straightened again almost instantly. "But, Dan . . ."

He picked up a pencil, drew up a sheet of paper, and said firmly, "Go home, Leda."

His mind was made up, she could see that. And maybe he was even right. But she didn't think so. Obediently, though, Leda turned and left the office, stepping past the tall, dark man just entering.

With every step she took, the feelings grew more intense. Leda *knew* that woman was up to something. There was something about her eyes. And the sudden fury she'd unleashed on Denny said quite a bit about her. Maybe, Leda told herself, if she kept an eye on the woman, she could learn something that Dan *would* listen to.

Hurrying her pace, Leda crossed the street, and scurried past the store, where Denny and Arthur were still sitting in the middle of the walk. She continued on past the bank, but paused for a moment outside Max's office. Max might help, she thought and glanced in the front window. There were several people waiting in the hall to see the doctor.

No telling how long he would be busy, she told herself. She would just have to go alone. If she was careful, the woman wouldn't even see her. Leda hadn't taken more than a step or two, though, when Denny's voice stopped her.

"Where ya goin'?"

Turning, she looked down and her eyes seemed to be drawn to the still red imprint of the woman's hand on his cheek.

"For a walk, Denny."

"Can me and Arthur come too?"

"Not this time, love."

"Ah, Leda . . ."

"I'll be back soon," she promised and smoothed her palm against his injured cheek. Then without another word, she started off down the path toward the trees.

A moment later Sean, clutching a wilted bouquet of wildflowers, walked up behind his younger brother. "Where's Leda goin'?"

"Followin' that mean lady."

"Huh?"

Dennis looked up at Sean, a disgusted scowl on his face. "That ornery lady that hit me! Leda's followin' her."

"How come?"

" 'Cause she don't like her any more than me and Arthur." Denny jumped from the boardwalk and yelled, "C'mon, Arthur! She might try to hit Leda too!"

The dog woofed, jumped from the walk, and trotted alongside his young master.

Sean snorted, as his youngest brother trailed after Leda. Then he rubbed the toes of his shoes against the backs of his legs and stepped into Max's office. Jenny was waiting.

"Hell, Mike," Dan said and tossed his friend Leda's gold-coin necklace, "it's prob'ly just another one of her 'visions.' "

"Maybe"—the other lawman nodded thoughtfully as he studied the coin—"and maybe not."

"Huh?"

"I don't know, Dan." Mike looked up and shrugged. "But we don't have much else. And the money taken in Red Deer *was* almost all new coins."

"That ain't any kind of proof at all. And you know it."

"Not proof, sure." Mike set the necklace down on a stack of papers threatening to spill across the desk. "But we got nothin' to lose by lookin' into it." He shoved his hands in his pants pockets. "Besides, there was somethin' kinda strange about that female, if you ask me."

"What's wrong, Mike? Didn't she fall at your feet like the rest of your women?"

The dark-haired man shook his head. "I don't mean that. It's just a . . . feeling, I guess. For such a pretty woman, she seemed awful *cold*."

"Oh, fine." Dan swung his feet down from his desk and stood up. "Now *you're* gettin' *feelin's*. Pretty soon, this whole damn town's gonna be reportin' visions and such." He snatched up his hat, pushed it down on his head, and started across the floor.

"Where *you* goin'?" Mike asked.

"To find Leda," Dan said with a glance over his shoulder. "And then that female. You comin'?"

"Hell, yes."

Max glanced in the open door and watched Sean and Jenny whispering together for a moment. Then smiling, he stepped back into the hall and motioned for his next patient to join him in the office.

Instinctively, he ducked beneath the bunches of herbs and told himself for the hundredth time that day what a lucky man he was. He had a successful practice, for the first time in his life he had friends, and he had Leda.

Hard to believe, but in only three days' time, he'd be a married man. Strange how things worked out, he thought wonderingly. He'd traveled halfway across the country to avoid the pain loving might cause, only to find a deeper, greater love than he'd ever dreamed existed. Proof enough, he told himself, that God did, indeed, look after fools.

"Max!"

"Excuse me," he said to the man just seating himself before the doctor's desk. Walking quickly to the hall, Max saw Dan and another, darker man waiting for him. "What is it?"

"Leda here?" the sheriff asked.

"No," Max said and felt the first flutterings of unease. "She was helping Garrett in the store today."

"She ain't now." Dan pointed at the man beside him. "We just left there."

"Is there something wrong?"

"Prob'ly not," Dan conceded in a grudging tone that did little for Max's well-being. "We just want to talk to her."

"We?" Max glanced pointedly at the other man.

"Oh," Dan said. "Sorry. This here's Mike Connor. A friend of mine. He's the sheriff over at Short Hill, Montana."

Max nodded briefly and turned back to Dan. "What's going on?"

"I don't know, really. It's just, Leda came to me a while ago with some wild tale about a woman named . . ." He glanced at Mike.

"Cecelia Standish."

Dan nodded.

"I don't know the name," Max said and, from the corner of his eye, saw Sean step into the hall, drawn by the voices. He ignored the boy and asked, "Is Leda in some kind of trouble?"

"I shouldn't think so." Dan shrugged. "We just want to make sure."

"I know where she went." Sean suddenly spoke up.

All three men looked at him. When he didn't speak right away, Max prodded, "Where, Sean?"

The teenager shrugged and looked from one to the other of the men. "Denny said she was followin' a 'mean lady.' Then him and Arthur run off to follow Leda."

The two lawmen exchanged wary glances and that small, uneasy feeling building in Max's gut flared into life.

"Where, boy?" Dan asked, a new urgency in his voice.

"Down the path to the lake. Through the trees."

Max slapped the boy on the back, and rushed through the door. He didn't even know why he was suddenly feeling so frantic. And he didn't stop to consider the question. Mike and Dan were just a heartbeat behind him.

Pine needles stuck to her socks and Leda winced as they jabbed at her instep. Hunched over behind an ancient pine, Leda watched her quarry and wondered again just what the woman was doing.

Curses and swears! she thought and fought the urge to straighten her aching back. Why in heaven would the woman stalk off into the woods? Then a chilling idea occurred to her. Could the woman be meeting someone? Perhaps the two strange men Leda'd seen the day before?

A sense of dread crept up her spine. Suddenly, the afternoon light filtering down between the trees seemed to dim. The small clearing where the mysterious woman paced furiously appeared to be more shadow-filled than moments before. Dry needles under the woman's feet hushed and sighed with her every step, and for the first time, Leda noticed that she didn't hear any other sounds.

No birds. No insects. Nothing. It was as if even the air had stilled, waiting.

Leda took one halting step back, farther under the tree, and jostled a small pine cone from its perch. It dropped to the ground with an unnaturally loud thud.

The woman across the clearing spun about and seemed to look directly at Leda as she dug into her bag and pulled out a small, deadly-looking gun.

"Whoever you are, step into the open."

Leda didn't move. She held her breath, knowing the other woman couldn't see her, hidden as she was by the pines.

In the silence, the distinctive click of a hammer being drawn back sounded out like a shot.

"I said," the cool voice announced clearly, "come out. Now."

But even if she couldn't be seen, she could very well be hit by a wildly aimed bullet. There was nothing else for it. Slowly, hesitantly, Leda straightened up, stepped out from behind the pine tree, and reluctantly walked into the clearing. When she stopped, there was a mere twenty feet of space separating the two women.

"You!" Cecelia gasped. Her gaze swept over the would-be gypsy and the helpless fury she'd been holding back all morning swept over her with the consuming force of a prairie fire. Even the other woman's appearance infuriated her.

Younger than Cecelia, Leda James also possessed a quiet confidence that surrounded her with an innate dignity despite her ridiculous attire. And if it weren't for *her,* Cecelia told herself, by this time tomorrow, she would have been a good deal richer.

But it wasn't only the money. It was the very fact that her plans had been shattered. Not through any sort of direct effort. But by a blind, stupid Fate! And now, the gypsy had the incredible nerve to look surprised!

"Do you have the slightest idea what your presence here has cost me?"

"I don't know what you mean," Leda said and glanced nervously from side to side.

"I don't suppose you do. And you needn't bother searching for help," Cecelia told her sharply. "Since you followed me here, you should be well aware that we are . . . *alone.*" She thought she saw the gypsy pale a bit and it did Cecelia's heart good. "That was very foolish of you, you know. Following me. Whatever caused you to do such a thing?"

"I . . . only wanted to see what you were going to do."

"Nothing!" Cecelia snapped and took two steps closer. "Thanks to your interference, both in Red Deer and here, I am doing precisely *nothing.*"

Leda took a half step back.

Cecelia waved the pistol's muzzle at her meaningfully. "Stand where you are, Miss James." Once the gypsy did as she was told, Cecelia glanced at the sheltering trees standing guard about the clearing. She smiled. "Perhaps you hadn't noticed, but I wandered off the footpath some time ago."

"I noticed."

"Good." Cecelia went even closer and she fancied she could see the damp sheen of sweat beading the gypsy's brow. "Then you'll understand when I say that it should take someone a day or two at least to find you, this deep into the woods."

"Find me?"

Oh yes. Cecelia smiled inwardly. The chit *was* frightened. A pleasant sense of satisfaction rippled through her. "Yes, Miss James. You see, I've decided to leave your little town on the morning stage. There is really no point in staying any longer . . . *now.* And I would hate to think that a visit from you to the town sheriff would prevent my trip. *Or* cause me any future problems."

A rustle in the woods to her right caught Cecelia's attention and she glanced toward the sound. But she didn't see anything. An animal, she assured herself. Nothing more.

Deliberately, carefully, she lifted the derringer and pointed it at the gypsy. "It's not very likely that my shot will be heard," she said congenially, "but I want you to know that even if caught—it will *still* be worth it to me."

Cecelia looked deeply into the gypsy's grass-green eyes and let her finger slowly tighten on the trigger.

Something huge exploded out of the trees and careened into Cecelia. The gun fired, the shot blasting into the otherwise still air. Almost at the same instant, the gypsy dropped to the ground limply. Cecelia lay flat on the forest floor, her left cheek pressed into the pine-needle-littered dirt.

On her back, a mountainous weight rested, and when she tried to shift out from under it, a massive head lowered itself to hers. A deep, rumbling growl thundered out around her, seeming to shake the very ground. She looked up into hair-covered brown eyes and what seemed to be hundreds of snarling teeth.

Cecelia groaned and lay carefully, quietly, still.

"Good boy, Arthur!" A little boy ran into her line of vision. The same boy she'd slapped such a short time ago. He hurried to the gypsy's side and anxiously began to call to her.

All at once, the woods were alive with sound. Voices, shouting came closer and she made one final effort to move. Arthur gripped her fashionable hat between his teeth and began to shake it and her, like a rat.

Cecelia screamed. *Anything* was better than being eaten alive!

Her wild eyes saw three men enter the clearing. One went to the gypsy. Two of them, one wearing a badge, ran straight to her. She closed her eyes.

"Leda!" Max shouted as his feet slid out from under him on the needle-strewn earth. He landed with a thud and felt his bones jar. Quickly, though, he scooted to her side, brushed a near hysterical Denny aside, and began to run his hands over her body, searching for injuries.

His heart had stopped when he heard the shot, and coming into the clearing only to see her prostrate form had almost finished him off.

Those damn visions of hers. Death. Dying. He clenched his teeth together to keep from screaming. It wasn't true, he thought furiously. He wouldn't *let* it be true.

"Leda! Dammit, wake up!" he shouted. "Don't you dare die three days before our wedding!" In the back of his mind, he noted the sound of Denny's cries and Arthur's deep-throated growls. He even heard the woman talking to Dan and Mike, but he couldn't pay attention. Everything in him was centered on the woman he loved, lying unnaturally quiet in the dirt.

"Max?"

His heart began to beat again.

"Max?" Leda's voice came a little stronger the second time and she tried to push herself into a sitting position. Denny stopped crying and threw himself at her. Instinctively, Leda caught the child to her and held him tightly. Then her gaze lifted to his and Max felt his world right itself again.

"Hello, Max."

"Good God, Leda!" he gasped and sat back on his heels. "I thought you'd been shot!"

"Shot?" She looked past him at the three people still struggling with Arthur. Then she turned back to him and grinned. "She didn't shoot me, Max. But the gunshot scared me and I think I *fainted*!"

Pine needles and leaves in her hair, dirt on her face, and a tangle of necklaces around her neck in knots.

Everything was just as it should be, Max told himself just before he pulled Leda and Denny into his arms.

EPILOGUE

Tanglewood—five years later

"Right over here please, Max," Leda called out from the side yard.

Max lifted the heavy basket filled with wet laundry and walked to the clothesline where she waited. He glanced at his two daughters playing in a splash of shade nearby. Even the shadows thrown by the pines couldn't dim the bright red hair they'd inherited from their mother. Love rushed through his bloodstream, thundering in his ears.

"You didn't have to carry it for me, you know," Leda told him and shook her head. "I'm only expecting a baby, I'm not ill."

"You're not to lift anything heavy and you know it," he chided.

She shook her head and absently rubbed her belly as if soothing the child within.

He stared at her and knew that he would never tire of watching her. Even after two children and well into her third pregnancy, Leda James Evans was as beautiful as ever.

Her rose-colored shirt hung outside her pink and black striped skirt and hugged her well-rounded belly. Her lucky coin shone brilliantly amid the ropes of necklaces hanging from her neck. Bare feet poked out from beneath the hem of her skirt and Max smiled when he thought about the socks she usually wore these days. She had no more need of her red wools.

Now, she favored blue socks, for Peace. And Joy.

He sighed and glanced up at the two-story frame house behind him. Only fifty feet from their office, the house was a world apart from anything else he'd ever known. Filled with his children's laughter, Leda's off-key singing, and quite often the barks and howls of Arthur's children.

It still struck Max as odd that a union between Arthur and August Haley's dog had produced only two puppies . . . both of which looked like their father. But, as far as Max was concerned, the big dog had the run of his house for as long as Arthur lived.

"Max?" Leda asked. "Are you listening to me?"

"Always, my love," he teased. He moved to stand behind her and snaked his arms around her widening middle. His unborn child gave him a good kick.

"I think this one's a boy, my love," she whispered.

He inhaled the scent of rosewater, smiled, and asked, "A vision?"

"No." She laughed and playfully slapped his hands away. "Just a feeling."

"Maybe it's a season for boys," Max countered and handed her the clothespins she needed. "Didn't Gladys's last letter say that Geraldine had had a boy this time?"

"Yes"—Leda laughed—"and I guess their daughter isn't too pleased with her new brother either."

"Papa," little Eileen shouted.

"Yes, sweetheart?" Max's heart swelled as he looked at the four-year-old replica of her mother.

"Sean's comin'!"

Max and Leda looked at each other curiously. The road into town couldn't be seen from their house. Besides, Sean and Jenny weren't due in until the weekend, for supper. Since their marriage a year before, the young couple had been living ten miles out of Tanglewood at the small ranch they'd purchased.

Leda shrugged and looked at her daughter thoughtfully.

"Jenny gots a baby!" Eileen added and brushed the dirt from her doll's skirt.

Leda smiled.

Max, though, said, "No, dear. Not yet. Jenny's baby will come *next* month."

"Uh-uh," Maggie piped up. The nearly three year old stood alongside Max, tugging at his pants leg. "He comed last night." She stuck out her tongue. "He's a boy."

Leda grinned, clapped her hands, then hugged her stomach excitedly.

Max's own stomach flopped over. Mouth dry, he said, "No, Sean would come and get me to help their baby come."

"Uh-uh," Maggie said again as she sat down on the toe of her father's shoe, telling him silently that she wanted a ride. "He come'd too fast. So Sean couldn't." Looking up at her father, she asked, "Is our baby gonna come soon?"

"Leda . . ." Max said helplessly.

She shrugged and looked from one to the other of her daughters, delight written on her features.

"Jenny gave him a name too," Eileen said as an afterthought.

"A name?" Max's voice broke uncertainly.

"Uh-huh," Maggie echoed then giggled as her father shuffled his foot for her. "Patrick."

Leda muffled her own laughter but not before Max heard it. "Leda, sweetheart, please tell me this isn't what I think it is . . ."

"From mother to daughter, my love." Her grin looked as wide as the lake. "In *my* family, this isn't strange at all."

"But, Leda—"

Then the sound of an approaching wagon shattered their thoughts. They turned as one to watch Sean drive up, cracking the reins over the backs of his horses. Before the buckboard could even come to a stop, Sean was standing up shouting. "The baby came last night! I have a son! And Jenny named him Patrick Garrett!"

The two little girls ran to greet their cousin.

"That's wonderful, Sean!" Leda called.

Max stood stone-still, horror stretched across his features. He looked at his beautiful daughters and whispered, "Good God!"

FREE
Romance
(a $4.50 value)

Send in the Coupon Below

To get your FREE historical romance and start saving, fill out the coupon below and mail it today. As soon as we receive it we'll send you your FREE Book along with your first month's selections.
